the Icing on the Cake

Hope it brings you laughter + joy!

Elodia Strain
2008

the Icing on the Cake

Elodia Strain

CFI
Springville, Utah

ISBN 13: 978-1-59955-011-4

Published by CFI, an imprint of Cedar Fort, Inc., 2373 W. 700 S., Springville, UT, 84663
Distributed by Cedar Fort, Inc. www.cedarfort.com

LIBRARY OF CONGRESS CATALOGING-IN-PUBLICATION DATA

Strain, Elodia Kay, 1979-
The Icing on the cake / Elodia Kay Strain.
p. cm.
ISBN 978-1-59955-011-4 (acid-free paper)
I. Title.

PS3619.T724I26 2007
813'.6--dc22

2006039286

Cover design by Nicole Williams
Cover design © 2007 by Lyle Mortimer
Edited and typeset by Kammi Rencher

Printed in the United States of America

10 9 8 7 6 5 4 3 2

Printed on acid-free paper

Dedication

To Jacob—you are a miracle in my life.

Acknowledgments

Thank you, Mom, for reading the early stages of the manuscript and telling me when it made you laugh, and for the giving, loving example you've set with notes in my lunch, dresses in my closet, and tons of cakes with buttercream icing. Thank you, Dad, for the humor you always brought to our home and for your example of living well amidst trials. Thank you, Miranda, Brian, and Brett, for the hilarious and wonderful things you've done that I was able to draw upon. I love you all.

Thank you, Nancy, for the edits and suggestions, and Jack for the support that made it possible for me to do what I've always dreamed of doing.

Thank you to the girls of the BYU 140th ward who were there through it all and who are truly my sisters.

Thank you to all the other family and friends who encouraged me.

Thank you, Kammi, for believing in the book from the beginning, and for being a fabulous editor.

And thank you, Jacob—it wouldn't have been possible without you. You are absolutely my best friend. Thank you for your endless support and for helping me make sure that my guys didn't sound like girls.

Prologue

When I was twelve years old, my mom bought me a diary. She called it a journal, but all my friends had diaries, so that's what I called mine. It was bright pink and had a little lock on the front and a key that, for some reason, I decided to hide in my retainer case.

On the first page of my diary I wrote:

These are the boys I like right now . . .

Brad Knightly (but pretty much every girl likes him)

Andrew Lawson

Robert Saunders

And on the second page, I wrote:

When I grow up I'm going to . . .

Go to college

Find a boy to love

Get married (in the temple, of course)

Well, I did go to college. But although I looked pretty much everywhere, I didn't quite find a boy to love and marry.

So, after college, I moved back to Monterey, California, my hometown, where I joined about my millionth singles ward, and used my journalism degree to secure a position as a food writer at a local magazine called *Central Coast Living*, a job that I thought was just perfect because it combined two of my greatest loves: writing and food. And the job was perfect—for the first two days.

But then the French Toast Fiasco happened.

For my first writing assignment, I was supposed to go to the Carmel Hills Bed & Breakfast and do a short write-up on the facility's stuffed French toast breakfast, which had received some big culinary award from a Bed & Breakfast association. I got the Bed and Breakfast's address from my boss, George Kent, and headed out there early one Monday morning.

When I arrived, I knocked on the door of the cute little cottage, and an elderly woman wearing a flowery robe answered the door.

"Hi, my name is Annabelle Pleasanton," I announced in a chipper voice. "I'm a writer for *Central Coast Living*, and I'm here to try your stuffed French toast."

The woman looked at me perplexedly for a moment before saying, "Of course, dear." Then she invited me inside, and I sat at a square table with a checkered tablecloth while she prepared me some French toast stuffed with a delicious cream cheese filling and perfectly ripe strawberries.

I ate the delicious breakfast, thanked the woman, and wrote down her name, which George had apparently gotten wrong. Then I wrote my article, and proudly emailed it to George.

Later that day, George called me into his office and informed me that I had not gone to the Carmel Hills Bed & Breakfast, but had harassed some random old woman and forced her to make me stuffed French toast.

As George yelled at me about how badly I had messed up and how he had to find something to take the place of my write-up, I suggested that maybe I could just write about the old woman because her stuffed French toast was delightful, and plus, she was really sweet. At that point, George kicked me out of his office and demoted me to recipe copy-editor.

Luckily though, George told me that it wasn't all over for me. He said that if I proved I could handle it, someday, maybe, if he was feeling really generous, he would give me another opportunity to write. So since then, I have been doing everything I can to prove myself to George. And that's kind of where this whole thing starts: me trying to prove myself to George with a cake.

And, well, still trying to find a boy to love.

Chapter 1

Okay. This is not good."

My best friend, Carrie, looked over at me. "What?"

I used the Red Vine in my hand to point to the store in front of us.

Carrie peered at the store and read aloud the big green words printed on the window. "Bob's Bait and Tackle."

I took a bite out of my Red Vine. "Mm hmm," I mumbled.

Now, being at Bob's Bait and Tackle would have been all fine and good if I was looking for bait and tackle. But I was looking for cake. Yes, that's right, cake.

You see, back in December I took a little trip inland to attend my Aunt Margaret's retirement party in the San Joaquin Valley town of Los Banos, and I was on my way home to Monterey when I realized I hadn't eaten much at the party and was quite hungry. Sure, I probably should have made the healthy choice and grabbed a salad or something, but as I drove down Main Street a cute little Portuguese bakery seemed to be calling out to me: "Annabelle, come try some tasty treats," and I couldn't resist. So I went into the bakery and bought two—okay, five—Portuguese sweet rolls for myself and a Portuguese sponge cake to take to the office Christmas party.

Well, my Portuguese cake was a big Christmas party hit,

especially with George, my boss. In fact, George liked the thing so much that now, six months later, he wanted me to get another cake—though he had no idea I would have to drive all the way to the San Joaquin Valley to get it—and bring it to the Anniversary Issue meeting on Friday.

Hence my problem. George, who I really needed to impress, was expecting me to show up at the meeting with a cake in hand, not a fishing pole and a big jar of bait. Or is it a can of bait? I don't know how it works.

"Are you sure we're in the right place?" Carrie asked in her soft, calm, perfect-for-a-yoga-video voice.

"Yep," I replied, cursing my ability to pick out a good dessert. If only I had just taken some stale green cookies to the Christmas party. "This was a bakery the last time I was here."

I turned off my car—a mid-nineties BMW that I got for really cheap at one of those impounded car auctions—and unbuckled my seat belt, which took a good minute since there was a piece of gum stuck in the buckle, compliments of the car's previous owner. "I'm going to run inside and see if anyone knows about the bakery. Maybe it moved or something. Do you want to come?"

Carrie put a finger to her pretty pink lips. "Sure."

The bait and tackle store was small and cramped and smelled like dead fish. As Carrie and I stepped inside, I noticed that we were the only ones in the store except for a large man who stood behind the counter. The man looked up at us briefly and then returned to the fishing magazine he was flipping through.

"Look at these," Carrie said. She gracefully approached the store counter and began inspecting a rack of colorful fishing lures.

I followed a few feet behind her, peering at a huge stuffed fish that hung on the wall. It seemed to be looking at me.

"Hey, you, girl with the brown hair," the man behind the counter called out to me. "Watch where you step. I think some of my worms got loose over there"

"Excuse me?" I gulped.

The man smiled a crooked smile. "Don't worry, they won't hurt ya."

I tried to put on my best of-course-I-know-they-won't-hurt-me face as I booked it to the counter, which was apparently out of the danger zone.

The man adjusted his camouflage hat. "Welcome to Bob's Bait and Tackle. I'm Bob." He offered me and then Carrie a rough, tan hand to shake. "You looking for a new fishing pole today? Or maybe some bait? I've got some fresh night crawlers. And if I can just find those worms . . ." The man looked down at the ground.

"Actually," I said, shuffling my feet in an attempt to keep the worms away, "we're looking for a place called Marcia's bakery. It used to be at this address and—"

"Sir," Carrie said, interrupting me, "I think I see one." Carrie calmly pointed to the ground a few feet away from us.

Bob moved to where Carrie was pointing and bent down to pick up not one but two slimy creatures. He placed the wriggling things in a Styrofoam container, which he set on the top shelf of a refrigerator marked "Live Bait." Then he returned to his position behind the counter.

"You've got a good eye," Bob said to Carrie. "You ever think about taking up fishing?"

Carrie shook her head, her golden hair swishing with the motion. "Not really."

"Well you should." Bob removed his camouflage hat and scratched his head. "So you're looking for a bakery?" he said to me. "I don't know anything about a bakery. Hey, Isaac, do you know about a bakery that used to be here?"

With this, a guy about my age of twenty-four years stepped out of some sort of storage room, a camera in his hand. And let me tell you, as I looked at him, all I could think was, "If guys like that are into fishing, then sign me up, baby."

The cute guy who Bob had called Isaac walked over to the counter. "What bakery are you looking for?" he asked, his eyes on me.

And I, who hadn't had a date in far too long, and had apparently lost all of my social skills in the meantime, just stared at him.

Carrie nudged me.

"Oh, uh, what?" I stammered.

"Which bakery are you looking for?" Cute Guy Isaac repeated.

"Oh, uh, Marcia's. It's, a, uh, Portuguese bakery." I sounded like I barely knew English.

"Marcia's? Oh yeah—it moved to a shopping center a few blocks from here. Let me get the phone book. The address is in there."

"Um, thanks, I really . . ." I began. But then I made a very big mistake: I looked into his eyes. They were the nicest hazel color I had ever seen. A little more green than brown and just incredible. "I, uh, oh, uh," I said, reverting to some sort of cavewoman language. I really have no idea what I was trying to say.

"No problem, weirdo," Isaac said.

Okay, so he didn't actually say "weirdo," but I'm positive he was thinking it.

"So . . ." Carrie said, turning toward Bob. "What is your best pole for catching trout?"

I looked at Carrie and furrowed my brow. Since when did she have an interest in catching trout?

Carrie smiled a secret-girl-code smile that let me know she had noticed me going ridiculously ga-ga over the cute guy I had just met, and was going to give me a little time to chat with him. Then she let Bob lead her over to a wall of fishing poles.

Once Carrie and Bob had gone, Isaac reached behind the counter and retrieved a phone book. He flipped through the book, circled a line of print, and slid the book across the counter toward me. "Here's the address," he said. "You just go out to Pacheco Boulevard, turn right, and it's a few blocks down."

I nodded and wrote the address on my hand. Then I attempted to slide the phone book over to Isaac in the cool way that he had slid it to me. But I pushed a little too hard and sent the book flying off the counter. It smacked him right in the stomach. He made one of those wind-knocked-out sounds that football players make when they get hit real hard.

"Oh my goodness," I gasped. "I'm so sorry."

"No problem," Isaac said, rubbing his abdomen. He picked the phone book up off the floor and placed it behind the counter. "You know, you're a lot stronger than you look."

"Sorry," I said, biting my lip.

Isaac put his thumbs in his pockets and leaned against the worm refrigerator to his right. It would have grossed me out if he hadn't looked so good doing it. "I'm Isaac," he said.

"So I heard," I replied. It was meant to sound all cute and coy, but it mostly sounded idiotic. "I mean, um, I heard Bob calling you that. I'm . . . I'm Annabelle."

"Are you from around here, Annabelle?" Isaac asked, and something about the way he said my name sent the tiniest shiver through my body.

"Actually, no," I replied. "I'm from the Monterey Bay area."

Isaac looked interested. "Really? My family lives in Monterey. You must be roasting out here. It never gets hot in Monterey like it does in this town."

Isaac then said something else, something about some house in Monterey, but I wasn't really listening because I was suddenly completely distracted, wondering why exactly he had made his "roasting" comment. Was my face a shiny ball of oil? Did I have sweat spots under my arms?

"Um, yeah, it's really hot here," I said, trying as inconspicuously as possible to check my underarms.

"So did you drive all the way out here just to go to Marcia's bakery?" Isaac asked.

"Pretty much," I replied. "I need a Portuguese cake to take to work tomorrow."

"Well, I hope you find your cake," Isaac said. Then he moved away from the worm refrigerator and headed back to the storage room. I wasn't really surprised that he wanted to get away from me and back to his work. I mean, who wants to hang out with a book-throwing cavewoman with sweaty underarms?

"Thanks," I replied, my voice a little weak. Then I looked over at Carrie, who was still talking with Bob. "Ready to go?" I called out.

"Sure." Carrie listened as Bob finished his story—complete with gestures and sound effects—about the biggest trout he ever caught, and then she came to my side.

"Thanks for your help," I said to Bob.

Bob nodded a no-problem nod.

Carrie and I headed toward the exit, watching for worms as we walked. My hand was on the door when Isaac's voice came to my ears.

"Do you want to be in the *Los Banos Enterprise?*" he asked.

I spun around. "The what?"

Isaac walked toward me. "It's the local newspaper. I'm shooting photos for an ad Bob wants to put together. Maybe you and your friend could be my models."

I looked down. "Oh, no, I'm nothing close to a model."

Isaac looked at me intently. "I'm not too sure about that."

My cheeks instantly turned pink. I hoped Isaac would assume it was due to the temperature, not his comment.

"I'll pay you each twenty bucks," Isaac offered. "You can use it to buy your cake."

"I don't know," I said reluctantly. I turned to Carrie. "What do you think?"

Carrie shrugged her petite shoulders. "It sounds fun."

Twenty minutes later Carrie and I were decked out in fishing gear, holding onto fishing poles, smiling I'm-so-glad-I-found-Bob's-Bait-and-Tackle smiles as Isaac shot pictures of us and Bob acted as photo director.

As Isaac took the photos, he talked and joked with me and Carrie, being in every way Mr. Charming. And even though the fishing outfit I was wearing smelled a little funny, I was quite disappointed when the photo shoot was over.

I finished removing my fishing gear before Carrie, and as Isaac and Bob discussed advertisement ideas, I made my way over to a wall filled with pictures of smiling people showing off huge fish. I was looking at a picture of a man holding a fish that for some reason reminded me of Jay Leno, when I heard a voice behind me. "Here you go."

I turned around to see Isaac holding out a twenty dollar bill.

"Thanks," I said, reaching for the twenty. "But you really don't have to pay me. I had fun."

"I had fun too," Isaac said. "But take the money; you earned it."

I took the money from Isaac's hand, and as I did, I caught a glimpse of his titanium watch. Without thinking, I grabbed onto his arm and moved it toward me so I could see the timepiece better: 4:38.

"I have to go," I said, my voice panicky. "Carrie! We have to go. I'm pretty sure Marcia's closes in twenty minutes."

Carrie quickly removed her fishing vest and followed me to the door. And Isaac—as if he hadn't already done enough things that made him irresistibly gorgeous—came to open the door for us.

"Good luck finding that cake," he said. Then he handed me a business card, "Bob's Bait and Tackle: Where the Catchin' is Good," and fixed his hazel eyes on me. "If you have any trouble finding the bakery, just call."

"Thanks," I said, feeling suddenly disappointed that I have a pretty good sense of direction and would most likely not have trouble finding Marcia's.

"No problem." Isaac swung the shop door open, his forearm flexing rather nicely.

And suddenly I had an idea.

I could give Isaac *my* business card and let him know that I was in the magazine business. *Central Coast Living* outsourced photography jobs all the time. I could just tell him that if he ever wanted some work in Monterey, he should call. It really was a good professional move, since it was obvious Isaac had talent.

All right, all right. So I didn't know at all if he had talent. He could have been the worst photographer ever. But come on, he was a charming, door-opening man with a sense of humor and the most amazing hazel eyes ever. That was definitely the kind of guy *Central Coast Living* needed. Needed to put on an assignment with me.

No, no, my brain instantly piped up. *Giving strangers your business card, which has your cell phone number on it, is not a good idea.*

He gave me one, I argued with my brain. *So basically, it's the polite thing to do.*

It's not a good idea, my brain warned.

Whatever, I shot at my brain. *Why should I listen to you now? Where were you when I was speaking Cavewoman and throwing phone books? Where were you then, huh?*

Ignoring my brain, I reached into my bag—a designer one I got for just twenty bucks at Macy's because one of the handles was nearly ripped off—to search for my business card.

Carrie and Isaac both looked at me, obviously wondering why I was fiddling with my bag and not going out the door, but I didn't care.

Quickly, almost frantically, I fished—no pun intended—through my bag, clutching its contents. A pack of sugar-free gum. A nail file. The ridiculously slippery hand lotion I got as a free sample and never used. But not a single business card. I must have given them all out. With a frown, I told myself that my brain was right after all, it probably wasn't a good idea to give Isaac my card, and zipped my bag shut.

"Thanks again for all of your help," I said to Isaac as I stepped outside.

"No problem," he replied, his lips turning up into a smile.

And of course, as my life goes, Cute Guy Isaac, who I would never see again, had a killer smile.

"I love you too, Milesy bear," Carrie said into her cell. She had been talking to her boyfriend, Miles, for the entire hour and a half ride back to Monterey, using numerous terms of endearment throughout the conversation.

I rolled the car windows down, acting like I didn't hear the kissing noises Carrie made into the phone as she said good-bye to Miles. The cool, coastal, Monterey Bay air blew against my face, refreshing me. I took a deep breath of the air, savoring the delicious scent of the sea.

"Home," I said as I peered at the Pacific Ocean in the distance.

I watched, mesmerized, as the turquoise and blue waters rolled into the sand. No matter how many times I saw the sight, it was still incredible.

Carrie put her hand out the window and played with the wind. "Home," she echoed.

When we reached the city of Monterey, I made a not-too-smooth exit off the highway and then glanced in the rearview mirror to make sure the Portuguese sponge cake was okay. The cake remained unharmed in its pretty pink box on the back seat of my car, the silver 50% off sticker on the box shining in the sun. Marcia had given me 50% off the price of the cake because I bought it at the end of the day—now that was my kind of cake.

I drove straight to the house Carrie inherited from her grandmother, located just two blocks up the hill from the famous Cannery Row in the city of Monterey. For those of you who are not Steinbeck fans, Cannery Row is this ocean-side street that used to house sardine packing plants but has since been turned into a sort of tourist strip and the home of the famous Monterey Bay Aquarium.

I parked in the driveway next to Carrie's Toyota hybrid and gazed at the organic herbs she had planted in wooden boxes in front of her house. While Carrie was checking her mail, I let myself into her house with the key I have on my key ring. Carrie has a similar key to my condo, which is also in Monterey. The condo eats up pretty much my entire salary in rent, but I live there because it's safe and quiet and beautiful. And because the alternative is living with my parents.

Once inside, I plopped down on Carrie's all-natural cotton living room couch and kicked my shoes off. Carrie glided into the living room, flipping through an issue of *Organic Woman.* She lifted my feet up off the couch, sat down, and then set my feet on her lap.

"Thank you so much for coming with me today," I said to her. "I know it wasn't a very convenient thing to do on a Thursday afternoon."

Carrie closed the magazine and set it on the coffee table. "I had a nice time. I like seeing new places."

"You know," I said, "I just remembered, it's Paint and Popcorn night. Do you want to buy a new shade of toenail paint? And maybe rent a movie?"

At Cal Poly, which Carrie and I attended together—Carrie majoring in fruit science, me changing my major three times and finally settling on journalism—Carrie and I started Paint and Popcorn night. This is where every Thursday night we paint our toenails and eat popcorn while we hang out, talk, and watch girl movies.

"Actually, Miles wants to do something tonight," Carrie said apologetically.

I frowned. Miles was a good enough guy. In fact, he was pretty much perfect for Carrie, but the peeling paint on my toenails was proof that he had begun to monopolize my best friend.

You know, I just realized that I've been telling you that Carrie is my best friend this whole time, but I haven't really explained. I should probably do that, huh? Okay, here goes.

It all happened at a youth conference when Carrie and I were both fourteen. I was in the bathroom, totally shattered because my nylons had a big hole in them that I noticed just as

Robert Beatty was walking toward me, about to sit next to me for the talk on missionary work.

In the bathroom, where she had been washing her hands, Carrie noticed my broken state and told me that the bare leg look was in, and besides, nylon was a manmade fiber that didn't let the body breath the way it was meant to.

So, I threw away my nylons, squared my shoulders, and went back to my chair in the gymnasium with Carrie's arm around my waist. Soon, Robert Beatty came back and sat next to me, and in the middle of the speaker's address he told me I had nice ankles.

That night, I went home and found my pink diary, which I hadn't used in quite a while, and made what I called a Pink Note. My first Pink Note.

> Pink Note #1
> Name: Carrie Fields
> Why she's noteworthy: Carrie saved me from a super-crisis at the youth conference. She is so sweet and so awesome. She's such a cool person. I hope that we will be friends forever.

Carrie and I have been best friends ever since.

And after I made that first note, I kind of made a tradition of my Pink Notes. I filled up my diary and then a couple of notebooks—all pink in the Pink Note tradition—with entries on people who inspired me, people who had an impact on me. And though I have a fair number of entries, I still look back to Pink Note #1 and smile.

So there you have it, the me-and-Carrie story.

Carrie and I sat on her couch and chatted until Miles called for Carrie. I got up from the couch after the three hundredth time Carrie called Miles her little "Milesy Muffin."

"Call me," I mouthed before heading to the door.

"Okay, love you," Carrie mouthed back.

I left Carrie's house and drove home.

As I drove, I found myself wishing I had someone to talk

with on the phone. I even entertained the idea of calling Bob's Bait and Tackle just to, you know, say that I found the bakery and thanks again. But I immediately discarded the thought. I would just go home and do what I always did: have a little date with Mr. Comcast and Ben & Jerry.

Chapter 2

I strode into the conference room at ten minutes to eleven on Friday morning. When I was about five steps inside the room, Arvin, my coworker who also happens to be on the singles ward activities committee with me, put a muscular arm around my shoulder. "Dude, what's up?" he asked.

Arvin works at *Central Coast Living* to supplement his professional surfing income, and he's pretty much the reason I got an interview at the magazine even though I had no experience outside of my college degree and a short-lived internship working on the weekly newsletter of an organization called Pets are People Too. He's a pretty cool guy. Although for every ward activity he suggests surfing.

But before you go thinking something like, "How cute would it be for Annabelle to get together with her fellow activities committee member?!" let me just tell you that Arvin and I would never and could never be a match. Arvin likes girls who are blonde and tiny and into surfing, none of which I am. And I like, well, a guy who doesn't call me "dude," for starters.

"Just delivering a cake George asked me to bring," I answered Arvin as I headed toward the buffet table in the back of the room.

Arvin followed me. "Did you make it?" He lifted the box's pink lid and looked inside.

"Nope. Bakery bought. George asked me to bring it."

Arvin nodded his head in understanding.

"Trying to impress the big boss, huh?"

I frowned at him. "Be quiet."

Arvin laughed in his laid back way. "Speaking of the boss, check this out." He held up a shiny silver key. "George asked me to do some things for his office remodel. I'm gonna change the whole vibe in there."

I raised my eyebrows. "I didn't know you were a decorator in addition to your many other talents."

Arvin glared at me. "Dude, do not call me a decorator. I'm a re-modeler."

"Sorry," I said. "I didn't know you were a *re-modeler*."

"What can I say; I've got skills," he said with a shrug of his surfing-sculpted shoulders.

When Arvin and I reached the buffet table, I carefully lifted the cake out of the box and set it down. I cocked my head to the right and examined the dessert. It was one good looking cake, if I do say so myself.

"It looks delicious," I heard a voice say from behind me.

I knew the voice was George's, and I turned around to face him. "George," I said, my voice sounding kind of like the squawk of a goose. I cleared my throat. "I, um, I'm glad you think so. I hope you enjoy it."

I smiled brightly at George and then flashed a smile at Gidget, George's teeny-tiny, always-perky assistant, who was standing beside him in a white suit and the cutest pair of shoes. "Great shoes," I said before turning to walk away.

Gidget called out a high-pitched "thank you," and Arvin began flirting with her.

I made my way to my usual meeting seat next to Patty Pearson, a short, feisty, single mother of three college students and associate food editor at *Central Coast Living*.

"Hey Patty," I said as I lowered myself into the seat. "What's up?"

"My children are torturing me." Patty said the words with melodramatic exhaustion. "You'll never believe what Elizabeth has chosen as this month's 'life ambition.'"

Elizabeth is Patty's youngest daughter, and I've heard quite a few interesting stories about her. And from what I've heard I think she and I might just get along. "What?" I asked.

"She wants to save the African flea. I told her, 'Honey if you want to save something, try the thousands of dollars I give you for college in hopes you'll earn a degree one of these years.'"

"What's an African flea?"

Patty shook her head. "I have no earthly idea."

I was about to ask Patty why exactly the African flea needed saving, when I noticed out of the corner of my eye that George, who remained by the buffet table in the back of the room, had picked up a white china plate and was placing food onto the plate.

I held my breath as he served himself chicken, then a roll, then some salad, then . . . a slice of the Portuguese sponge cake. I smiled and released a long breath. And then my smile grew into this huge, face-swallowing thing—which I think may have scared Patty—as I watched George add a second slice of the cake to his plate.

When the meeting was over, I decided it was time to visit the buffet table one more time—the dessert area of the buffet table to be exact. Right after I had placed a slice of chocolate silk pie on a plate, I was approached by George.

"Pleasanton," he said. He always refers to me by my last name for some reason, kind of like I'm the center on his football team or something. "I need to see you in my office."

"Oh, okay." I disappointedly put the pie back onto the glass serving platter and hoped that the treat would still be there when I returned.

I followed George to his office. Once inside, I took a seat

in the blue canvas-covered chair facing the desk, and George settled into his leather swivel chair.

"Well, Pleasanton," George began. "I have been very impressed with you lately. You have been willing to step up and do what is required of you. When I asked you to bring that Portuguese cake to the meeting today and gave you very little notice, you took it all in stride and remained impressively poised. You have proven you can meet a deadline, and deadlines are what the magazine business is all about."

"Oh," I said. "I'm glad you liked the cake. I—"

George cut me off. "This isn't just about the cake. It's about you."

I looked at George in confusion. He must have sensed this, because he continued speaking. "I need you to write a piece for the Anniversary Issue. Patty is having surgery tomorrow, so she won't be able to write. She's taking three weeks of sick leave."

"Oh, no," I said. "Is Patty okay?"

"Patty's fine. It's an elective procedure, if you know what I mean." George gave me a weird look.

"Oh," I said. I wasn't sure I did know what he meant.

George continued. "The article is to be on the restaurant La Bonne Violette in Carmel and its owner and executive Chef, Jean-Pierre Poitier. Jean-Pierre—that's how he prefers to be addressed—has agreed to do an exclusive interview for the article. This could quite possibly be the best piece ever to appear in the *Central Coast Living* Cuisine section." George's eyes lit up.

I stared straight ahead, a dumbfounded look on my face. George was asking me to write an article on La Bonne Violette? La Bonne Violette was the most posh restaurant in the area. Only the rich and famous dined at La Bonne Violette. And Chef Jean-Pierre was a huge deal. In fact, just a few days earlier I had seen a little blurb on him in one of those weekly celebrity magazines as I was reading it over the shoulder of the lady in front of me in the grocery store line. This was a big-time assignment. And it was mine?

George smiled at my state of speechlessness. "Okay, Pleasanton, you have a lot of work to do. I've set up a meeting with Jean-Pierre for an hour from now. A photographer will meet you at the restaurant."

"You mean I need to get started in an hour?" I asked. "What about research, what about—"

"That's the magazine business for you," George said. "Is it too much for you to handle? If it is, I can give the assignment to Arvin in subscriptions. He's always trying to tell me he can write."

"Oh, no, I can handle it," I said emphatically.

"All right then. Your deadline is two weeks from Tuesday. I'm giving you a little extra time since you'll still be expected to do your editing. And I'd like you to bring me a draft on Wednesday, by five o'clock. Just so I can check your progress."

"I will," I promised. "Is there anything else?"

"No. Now get to work."

George flashed me a thumbs-up sign and I awkwardly flashed one back before getting up to leave.

Back at my cubicle, I did some quick internet research on La Bonne Violette and Jean-Pierre. As I looked at stunning pictures of the restaurant, my stomach felt all fluttery, and I found myself looking forward to stepping foot into the glamorous restaurant. And I was totally excited to meet Jean-Pierre.

Of course, that was until I actually did meet Jean-Pierre.

The first thing I noticed about La Bonne Violette was the floor. It was made of this beautiful cobblestone that made me feel like I was at an outdoor French café. Natural light and the sparkle of the ocean poured in through the restaurant's spotless windows, and this added to the outdoor effect.

No wonder all the celebrities come here, I thought as I peered into the dining room. I was slightly disappointed that no one was sitting at the white-linen-covered tables. I mean, it would have been cool to get a peek at Jen or Colin.

Within seconds, I was greeted by a tall, thin maître d' dressed in a white tuxedo shirt and black pants. "Bonjour, Mademoiselle," the maître d' said. "What can I do for you?"

"I have an appointment with Jean-Pierre at one o'clock."

The maître d' consulted a book on the podium in front of him. "Are you from *Central Coast Living*?"

"Yes," I answered. Both excitement and anxiety began to bubble inside me.

"May I have your name?"

"Annabelle Pleasanton."

"Right this way."

The maître d' led me through a set of doors into the kitchen where sous chefs were busy at work, and the sounds of washing, chopping, and speaking—both in French and English—filled the air. The maître d' led me to a large chrome range and presented me to a medium-height man with a protruding belly and a bushy mustache. His white chef's uniform had a large red food stain on the front.

"Jean-Pierre, Mademoiselle Pleasanton from *Central Coast Living*," the maître d' introduced me.

"Merci, Joseph," Jean-Pierre said without taking his eyes off the food he was sautéing on the range in front of him.

The maître d' walked away, and Jean-Pierre quickly shot me a look that told me I had not come at a convenient time.

I cleared my throat and searched for words. "Good afternoon, Jean-Pierre. I understand you spoke with my boss, George Kent, and agreed to do an interview," I began. With shaky hands, I retrieved a yellow notebook from my black leather satchel.

"Oui," Jean-Pierre responded. Then, as if I weren't even in the room, he headed toward a walk-in refrigerator and went inside.

I followed on his heels, notebook in hand.

Inside the chill of the refrigerator, I opened my mouth to

ask my first interview question, the one I had practiced over and over in my car as I drove to the restaurant.

But Jean-Pierre spoke before I could. "You are in zee way," he said in a thick French accent as he reached for something on the shelf behind me.

"Oh, I'm sorry," I said as I took a quick step to the left. Too quick of a step.

My left foot caught the edge of a box of produce on the floor and I lost my balance. As I fell forward, I put my hand out to break my fall. My hand, in turn, grabbed onto a metal shelf, and the whole set of shelves began shaking.

Before I had time to process what was happening, the contents of a bowl filled with mixed greens, juicy tomatoes, and some crumbly cheese fell on me like some sort of salad shower.

Jean-Pierre watched as the red tomatoes splattered against my pale blue cashmere sweater—which I bought for just fifteen bucks at a consignment store—and the cheese and salad greens sprinkled my hair and shoulders. Then he let out a string of French words, which I don't think meant, "My, what a wonderful girl you are."

I bent over and attempted to clean up the mess, apologizing like mad and assuring Jean-Pierre that I would pay for the food.

As I was cleaning, a woman with kind eyes and a French accent not quite as pronounced as Jean-Pierre's appeared in the refrigerator doorway. She took one look at me and shot me a compassionate glance. "Everything all right?" she asked.

"Well, I—"

"She's fine," Jean-Pierre snapped. "But look at this mess."

"There is a bathroom to the right of the salad prep area," the woman whispered to me kindly. Then she turned to address Jean-Pierre. "The photographer for *Central Coast Living* is here to see you."

"I do not have time for this," Jean-Pierre grumbled. "I called Ingrid and asked her to change these appointments!"

"I, um, I could come back later, and I'm sure I could talk to the photographer and . . ."

"It is too late now," Jean-Pierre growled. Then with a heaving sigh he followed the woman out of the refrigerator.

Feeling completely terrified that this assignment was going to turn out worse, not better, than my first one, I cleaned up the mess the best I could. Then I picked salad greens out of my hair and wandered back into the massive kitchen in search of the bathroom, where I would try to fix myself up before I went to talk with the photographer.

As I tiptoed through the kitchen, I noticed that the photographer was taking candid shots of the kitchen and staff. His back was toward me, so I couldn't see him very well. Then he turned slightly to get a better angle for a shot, and I noticed that he looked vaguely familiar.

No way, I thought, narrowing my eyes. *It couldn't be.*

But it was. It was Isaac. The guy I had met at Bob's Bait and Tackle. The guy who lived nearly a hundred miles away from me. The guy I was sure I would never see again. This weird excited feeling suddenly came over me, and I began walking quickly toward Isaac to say hello.

But then I smelled myself. I stunk like a mix of acidic tomatoes and horrifically smelly feet. Thinking better of my idea to go talk to Isaac, I quickly ducked behind a tall bread warmer and held my breath. Partly because I was nervous that Isaac would see me and partly because I really did stink.

"Annabelle? Annabelle the cake girl?"

I spun around and saw Isaac looking at me, his face registering both disbelief and delight.

"Uh, hey, what are you doing here?" I asked, backing away from Isaac slowly.

"I'm taking photos for a magazine article," Isaac explained, moving two steps toward me for every one step I took back. "Have you seen a writer from *Central Coast Living* around here?" Isaac looked at my shirt and saw the tomato stains. He furrowed his brow. "Do you work here?"

"No, I don't work here." I looked down at my soiled shirt. "I'm actually the writer you're looking for."

"Really? You write for *Central Coast Living*?" The corners of Isaac's mouth turned up slightly.

"Probably not for long," I replied somberly.

I realized a little too late that Isaac had moved very close to me. And as soon as he was in the new close-to-me position, he scrunched up his nose and began sniffing the air around me. "Have you been eating . . . cheese?" he asked, his nose still all scrunched up.

My face grew hot with humiliation and in a reflex reaction I pushed Isaac away. "There was a little accident in the refrigerator locker," I said. "I haven't been eating cheese. I just kind of, you know, smell like it." Then, to get the subject off my cheesy-smelliness, I said, "So wait a minute? You're working for the magazine. But you live in Los Banos. That's quite a commute."

"I grew up there, but I live here now. I think I told you that yesterday."

I opened my mouth to respond, but I suddenly found myself lost in the hazel color of Isaac's eyes. And for a good thirty seconds I forgot how to speak.

The sound of Jean-Pierre's voice in the distance brought me back to reality. I pulled my eyes away from Isaac's. "I'm going to go figure out what to do about interviewing Jean-Pierre. Will you excuse me?"

"After you talk to Jean-Pierre, do you want to get some lunch?" Isaac asked. "I think it would be good for us to talk about the article. I can meet you out in the dining room when I'm done back here, and we can go grab something."

Now, it was true that I had already eaten lunch at the meeting at work, but I really wanted to hang out with Isaac, so I accepted. "Lunch sounds great," I said. "That is, if you don't mind how I look."

"I definitely don't mind how you look," Isaac said as he turned to walk away. Then I think he may have winked at me, but I'm not sure. He may have been grimacing at my smell.

With a happy little grin on my face, I approached Jean-Pierre, who had returned to his spot in front of the range. "Jean-Pierre, is there a better time for us to meet?" I asked.

"I am going out of town. Come back on Wednesday. Nine o'clock in the morning."

That's just hours before George wants to look over my draft, I thought fearfully. "Maybe we can do a phone interview," I suggested.

"Come back Wednesday," Jean-Pierre repeated in a tone that said he was used to giving orders.

"Of course," I answered.

I could make it work. I could do as much of the research and writing as possible beforehand and then just add the interview stuff in. It would be no problem. No problem at all.

I found the restroom the woman had directed me to, where I scrubbed my face and arms with a floral scented soap, hoping this would get rid of the cheese smell. Then I washed my hair right there in the sink with the same soap and dried it with one of the towels in the basket on the counter. I sniffed myself and noted that I smelled slightly better. Kind of like flower scented cheese.

I combed my hair back into a bun and put a touch of makeup back onto my face. Unfortunately, not much could be done about my clothes. But hey, if holey, grease-stained jeans can sell for $150—and I know they do because I saw them at the mall— then my tomato-soiled cashmere sweater had to be worth like $100, right?

I went into the dining area and sat down at a table just outside the kitchen doors. I stared at the fresh violets in an antique vase on the table and pretended to take some notes. But there weren't many notes to take. So instead I drew Jean-Pierre's head with a whole bunch of tomatoes squished all over it.

As I doodled, a guy in a wheelchair approached the table

where I sat. I immediately put my hand over my drawing.

"Hello," the guy said to me. He smiled a friendly smile as he buttoned the top button of his tuxedo shirt. "You wouldn't happen to have seen a photographer around here, would you?" he asked.

"Actually, yes," I replied. "He's in the kitchen."

"Thanks." The guy smiled at me again before disappearing into the kitchen.

A short while later he returned side by side with Isaac. The two were laughing and gesturing in a way that suggested they knew each other.

Isaac approached me and put his arm around the guy's shoulder. "Annabelle, meet my brother, Ethan."

I raised my eyebrows. "Brothers, huh?"

"Unfortunately," Ethan joked. He then glanced at a watch on his wrist. "I'd better go. I'm on pretty soon."

"Do you work here?" I asked.

"I play the piano every so often."

"Cool," I said. "I'd like to hear you play sometime."

"Well, I'm here every Friday," Ethan told me. Then he said a quick good-bye to me and Isaac, leaving us alone at the table in the dining area.

"How did it go in there?" I asked, nodding toward the kitchen.

"Pretty good."

"Well good for you," I said, my tone slightly sarcastic.

"Thanks," Isaac said with a grin. "So, ready for lunch?"

"Sure am."

"Where do you want to go?"

"Well . . . there's a great café that sells smoothies and really yummy croissant sandwiches a couple of blocks from here. We could go there if you'd like."

"Smoothies and croissant sandwiches it is," Isaac replied without hesitation.

Isaac and I walked side by side to the café. Once, my swinging hand brushed against his and I immediately apologized. But secretly I enjoyed the little chill I got when it happened. Hey, a bit of harmless photographer-flirting never hurt anyone.

As we reached the entrance to the café, I noticed a group of women dressed in exercise wear of various pastel colors sitting around one of the wooden tables inside. I immediately recognized the group. It was the Jazzercisers.

The six women, ranging from age thirty-nine to sixty-five, meet three times a week to do Jazzercise in the gymnasium inside the church building in Monterey. Afterwards, they reward themselves with smoothies at various cafés and smoothie shops in the area. I knew this group because one of its members, today dressed in a lavender warm-up suit and bright white sneakers, was my mother. And I also knew that if I showed up in the café with Isaac by my side pandemonium could quite possibly ensue. So I had to act quickly.

"Isaac, it looks pretty crowded in there," I said. "I don't, uh, really have a lot of time for lunch today. So maybe we should try somewhere else." I took a few steps away from the door of the café.

"There isn't even a line inside," Isaac said, opening the door for me.

I stood in place and tried again. "But I think I'd like someplace more quiet."

Isaac let the door close and stepped to the side. "It's up to you."

I nodded and looked around for an alternative lunch location. And just when I had spotted a restaurant that didn't have the best food, but was attractive due to its lack of pastel-sweat-suit-clad women, I saw six hands waving wildly at me from inside the café. For a second I thought about ignoring the hands and dashing toward the other restaurant, but Isaac interrupted that thought.

"Do you know those people?" he asked.

"Yes," I responded with a sigh. "And you're about to."

As we walked into the café, I heard the sound of blenders and coffee grinders behind the counter and the buzz of six women greeting me and Isaac. I approached the Jazzercisers' table, and bent down to hug Mom. Her shoulder length curls brushed against my face.

She looked from me to Isaac and then fixed her eyes—which are nearly the exact shade of maple-syrup brown as mine—on me. "What happened to you?" she asked.

I ignored the question and introduced Isaac to Mom. I told her he was the photographer assigned to a new article I was working on. Mom and Isaac shook hands. Then I went around the table introducing the rest of the women: "Loraine, Lynn, Suzanne, Maria, and Janet."

"Why don't you two sit down," Mom suggested immediately. Lynn and Maria borrowed two chairs from a nearby table for us to sit in. I tried to gauge Isaac's reaction to everything, and thought he was handling the estrogen overload quite well.

"So, Isaac, where are you from?" Mom asked the second Isaac and I were seated.

Isaac set his camera case beneath his chair. "Originally I am from a little town in the San Joaquin Valley called Los Banos, which is where I met your daughter." Isaac smiled at me. "But I live in Monterey now."

"Oh, and what brought you to Monterey?" Mom asked.

Isaac paused for a moment before answering. "My younger brother was in an accident. My parents moved out here to live closer to my uncle, who is a doctor. I decided to move out here too."

I looked at Isaac, and was tempted to ask for more details about what happened to his brother, but I knew it wasn't the right time or setting to ask.

With the where-are-you-from stuff taken care of, Mom and her friends dove in on Isaac like vultures. They asked him about his family, his education, his job, and even—I'm telling you these women are shameless—his dating status.

I listened in.

He had twin sisters who were in high school, and Ethan was his only brother. He double majored in business and photography at San Jose State. He worked for a newspaper in Los Angeles and then moved to Monterey, where he does mostly freelance. And as for his dating status: single. I listened carefully to that part.

As Mom and her friends interrogated Isaac, I watched him carefully, waiting for a get-the-questions-to-stop signal, but he never sent me one. He was the picture of graciousness.

Finally Mom hugged me and said in a tone that made my cheeks turn pink, "Well, I guess we'd better leave you two alone." Then she turned to Isaac. "It was a pleasure to meet you."

"Good to meet you too," Isaac replied genuinely. He then nodded toward Mom's friends. "It was good to meet all of you."

The women took turns bidding me and Isaac good-bye and giving me little he's-a-cutie looks behind Isaac's back, and then they were off in one pastel swoop.

"I'm so sorry about that," I said once Isaac and I were alone.

"About what? They were great."

"They sure liked you," I said.

"Your Mom's real nice. Now I can see where you get it."

I looked down at the floor. "We should get some food," I said quickly. I picked up the leather-bound menu that was on the center of the table and began looking it over.

"So, this place isn't too crowded for you after all?" Isaac asked with a grin.

"No, it's just right," I answered meaningfully.

Isaac and I looked over the menu and decided to split a turkey croissant sandwich.

As we ate, we made small talk and then talked about the article. Then, as we sipped on smoothies—mine a Pineapple Mango Delight, Isaac's a Strawberry Banana Dream—the conversation turned more serious.

"Can I ask you a question?" I asked Isaac.

"Okay."

I tried to form the question in my mind before asking it, so it didn't sound like I was prying. "Can I ask what happened to your brother?"

Isaac leaned back in his chair. "Sure you can ask that. When he was on his mi—I mean, when he lived in Guatemala for a couple of years, he got hurt trying to save a girl during a flash flood." Isaac managed a weak smile.

I carefully chose my next words. "That must have been terrible."

"Yeah, but he's a rock. He's handled it better than I ever could have." It was obvious in Isaac's voice that he really admired his brother.

I nodded silently.

"Thanks for coming to lunch with me," Isaac said, sounding pretty eager to change the subject.

"Thanks for the invitation."

"Will you have dinner with me sometime?" he asked out of nowhere.

I played with the straw in my smoothie as I considered the question.

Annabelle, you're setting yourself up to get hurt, my brain immediately piped up. *No sense dating a guy if he can't take you to the temple.*

Everyone has to eat, I told my brain.

I could eat dinner with a work colleague if I wanted to. And if he just happened to be gorgeous and charming, well, there was nothing I could do about that now was there.

"I would like that very much," I answered.

"How about tomorrow night?"

"Tomorrow is perfect," I replied, still playing with my smoothie straw.

"Pick you up at six?" Isaac looked over at me in a terribly adorable way.

I listened carefully to my feelings. In this day and age a girl can never be too careful, and Dad has always told me to exercise caution when it comes to letting men pick me up at my home. Luckily for me, I didn't have any uneasy feeling about Isaac. In fact, I had some pretty good feelings about him.

"Six would be wonderful," I said. I wrote my cell number and address on a sugar packet and resisted the urge to draw a big heart on it before handing it to Isaac.

"Great," Isaac said as he simultaneously put the sugar in his pocket and stood up from the table. He offered me his hand and helped me out of my chair.

I moved toward the door, and Isaac followed close behind, opening the door for me. I've found that this is a tricky maneuver for most guys, but Isaac handled it perfectly.

Outside the café, Isaac told me he was going to go to a nearby store, and I explained that I was heading back to La Bonne Violette to get my car. Then I stood still on the sidewalk for a moment trying to figure out how to say good-bye. Should I hug him? Should I shake his hand? Should I give him a little punch on the shoulder? I finally settled on a nice, "I'll see you tomorrow," accompanied by a wave and a warm smile.

Isaac reciprocated with, "I'll be looking forward to it," and a wave and smile of his own.

I spun on my heels and walked away. And then when I just couldn't stand it anymore I turned around to look back at Isaac.

He was watching me walk away.

Chapter 3

"Hello?" I answered my cell.

"Hello, Annabelle, this is Miles speaking. I was calling to inquire what you are doing this evening."

I think this is a good time to mention that Miles talks properly all the time. Sometimes it almost sounds like he has an English accent, which I know is impossible because he's from Idaho.

"I'm on my way to have dinner at my parents' house," I answered.

"Excellent. Thank you very much. Good-bye."

"Bye." I hung up the phone, furrowing my brow in what-was-that-all-about confusion.

When I arrived at my parents' house, Mom and Dad were sitting on the porch swing in front of the single-story, pale-blue home they have lived in since before I was born. They were holding hands and gazing out at the glittering ocean in the distance.

I approached them and sat down next to Mom on the swing. I could immediately smell the scent of the freesia fragrance she wore.

"Hi, hon," Mom greeted me.

"Hey," I said, putting my head on her shoulder.

"Hi, Bellie," Dad said. That's his nickname for me. It's short for Annabelle, and has no reference to my stomach—just so you know.

"Hi, Dad." I lifted my head off Mom's shoulder and smiled at him.

"I'm going to go check on dinner," Mom announced, standing up from the swing.

Dad and I followed Mom into the house, which smelled delicious, as it always does around dinner time.

I was washing my hands in the bathroom next to my old bedroom when I heard Mom's voice call out to me. "Annabelle, someone is here to see you."

My heart stopped. More than once when I've come to my parents' house for a casual Friday evening dinner Mom has invited an acquaintance of hers to join us. A single, male, twenty-something acquaintance.

There was the stockman from the grocery store who to everyone's surprise turned out to be a seventeen-year-old stock-kid.

There was the pool guy who announced during dinner that he hoped to marry a rich woman so he could quit his job and try to sell the collection of bugs he removed from his clients' pools over the years.

Then there was a guy I actually liked. Mom had met him at church in her and Dad's ward. He was cute, interesting, and had no overt quirks. We went on a couple of dates, and I thought things were going well. Then he came to attend church in the singles ward with me, took one look at the cute redhead who was leading the music, and was gone. The two of them were married last month. Mom and I made some chocolate dipped strawberries for the reception.

"Annabelle, where are you?" Mom called out again.

What was Mom up to? Had she decided that Isaac was not suited for me when she met him at the café, and gone out in search of a replacement man? I thought about locking myself in the bathroom, but before I could, Mom appeared in the doorway.

"Miles is here," she announced.

Miles. Oh, thank goodness.

"What is he doing here?"

"He needs your help with something," Mom replied, sounding like she had a very juicy secret.

"Oh." I bit my lip in puzzlement.

I smoothed my hair as I followed Mom into the living room. Dad was sitting comfortably in his recliner, which is just about as old as me, and Miles was sitting on the well-worn plaid couch. Mom perched on the arm of Dad's recliner, and I plopped down on a giant bean bag on the floor and listened carefully to Dad and Miles discussing homerun records and traded baseball players. Since knowing baseball facts can sometimes give a single girl like me an advantage in the dating world, I listened carefully.

"Hey, Miles," I said in a break in the conversation. "Mom says you need my help with something?"

"Yes, indeed. I need you to accompany me as I go ring shopping."

"Why don't you ask Carrie to come with you?" I asked dumbly.

Two seconds later, I figured it out. "No way!!" I screeched. "Are you going to . . . I can't believe you're . . . Does Carrie know about . . . Of course I'll come shopping with you!"

"I was considering going tomorrow morning." Miles spoke calmly as if to demonstrate that he was completely cool about this whole thing, not at all screechy and unable to form sentences like I was.

"Yeah, sure," I agreed. I tried to catch my breath. "Where do you want to meet?"

Miles reached into his pocket and took out a neatly folded piece of linen paper. He handed me the paper. "I have a list of jewelry stores I have researched," he said. "I think we should meet at the first one on the list."

I looked at the paper. John Wilfred was first on the list. I swallowed hard. John Wilfred is *the* place to buy jewelry in the Monterey Bay area.

"What time do you want to meet?" I asked.

"Would ten o'clock be suitable for you?"

"Yeah, ten is great." I returned the list to Miles.

"Splendid," Miles said.

Miles started to get up from the couch and Mom immediately objected. "Sit down and stay for a while, Miles. I've just finished dinner, and you're welcome to stay."

"Thanks for the invitation Marjorie, but I have dinner plans with Carrie."

Mom shot Miles a disappointed look.

So, being the kind guy that he is, Miles said, "On second thought, it would be quite a pleasure to stay a while."

"Great," Mom said before disappearing into the kitchen.

Miles and Dad started right back in on their baseball talk, and I quietly considered the information I had just been given. I couldn't believe it. Miles was going to ask Carrie to marry him, and of course she was going to say yes. I couldn't have been happier for anyone in the world.

Then, suddenly, I found myself wishing Miles was my boyfriend. Okay, not technically Miles, no way, but a Miles of my own. I wished I were at my parents' house with a guy Dad could talk with, a guy Mom would invite to stay for dinner, a guy who wanted to buy me a John Wilfred diamond ring. I was happy for Carrie and Miles, I really was. But couldn't I be happy for them and sorry for myself at the same time?

"Is everyone ready to eat?" Mom asked, bringing me back to reality.

Everyone nodded, uttered various forms of "I'm starving," and followed Mom to the dining room where I proceeded to drown my sorrows in twice baked potatoes and Mom's famous raspberry cheesecake.

Okay, I know that diamonds probably shouldn't be a girl's *best* friend because that would be entirely too materialistic. But maybe they could be a girl's *really good* friend. I mean, that would be okay, right?

"Of course that would be okay." The diamonds honestly seemed to be whispering those words to me as Miles and I walked into John Wilfred at ten o'clock Saturday morning.

The place was a world of luxury. Deep-green plush carpeting. Golden light that cast a warm glow on everything. Gourmet chocolates and bottles of mineral water arranged beautifully on a large mahogany table. Spotless glass display cases filled with diamonds and other precious jewels. It was all just so incredible.

"Where shall we start?" Miles asked me after a moment.

I was torn. Did I want to start with the jewelry or the chocolates? Yes, I know I was technically there to shop for Carrie, but I might as well enjoy myself while I was at it, right?

Miles and I were promptly greeted by a short, dark-haired man in a black suit.

"How are you two today?" the man asked as he shook both of our hands firmly.

"Very well, thank you," Miles replied.

I smiled politely and tried to stop my eyes from wandering to the display of diamond jewelry to the left.

"I'm Bryce," the man introduced himself.

Miles and I both told Bryce our names.

"Are you looking for something in particular?" Bryce asked.

"Yes indeed," Miles said. "We are searching for an engagement ring."

A bright smile formed on Bryce's face. "You've come to the right place. Why don't you come this way and we can take a look at the catalogue to get a good feel for what we're looking for." Bryce gestured toward the back of the store.

"All right then," Miles said. He turned toward me to see if I was going to follow.

"I'll just wait here," I said. *And check out these rocks.*

Miles nodded, and he and Bryce took off toward the back of the shop.

I immediately dashed over to the diamond display case. I bent forward, closely examining delicate rings and necklaces, earrings shaped like squares and tear drops, and tennis bracelets that no sensible woman would ever wear while playing tennis.

Absorbed in the world of sparkly beauty, I was unaware of a saleswoman approaching me until I saw a reflection of her knee-length black skirt and slender legs in the glass.

"Hello," the woman said in a milky-smooth voice.

"Hi," I responded, looking up from the display case. The woman had dark curly hair and an ivory complexion.

"Lisa Toriani." The woman held out her hand for me to shake.

"Annabelle Pleasanton," I said, shaking Lisa's hand a little too loosely.

"Would you like to start trying some rings on while your fiancé is in the back?" Lisa asked me.

I let out a small chuckle. "Oh, no, he's not my . . ." I let my voice trail off.

Yes, I should have finished the sentence with, "He's not my fiancé. He's going to propose to my best friend, and I'm here to help pick out her ring." But instead, my good sense left me and I thought, *I wonder what it would it feel like to be ring shopping for my own ring rather than my best friend's ring?* And before I knew what was happening, the word "sure" was coming out of my mouth.

"Do you prefer a platinum or gold setting?" Lisa asked me.

"Platinum," I answered. I knew full well that Carrie wanted gold.

"Our platinum is in this case right here." Lisa's calf muscles flexed as she moved behind the display case I had been examining. "What type of cut would you like?" she asked as she unlocked the case.

"Definitely princess," I answered, though I knew Carrie wanted a round.

Lisa slid the display case door open, and immediately my left ring finger started to itch.

"Most of our display rings are a size six. Will that be all right?" Lisa asked me.

"Oh sure, that's fine," I replied even though I wear a size seven. *Six, seven; there can't be that big of a difference. I want to try on some of these rings!*

"So where shall we start?" Lisa asked.

I took my time gazing at the rings, which ranged from nice-looking pebble to heart-stopping rock.

Then I saw it. A princess cut, heart-stopping rock set in a thick band made of the shiniest platinum. I felt my breath get caught in my lungs.

"That one," I said breathlessly as I pointed to the ring.

Lisa removed the ring from the case and handed it to me.

I began to slide the ring onto my finger slowly, carefully. As I did this I pictured my dream man on his knees in front of me. I pictured that it wasn't me slipping the ring onto my finger, but him. And the weirdest part is the dream man I was picturing looked an awful lot like Isaac. But before I could get the ring all the way on and imagine myself exclaiming "Yes!" and kissing my dream man, the thing got stuck on my knuckle.

I forced a smile at Lisa as I tried to jam the ring onto my finger. Finally it moved. But the wonderful moment of at last having the ring on my hand was overshadowed by the fact that my finger began to go numb. And it kind of started to turn blue. Lisa looked at the ring and told me how gorgeous it looked on me. But all I could think about was what would happen if I lost my finger.

I was thinking about how much my life would change if I were left-ring-finger-less when I heard Miles's voice, and it sounded close. "There she is," he was saying.

I looked up and my eyes grew wide with panic. My pretend fiancé was heading toward me.

"Hi, Miles," I squeaked when he reached my side.

"I believe I know where we should start," Miles said to me. Luckily for me he was too focused on finding the perfect ring to notice how flustered I was.

Bryce the salesman pointed to the right. "Our high quality gold is this way," he explained.

"Oh," I said.

"Bryce," Lisa said to the salesman in a women-know-best tone, "she has already indicated a preference for platinum."

"She has?" Miles asked confusedly.

"Um, yeah, maybe," I stammered. "What do you think about this ring?" I held my hand out like it was completely normal for the single friend to try on the rings.

Miles looked at the ring for no more than a second. "No," he said briskly.

Lisa shot me a look that said I'm-so-sorry-you-have-such-a-horrible-fiance-who-won't-buy-you-the-ring-of-your-dreams.

"Yeah, you're right," I said to Miles, wrinkling my nose at the ring. "Why don't you go look at the gold collection. I'll be right over."

Miles nodded a perplexed yet complying nod, and he and Bryce went to the right to look at the gold jewelry.

"Well," I said to Lisa, "I guess that's that." With a sad look on my face, I tried to remove the ring from my finger. But it wasn't budging.

Forcing an everything-is-all right look onto my face, I leaned down and pretended to examine the other jewelry in the display case. As I did this, I hid my hand and yanked on the ring a few more times. The thing would not come off.

My mind began to race with ideas for how to get the ring off my finger. I went over the options in my mind.

Option One: Find some string and tie it to a doorknob and then slam the door shut.

No. That's for loose teeth not tight rings.

Option Two: Ask Lisa to give the ring a tug.

No. I don't think that will go over too well.

Option Three: Use the slippery hand lotion in my bag to coat my finger, then tug and hope for the best.

Okay. I'll give that one a try.

With my left hand resting on the top of the glass case and my eyes still searching the case to keep up the pretense that I was perusing the jewels, I reached into my bag with my right hand. I clutched the slippery hand lotion after only a moment. Then, so my hand would not be in Lisa's line of vision as I attempted the ring-removal, I asked her to grab a ring from the very corner of the display case.

As soon as Lisa went in for the ring-retrieval, I squirted an ample amount of the lotion onto my left ring-finger. I pulled on the ring as hard as I could, and it went flying onto the floor. I swiftly bent down to pick up the ring and met Lisa's eyes through the glass. She was looking at me as if I had absolutely no class and did not belong in a place like John Wilfred.

"My lotion is a little slippery," I explained sheepishly as I straightened myself up. I handed Lisa the ring and noticed that the lotion had made a coating on the band. I avoided making eye contact with Lisa. "I think I'll go look at the gold collection now," I said.

I walked quickly toward Miles and Bryce, and out of the corner of my eye I saw Lisa cleaning the slimy lotion off the ring with a cloth and jewelry cleaner.

When I reached Miles, he was holding up a delicate gold ring with a round-cut diamond that looked like it was floating in the air. It was so Carrie.

"This is the ring," Miles said to Bryce, his polished voice filled with emotion.

"It sure is," I agreed as I approached.

Miles looked up at me and smiled the biggest smile I have ever seen.

Chapter 4

One of my job perks—actually, come to think of it, pretty much my only job perk—is a free gym membership.

Most of my coworkers use their gym memberships enthusiastically for the month of January and then quit. But not me. Since I am physically unable to pass up a bargain, I am at the gym, using my free membership, five times a week. Okay, more like three times a week.

The crazy thing is—and don't tell Carrie I said this, because she has been trying to convince me of this for years—working out makes me feel great. I mean, now I can walk up long flights of stairs without huffing. And one time, when I saw this lady at the grocery store trying to pry two shopping carts apart from each other, I offered to help and just pulled those babies right apart.

So, after saying good-bye to a very content Miles in the John Wilfred parking lot, I headed to the gym for a little pre-dinner-with-Isaac workout.

After checking in with the extremely muscular guy at the front desk and changing into my workout wear, I headed to the cardio room where I saw that my favorite treadmill was free. And by favorite treadmill I mean the one from which I can hear the radio the best.

I hopped onto the treadmill, set the speed to 5 mph, and began jogging comfortably. As I jogged to the sound of an eighties pop song, I found myself thinking about Isaac. I probably should have stopped the thoughts, since they were potentially dangerous, but I just couldn't.

I couldn't stop thinking about that smile. Those hazel eyes. And I couldn't get out of my head the fact that even though I barely knew the guy, when I was with him I felt, I don't know, something.

A bit of sweat began to form on my forehead, and I dabbed at it with my fuzzy blue towel. I was in the middle of dabbing when I saw a woman I recognized enter the cardio room. A woman named Rona Bircheck.

Male heads turned as Rona sashayed into the room, her workout clothes clinging to her toned figure. Her shiny auburn hair was tied back in a perfectly smooth knot, and her green eyes were peering in my direction.

I quickly began rubbing my face with my towel, hoping this would conceal me from Rona's view, but unfortunately, she had already spotted me. She swung her hips as she walked toward me.

I think it's imperative that I tell you a little about Rona.

Rona moved to the Monterey Bay area from Alpine, Utah, around the end of my senior year in high school. Rona was LDS, and Carrie and I were happy to finally have another LDS girl to hang out with. We quickly welcomed her into our circle of friends.

Being the end of our senior year, the prom was on everyone's minds. Especially mine. I had been asked by Alex Michaels, the guy I had been crushing on for months, and I couldn't wait. I think I looked at my dress, a black sequined beauty with cap sleeves—which I got on clearance at the mall—about fifty times a day. And I tried it on at least ten.

Well, Rona decided that she wanted Alex Michaels to be her boyfriend, and she didn't wait until after the big dance to make it happen. I ended up spending prom night playing croquet with my parents in our backyard. Ever since then, things have been kind of . . . tense between us.

"Hi, Annabelle," Rona said in her breathy voice as she approached me.

I stopped the treadmill and stepped off. "Hi, Rona."

"So, I hear Carrie is getting married," Rona said. Although Rona ruined my last year of high school, she's never done anything rotten to Carrie, so she and Carrie are still pretty good friends. In fact, Carrie thinks Rona is wonderful.

"How do you know that?" I asked, stunned.

"Miles asked me to help him out with his proposal. I had access to a lovely beach front property, and I arranged for him to propose there. He's there now."

"Oh," I said flatly. I tried to squash the envious feelings. Why hadn't Miles asked *me* to help with the proposal?

"I'm engaged too." Rona flashed a huge diamond in my face. "His name is Tristan. I was on vacation in Rio de Janeiro and I met him at a church branch I attended down there. I extended my vacation, and we spent every waking moment together. He asked me after just three weeks."

"Congratulations," I said, forcing cheeriness into my voice.

"He's a doctor. He's still in Brazil teaching seminars on improving medical care." She sounded like a girl showing off her Barbie dream house. "We're having a short engagement. Just one month."

"That's great," I said. "Well, Rona, my heart rate is going down. I should get back." I gestured toward the treadmill.

"Of course," Rona replied. "Oh, but wait, there's one more thing. I'm throwing Carrie a surprise bridal shower in three weeks. I thought that I should probably include you in the plans since you two are so close."

Excuse me? Excuse me?! You're throwing my best friend a bridal shower and you thought *you should include me?!*

I forced a smile. "I would love to help."

"I thought that since you work for the food section at

Central Coast Living, the perfect job for you would be to find a caterer and plan the menu," Rona told me.

"Great," I said through my gritted teeth.

"Great," Rona echoed. "I'll be in touch. Tell Carrie congratulations for me, if I don't see her first." And with that, Rona sashayed off.

I stepped back onto the treadmill, fuming. I hadn't even had time to digest Carrie's engagement let alone think about throwing her a bridal shower. And now Rona was throwing it? Rona who spoke to Carrie, what, like once a week?!

Fueled by the fury inside of me, I turned on the treadmill and began to run faster than I had been running before. In fact, I ran faster than I *ever* had before. As the machine sped up to the 8mph I had set it to, I realized just how fast this really is.

I threw my legs forward wildly, trying desperately to keep up with the treadmill belt as it moved below my feet. I'm certain that I looked like an ostrich trying to sprint. I kept running, the anger still flowing through my limbs. But after only a few minutes, I started to feel ill. My heart was pounding much faster than I think it should have been. And I began to find it hard to breathe.

Gasping for air, I jumped off the machine and bent forward over my knees, taking huge, gulping breaths. The pain in my heart and lungs was so bad, I felt like I might pass out right there in the gym. It was some of the worst pain I have ever experienced.

And it was all Rona Bircheck's fault.

"So, where are we going?" I asked Isaac.

"You'll see," he responded with a glint in his eye.

Isaac was driving me to dinner in his black, classic, 1968 Firebird. Mellow alternative rock music was playing on the car stereo. The evening was cool and breezy, and the bay was shimmering like glitter. The whole scene made me feel like I was in a music video or something.

"Will you tell me if I guess it?" I asked, peering over at Isaac.

"You'll never guess it," Isaac responded in a joking tone.

I faked an I'm-extremely-offended-that-you-have-no-faith-in-my-guessing-abilities frown. "Fine then," I said.

Isaac pulled the car onto Highway 1, and the increase in driving speed sent the wind whipping through my hair. I took my hair into my hand and held it in a loose ponytail on the top of my head.

Isaac looked over at me. "Have I told you yet how gorgeous you look?"

I averted Isaac's gaze and began playing with the seam on my favorite jeans—a $110 pair I got for $30 at Macy's because they had a tiny hole in one of the pockets. I didn't respond to Isaac's question.

"Well you do," Isaac said. "People are going to wonder what you're doing with me."

"I seriously doubt that," I countered. Isaac was looking pretty amazing himself dressed in a pair of loose-fitting pants and a surfer-style polo shirt. His thick, dark hair was slightly tousled as if he had combed it with his fingers while driving with the windows down. The whole look was quite appealing. Dangerously appealing.

Isaac removed his right hand from the steering wheel and changed the CD changer to a new CD. "This is my favorite band," he said as he advanced the CD to track three. "They're called Gidget Goes Graceland."

I held back a giggle as the band's name conjured up an image of George's assistant Gidget going to Graceland and coming back with a huge Elvis mug that she put on her desk.

The song Isaac played for me was soft and melodic and, of course, about a girl, and I quickly decided that I liked Gidget Goes Graceland. Just as the song ended, Isaac pulled the car into the parking lot of a shabby-looking hotel. He got out of the car and walked over to open my door for me.

"Here we are," he said, extending his arm to me.

"And where is here exactly?" I asked apprehensively. It's not my practice to enter shabby-looking hotels with men I don't know all that well.

"Vaz Plaza. It's a hotel and Portuguese restaurant. And they have Portuguese sponge cake. I wasn't sure what kind of food you like, so I went with the one thing I know: You were willing to drive a hundred miles for Portuguese cake, so it must be pretty good."

I couldn't help smiling. I mean, Isaac had considered what food I like. That was a big deal to me considering I once dated a guy who for every date took me to Big Bernie's Buffet because he had a year's worth of coupons for the place.

"It sounds great," I said. Then I paused. "But wait a minute. You're telling me that there's a place right here in the Monterey Bay area that sells Portuguese sponge cake?" I shook my head. "I wish I would have known that before I drove all the way out to Los Banos."

"It may be selfish of me," Isaac began, "but I'm glad you didn't know about this place. I'm glad you had to drive all the way out to Los Banos." Isaac's lips curved up into a delicious smile.

I quickly looked away from him and began fiddling with one of the tiny beads on my black silk-chiffon top.

Isaac offered me his arm and led me toward the restaurant. As I rested my hand on his muscular forearm, my heart began to speed up, and my temperature rose slightly. And that's when my brain piped up, and the two of us, me and my brain, began a silent conversation.

Brain: Annabelle, be careful.

Me (innocently): What are you talking about? I'm just heading into a restaurant with my colleague Isaac. Why do I need to be careful?

Brain: Because you're starting to like him. And you're just setting yourself up for heartache.

Me: Heartache? Since when did an innocent dinner with a work colleague cause heartache?

Brain: You know this isn't an innocent dinner. This is a date. Need I remind you that when you were sixteen you made a commitment to only date guys who share your religious views? You need to stop this before it's too late.

Me (angrily): Fine. This will be the last time I go out with Isaac, okay! Now please stop bothering me.

Brain (satisfied): All right.

Isaac and I reached the restaurant's entrance, and he held the door open for me as we stepped inside. Vaz Plaza was charming and warm. Solid wooden tables covered in embroidered tablecloths dotted the floor, each table lit by a delicate candle in a golden glass globe. A hostess with graying hair appeared in front of Isaac and me, carrying two menus. She led us to a table in the corner of the dining area and set the menus on the table as Isaac pulled out my chair for me.

The conversation between me and Isaac was easy as we split an appetizer and then enjoyed our main courses. When we had finished our meals, our waitress, a young, dark-haired woman, instantly brought out two slices of Portuguese sponge cake. I immediately began enjoying my slice.

"How do you like the cake?" Isaac asked, his voice expectant.

"Actually, I think I like it even better than Marcia's," I answered honestly.

"Really?"

"Yeah. I mean, it has more icing. And everyone knows the icing is the best part."

"Oh yeah?" Isaac asked, raising an eyebrow slightly.

"Yeah." I took a spoon off the table and filled it with a large amount of the cake's sugary icing. I placed the spoon in my mouth and let the icing melt on my tongue. "Definitely the best part," I said, my tongue sticky and satisfied.

Isaac leaned back in his chair and wiped his mouth with a cloth napkin. "Maybe I should have asked them to forget the cake and just bring out some icing." He smiled into the napkin.

I twisted my lips embarrassedly. "Very funny."

Isaac and I continued to talk and joke with each other as I finished my slice of cake and then enjoyed a few bites of Isaac's. Okay, nearly half of Isaac's.

Then the water I had sipped during dinner suddenly caught up with me. "Would you excuse me for a moment?" I asked Isaac. "I need to make a trip to the ladies'."

"Of course."

I took one last bite of Isaac's cake before walking to the restroom.

While in the ladies' room, I checked my teeth for anything unsightly that may have crept between them during dinner. After my teeth-check, I began practicing smiles in the mirror, trying to decide which one to flash at Isaac when I walked back out to the table. Not because I liked him and was practically bursting with flirtatious energy that I absolutely had to get out. Of course not. Just because it was the last time we would go out and I might as well make it pleasant for him.

I was practicing a smile I thought was the perfect mix between flirty and mysterious when a thirty-ish woman entered the bathroom. She saw me smiling at myself in the mirror and looked at me like I was a nut.

"Just practicing," I said sheepishly.

I quickly exited the ladies' room and headed back to the table, flashing my flirty-yet-mysterious smile at Isaac. I was pleased to see that Isaac was smiling too. But it only took a second for me to realize that he wasn't smiling at me. No, he was smiling at a woman who was sitting in my seat. A gorgeous woman with lovely green eyes and shiny auburn hair.

He was smiling at Rona Bircheck.

The smile fell from my face, and I moved my feet quickly toward the table. "Rona what are you doing here?" I asked when I reached the table. I glanced at Rona's left hand and noticed that the huge diamond ring she had flashed at me just hours earlier was no longer on her finger.

"I was just finishing dinner with a friend when I saw you two come in. I came over to meet your handsome date." Rona smiled nauseatingly at Isaac. Engaged or not, she was the same Rona.

"This is Isaac," I said, plastering a friendly expression onto my face.

I waited for Rona to give me back my seat. But she didn't. So, since it was a two-person table, I had to grab a chair from a nearby table and squeeze in next to Rona. It was ridiculous.

"Yes, he already told me his name," Rona said. "He also told me that you two are working together on some article. It's nice to see that you're writing again after what happened last time."

I bit my tongue. And not figuratively either. I literally bit down on my tongue. Pretty hard, too. It was the only way I could stop myself from saying something less-than-nice to Rona. I mean, she knew what had happened with my last writing assignment because Carrie had told her, and it was just like her to bring it up in front of Isaac.

"My photographer has been letting me down lately," Rona said, talking to Isaac more than to me. "So, I've asked Isaac to bring a portfolio down to my office. I bet he could help me sell houses."

"I'm sure he could," I said.

"Here is my card, Isaac." Rona handed Isaac an ecru business card. "Call me and we'll get something arranged." She put extra emphasis on "call me."

"Sounds good," Isaac responded politely.

With her trademark poise, Rona stood up from the table and swayed off without another word to me.

"This is great," Isaac said after a moment. "I could really use some more work."

"Well good," I said flatly.

"So how do you two know each other?" Isaac asked.

I wanted to say, "She stole my prom date and ruined my last year of high school." But instead I said, "She's a friend of a friend," which was true. I wanted to add, "And she's engaged, so don't fall for her like pretty much every male on the planet does," but, unfortunately, I just couldn't find a way to work it into the conversation.

"I'm really glad she was here tonight." Isaac glanced around the restaurant as if he were looking for Rona.

I nodded my head emotionlessly.

For the remainder of our date, Isaac seemed distracted. We exchanged small talk as he drove me back to my place, but that was about it. We didn't talk and laugh like we had before. And as Isaac walked me to my condo, he didn't offer me his arm like he had at the beginning of our date as we walked into the restaurant.

I didn't know what had happened. Had he taken one look at Rona and wondered what he was doing with someone like me? Or worse, had Rona acted completely un-engaged and charmed Isaac, leaving him interested in her? Or had Rona told him I had some sort of communicable disease? Because I wouldn't put it past her.

"Thanks for everything," I said when we reached the top of the steps outside my condo. "It was all so thoughtful of you."

"I'm glad you enjoyed yourself," Isaac said briskly. And with that he gave me a hug of the variety that little boys give to distant relatives they are meeting for the first time. "I'll call you," he said in a noncommittal tone.

"You still have my cell number right?" I asked.

"Yep," Isaac answered. Then he practically ran into the night.

Well, I thought as I opened the door and stepped inside, *looks like you got what you wanted after all, brain.*

Chapter 5

Singles ward, Sunday morning.

I strutted through the front doors dressed in a grey wool pencil skirt and my cutest pink top—which a girl had eyed covetously and then nearly ripped out of my hand when I was at Cheap Chic's annual blowout sale a week earlier. On my feet I wore a pair of open-toed heels and a killer pedicure.

I paid such attention to my appearance partly because I believe in donning my Sunday best and partly because I have read quite a few magazine articles that say one of the best places to meet a mate is in church. And since I had been reminded of how great it felt to go to dinner with a kind, attractive, intriguing guy, I was really hoping I would meet another one soon. One I could actually date.

I have a pretty good idea of how my mate-meeting in church will occur. I will walk into the chapel, and there will be a handsome guy leaning over in his seat reading his scriptures. Then, as I walk gracefully past the handsome guy, a gleam of light will shine in through the window and make my hair appear impossibly shiny and make my face look all dewy and glowing.

The handsome guy will look up from his reading and our eyes will meet. We will fall madly in love, and we'll print the passage of scripture he was reading the moment we met on our wedding invitations. Yes, I'm quite certain that's how it will go.

As I moved my pedicured feet into the church foyer, I noticed a group of females standing near one of the couches. I could hear them giggling and speaking in higher-than-usual voices. In my experience this can only mean one thing: a new guy.

Just as I had guessed, as I walked closer, I noticed a pair of suit-pant-clad legs extending from the couch. I turned my head away from the scene quickly as if to say I was much too grown-up to be hovering over a new guy. Especially one who was not leaning over in his seat reading his scriptures. It was then that I heard it.

"Annabelle?"

I turned around to see the suit-pant-clad legs walking toward me. And you'll never guess whose legs they were—they were Isaac's.

"Annabelle? What are you doing here?"

The girls in the group flashed me narrow-eyed stares as Isaac came to my side.

I tired to speak. "I-I'm going to church. W-what are you doing here?"

The group of girls dispersed, casting disdainful glances in my direction as they walked past.

"I'm going to church too," Isaac answered, staring at me incredulously.

"Wait a minute? Are you LDS?"

"Yes I am," Isaac answered. And when he did, something very strange happened inside of my chest. It was kind of a warm, almost burning feeling.

"I had no idea," I said. "I thought that I could never—" I stopped myself. How was I going to finish that? "I thought that I could never date you because you weren't LDS, and now I find out you are, and this makes what happened on our date important again, so now I have to ask if you lost interest in me and gained interest in Rona Bircheck." Yeah, right. I was not finishing the sentence like that. First of all it was entirely too long, and second of all, it was entirely too revealing.

So instead I said, "I thought that I could never find out something like this." It was quite possibly the worst sentence ever formed, but hey, I didn't exactly have a lot of time to come up with it.

"This is crazy," Isaac said. "And I was planning on calling you today and telling you we shouldn't, you know, go out again because I only date girls in my church." He laughed uncomfortably. "In fact, last night after we ate dessert, I realized that I was, probably, you know, leading you on or something by the way I was acting, so I tried to get up the guts to tell you that we probably shouldn't go out again, but I couldn't."

I smiled. So maybe he wasn't acting weird because he had experienced love-at-first-sight with Rona. From the sound of it, he had decided it was our last date, too.

"Well, now I'm kind of hoping we will go out again," I said. I was shocked and embarrassed that the words had come out of my mouth, so I gestured toward the chapel and quickly added, "So, um, I guess we should probably get in there."

Isaac nodded and followed me into the chapel. I felt my pulse quicken as he walked beside me. I scanned the chapel and found Carrie and Miles sitting in their usual bench and went to sit next to them. Isaac took a seat next to me. My pulse got even faster.

Isaac recognized Carrie and smiled at her. Then he gave one of those silent nodding greetings to Miles. Carrie looked at me then Isaac and then back at me, her eyes quizzical.

"I'll tell you later," I mouthed, making sure Isaac didn't see me.

"Okay," Carrie mouthed in reply. Then, with a beaming smile on her face, she held up her left hand, showing me her gorgeous ring.

"It looks so good on you," I said a little too loudly. The

organist shot me a scornful glance over the top of her music.

"You'll be such a beautiful bride," I said, lowering my voice to a whisper.

"And you'll be such a beautiful maid of honor," Carrie whispered.

"Have you guys decided where you're going to be sealed?" I asked.

Carrie beamed. "The Oakland temple. And we'll have a small reception in Oakland afterwards."

I smiled and squeezed Carrie's ring-decorated hand.

The meeting was wonderful. The talks were uplifting, and there was a gorgeous musical number by a blonde girl who, Carrie whispered to me, is now dating Arvin.

As the congregation sang the closing hymn, I got the sense that someone was looking in my direction. Pretending to stretch my neck, I darted my eyes around the room, and my eyes soon fixed on the person looking at me: Rona Bircheck. I quickly looked away.

When the meeting was over, Rona approached the bench where my friends and I sat. She looked absolutely perfect and smelled like warm vanilla. And again there was no trace of her ring.

She sat down on the bench behind us and talked to Carrie and Miles for a second, congratulating them on their engagement and cooing over Carrie's ring. Then she greeted me with a quick hello.

I smiled a mostly genuine smile and said hello back.

As Rona stood up to leave, she looked at Isaac. "We're still on for lunch at one o'clock right?"

Isaac nodded, and Rona smiled charmingly before turning to walk away.

Lunch? They were having lunch? Why were they having lunch? It couldn't be a work lunch; it was Sunday. Okay, I realize I just said the word "lunch" a ridiculously large amount of times, but seriously, what was Rona up to?

With Rona gone, Isaac turned his attention to me, and

I clenched my jaw with the strength of a wolf. The wolf is known for its jaw strength, right? Anyway, I clenched my jaw with the strength of an animal known for having a strong jaw, wolf or otherwise.

I did this to keep my mouth from blurting the countless things I wanted to say: *Isaac keep away from Rona. Even though she obviously isn't very true to him, she already has a man. She's a thief. She's pure evil. She . . .*

I kept my jaw tight and pretended to be listening to something Carrie was telling Miles. But after a moment Carrie and Miles bid me and Isaac good-bye and got up from the bench, leaving the chapel completely empty except for Isaac and me.

Isaac looked at me as if he could tell something was wrong. Or maybe he was wondering if I had lockjaw problems; I don't know. Before he could say anything, I unclenched my jaw slightly and questioned, "Are you going to Sunday school?"

"I'm actually taking off for the Spanish ward. My brother attends that ward, and he's giving a talk today. I won't understand a thing, but I still want to go. So, I'll see you around."

I'll see you around? Clearly, that would not do if he was planning on having lunch with Rona Bircheck. I needed to step up my game.

So, I quickly blurted, "Will you come to my parents' house for dinner tonight?"

"I would like that," Isaac answered. And then he smiled his devastatingly gorgeous smile and got up from the bench.

According to the ancient grandfather clock in my parents' living room, Isaac was ten minutes late. Maybe he was lost. Or maybe he had car trouble. Or maybe he had fallen in love with Rona Bircheck over lunch and thus decided he had no time to waste on me.

"Mom," I called out, a sudden urgency in my voice, "are

your clocks fast?" I hurried into the kitchen where Mom was putting the final touches on dinner.

"No," Mom replied with a grin. From the moment I arrived at my parents' house and told them that I had seen Isaac at church and invited him to dinner, Mom had been grinning at me like that.

"Could you take the rolls out of the oven?" Mom asked me. "I don't have any free hands."

"Sure," I agreed halfheartedly as I looked at the sail-boat-shaped clock on the kitchen wall.

As I stared at the clock a vision began to form in my mind. In the vision, Rona set an obviously overcooked lunch in front of Isaac. But Isaac didn't notice how completely disgusting the food looked since Rona brushed her hand against his as she handed him a fork. Isaac looked up, surprised by the touch. Then Rona began leaning in toward him and . . .

"They'll burn if they stay in much longer," Mom's voice came into my ears.

"Oh, okay," I said, snapping out of the vision. I slipped an oven mitt—a red mitt in the shape of a crab claw—onto my hand and reached into the oven.

"You know, Annabelle, those rolls are my own invention." Mom nodded toward the pan of rolls as I removed it from the oven. "The secret ingredient is a little bit of pure molasses." Mom spoke as if she were telling me the secrets of the universe.

"They look great," I responded with a smile.

Every Sunday night, I have dinner at my parents' house. And ever since I started editing recipes for *Central Coast Living*, it seems Mom has put just a little extra effort into our Sunday night meals. She would never admit it, but I think she secretly hopes that someday, in the middle of the meal, I will throw my cloth napkin onto the table and declare, "This food is marvelous! It has to go in the magazine!"

I've never had the heart to tell her that I really have no say what recipes go into the magazine. I just edit whichever ones George tells me to edit.

I was lazily placing the rolls into a basket when I heard the sound of a car outside. I quickly tossed the last few rolls into the basket and hurried to the front window. I looked outside, expecting to see Isaac's Firebird. But I didn't see the Firebird. No, I saw a fancy, silver Mercedes convertible. I would recognize that car anywhere. It belonged to Miss Rona Bircheck. I stared at the car in disbelief. *What in the world is she doing here?* I wondered, my eyes beginning to narrow.

I continued to watch the car. After a while, I saw Isaac get out of the passenger's seat. As he exited, I could see Rona, looking like a fashion model in a pair of stylish sunglasses. She leaned over, gave Isaac a saucy little wave and called out loud enough for the whole neighborhood to hear, "I'll see you in awhile."

Isaac responded with, "Okay, see ya."

What? What are they doing later?

Finally, Rona zoomed away and I was relieved, but still confused. Why had she driven Isaac to the house? And how was he going to get home? Was he planning on asking me for a ride? Because that would be nice.

I watched Isaac follow the sidewalk up to the house. He had changed out of his suit and was looking yummy in a pair of dark blue pants and striped polo shirt. Was he trying to look that good? And if he was, was it for Rona's sake or for mine?

Isaac's pace quickened as he drew nearer to the door, and I jumped away from the window for fear that he would spot me. He rang the doorbell.

"Dad, he's here," I called out as I rushed to the kitchen. "Will you get the door for me?" Dad, who had been setting the table in the dining room, shook his head.

"Three grown girls and I still don't understand why you all can't just get the door yourselves."

He answered the door anyway.

I listened as Isaac and Dad exchanged greetings, and then I entered the living room, followed by Mom.

"Hi, Isaac, I'm glad you made it," I said, feeling slightly giddy at the sight of him. He was seated on the couch, looking terribly gorgeous, and I sat down next to him. My pulse immediately quickened.

"So did you find the place okay?" Mom asked, leaning against Dad's recliner.

"Actually, Rona Bircheck drove me here so I wouldn't get lost," Isaac replied matter-of-factly.

So that was it? That was why she drove him? Oh, please. Hadn't she ever heard of MapQuest?

"That was nice of her," Mom said.

Yeah, real nice, I thought bitterly.

Isaac regarded me for a moment. I had changed into a pair of slim black pants that I got for less than thirty bucks at Nordstrom Rack, and a pale blue top. "You look pretty," he said quietly, his eyes sparkling.

"Thanks," I responded. "You look good too." And oh boy he did.

Isaac moved his eyes away from me and surveyed the room. "You have a very nice home," he told my parents.

"Thank you," Mom said.

Then, spotting Dad's prized chess set, which was on the coffee table, Isaac asked, "Who's the chess player?" Mom and I simultaneously pointed to Dad.

Dad, who had beaten every overconfident Scout at a chess tournament at Scout camp a month earlier, shrugged his shoulders. "I play a little."

Mom excused herself and disappeared into the kitchen, and Dad and Isaac talked a bit about chess. I sat there watching Isaac as he and Dad talked. I couldn't help it. He was just so handsome with his gorgeous hazel eyes and slightly mussed dark hair. And that smile. Oh, that smile.

After I had been shamelessly staring at him for quite a long time, he seemed to notice, and turned his head toward me. I quickly turned away and pretended to be enthralled by a piece of lint on my pants. Thankfully, at that instant, Mom came into the room and announced that dinner was ready.

"I know I'm hungry," Dad said, patting his stomach.

We all moved into the dining room. Dad and Mom sat down in their usual places at the six-seat table, Dad at the head and Mom to his right. I sat next to Mom, and Isaac sat across from me. I eyed the steaming food eagerly.

"Isaac, would you offer the blessing on the food?" Dad asked.

I quickly shot Dad a what-are-you-doing glare, but he ignored me. I turned my eyes down to avoid making eye contact with Isaac.

"Of course," Isaac said.

Isaac bowed his head and offered a reverent and sincere prayer. When he had finished praying, I opened my eyes slowly and turned them upward to look at him. He met my gaze and our eyes locked for a moment. I gave him a tiny smile. Then I thought I felt his foot touch mine under the table. But I'm not quite sure—it might have been Mom's.

"Did you serve a mission, Isaac?" Dad asked as he served himself some drizzled chicken and passed the dish to Mom.

I shot Dad another look, but I was ignored again.

"Yes, sir, I served in the Philippines," Isaac answered.

"What year did you get home from your mission?" Mom asked, sounding interested. She handed me the chicken.

"I've been home for about four years now."

As I dished up some chicken, I did some quick math in my head. I figured out that if Isaac had gone on his mission when he was nineteen, then he was likely about one year older than me. Not too shabby.

Mom obviously did some math in her head as well because seconds later she started listing off the names of anyone and everyone she knew who had served a mission in the Philippines during the years Isaac had served there.

I always find it funny when people do this. And I find it even funnier that they usually discover they have a friend or an acquaintance in common. It turned out that Mom's previous visiting teaching companion had a daughter whose ex-fiancé served in Isaac's last area. Mom and Isaac talked about him for a moment.

For the remainder of the meal, the conversation stayed mostly on Isaac and his mission. I listened intently as he spoke about what he learned and experienced in the mission field. I felt my admiration for him growing as he shared his stories and his thoughts with my family.

When we were through eating, Dad, remembering Isaac's earlier interest in his chess set, asked Isaac if he would like to play.

Isaac looked at me as if asking for permission, which I thought was really adorable. "Go ahead," I said. "I'm going to help clean up." I stood up and started clearing dishes from the table.

"Are you sure you don't need help?" Isaac asked in a way that let me know he really wanted to play chess.

"I'm sure. Mom and I both hate chess, so he doesn't get a chance to play much. Go play."

I put my hand gently on Isaac's shoulder and suddenly felt an electric-like sensation that began in my fingers and spread all the way into the center of my chest. I moved my hand away quickly, but couldn't help smiling sweetly at Isaac as he stood up from the chair. He returned my smile with a look that let me know he had enjoyed the simple touch as much as I had.

Dad and Isaac set up their game in the living room, and I helped Mom with the dishes. In the privacy of the kitchen, Mom and I talked.

"I really like him, Annabelle," Mom said with a smile. "I liked him the second I met him at the café."

"I really like him too," I whispered dreamily, leaning against the counter.

"How does he know Rona Bircheck?" Mom asked with a hint of skepticism in her voice. Mom became a little wary of Rona after she watched me attempt to play croquet in my black prom dress.

"She asked him to take some photos for her," I said in a

resent-laden voice. "And now she won't go away. She has some big-shot world-saving doctor for a fiancé, but she insists on spending time with a guy who may possibly be interested in me. I don't know. She's up to something."

"Well, Annabelle, as your father and I have always told you: Leave it in the Lord's hands, and everything will turn out the way it should."

"I don't want everything to turn out the way it should if it includes Isaac and Rona Bircheck being together." I smiled to let Mom know I was joking. At least, halfway joking.

Mom and I heard a victorious holler coming from the living room. Grinning, we went to see what was going on.

Isaac looked up at me as I entered the living room. "Your Dad's beating me."

"Don't give up hope," I encouraged, standing behind Isaac. Without thinking, I began rubbing his shoulders the way I've seen trainers do to boxers in the movies. And there was that electric feeling again. I quickly moved my hands away.

Dad ended up winning the chess game, and Isaac accepted the defeat wonderfully. We were all talking and laughing as we ate strawberry shortcake in the living room when we heard the doorbell ring.

"Oh man, is it already eight o'clock?" Isaac asked, looking at the grandfather clock in surprise. "I told Rona to pick me up at eight. I didn't want to overstay my welcome." He sounded apologetic, regretful even.

I closed my eyes and tried to think good thoughts about Rona.

Mom got up and answered the door. "Rona, please come in," she offered kindly. Just like me, Mom has never been unkind to Rona, just a little . . . cautious.

Rona reluctantly entered the house, and I forced a smile onto my face. *Good thoughts,* I reminded myself. *Good thoughts.*

"Would you like to join us for some shortcake?" Mom asked.

I turned my head away so no one could see the how-can-you-possibly-invite-her-to-have-shortcake-with-us look on my face.

"All right," Rona replied slowly.

Mom sent Dad into the kitchen to serve the shortcake. Then she invited Rona to sit down. "Annabelle tells me you are engaged," she said as Rona lowered herself onto Dad's recliner. "Congratulations."

Isaac looked at Rona like he was hearing the news for the first time, and silently I profusely thanked Mom for finding a way to reveal the news to Isaac.

"Yes, uh, I, uh," Rona stammered, her eyes suddenly taking on a strange look. Then, without finishing her rambling sentence, she said, "My mom and sister threw me a surprise party yesterday. It was supposed to be a bridal shower, but it was more of a, well, anyway, it was down at Pebble Beach. The band Gidget Goes Graceland played. My mom surprised me with that. They had a show in San Jose last night, so she arranged for them to play at my party first."

I looked at Rona. Was her little party supposed to impress us or something? I mean, sure it's impossible to have a function at Pebble Beach unless you're extremely rich or extremely famous, and it's pretty much the most coveted party location ever. But who was this "Gidget Goes Graceland?" It didn't even sound like a real band.

Then I remembered. That was the name of the band Isaac had played for me on our way to Vaz Plaza. His favorite band.

"That's my favorite band," Isaac said, his eyes wide with excitement.

Rona angled her body toward Isaac. "Really?"

"When does your fiancé get back?" I blurted out. The room grew extremely quiet, and everyone looked at me like my head had just fallen off. I shrugged my shoulders in it-was-just-an-innocent-question fashion.

A look of confusion came over Rona's face. "I'm not quite sure, but . . ."

Then Mom attempted to save the day. "Speaking of bridal

showers, Annabelle says you're throwing Carrie a surprise bridal shower."

"Yes," Rona replied, obviously eager to change the subject. "Annabelle is arranging the menu for the shower."

"Really, Annabelle?" Mom looked at me with surprise.

"Mm hmm."

"By the way, how is that progressing?" Rona asked, taking the opportunity to put the hot lights on me.

Okay. It was bad enough that Rona was planning my best friend's bridal shower instead of me. But now I was her underling. Now I had to report my progress to Rona Bircheck. My progress on the menu for *my* best friend's bridal shower!

Mom, Dad, and Isaac all looked at me expectantly, waiting for me to respond to Rona.

"It's going great," I answered. It wasn't a complete lie. I had bought a bridal magazine on the way home from the gym the day before. And I had intended to look through the magazine for tips on organizing the food for a bridal shower. It wasn't my fault all the gorgeous dresses in the magazine distracted me from the task.

"Good. Since the party is so soon, I was worried it might be a little bit difficult."

"Nope. Everything is going just fine," I responded breezily.

"So you've decided on a caterer then?" Rona asked.

A caterer? I was planning on some nice fruit, veggie, and meat trays from the grocery store and a jumbo bag of Costco rolls. She was expecting me to get the party catered? "Oh, well, I haven't found one yet, but I'm close," I answered. It was basically true. Now that I knew I was supposed to be looking for a caterer, I was one step closer.

"Good," Rona said. "Oh, and I forgot to tell you, plan for about twenty people. And as far as the budget, I was thinking about ten dollars per plate, so that's two hundred dollars. I can put in a hundred and you can put in a hundred."

"Okay," I answered. "Anything for Carrie."

"Just don't dilly dally too long," Rona instructed, standing up from her seat abruptly.

Dilly dally? Who says that?

"We'd better go," Rona announced.

She looked toward Isaac who was still sitting comfortably on the couch. He looked at her like he wanted to say something, but he didn't. He stood up slowly and thanked my parents for dinner.

I opened my mouth to offer Isaac a ride home, but Rona interrupted me, almost as if she knew what I was going to say and she wanted to prevent me from saying it. "Thank you for the shortcake," she said to my parents. She gingerly set her plate down on the coffee table and I noticed she hadn't taken a single bite. This really bothered me for some reason. Probably because I would have happily eaten her serving.

Rona made her way to the front door, and the rest of us staggered behind her. I was still trying to find the words to offer to drive Isaac home.

"Goodnight Brother and Sister Pleasanton," Rona said as she reached for the brass doorknob.

To my disappointment, Isaac said good-bye to my parents as well.

But then, after letting Rona open the door and walk out ahead of him, he spoke softly to me. "Will you be here for another twenty minutes?"

I stared at him blankly. "Yeah, probably."

"Good. I'll be back."

"What?" I asked, completely confused.

But Isaac was already jogging toward the car, grinning at me over his shoulder as he went.

After Isaac and Rona left, my parents and I cleared the chess set off the coffee table and set up a game of Scrabble in its place. Mom and I were in the process of telling Dad that *tonsilectomist* is not a word when the doorbell rang. Laughing at Dad, who was looking the word up in an online dictionary, I went to answer it. I swung the door open and the person on the doorstep immediately began speaking.

"Hi, Annabelle. I didn't get a chance to say good-bye the way I wanted to with Rona around, so I decided to come back." It was Isaac, and he was a sight to behold.

I blinked a few times. "You came back to say good-bye?"

"Not quite this second, but yeah, basically."

I smiled a pleased smile and invited Isaac in.

Dad, spotting Isaac, called out, "Tell my girls that *tonsilectomist* is a word."

Isaac looked at the board game on the coffee table and chuckled. "I definitely think I remember taking photos for an article about a tonsilectomist," he said to Mom and me.

I rolled my eyes playfully. "Well, until you can settle this one, Isaac and I will be on the front porch."

I led Isaac out onto the front porch where I sat down on the porch swing. Isaac sat down next to me. Quite close to me, I might add. "I couldn't believe it when I saw you at church today," I said because it was the first thing that I could think of to break the silence. "If you live around here, why haven't you ever been to singles ward before?"

"I've been staying away from singles wards for a while."

I raised my eyebrows as if to ask "why?"

"It's too long of a story to get into now," Isaac replied dismissingly. "But today, I don't know, I just felt like I should go to the singles ward."

"I'm really glad you did," I said.

"So am I."

Isaac and I peered out at the bay. The city lights of Monterey illuminated the shoreline, and flickers from a handful of boats looked like fireflies dancing on the sea. I closed my eyes and breathed in the sea air. When I opened my eyes, Isaac was looking at me. I turned my head away quickly.

"Tell me something I don't know about you," he said.

"Okay. Well, I'm the youngest of three girls. Both of my

sisters are married with kids, and I think my parents are wondering if I'll ever get married and . . ." *Oh my goodness. Did I really just say that my parents are wondering if I'll ever get married?* Swiftly I tried to recover by saying the first thing that came to my mind. "And I once ate grass because I thought if it was good enough for cows it was good enough for me." *Grass eating?! Now I'm talking about grass eating?! Isaac's probably agreeing with my parents about me never getting married!* I bit my lip in complete humiliation.

But Isaac just smiled. "I ate hay because I was convinced it would make me strong like a horse."

"Oh good, so I'm not the only one who did something like that," I mumbled, still totally embarrassed.

"Did you grow up around here?" Isaac asked.

"Yeah, I did. I've lived in the Monterey Bay area for my whole life with the exception of my four, well really more like five, years at college."

"What did you major in?" Isaac asked with interest.

"Journalism," I answered. In an act of self-censorship, I didn't mention the rest of my long list of majors. "I think I was too idealistic about it though."

"What do you mean, too idealistic?"

"Well, I had this crazy idea that I could make a difference in the media. Sort of counteract the junk that's out there with positive stories. But I've discovered that things don't work out that way. I mean, my boss is interested in glitzy stories about famous chefs and award-winning restaurants, not sweet little old ladies who make great stuffed French toast."

Isaac looked at me in confusion, and I waved my hand in a never-mind gesture.

"I don't think you should give up on the idea of making a difference in the media," Isaac said. "I think it's great."

"Maybe someday . . ." I let my voice trail off. With the way my current writing assignment was going, I'd better get used to the idea of editing recipes for the rest of my life.

Feeling a bit discouraged, I changed the subject. "What

about you? Tell me something I don't know about you."

"Actually, I think I need to learn a few more things about you first. You're already way ahead. Your mom and her friends pretty much got my entire life story out of me." Isaac smiled.

"Yeah, I guess that's true." I tilted my head downward, feeling suddenly nervous.

Isaac lifted my chin gently with his hand. "I like the Giants, though they've been letting me down this season, and I play a little tennis."

"Thank you," I said, feeling breathless at Isaac's touch.

"In fact, why don't we play tennis sometime," Isaac suggested.

I thought for a moment. I once played tennis with Carrie and Miles, both expert tennis players, and suffice it to say, I can't play any game that involves a flying object. Unless maybe it's a Frisbee. But even that's pushing it. "I don't know if we should play tennis together," I told Isaac. "After you see the way I play, you probably won't like me very much."

"Oh, I'll still like you," Isaac replied with a meaningful smile.

I returned the smile.

After that, Isaac and I talked the hours away. We talked about our favorite foods. I told him that mine was Mom's lasagna, and he told me his was any and all pizza. I was sure it meant something that both of our favorites were Italian dishes. Pizza is Italian right? I've heard conflicting information.

Then we talked about the place in the world we want to travel someday. He said Barbados, and I said St. Lucia. Again, I was sure it meant something that both of our choices were in the same sea.

We even talked about our most embarrassing moments. His involved a Valentine that was meant for a girl in his fourth grade class, but was accidentally placed in the cubbyhole of a boy named Nathan Baxter, and mine involved a speech I had to give in speech class the day after I had my wisdom teeth removed.

Isaac and I were laughing about our embarrassing moments

when I noticed the lights inside my parents' house go off.

"I guess I should go," Isaac said. "I'll give you a call so we can get together for our tennis match." He stood up from the swing and then helped me up.

I looked into Isaac's tasty hazel eyes. "Thank you for coming back," I said.

"I couldn't help it," Isaac said, his deep voice making me feel dizzy.

Then he leaned in toward me until his lips were nearly touching my cheek. "Goodnight, Annabelle," he said softly into my ear. Chills ran up and down my spine.

"Goodnight," I managed to say somehow.

I stood frozen in place as Isaac moved away from me, walked to his car, and gave me a wave before driving away.

A good night it was indeed.

Chapter 6

I really wanted to talk to Isaac.

So, just before my lunch break on Monday, I sat at my desk and typed up a comprehensive list of excuses to call him.

Excuse 1: I could call to tell him I had a nice time on the porch swing.

Reason not to use Excuse 1: "I had a nice time with you on the porch swing" is the dorkiest thing I've ever heard.

Excuse 2: I could thank him for coming back to my parents' house last night.

Reason not to use Excuse 2: Talking about my "parents' house" will make me sound like I'm about thirteen years old.

Excuse 3: I could ask him what kind of photos he got on Friday. After all, that will probably help me with my article.

Reason not to use Excuse 3: Actually, I really like Excuse 3.

I picked up my cell phone and dialed Isaac's number—which he had given me as we talked on my parents' porch. My heart rate increased with every ring.

"Hi, this is Isaac," Isaac's voice came onto the phone.

"Hey, Isaac, this is Annabelle, I was just calling to say—"

"Sorry I can't take your call right now. Please leave a message, and I'll get back to you as soon as I can." It was Isaac's voicemail, not Isaac.

Then, giving me no time to gather myself and come up with a message that made me sound irresistibly cute, the tone sounded.

"Um, Isaac this is Annabelle. I was calling for . . ." *Wait a minute. What was I calling for again?* I suddenly couldn't remember. "I was calling to . . . I was calling to say I had a nice time on the porch swing." *What?!* I hung up the phone in horror. Then I just sat there staring at it, willing an erase-the-message-just-left-on-cute-guy's-voicemail option to appear, but no such option appeared. I knew I should have switched to Verizon.

I gathered myself and decided to call back and finish the message as if I had been cut-off by something other than my own panic. This time, though, I was careful. I took a minute to think about what I was going to say before I made the call.

Once I had a good monologue in my mind, I dialed the phone number again. After three rings, I heard Isaac's familiar "Hi." I waited for the rest of Isaac's outgoing message, but strangely I only heard silence. *It wasn't this long of a pause,* I thought.

"Hello?" Isaac's voice spoke again. "Are you there?"

What in the world? Why was Isaac answering the phone? I wasn't ready for a conversation with the real Isaac. I had a monologue for the electronic Isaac.

"Oh, uh, hi," I stammered, sounding about fifty times more asinine than I had on the message I had just left. "I just left a message, but I got cut off or something."

"I just listened to your message," Isaac said.

"You did?"

"Yes, I did."

"I really wish you hadn't."

"You don't need to wish that. It was cute. A cute message from a cute girl."

Did he just call me a cute girl? "Oh," I said, unsure of what else to say. "Well, I was actually calling to see what kind of shots you got at La Bonne Violette on Friday."

"Why don't I come to your office and bring the photos and we could look them over," Isaac suggested.

I found myself extremely relieved that he wanted to see me even though I was obviously conversation-impaired when it came to him. "Sure," I said. "I'll be here all day."

"How about two o'clock?"

"Okay," I answered. I'd kind of been wishing he would say twelve-thirty, seeing that it was currently twelve-twenty.

"I'll see you at two o'clock then," Isaac said

"See you at two." I was about to hang up the phone when I added, "Oh, and Isaac, I really did have a nice time on the porch swing with you last night."

"I did too," he said.

After I hung up with Isaac I tried to get some work done. But I was useless. I decided it was probably because I was hungry. So I called for a ham sandwich from a deli down the street and began flipping through the bridal magazine I had bought on Saturday.

I was imagining what I would look like wearing one of the flowing gowns in the magazine, and I was picturing Isaac standing beside me in a black tux, when I noticed an article entitled "Planning the Perfect Menu for All of Your Bridal Events."

I skimmed the article, which suggested using an event planner to help set up the details for all kinds of bridal get-togethers. The text explained that event planners can negotiate deals and can take the stress out of the planning process. So, thinking that might be a good idea, since 1) I had no idea how to find a caterer and 2) I really needed to focus on my article over the next weeks, I searched an online directory for event planners in the area and made a list of the ones that looked the best to me.

After not too long, I had a pretty long list. I decided to narrow it down and maybe even call a few of the planners. Pen in hand, I went over my list.

1) Perfect Parties. *Nice alliteration, but no.*
I crossed it off.
2) Anna Medici and Company. *Sounds classy, and kind of rolls off the tongue when said out loud.*
I circled it.
3) Fun Guys Party Planning. *No, just no.*
I crossed it off.
4) Gather Together Parties. *Hmm, it has a nice sound to it.*
I circled it.
5) Beverly, Ross, and Alexander, Event Planners. *Sounds a little like a law firm.*
I circled it.

I decided to call the first company I had circled: Anna Medici and Company. A woman with a smooth voice answered on the second ring. "Thank you for calling Anna Medici and Company. This is Lily; how may I direct your call?"

"I'm just calling for some information about catering for a bridal shower," I replied.

"I'll put you through to Brenna; she's over bridal." Lily patched me through.

"This is Brenna," a voice that reminded me of a kindergarten teacher answered.

"Hi, I'm interested in finding a caterer for my best friend's bridal shower," I said.

"Just a shower, dear? Do you already have catering for the rehearsal dinner and reception?"

"The wedding and reception are going to be in Oakland actually. But the shower is going to be here. So I just need a caterer for the shower."

"Oh, I see. If you would like, you could come by and take

a look at our catering portfolio. I have an opening today at six o'clock."

"Okay, sure."

"What's your name?"

"Annabelle Pleasanton."

"Okay, Annabelle, we'll see you at six o'clock. Good-bye"

"Bye." I hung up the phone with satisfaction—only a teensy bit of that satisfaction due to the fact that I was going to show Rona Bircheck that I could get the best caterer ever for Carrie's shower.

My sandwich arrived as I was writing Anna Medici and Company's address in my planner. Feeling quite ravenous, I attacked the sandwich the second the delivery boy was gone.

"Good sandwich?" I heard someone say.

I looked up. Isaac was standing in the doorway looking handsome in a pair of slacks and a green-hued dress shirt that brought out the color in his eyes and hung perfectly on his strong shoulders. "I know it isn't two o'clock yet, but I had a bridal photo cancel on me."

"Mm mm?" I hummed with my mouth full, attempting to make the sound of the word "Really?" I could feel my face burning with embarrassment.

Isaac smiled. "She got her eyebrows waxed, or whatever it's called, and she had a bad reaction to it."

I nodded knowingly. The things we women endured. Nicked legs. Fried hair. Oompa loompa self-tanner incidents. I swallowed my bite of sandwich and spoke. "Her misfortune is my fortune," I said sweetly.

Isaac took a seat in the spare chair in my office. "So what are you up to?"

I spun my chair around so I was facing him. "Lunch. I just called an event planning place. They're going to help me find a caterer for Carrie's shower."

"That's great," Isaac said. "So, do you want to look through the photos?"

No, not really, I'd rather just sit here all day and talk to you.

"Sure," I answered.

I looked through the photos Isaac had taken, and they were very good. Gorgeous shots of the restaurant. Some nice shots of Jean-Pierre at work in the kitchen. And brilliant photos of the food.

"These are really good," I said.

"Thanks. But here is my favorite one." Isaac showed me a picture of myself. My mouth was slightly open, a single salad green was stuck in the back of my hair, tomato juice was all over my clothes, and crumbly cheese was dotting me like snow.

I grabbed the picture. "Give that to me," I shouted. I shoved the photo into one of my desk drawers and made an angry face at Isaac. "When did you take that?"

Isaac shrugged his muscular shoulders. "I didn't realize I did until I had them developed. I must have snapped it by accident."

"Well you should have ripped it up," I said in a scolding voice.

"Why?" Isaac asked innocently. "You looked beautiful. You always look beautiful."

I suddenly felt like someone had turned the heater in the office up. Way up. I resisted the urge to fan my face with my hand.

Isaac and I continued to chat for a while, until, unable to bear the guilt of getting paid for flirting, I looked at Isaac and said, "I should probably get to work."

"I thought we were working," Isaac said with a grin. "No, you're right. I'll call you later. We still have to arrange our tennis match."

"Yeah I guess we do," I responded.

Isaac stood up from his chair and looked into my eyes. "Annabelle, this is the best assignment I have ever had." And with that, he disappeared from sight.

"Me too," I whispered.

Anna Medici and Company was even more elegant than I had imagined. Walls the color of caramel were complimented by plush carpeting about three shades lighter. A beautiful chandelier hung in the middle of the vaulted ceiling, and heavy velvet curtains perfectly framed the windows that gave a view of the Monterey Bay, which at six o'clock was a twinkling wonder.

I approached the front desk, behind which stood a woman dressed in an immaculate silk suit.

"May I help you?" the woman asked, flashing me a toothpaste-commercial smile.

"I have a six o'clock appointment with Brenna."

"Your name?"

"Annabelle Pleasanton."

"Okay, have a seat and I'll see if she's ready for you." The woman pointed me to a brocade couch that faced the large, spotless windows. On a table in front of the couch sat a golden tray filled with fancy chocolates. I eyed the chocolates eagerly. I wondered if they were free. I almost asked the woman at the desk, but I didn't want to sound tacky.

I leaned my back gently into the couch and gazed out at the bay. I watched as the white-capped waves crashed into the sand. It was absolutely gorgeous, a gift of beauty from a loving God.

"Annabelle, Brenna is ready for you," the woman at the desk informed me. "Just go up the stairs, and hers is the third office on your left."

"Thank you," I said.

I walked up the plush stairs toward the office. It was marked with an engraved name plate. I knocked softly on the door.

"Come in," a woman's voice said from within the office.

As I walked inside, I smiled at the woman who was probably in her mid-thirties and had full hair and small blue eyes.

She stood up and offered me her hand to shake. "You must be Annabelle," she said.

"Yes," I replied, extending my hand.

"Brenna Lockman. Nice to meet you, dear."

"Nice to meet you too," I echoed.

Brenna sat back down on what looked like the most comfortable office chair I have ever seen. "So, you're throwing a bridal shower for your best friend?"

I took a seat. "Yes."

"And you'd like to look through our catering portfolio?"

"Yes."

"All right," Brenna said, rising from her chair. She plucked a portfolio from a bookcase and sat back down. "How large is the party?"

"Probably about twenty people," I answered.

"Okay."

"I do have one question though," I informed Brenna. "What is your fee for arranging catering?"

"It's very minimal," Brenna assured me. I wasn't sure if it was a good thing that Brenna had said "minimal" instead of giving me a number.

"Would you like to go ahead and take a look at the portfolio?" Brenna asked.

"Yes," I answered, pushing my worries about the fee aside.

"Here is a list of the caterers we usually use, and some photos of their fare, but if there is something else you have in mind, we can usually arrange just about anything. In fact, just this past Saturday I had a local sushi place set up a mobile sushi bar in the shoe department at Macy's."

"Wow," I said. I began flipping through the glossy pages of the portfolio. My mouth watered at the sight of the delicious food. "This all looks great. Maybe we should talk about price now."

"Just remember, anything can be worked out," Brenna said. I was beginning to get worried at the way she seemed to dance around the subject of price.

"Well," I said, "I need to keep it right around two—"

Brenna smiled broadly and cut me off. "With that amount, you can pretty much have your pick from all of these places."

"Really?" I asked, my worry suddenly replaced by

excitement. The food at Carrie's shower was going to be incredible.

"Yes, definitely," Brenna assured me, a smile on her face. "Here are the price lists." Brenna withdrew a stack of papers from the back of the portfolio.

Eager to get the catering all set up and find a caterer who could provide the all-natural foods that Carrie liked, I took the papers from Brenna.

As I looked at the price lists, I decided that Brenna really should have let me finish telling her what my budget was, because the caterers in the portfolio could cater a party of twenty for *two thousand* dollars, not two hundred dollars.

I began to feel incredibly dumb for coming to Anna Medici and Company. I should have known. People who came to places like this were looking for extravagance, not bargains. "Brenna, thank you for your time, but I really don't think I'll need your services after all," I said.

"What is the problem, dear?"

"I can't afford this." I stood up to go.

"Tell me your rock bottom price," Brenna instructed without budging from her chair.

"Okay, about two hundred dollars. Two zero zero, the end."

"Oh dear," Brenna said slowly. "That is quite a problem. I can only think of one place that could possibly cater for two hundred dollars."

Brenna flipped to the back of the portfolio to a picture of a beautiful restaurant called The Blue Wave. On the next page, there were photos of the restaurant's food; it all looked delicious.

"Wow, this looks great. They could cater for two hundred dollars?" I asked, feeling hope well up inside of me.

"Oh, no, not The Blue Wave," Brenna said. She pointed to the corner of the photo. "I can get you *that* for two hundred."

I squinted, trying to make out what she was pointing to. There were two golden arches in the back of the photo.

"Oh," I said, forcing a laugh.

Brenna stood up slowly. "I wish you luck in finding a

caterer." She walked toward the door as if to cue my exit. I thanked her and left.

As I walked down the stairs, I kicked myself for being so naïve. I should have known the second I set foot in the place that I should turn my sale-rack shoes right around.

I glanced at the tray of chocolates in the waiting area as I made my way to the door. And just to spite the place, just to say "I am frugal and proud of it," I asked the desk lady if the chocolates were free.

Sure enough, she looked at me like I was the tackiest of the tackies. "Yes, they are . . ." She tried to force the word "free" out of her mouth, but she couldn't. "They are complimentary," she said finally.

I walked over to the chocolates and popped one of the treats into my mouth. Then, because I have never been able to turn down free chocolate, I put two more in my bag. I think I heard the woman at the desk gasp at my terribly un-classy move.

As I strolled out to my car, I began to feel a little worried about the whole finding-a-caterer thing. It certainly wasn't off to a very good start. I sighed heavily when I reached my car and slowly got inside. Then I started the engine, turned the radio up really loud, and headed somewhere I knew I would find some comfort. Hopefully in the form of something home-cooked.

Chapter 7

"Mom," I called out as I walked through the front door.

"In here," Mom hollered from the kitchen.

I walked into the kitchen and found Mom decorating a two-tiered cake. Mom makes the most amazing special occasion cakes. They have the rare combination of being both good to look at and delicious. People are constantly asking her to make cakes for this or that occasion, and she gladly accepts. Then when she is offered cash for her creations, she graciously declines.

"What's the cake for?" I asked, taking a spoon to a bowl of Mom's famous buttercream icing.

"A bridal shower tonight," Mom answered. She bent down slightly and continued to ice the cake, which had been decorated to look like a white basket. Fresh flowers sat on top of the cake, adding to the basket affect.

"On a Monday?" I asked, my mouth full of icing.

"It's the only evening the bride has off work," Mom answered.

"Do I know the girl?" I asked.

"No, I don't think so."

"What's her name?"

"Elise Stapleton," Mom replied. "I actually don't know her

at all. She's Bev Stapleton's daughter. Bev goes to the same church as Maria. You know Maria; she's in my exercise group. Anyway, Bev saw the cake I did for Maria's fiftieth birthday, and asked me to do a cake for her daughter's shower."

I suddenly had a great idea. "So you're going to a bridal shower tonight?"

Mom shrugged. "I'll probably just drop off the cake."

"Can I go?" This could be the perfect opportunity to check out the menu at someone else's shower. Do a little research.

"Sure. I could actually really use your help."

Good. We would both get something out of my going. "What time do we have to leave?"

"In an hour or so," Mom replied.

I freshened up in the bathroom, and when I was through, I found Dad in the kitchen with Mom. He was home from work, where he does something I've never really understood—investments or investing or something like that.

"Hey, Dad." I smiled when I spotted the spoonful of icing in his hand. Like father, like daughter.

"Hi, Bellie. Will you be around for family home evening tonight?"

"Aren't I always, Dad?" Since the first Monday after I graduated college and moved back to Monterey, I have had family home evening with my parents. Usually, I go to the one at singles ward and then go to my parents' house afterwards.

Dad smiled. "Yes, but you have a boyfriend now. I thought maybe you'd just go to singles ward and then spend some time with him."

"What?! Dad, Isaac isn't my boyfriend!" Although I did kind of like the sound of that. "You can't go around calling him that, okay?"

"Okay," Dad said, raising his hands in acquiescence.

Mom looked up from her cake and smiled at the two of us.

"Plus, the singles ward isn't having FHE tonight," I explained.

"Annabelle is going to come with me to Bev Stapleton's

house to drop off the cake," Mom said. "We'll be back at about eight o'clock. I know it's a little late, but they asked me to do this cake at the last minute. I didn't have time to plan as well as I would have liked."

"It's a beautiful cake, Marjorie." Dad kissed Mom gently on the top of her brown curls.

Mom put the finishing touches on the cake and declared it finished. She asked me to put some frozen stew into the microwave for dinner while she changed out of her cake-making clothes.

Mom emerged from her room in a floral skirt and a short-sleeved sweater set. Her hair was freshly combed, and she had put on a creamy shade of lipstick. She looked lovely. Dad obviously thought the same thing because he whistled at her. Mom responded to the whistle with a grin and a "Stop, Walter."

As Mom and I prepared to leave for the shower, I found that everything was making me think of Isaac. As we ate our stew I saw a carrot that was in the exact shape of Isaac's Firebird. Mom and Dad didn't quite see the resemblance, but I'm telling you, it was there. Then as Mom and I were loading the cake into the back of the station wagon, she said to me, "Watch out for this icing," but for a split second I thought she said, "Watch and then kiss Isaac."

Oh, man. I was falling fast.

I stepped inside the gigantic Carmel home where the final touches were being put on Elise Stapleton's bridal shower. I helped Mom carry the cake through the marble-floored entryway and into a kitchen that looked much different than the bridal shower kitchens I'm used to. No stacks of dishes. No sauce spills. No hurried women bumping into each other as one pours bottles of Sprite into a punch bowl while the other stirs in the limeade. All I saw was a huge, spotless kitchen filled with gourmet foods and people with focused looks on their faces and neat uniforms on their backs.

Inside the kitchen, a woman in a cream-colored dress greeted Mom. "Marjorie," she said. Then she glanced at the cake and gushed, "How lovely. Let's take that out to the ballroom."

On the way to the ballroom, which I thought was a room that only existed in old movies and the game of Clue, Mom introduced me to the woman in the cream-colored dress: Bev Stapleton. We exchanged greetings.

As Bev, Mom, and I entered the ballroom, my eyes grew wide. This was not a bridal shower, it was a bridal storm.

The first thing I noticed, probably because we were standing right next to them, were the cakes. Three of them. Mom and I placed our cake on the large table decorated with fresh flowers and greenery, and I stared longingly at the other cakes. One was a fancy chocolate confection complete with perfectly placed red raspberries. The other appeared to be a simple white cake.

Just as I was looking, and wondering if it would be rude to ask if we could stay long enough to have cake, a woman dressed in a sky blue suit whizzed by and placed cards written in calligraphy in front of the cakes.

I read the cards. The one in front of Mom's cake read: Classic White with Buttercream Icing. The chocolate cake was labeled: Double Raspberry Mousse with Swiss Chocolate Icing. And the label for the third cake read: Low-Cal Vanilla with Low-Cal Icing. Low-calorie cake? It just didn't seem right to me.

I should take notes, I thought suddenly. But since I hadn't brought anything to write on, I had to resort to the mess of receipts that had accumulated in my bag. I took out the receipt for *Today's Bride* magazine and wrote: have a variety of cakes.

"Hi," I heard a woman's voice behind me. I shoved the receipt back into my bag.

"Hi," I said back.

"I'm Olivia."

"Annabelle," I said as I looked into Olivia's nearly purple eyes.

"Are you Elise's friend?"

"Uh, actually, my mom made one of the cakes, so I'm just here to help her."

Olivia looked around as if trying to find someone else to talk to. "Well I think I'm going to go take a seat," she began, "though I hate to sit alone."

"I'll sit with you," I said. Mom was chatting with Bev, so I could sit for a while.

"So, how do you know Elise?" I asked Olivia as we sat down. That was always a good question because it usually led to a long story, thus filling in the moments of otherwise awkward silence.

"I met her in . . . EEEEE!" Olivia let out an ear piercing screech as she looked at something over my shoulder. I followed her line of vision to the entrance of the room and saw two women—one petite with glossy brown hair, the other extremely tall and skinny—rushing toward the table. Olivia stood up to hug them. The three women sort of jumped up and down all talking at once. What I picked up from the conversation went something like this:

"You look so . . ." Tall and Skinny said.

"I know, I love your . . ." Petite and Glossy interrupted.

"Oh, no, you're the ones who . . ." Olivia began.

"Have you seen the rock on Elise's . . ." Tall and Skinny started to ask.

"My gosh, it's like a . . ." Olivia tried to finish.

"I know, I saw it and just about . . ." Petite and Glossy said.

"Totally," Tall and Skinny and Olivia said in unison.

"Totally," Petite and Glossy added.

"Come sit with us," Tall and Skinny said to Olivia. With a little wave in my direction, Olivia was off.

I peered over at the buffet table. Large china platters held fancy-looking food. I saw the back of the woman who had whizzed past me while I looked at the cakes. She was putting labels written in calligraphy in front of the platters. I waited until the woman was gone and then pulled another receipt out of my bag, making my way over to the buffet table.

I copied down the cards, well, minus the calligraphy. Beef Tenderloin with Garlic and Rosemary. Roast Duck with Port Wine Glaze. Steamed Leeks with Mustard Vinaigrette. Roasted Mushrooms with Thyme. Ancient Grains Bread. Whole Wheat Bread. And, of course, Low-Cal Asian Salad.

With my list tucked in my bag, I made my way back to my seat. I glanced around the room in search of Mom and noticed that the room was filling up quickly with chatting, giggling women. Three such women had taken seats at the table I had been sitting at. I smiled at them and lowered myself into my seat.

Just then, Olivia, who was standing in the front of the room, clanked a silver spoon against a crystal glass and the chatter in the room came to a hush.

"Before Elise gets here we need everyone's help with a surprise gift." At this, a collective "Ah" sounded in the room. "Sierra," Olivia pointed to Tall and Skinny, "will be coming around with a camera to film your words of marriage wisdom for Elise and Dominic."

Olivia surveyed the room. "We'll start back there," she said, pointing at my table. Then she put her glass down and disappeared from view.

I stood up to go find Mom. "Oh, no you don't," a redheaded woman seated at the table said to me. "If we have to be on camera so do you."

"But I don't—"

"So who's first?" Tall and Skinny, a.k.a. Sierra, asked as she approached the table.

"She is." The redhead pointed to me.

"Okay, when the red light is on, go ahead."

"But I don't even—"

"I know, I know, I hate being on camera too. But do it for

Elise," Sierra said, sounding slightly agitated.

I felt a whole bunch of eyes on me. I think I even heard someone whisper, "Who's she?"

"Listen, I'm just here for the cake," I said, trying to explain.

"Aren't we all," the redhead said with a laugh.

I opened my mouth to try to clarify, but Sierra spoke up first. "Listen, you're holding up the program."

"Okay," I relented. I cleared my throat, and watched for the red light.

"Hey Elise," I began. "The words I would like to offer are . . ." My mind went blank. I had nothing. Why did I have to go first? Or at all for that matter? I didn't even know the girl. "I would like to say . . ."

My mind raced through some quotes. An apple a day . . . No. People who throw stones . . . No. Turn off the water while you brush your . . . No. I felt myself starting to sweat.

Then I saw Mom.

She was walking into the room with Bev. Her hair was brushed behind her ears and her smile was radiant. "Look Elise, I don't think you even know me, but I can tell you this: I know two people who have been married for a very long time. And from what I can tell, love looks a lot like friendship. It's sitting on the couch playing Scrabble together. It's eating stew on a Monday night. And it's sweeter than a big spoon of buttercream icing." I smiled, feeling myself starting to tear up. "Okay that's it," I said quickly, before my blubbering was caught on tape.

Sierra turned off the camera. "Okay, who's next?" she asked, moving on to the redhead.

I looked for Mom, but she had disappeared. So, interested in what was on the drink menu, I made my way to the drink table. Three silver fountains were flowing with frothy drinks. Tall glasses filled with ice cubes with raspberries frozen into them stood next to the fountains. And sure enough the drinks were labeled by calligraphy cards.

I took out another receipt, this one for a stick of deodorant I had bought before my dinner date with Isaac. I copied down the names of the drinks. They were probably alcoholic, but the alcohol could easily be omitted, making the drinks better for the body and taste buds alike.

After I wrote the names of the drinks on the receipt, I pulled the rest of my receipt-notes from my handbag. I was looking over them and fixing my t's and i's when I was aware of the whizzing woman coming up behind me.

"What are you doing?" she asked.

"Oh, I'm just . . ." I looked up and immediately recognized the woman. It was Brenna, the event planner.

Suddenly I had a flashback to getting caught writing a note to Melissa Mission during class in fourth grade, and though I'd like to think I am much brighter than my fourth grade self, I hid my receipt-notes the same way I hid my note to Melissa—I put them down my shirt. Unfortunately, although my ten-year-old self wore her shirts tucked in, my twenty-four-year-old self did not, and the notes went directly to the floor.

Brenna picked them up before I could. She surveyed my messy handwriting. "You're taking notes? Why would you . . ." Brenna looked up at me. "Wait a second? Aren't you that girl who came into my office earlier today? Did you follow me here so you could write down the food I was serving?" She looked at me like I was some kind of lunatic.

"No. Of course not. I—"

Just then, a girl wearing a crystal tiara atop her smooth blonde hair approached me and Brenna. I eyed the tiara. *Must be the bride*, I thought.

"What's going on over here?" the girl in the tiara asked. Then she glared at me. "Who are you? I don't know you."

"I was just taking care of it," Brenna said.

Elise eyed me suspiciously and stepped in front of Brenna. "Actually, Brenna, I just realized I know who she is. Why don't you go make sure the DJ is ready to start? I'll take it from here." Her voice was menacing.

Brenna nodded and walked away, my receipt-notes still in her hand.

Elise put her hands on her hips and gave me a scathing look. "You're Dominic's ex-girlfriend aren't you? The one who's been sending me all those nasty emails."

"What? No." I noticed that a crowd had begun to form around us.

The redhead from the table I had been sitting at, through with her video appearance, walked over to see what the commotion was about.

"Hey, Scarlett, you've seen Dominic's ex-girlfriend, haven't you?" Elise asked.

"Yeah, once briefly," Scarlett answered.

"Is this her?" Elise pointed at me in disgust.

Scarlett narrowed her eyes and looked me over. "It could be, but I think his ex-girlfriend was fatter."

"She could have gone on South Beach," a girl who had just joined the crowd chimed in, giving me a scathing look.

"Look," I said, "I'm not Dominic's ex-girlfriend on South Beach."

"Then why are you here?" Elise asked, getting in my face.

"I'm here because my mom made the cake."

"Oh, really?" Scarlett said accusingly.

"Yes, really," I said, wondering why she was talking like she thought she was Nancy Drew.

I watched as Scarlett whispered something into Elise's ear. Elise then turned her mouth into an angry shape and daintily removed her tiara and placed it in Scarlett's hand. Before I knew what was happening, Elise grabbed the back of my hair and yanked. Then, the angry shape of her mouth intensifying, she balled up her fist and took a swing at me. I shielded my face and awaited the punch.

But an arm came out of nowhere and, with cat-like quickness, stopped Elise in mid-swing. I moved my hands away from my face to see who had just saved me.

It was Mom.

And next to Mom stood Bev Stapleton, looking in shock at her daughter who still had a chunk of my hair in her French-manicured hand.

"What is going on?" Bev directed at her daughter.

"This is Dominic's ex-girlfriend, Mom." Elise shot me a nasty look.

"No, Elise, this is Marjorie Pleasanton's daughter, Annabelle."

I nodded at Elise. She let go of my hair. "But . . . she said her Mom made one of the cakes," Elise protested. "And Scarlett told me that Dominic's ex-girlfriend's mother works at Confection Perfection, which is where we got the chocolate raspberry cake."

"Yes," Mom said, obviously trying hard to resist the urge to let Elise have it. "But I work for Marjorie Pleasanton bakery, and I made the white cake with buttercream icing."

Elise turned her mouth into a pout. "Sorry," she said without conviction. Then she put the crown back on her head and without another word walked away with her nose slightly in the air. The musicians, who had stopped playing so as not to miss the unfolding fight, began to play again. The guests whispered amongst themselves about what had just happened.

"I am so sorry," Bev apologized to both Mom and me.

"It's not your fault," Mom said graciously.

"Can we get out of here?" I asked Mom as I rubbed the back of my head, checking for a bald spot.

Mom put a protective arm around me. "Sure, let's go."

I looked at the floor as Mom and I made our way out of the house. We climbed into the car, and I thought about how Mom had saved me in there. "Hey, Mom," I began. "Where did you learn to stop a punch like that?"

Mom sighed. "Three girls with one bathroom to share. You pick these things up."

Chapter 8

The red blinking light of my answering machine greeted me inside my condo.

I pressed Play on the machine and popped open the rubber food container that Mom had sent home with me. It was filled with cake scraps and a generous amount of buttercream icing. I smothered a chunk of the cake with icing and ate it with my fingers while I checked my messages.

The first message was from Carrie.

"It's me. Could you call me? Please."

The tone of Carrie's voice worried me, so I quickly dialed her number. The phone went directly to voicemail, which meant she was on the line. So while I waited for the line to free up, I checked my other message. And that message was from Isaac.

"Hi, Annabelle, it's Isaac. I'm just trying to figure something out so will you . . . call me when you get this message."

Trying to figure something out? I silently hoped it wasn't one of those crossword puzzles in the newspaper. I am really not good at those. I dialed Isaac's number.

"Hi there," Isaac said, obviously recognizing my number on the caller ID.

"Hi," I said, pleased by Isaac's greeting. "What are you up to?"

"Just watching a little ESPN."

"Cool. I got your message about trying to figure something—"

My call waiting beeped. It was probably Carrie.

"Oh, that's the other line," I said to Isaac. "Is it all right if I put you on hold and get it really fast, honey?"

Oh. My. Goodness. My mouth flew open in what-in-the-world-did-I-just-say panic. *Did I seriously just call Isaac honey?*

"I mean . . . uh . . . homey . . ."

Homey? That's worse than honey!

Flustered, and not knowing what else to do, I switched over to the other line.

"Hello?" I answered.

The person on the other end of the line didn't answer.

"Hello?" I said again.

Still no answer.

I clicked back over to Isaac. "Sorry about that," I said. The sound of me calling him honey and then homey was still echoing in my ears.

"That's all right . . . homey."

Thank goodness Isaac couldn't see how pink my cheeks turned, because they were pretty darn pink.

"So I heard you went to an interesting bridal shower tonight," Isaac said.

"How do you know that?"

"My sister Ally told me about it. Elise Stapleton is her cheer coach, and she invited the whole cheer team to her bridal shower. Ally told me that Elise got in a fight with a girl named Annabelle Pleasanton. I don't know a whole lot of Annabelle Pleasantons, so I thought it might be you."

"Oh," I said, drawing the word out. "First let me just clarify that we didn't get in a fight. She nearly punched me. There's a difference."

"Ally said it was over a guy?"

"Isn't it always," I said with a sigh.

"So it's true?" Isaac sounded concerned.

"Yeah."

"That doesn't seem like you," Isaac said, sounding like he had just discovered that I was a hardened criminal.

"Wait? What?"

"To show up at a bridal shower uninvited because you still have a thing for an ex-boyfriend."

"Huh? That's not what happened."

"But you just said it was."

"I did not," I argued. "I said that the fight was over a guy. Elise thought that I was her fiancé's ex-girlfriend. But obviously I'm not. I was there because I helped my mom deliver a cake. And plus, I haven't dated anyone since this guy named Hadwin who I broke up with six months ago because he started talking about how he and I should try to be the first human inhabitants of Jupiter's moon Io." *Okay. That may have been a little too much information.*

"So you don't still have a thing for an ex-boyfriend?" Isaac asked again.

"I just told you I didn't," I said, feeling slightly offended. How many times did I have to repeat myself?

"I know, but you're not just saying that because you don't want me to stop calling you and stuff, are you?"

"Okay, that sounded both conceited and rude," I said. Now I was really offended.

"I'm sorry, that came out wrong, I—"

My call waiting beeped, cutting Isaac off.

"That might be Carrie," I said briskly. "I really need to get it. Hold on a second." My voice definitely wasn't the nicest I've ever heard it. But I couldn't help it. I was a little hurt by the things Isaac was saying.

"All right," Isaac said slowly.

I clicked over to the other line. "Hello?"

"Oh, Annabelle, thank goodness." Carrie sounded exasperated.

"Carrie, are you okay?"

"No," Carrie answered. "Miles and I had a terrible fight."

"Oh, Carrie," I said, sensing the distress in her voice. "Hang on just one second."

I clicked back over to Isaac.

"Listen Isaac, I have to go."

"I didn't mean to upset you," Isaac said.

"I'm sure you didn't," I said softly. "But you still kind of did."

"I'm really sorry," Isaac began. "Let me explain. I—"

"Let's talk about this later," I said, cutting Isaac off. "I really need to get back to Carrie."

"All right. So we'll talk later then." Isaac's words were more of a question than a statement.

"Yes, we'll talk later," I agreed. Then I clicked back over to Carrie.

"I'm sorry," I said to Carrie. "I was on the other line with Isaac. Now, tell me what happened."

"Oh, Annabelle. We had such a horrible fight. I tried everything to stop myself from getting upset. I tried some yoga breaths. I took some St. John's Wort. But nothing helped. I don't think he wants to marry me anymore. And we've only been engaged for two days." Carrie was crying.

I was taken aback. It took a lot to upset Carrie. Normally she was the Queen of Calm. "What happened?" I asked.

"It was so dumb, Annabelle," Carrie sniffled. "Miles is very practical, and I love that about him. But with some of the wedding details I want to be sentimental, not practical. So today I wanted to go and look at wedding dresses. We set the date for two months from now, so we don't have a whole lot of time.

"Well, I found this gorgeous dress—it was even modest—but Miles took one look at the price and said, 'Should you really spend this much on something you'll only wear once?'" Carrie paused and sniffled.

"Oh, Carrie, I'm so sorry. Men are so dumb sometimes," I

said, suddenly wanting to smack both Isaac and Miles upside the head.

"But that's not the worst of it," Carrie said.

"What else?" I asked.

"I got upset by what Miles said and then . . . and then he told me he thinks we should postpone the wedding so we can have more time. He said two months isn't enough time, and that if it's going to put too much stress on us we should postpone the wedding. Oh, Annabelle. Why would he want to postpone the wedding? Do you think it's because he doesn't want to marry me anymore?" Carrie's cries increased in intensity.

"Carrie, Miles loves you," I assured her. "Of course he wants to marry you. I'm sure he just doesn't want you to be stressed about the planning, so that's why he made the postponing suggestion. Dumb as it was."

"Do you think?" Carrie asked with a small sniffle.

"Oh, yeah," I answered. I looked at the shiny chrome clock in my living room and had an idea. "Carrie, what are you doing tomorrow?"

"Not much, just work," Carrie responded, her voice sad.

"Is there someone that can run the store in the morning?"

"Yes, Moonbeam will be there."

"Okay," I said, smiling. "I'm coming over. I'll be at your house in fifteen minutes. And pack a bag. I know it's Monday, but we're going to The Golden Artichoke."

"We haven't been there since you broke up with Hadwin," Carrie said, her voice brightening.

"Then I think we're due for a visit. See you soon. Love you."

I hung up the phone and raced to my room. I packed a small suitcase for the night and grabbed my keys, handbag, and cell. Then I called Mom and left a message on my parents' machine, letting Mom know where I was going to be.

Yes, I still call my mother when I disappear for the night. Otherwise, the next day I come home to tons of frantic messages from Mom, the last few telling me that she is going to call Search and Rescue if she doesn't hear from me within an hour.

Rolling my suitcase behind me, I excitedly jogged to my car. Then, with the radio blaring, I drove to Carrie's house, gearing up for a girl's night at The Golden Artichoke.

Carrie and I emerged from my car in the parking lot of The Golden Artichoke and immediately smelled the familiar scent of French-fried artichoke hearts. Breathing in the intoxicating smell, we walked through the door, which is in the shape of a gigantic artichoke, and entered the lobby of our favorite inn and restaurant.

"Do you have any rooms available?" I asked the woman at the front desk. I was pretty sure they would on a Monday night.

"How many adults?" the woman asked.

"Two," Carrie answered, her puffy eyes focused on the desk clerk.

"Okay." The woman pressed some keys on her computer. "Do you want a Jacuzzi-balcony room?"

"Yes," Carrie and I answered in unison. We always got a Jacuzzi-balcony room.

"Smoking or non?"

"Non," I said.

"Ocean or artichoke-field view?"

"Ocean view," Carrie responded.

The woman typed a few things into her computer, handed us a key on a golden keychain with a dangling artichoke charm, and sent us up to our third-floor room.

You may be thinking that an artichoke inn and restaurant is the weirdest thing you've ever heard of, but here on the Central California coast artichokes are a huge deal. And The Golden Artichoke makes an art out of showcasing all things artichoke.

Carrie and I walked up to the third floor of the inn—which looks like a huge beach house with a fresh coat of clean white paint. We entered our room and immediately dove for the two golden vouchers on the table in the sitting area. The vouchers read: Good for one large order of French-fried artichoke hearts.

"French-fried artichoke hearts 24 hours a day; there's nothing better," I said, giving my voucher a little kiss.

"They're so good, I forget about my heart and health and eat hydrogenated oils, refined flour, and dairy," Carrie declared with a smile.

"They're so good," I said, "I can forget that Isaac was a total punk on the phone tonight."

"He was?" Carrie asked, looking at me empathetically.

"Yeah, it must be National Punk Day." I plopped down on one of the two queen beds in the room. I ran my right hand across the deep green satin comforter and used my index finger to trace the golden artichokes that were embroidered perfectly into the fabric.

Carrie lounged on the other bed. "What happened?"

I quickly recounted the bridal shower story for Carrie. She completely believed every word of my side of the story, as a good human should. Then I told her that Isaac, for some reason, had trouble believing that I wasn't a psycho ex-boyfriend's-fiancé stalker and that he had said some pretty hurtful things to me.

Carrie shook her head in sisterly solidarity.

"Let's go, our artichokes are waiting," I said, pushing Isaac out of my mind. I held out my hand to help Carrie off the bed.

We walked downstairs to the 24-hour restaurant attached to the inn. Once inside, we were seated immediately because, other than a group of teenagers, we were the only customers. As soon as the waitress, a thin, harried-looking woman, came to the table, we handed her our vouchers and ordered our artichoke hearts with extra ranch dipping sauce.

"This puts me in a much better mood," Carrie said. She sounded like she was trying to convince herself.

"Don't worry, Carrie," I consoled. "I hear that engaged couples fight a lot."

"From who?"

"Oh everybody knows that," I replied. I wasn't quite sure where I had heard it from.

"But Miles and I have never fought before," Carrie said in a far-off voice.

"There must be something in the air, then," I said, remembering yet again my conversation with Isaac.

"There must be," Carrie said. "So what's going on with you and Isaac?"

"Well, we hung out a lot this weekend, but every time we were together it seemed like Ro—" I stopped myself. I couldn't say that Rona Bircheck was sabotaging all my dates with Isaac. Remember, Carrie thinks Rona is great. "Ro . . . Roman candles are always going off," I said, finishing my sentence.

Carrie looked at me weirdly. "Roman candles?"

"Yeah, you know, it's almost the Fourth of July and those kids, they just don't wait."

Carrie looked at me like I was insane. But luckily for me, before she could say anything our waitress appeared with our order, and by the time our food was set in front of us Carrie had forgotten about the Roman candles.

"Okay, so you've been hanging out with him a lot. But how do you feel about him?" Carrie asked, taking a bite of a steaming artichoke heart.

"It's been just a few days, but I have to tell you, I feel like . . . like if I could have one thing in the world, I would want more time with him." I bit into an artichoke heart and stared into space dreamily.

"I think he's good for you," Carrie told me.

I snapped out of my dreamy state, and looked at Carrie. "You've only spoken to him twice. How can you know he's good for me?"

"Because you're still the same."

"What?" Carrie was completely losing me.

"Remember the last time we were here?"

"Yes," I said as I dipped another artichoke heart into the thick ranch dipping sauce.

"I have something to tell you about that," Carrie said.

"What?"

"I was relieved when you broke up with Hadwin," Carrie confessed, sounding apologetic.

"Really? Why?"

"Because you let him change you," Carrie explained.

"I did?"

"Yeah," Carrie began. "Let me ask you this: Do you really think that *Space Traveler III* is the best movie ever made? Or that when you get married you want a moon rock instead of a diamond ring? Because I'm quoting you here, Annabelle."

"No," I answered, embarrassed.

"Do you still play those video games you two used to play together?"

"No," I replied.

"Because three days after you started dating him, you told me you loved those video games."

I made a face. "Why didn't you ever say anything to me?" I asked Carrie. I mean, isn't a best friend supposed to intervene the second you start talking about not wanting a diamond?

"Because I knew that eventually you would realize he wasn't right for you. And that who you were trying to be wasn't right for you either."

I looked at Carrie. Had she been taking some new wisdom herbs or something?

"I don't know why I'm always trying to do and be what I think others want me to do and be," I said softly.

"You don't seem to be worried about that with Isaac," Carrie said.

"That's because even if I knew what he wanted, I wouldn't be able to give it to him because he always sneaks up on me. He's already seen the good, the bad, and the ugly."

"And that's good," Carrie said.

"I guess," I responded, not really convinced.

"What would you do if you saw Isaac right now?"

"Let's see. First I would tell him that I am not the kind

of girl that gets obsessed with an ex-boyfriend. Then maybe I'd throw something at him." Okay, so I wouldn't really throw something at him, but I was getting into the moment.

"Nothing sharp and pointy I hope," I heard a male voice say from behind me. It sounded an awful lot like . . .

"Isaac," I said, my eyes growing wide as I turned around.

Isaac stood behind me holding a package of Milk Duds with a white bow on them.

"Milk Duds are my favorite," I exclaimed, eyeing the candy with a smile growing on my lips. Then, remembering that I was still a bit upset with Isaac, I wiped the smile off my face.

"I know," Isaac said.

"How do you know?" I asked, pretending like I really didn't care.

"Your mom told me."

"When did you talk to my mom?"

"Well, I tried to call you back at your house and got no answer. Then I called what I thought was your cell number, but it was actually the number you gave me for your parents' house. So, since your Mom and I are pretty tight, I asked her what your favorite candy bar is, and asked if she knew where I could find you and deliver my peace offering. So here you go, some Milk Duds to say I'm sorry for being a dud." Isaac smiled, obviously enjoying himself for coming up with that.

"That's the sweetest, corniest thing I've ever heard." I stood up to give Isaac a hug. But then I stopped. "So do you still think that I'm a crazy, ex-boyfriend-obsessed stalker?" I asked gruffly.

Isaac put his arms around me and said, "Not one bit."

I smiled as I let Isaac hug me. And let me tell you, being in his strong arms was better than eating chocolate silk pie. While reading a great chick book. In a bubble bath.

Carrie was eyeing us sadly. I felt terrible for her. Miles should be at the restaurant too, giving Carrie a whole truck load of her favorite candy bar. Talking about postponing the wedding. The nerve of that guy.

"Thank you, Isaac," I said, pulling away from him. "It was really sweet of you to come out here, but tonight is ladies' night. Carrie and I are going to hang out. But I'll call you later."

"Okay, but there's one more person you're going to have to send away. I found him wandering around the parking lot when I got here."

"Who?" I asked.

Just then Miles appeared carrying a bouquet of lilies, Carrie's favorite flower. Miles rushed to Carrie's side and knelt beside her.

"I called Annabelle's condo in search of you," I heard Miles whisper as I pretended like I wasn't listening. "Then I telephoned your mother. Then, desperate, I telephoned Annabelle's mother. She informed me that I could find you here. I am so sorry, my love. I was terribly insensitive."

Sweet, I thought. But I preferred a man who referred to himself as a dud.

Isaac and I quietly sat down and started talking as Carrie and Miles continued to whisper to each other. Soon the whispers turned to kisses. Apparently their fight was over.

Sighing, I opened my box of Milk Duds, and popped a Dud into my mouth. I smiled at Isaac appreciatively as I savored the treat. Isaac smiled back at me. Over the top of his head I noticed that the large artichoke-shaped clock in the restaurant had changed to 12:01 AM.

National Punk Day had officially ended.

Chapter 9

Tuesday morning, I was sitting in my cubicle, about to take a bite out of the Krispy Kreme maple iced doughnut that I bought on the way to work, when my cell rang.

"Hello?" I answered.

"Good morning, beautiful," Isaac's voice came onto the line. "How did you sleep last night?"

Beautiful? A pleasant shiver went up my spine.

"So good," I answered. "Carrie and I got in the Jacuzzi before bed, and my muscles melted into oblivion. I just wish I could have slept longer, but I got to work late as it was."

"Yeah, I got a pretty late start too," Isaac admitted. "Listen, Annabelle, there's something I need to talk to you about. I was hoping you could come over to my place after work."

Something he needed to talk to me about? I felt my heart kind of stop in my chest. In my experience, those words are rarely the prelude to anything good.

"Um, yeah, I can come over right after work," I answered, trying to hide the anxiety in my voice.

"Great," Isaac said. He proceeded to give me directions to his home in Monterey and ended the conversation quickly.

As I pushed End on my phone and placed the directions

to Isaac's house on my desk, I noticed my hands were shaking slightly.

"Hi, there," Isaac greeted me through my open car window, looking very handsome in a pair of jeans and a t-shirt. The shirt had a small grease stain on the hem, due to the fact that Isaac had been working on his Firebird when I drove up.

"Hi," I said, winking at him. At least, trying to wink at him—my eyelid was a little shaky due to my nervousness.

I parked my car at the end of the dirt driveway, in front of a structure that looked like a garage. To the left of my car was Isaac's Firebird, shiny in the sun.

Isaac wiped his hands on a rag and helped me out of the car.

"This place is amazing," I told Isaac as I looked around. If I hadn't known Isaac lived there, I might have assumed it was one of the Monterey Bay's many gorgeous, exorbitantly priced vacation rentals. I spun around, inspecting the lush trees that gave the place a tranquil feeling, the beautiful house that looked like it belonged on a resort, and the large backyard complete with a tennis/basketball court.

"Is it all yours?" I asked Isaac.

"Mine and Ethan's," Isaac answered. "The lot belonged to our grandfather, and he sold it to us cheap. We built everything on it, with a little help from professionals, of course."

"Really? It's great." I paused and took a deep breath. "So . . . what is it you wanted to talk to me about?"

Isaac turned his eyes toward a large wooden deck that jutted out from the back of the house. "How about we go sit on the deck," he suggested.

"Okay," I responded apprehensively.

Isaac and I walked silently up the stairs onto the deck and sat down next to each other at a table with a massive blue umbrella looming over it.

"My sister Ally called me back last night to tell me that she was wrong about you still having a thing for an ex-boyfriend," Isaac began, wasting no time. "I'm sorry I said all that stuff last night. I really didn't mean to be such a jerk. But I think there's something you should know."

I held my breath and remained silent.

"I was engaged once," Isaac stated simply. He searched my face for a reaction.

My eyes widened a bit, but I remained silent.

"Her name was Ashley. She was in my singles ward when I was at San Jose State. I knew her for a while, but we didn't start dating until after she broke up with a guy she had been dating for a long time. The first few months, all she did was talk about her ex-boyfriend. She'd say, 'You're so much sweeter than Spencer,' and, 'Spencer would have never done that for me.'

"We dated for six months, and it seemed like Spencer was history, and I felt that it was right to ask her to marry me, so I did. But looking back, I think I was just in love with the thought of having a marriage and a family. Anyway, she said 'Yes,' and we started planning the wedding.

"Then, three weeks before the wedding, she showed up at my apartment, handed back the ring, and admitted that she had been seeing Spencer behind my back for about two months. She told me that at first it was just as friends, but then she had realized she was still in love with him. Can you believe that? While we were planning our wedding! She was seeing him while we were planning our wedding!" Isaac's voice was filled with traces of pain.

Hesitantly, I put my hand on Isaac's forearm as I tried to process the news. Isaac had been engaged before. To a girl named Ashley. In my mind, I tried to come up with what Ashley might have looked like. For some reason, I saw a perky brunette in a size four drill team uniform.

"Anyway she . . . she messed me up, Annabelle. So when Ally told me that stuff about the bridal shower and said that you were still hung-up on an ex-boyfriend, it just shot me back to that, and I remembered that feeling of being betrayed. And

I just thought, 'If Annabelle has a thing for another guy, then I need to stop things right now, because I'm starting to . . . '" Isaac paused for a moment. "Anyway, I just wanted you to know where I was coming from yesterday."

I looked off into the distance, trying to gather my thoughts. "I really . . . appreciate you telling me all of this. I'm so glad you trust me enough to share something so personal with me."

"I can't help it," Isaac said. He leaned close to me, locking his eyes with mine. "There's just something about you. Something that makes me feel like I've known you for years. And I know I probably shouldn't say things like this since we haven't actually known each other for years, but you are the most fascinating, alluring, breathtaking woman I have ever met."

A feverish, lightheaded feeling suddenly took over my body, and the feeling greatly increased when Isaac took a hold of my hand and laced his fingers in mine. With our hands linked, we looked out at the green trees of the property, silent because there was no need for words.

The silence was finally broken by Ethan.

"Hey, guys," Ethan called out to us from the doorway of the garage at the end of the driveway.

"Hey," Isaac shouted back.

I watched as a van pulled up into the driveway. An older man with dark skin and dark hair exited the driver's seat. He moved to the back of the van, removed a small, motorized wheelchair, and placed it on the ground. He then opened the passenger side door and picked up a small boy and carried him to the wheelchair. The little boy proceeded to drive the wheelchair around expertly, his wide smile visible even yards away. Ethan greeted the man and boy, and the trio went inside the garage.

"Why are they going into the garage?" I asked Isaac.

"Oh, that's not a garage. It used to be, but now it's Ethan's piano studio," Isaac said. "That's one of Ethan's piano students, Angel, and the man with him is his grandfather, Julio."

"Ethan teaches piano lessons?" I asked.

Isaac nodded, straightening his back. "Ethan is, well, he's a far better guy than I'll ever be."

"What makes you say that?" I asked. "Though I'd have to disagree with it."

"Ethan was a football player, an all-American in high school. He was first-string quarterback when he was a college freshman. Then he went on his mission and was in the accident, and everyone knew he probably wouldn't ever play football again.

"So the first few months after his mission, he was pretty messed up. I remember he'd sit in his wheelchair in my parents' garage and hit a punching bag until his knuckles were bloody. I was really worried about him for a while. But then one day he said to me, 'You know Isaac, I'm done. I don't think God wants me to be like this. I think he expects something better out of me.'

"So from then on he tried to make the best of his disability. He set out to perfect another talent of his: his music skills. And that was easy since he was as good of a musician as he was a football player. Ethan's music and story got really popular. He was even in the papers and stuff. Recording artists started buying his songs like crazy, and fancy restaurants like La Bonne Violette were offering him hundreds of dollars per hour just to play there."

"If he makes all that money, why does he need to teach piano lessons too?" I asked.

"He doesn't need to," Isaac answered, a look of admiration on his face. "After he started making a decent living, he came to me with an idea. He asked me, 'What would you think about me turning the garage into a piano studio? I want to teach music to kids with disabilities.' I thought it was a great idea, so for the next few months we worked on turning the garage into a studio, Ethan working about four hours to every one of mine. And now he has six students that learn piano from him."

"Wow," I said, unable to find a better word. What an incredible thing to do. Rather than becoming bitter, Ethan had made something wonderful come out of something so devastating. And now, in that little garage at the end of the driveway, he was making a difference in the lives of six children.

"I'd love to see the studio sometime," I told Isaac.

"How about now?" he suggested, standing up from his chair.

"But won't we interrupt the lesson?"

Isaac shook his head. "There's a nice little waiting area inside. We can sit there until the lesson is over."

"That sounds good," I said as Isaac helped me up from my chair.

The door to the studio creaked slightly as we pushed it open.

The little boy Isaac had called Angel was sitting at a shiny black grand piano in the east side of the room, and when the door creaked, he looked up, losing his place in his music.

I scrunched up my face in apology. "Sorry," I whispered.

"It's just my brother and his friend Annabelle," Ethan told Angel.

The small, dark-haired boy nodded and resumed plunking the keys on the piano.

Isaac and I tiptoed toward a leather couch in the large waiting area of the room and nodded hello to Angel's grandfather, Julio, who was already seated on a leather chair.

I looked around the studio from my seat on the couch. It was gorgeous. The high ceilings gave an open, airy feel to the room and the warm color of the stained-wood walls gave the place a feeling of natural elegance. Four large windows displayed a view of the beautiful landscape outside and the walls were decorated with incredible photos. Some of the photographs featured smiling children playing the studio's piano, and others were artistic shots of the studio's architecture.

When Angel had finished the song I recognized as

"Michael Row Your Boat Ashore," I clapped quietly. I couldn't help it—he was just so adorable sitting there at the piano, a huge smile on his face.

Angel looked over at me appreciatively and quickly turned the page in his piano book to his next song. He began playing the song and singing the words loudly. I immediately recognized the tune: "La Cucaracha."

As Angel played, Isaac took a hold of my hand. I looked over at him and smiled—I was enjoying this new handholding thing like crazy. Isaac and I watched and listened as Angel performed his song. He moved his small, feeble fingers from key to key with impeccable focus and determination, and he sang seemingly with all the joy in his little heart. He was obviously enjoying playing for his small audience, and it was terribly cute.

But there was something more. As I watched him play, I knew that I had something to learn. Here was this little boy who lived with limitations I could not imagine, and yet he was filled with joy. A joy that radiated from his face. A joy that was apparent in the determined way he plunked those piano keys. A joy that echoed in the sound of his voice.

When Angel was finished with his rendition of "La Cucaracha" I clapped again, this time the applause not only for the song, but for the little boy who had touched me through the way he played it. Everyone in the room joined in on the clapping, as if they too somehow knew what the applause was truly for.

After a couple more songs, Ethan told Angel that he had played his songs very well, told him to remember to practice, and helped him place his piano books in a SpongeBob backpack. Angel zoomed over to the sitting area, followed closely behind by Ethan.

Julio stood up from his seat. "Good job, Angel," he said with a heavy Spanish accent as he secured the SpongeBob backpack to Angel's wheelchair.

"I only messed up once on 'La Cucaracha,'" Angel said excitedly.

"Yes, I know," Julio said.

Ethan politely introduced me to Julio and Angel, and I shook Julio's hand and told him it was a pleasure to meet him. Then I looked at Angel. "You are an excellent piano player," I praised.

"Thank you," Angel said bashfully. "Will you be here for my next lesson?"

"Um, I'm not sure," I answered, looking over at Isaac.

"Maybe you can come to my recital," Angel suggested in his adorable little-boy voice.

"It's this Friday at seven," Ethan informed me. "You're welcome to come."

I nodded my head. "I would love to come. I'll check my schedule."

"Okay, bye," Angel said to me. He zoomed toward the door where his grandfather helped him outside.

I waved to the boy. "Bye."

Isaac and Ethan started chatting about the recital, and I stepped toward the large windows and watched as Julio gently lifted Angel out of his wheelchair and secured him into the seat of the car.

As I watched the van bounce down the dirt driveway, the late afternoon sun poured in through the window, warming my face. And a stronger, different kind of warmth filled my chest, letting me know that on a simple Tuesday afternoon I had been given the gift of meeting a remarkable child of God.

Back on the deck, I opened the pink notebook that I carried in my bag and made two additions to my Pink Notes while Isaac was inside the house pouring glasses of lemonade.

Pink Note #125

Name: Ethan Matthews

Why he's noteworthy: Ethan was in an accident that left him confined to a wheelchair. He makes something good come out of that trial by teaching piano to children with disabilities. Not for the money or anything; just because he does.

Pink Note #126

Name: Angel

Why he's noteworthy: Angel is one of Ethan's piano students. His body is weak and fragile, but he is not. His joyful smile reminds me that I need to stop getting down about the things that I don't have, the things I can't do.

"What are you writing?"

Isaac's voice startled me, and I quickly closed my Pink Notes. "Oh, nothing, just notes," I answered as Isaac set a glass of lemonade in front of me.

The thought of Isaac seeing my Pink Notes was terrifying. No one who doesn't know my middle name had ever seen them. Meaning only my immediate family and Carrie had seen them since I have never, ever, told anyone outside my family, except for Carrie, my middle name.

Okay, okay. Since I know you're just going to wonder, and won't be paying attention to the next part of the story—which gets pretty juicy, I must say—I'll tell you, as long as you promise to keep it a secret for all of your days.

You promise?

Okay.

It's Methuselah. Which is actually the name of a man in the Bible who lived to be really old, but in the delirium of an un-medicated, thirty-two hour labor, Mom thought it sounded like a pretty name for a little girl. I'm just lucky it isn't my first name.

"You really don't want me to see that notebook, do you?" Isaac asked, mischief in his eyes. Then, without giving me any warning, he reached for the notebook, splashing lemonade onto the deck as he did so.

"No," I hollered. I quickly put the notebook back into my handbag and clutched the bag tightly to my chest.

Isaac set his glass of lemonade on the table and raised his hands in surrender. "Okay, okay, fair enough."

Isaac sat down next to me, and his cell phone began ringing from within his pocket. "Excuse me," he said to me before answering the call.

I sipped my lemonade, which was a little heavy on the sugar, as Isaac talked.

"Of course," Isaac said to the person on the line. "You can come pick them up here, if you'd like. I can have them ready in twenty minutes. Okay, sure. See ya." Isaac hung up the phone. "Annabelle, I have to go get some photos together really fast. Do you mind waiting for a minute?"

"No, that's fine," I answered.

Isaac picked up the glasses of lemonade he had just set on the table. "Would you like to come inside?"

"All right."

Isaac led me through the sliding glass door and into the house. Inside, the house was obviously well designed, but as can be expected with two brothers living together, under-furnished and undecorated. Just inside the sliding door was a dining room that contained a sturdy dining table and little else. To the left was a simple kitchen with solid wood cabinets and black appliances.

Isaac went into the kitchen and placed the lemonades on a low breakfast bar. Then he reached into the refrigerator and grabbed a pitcher full of lemonade from the bottom shelf. This left the refrigerator bare except for a large pizza box, a bag of oranges, a gallon of milk, and a door full of condiments.

Isaac placed the pitcher on the breakfast bar. "Just in case you want more," he said.

"Thanks," I responded sweetly.

"You're welcome." Isaac flashed me an adorable smile.

When Isaac had gone, I wandered into the living room with my glass in hand and sat down on the couch. I fumbled through a stack of magazines on the coffee table: sports magazines, photography magazines, the *Ensign*.

I had just begun reading an *Ensign* article when Isaac strolled into the living room and sat down next to me on the couch. "You look so beautiful sitting here reading the *Ensign*," he said in a low voice.

I closed the magazine and batted my eyelashes playfully.

"So, are you up to a game of tennis?" Isaac asked.

"I'm not exactly dressed for tennis," I answered quickly.

Isaac looked over at my khaki pants—a pair I got a fabulous deal on at an outlet store—and black knit top. "We'll just hit the ball around a little," he said.

"Okay," I relented with a weak smile.

"Great, I'll go get the rackets," Isaac said, rising from the couch.

As Isaac rummaged through a nearby hall closet, my eyes turned to the stone fireplace located front and center in the room. I let my mind wander and began imagining me and Isaac sitting in front of the fireplace, holding hands and talking about everything, sipping the most delicious hot cocoa with whipped cream and chocolate sprinkles, and . . .

Above the fireplace, I noticed a black and white photograph of a farm worker dressed in a button down shirt and a cowboy hat. He was leaning against an old truck. In the background, Watsonville strawberry fields stretched out with no visible end. It was really an amazing photograph. I got up from my seat and stood in front of the fireplace, looking up at the photo.

"Did you take this?" I asked Isaac when he came to my side, rackets in hand.

"I sure did," Isaac answered.

"You have a way of capturing people," I said, continuing to admire the photo.

"People are my favorite subjects. When a person inspires me, I capture a moment in their life, so I can remember."

I narrowed my eyes pensively and thought about Isaac's comment. I wasn't a photographer, but I did the same thing with my Pink Notes. I captured people, so I could remember them. So I could remember the impact they had on me.

I turned and looked at Isaac. "I know exactly what you mean," I said.

Following my words, there was a thick silence and the air in the room seemed to grow extremely hot. Wordlessly, Isaac looked into my eyes and put his arms around me gently. He pulled me close to him, and my heart began to beat heavy in my chest. I wondered if he was going to kiss me. I closed my eyes and waited for what was going to happen.

Knock, Knock, Knock.

Isaac and I both jumped at the sound of a knock at the door. Isaac quickly released me and cleared his throat as he walked to the door. I was curious to see who I could blame for interrupting our moment, but my view of who was at the door was blocked by a large wall.

"Come on in," I heard Isaac say. "I just have to go get the photos."

I heard the door close, and seconds later I was standing face to face with the interrupter.

None other than Rona Bircheck.

"Annabelle," Rona said, surprised to see me. "What are you doing here?"

I couldn't speak. I could barely think. Yet another me-and-Isaac moment ruined by Rona Bircheck. It was like she planned it. In what had become a reflex reaction, I looked at Rona's left hand—no ring. Why wasn't she wearing it?

"Annabelle and I were just about to play a game of tennis," Isaac said, responding to Rona's question.

I glared at Isaac. He made it sound so nonchalant. Like we were just two buddies about to play a good ole game of tennis. How could he sound so casual after we maybe almost kissed?

"How nice," Rona responded slowly.

"I'll be right back," Isaac said, glancing at the two of us.

I nodded woodenly.

Rona smiled.

Rona and I stood in silence as Isaac disappeared to retrieve the photos he was apparently going to give to Rona. The time passed excruciatingly.

"So, have you found a caterer?" Rona asked, obviously unable to deal with the silence.

"I've looked into some," I answered.

Another long silence followed.

Finally, Isaac returned, carrying a stack of photos. I saw the first one on the stack: a house big and fancy enough to be a hotel.

Rona flipped through the pictures. "These are great, Isaac. I just may have you replace my photographer permanently."

Isaac's face lit up. "I'm glad you like them."

I clenched my jaw tightly and tried to push the unkind thoughts I was having toward Rona out of my mind using the trusty old think-of-a-hymn technique. *Put your shoulder to the wheel, push along.* The tune sounded in my mind. Only that wasn't a very good choice of song, because I immediately had a vision of Rona struggling to push a handcart, and me adding extremely heavy rocks to it when she wasn't looking.

The three of us stood awkwardly for a moment. I smiled inside when I noticed that Isaac was standing much closer to me than to Rona. I know, I'm horrible.

Then Rona turned toward the door to go. "I guess I had better go. Unless . . ."

No. No unless. Stick with "I had better go," I thought desperately.

"Unless you could use a third person for your tennis game."

Uh, no, we couldn't. It's tennis. You know, singles or doubles. There is no tribles.

"It's Annabelle's call," Isaac replied, looking at me.

I groaned to myself. Of course I couldn't say no now. I mean, I'd look like a total jerk. I could endure Rona for one lousy tennis game.

"Fine by me," I said, looking directly at Rona. I was determined not to let her know she was getting to me.

"Great. I'll go grab another racket," Isaac said with enthusiasm before jogging down the hall.

He was adorable. He was kind. He was artistic. And he was as dense as Monterey Bay fog in November. Didn't he know that you don't invite one girl over and maybe almost kiss her and then let another girl play tennis with you and the girl you were maybe almost about to kiss?

Obviously not, I thought when Isaac returned with the third racket.

"How do you want to coordinate this?" Isaac asked. He opened a brand new container of tennis balls and bounced each ball, one after the other, on the deep green surface of the court.

"Why don't you two play and I'll watch?" I suggested. I might as well use Rona's untimely appearance to get me out of playing tennis.

"I don't think so," Isaac said, smiling. "How about we play girls against guy?"

I glanced at Rona. "Okay," I agreed quickly, still keeping up the of-course-Rona-isn't-bothering-me pretense. "That is, as long as it's okay with you," I said to Rona.

"Okay," Rona concurred.

We all took our places on the court, and I bent at the knees the way I had seen tennis players do on TV. I hoped this made me look like I knew what I was doing. I'm not quite sure it did though, because Rona gave me a strange look.

Isaac served first, and what followed was a long rally between Rona and Isaac. Rona was both powerful and graceful on the court. She buzzed beside me, behind me, and even in front of me as she returned each of Isaac's hits. Finally, Isaac hit a ball that was clearly out of Rona's reach.

"It's yours!" Rona called out to me.

I saw the ball whizzing toward me and although I knew all about the importance of the phrase, "Keep your eye on the ball," I shut my eyes in a reflex reaction. I mean, the thing had to be going at least sixty miles per hour. With eyes closed, I swung the racket as hard as I could.

Then I heard a beautiful sound: the sound of the racket hitting the ball. I opened my eyes to see how the rest played out. The ball flew toward Isaac and he hit it back to our side. It landed about a foot out of bounds.

"Our point," Rona announced.

I jumped up and down, much too excited over one point.

"Nice shot, Annabelle!" Isaac called out across the net.

Then, in a moment of I-just-made-a-point-in-tennis induced insanity, I put my hand out toward Rona for a high five. Reluctantly, she clapped her hand to mine.

I took a second before I served the ball to think about what was going on. Rona and I were playing tennis. Together. On the same team. And I had just given her a high five. And, come to think of it, she didn't really seem to be making a play for Isaac. Perhaps it was time to let bygones be bygones. Bury the hatchet. Time for Britney and Christina to sing a duet.

I attempted to serve and faulted. I tried again and faulted again. I glanced at Rona, and she didn't look too pleased.

So, again it was Isaac's serve, and again it was the Isaac and Rona show. I watched as the two of them hit the ball back and forth. Then, since I wasn't getting any hits, my mind left the game for a second. Of course, it was at that precise second that a ball headed straight toward me.

"Look out!" Rona shouted.

But it was too late.

The ball hit me right smack in the mouth, and the shock of the impact made me lose my footing, and I went tumbling to the ground.

Isaac came rushing toward me. "What happened?" Isaac asked Rona.

"I must have gotten a bad spin on the ball," Rona answered.

Wait a minute! Rona was the one who hit me? I was confused.

"Are you all right, Annabelle?" Isaac asked, his voice full of concern.

"I'm fine," I replied, standing up. My favorite khakis were torn, revealing cut knees, and I could taste blood in my mouth. But worse than all of that, I felt like a complete idiot.

"I'm sorry," Rona said.

"It's cool," I responded. But inside I was pretty miffed. It didn't look like a coincidence that the ball she hit had smacked me in the mouth, leaving me looking like a complete mess while she was looking flawless. Even the sweat on her face made her look all glistening and gorgeous. I'm not exactly saying Rona hit me on purpose. But I don't know. "A bad spin on the ball"? It sounds a little iffy if you ask me.

Isaac helped me as I limped into the house. Rona followed behind us. Isaac led me to a spacious bathroom with shiny fixtures, a dark blue shower curtain, and dark blue towels. I sat on the lid of the toilet and rolled up my pants.

Seeing my bleeding knees, Isaac immediately began searching the medicine cabinet for some disinfectant and bandages. He then went to fetch an ice pack for my mouth.

When Isaac had gone, I stood up slowly and inspected myself in the bathroom mirror. My mouth was already beginning to swell. My makeup was running. My clothes and hair were in shambles.

Isaac returned with the ice pack while I was still staring in the mirror. I looked away from my reflection and said, "I think I'm going to go home."

Isaac moved close to me. "Please don't go. I was hoping you would stay for dinner."

I was about to ask Isaac if he was planning on asking Rona to stay for dinner as well when Rona appeared in the bathroom doorway and said she was going to leave.

"Bye, Annabelle," Rona said cautiously. "I'm really sorry." I listened for signs of remorse. I wasn't sure if I could detect any or not. Of course, as much as I hate to admit it, I'm not sure I wanted to.

"Don't worry about it," I responded with a wave.

I sat down on the toilet again and began disinfecting my

knees while Isaac walked Rona to the door. I strained to hear how the two of them said good-bye to each other, but Isaac's house was too big for that kind of eavesdropping, and I finally gave up.

When Isaac returned to the bathroom, I was rubbing my hands over my once beautiful, now torn khakis.

"I have something you can change into," Isaac said.

I looked at Isaac who was much taller, and much more muscular than I. "Nothing you have is going to fit me."

"True. But that's what drawstrings are for," Isaac said with a smile. "I'll be right back."

When Isaac was gone, I smoothed my hair and made it into a knot at the base of my neck. I rinsed my face with cool water, removing traces of blood and makeup at the same time.

Isaac returned carrying a pair of flannel drawstring pajama pants that were still in the package. "My mom bought these for me for Christmas, but they're too small for me." Isaac handed me the package.

The pants may have been too small for Isaac, but they still looked huge to me. I decided, however, that I preferred huge to holey and bloody.

Isaac left me alone to change, and after a few moments of securing the pants so they wouldn't fall off, I emerged from the bathroom and found Isaac waiting in the living room.

Isaac looked me over. "You look adorable," he said.

I humored him by giving him a spin, knowing full well that I looked ridiculous and not adorable.

"You want to order pizza?" Isaac asked me.

"Mmmm, pizza," I hummed.

"Is that a yes?"

"A definite yes."

Isaac and I made our way to the kitchen where Isaac opened a drawer and pulled out a bunch of pizza parlor menus. I guessed from the size of the stack of menus that Isaac and Ethan must order pizza a lot. "These are the ones that deliver out here," Isaac said. "You pick whichever one looks good to you."

Ethan, who had suddenly appeared as soon as the word

pizza was mentioned, pointed to one of the menus. It was for a place called Stuff Your Face Pizza.

"That place is Isaac's favorite," Ethan whispered to me.

"I choose this one," I announced, pointing to the Stuff Your Face Pizza menu.

"Hmm, I wonder how you came to that decision," Isaac said, looking at Ethan through accusing eyes. "That just happens to be Ethan's favorite."

I jokingly waved a finger at Ethan. "Shame on you. You shouldn't use your brother like that."

The three of us sat at the breakfast bar, scanning the menu. We finally settled on The Mouthwaterer. This pizza was topped with extra cheese, pepperoni, Canadian bacon, green pepper, and mushrooms, and true to its name, the very thought of the pizza made my mouth water. Isaac called and placed the order, and we were assured that our pizza would arrive within thirty minutes.

"What happened to your lip? And why are you wearing pajamas?" Ethan asked, able to focus on other things now that the pizza had been ordered.

"Yeah, well, there was a little mishap on the tennis court," I explained, trying to sound light.

"Rona accidentally hit Annabelle in the mouth with a tennis ball," Isaac said.

"Rona's here?" Ethan asked.

"She was here," Isaac clarified. "She left a minute ago."

"I wish I would've known she was here," Ethan said.

"Yeah, just because you think she's cute," Isaac ribbed his brother. "You should just ask her out."

"But, Isaac, haven't you told Ethan that Rona's engaged?" I asked, leaning forward against the breakfast bar.

"You mean you haven't heard?" Isaac asked me.

"Heard what?"

"Her fiancé broke it off."

"What?" I choked out.

"Yeah. He fell in love with some Brazilian model." Isaac

spoke in a tone that said isn't-that-just-awful.

And it was awful. It was horribly awful because now nothing was going to keep Rona from going for Isaac. "When did they break up?" I squeaked.

"Last Saturday. The day we saw her at the Portuguese restaurant."

I sat paralyzed. This meant Rona was not only a free woman, but a woman with a broken heart that probably needed mending.

And that could quite possibly mean disaster.

Chapter 10

Okay, okay, clean slate.

I repeated that phrase over and over in my mind as I drove to La Bonne Violette Wednesday morning, gripping the steering wheel tightly. I was dressed in my very best suit, a gorgeous silk one that I got really cheap at a boutique downtown when it was going out of business. And I was armed with an arsenal of questions I had written during the night since I wasn't getting much sleep anyway.

And, why, you ask, didn't I get much sleep? Well, not only was I nervous about going back to La Bonne Violette, but also, now that I knew that Rona was a single girl again, my mind was filled with questions about Isaac's actions: Had he let her play tennis with us because he felt sorry for her? Or was there another reason? Had he looked so happy that Rona liked his photos because he enjoyed the praise professionally? Or was it more personal than that? Yes, those were the questions that had plagued me until I finally fell asleep around 2 AM.

I pulled into La Bonne Violette's parking lot and took a deep breath. I tucked my car keys into my pocket because my handbag—my very best only-for-special-occasions handbag that I got at a consignment shop—was gorgeous, but not very roomy.

My heart was pounding as I opened the restaurant's heavy front door. After greeting me, the maître d' led me to Jean-Pierre who was in a tiny room in the back of the kitchen, caramelizing little ramekins of crème brûlée with a small blow torch.

"Good morning, Jean-Pierre," I said in my most professional tone. "I don't know if you remember me. I'm Annabelle Pleasanton from *Central Coast Living*, and I am here for our nine o'clock meeting. I would like this to be a very informal interview. I have just a few questions for you." I reached into my handbag and pulled out my notepad.

"Jean-Pierre! Jean-Pierre!" A young man rushed into the room, speaking hurriedly in French.

After hearing what the young man had to say, Jean-Pierre's eyes opened wide in shock, and he shoved the blow torch into my hands, flame still burning, and rushed out of the room.

I looked at the blow torch in my hand, and wondered what to do. Should I turn it off? Should I put it down? Or . . . should I finish caramelizing the crème brûlée, and then Jean-Pierre would be so impressed at how industrious I was he would be the most cooperative interviewee ever and give me tons of great quotes for my article? Yes, I decided, that's what I should do.

So, I put my notepad back into my handbag, set the bag on a nearby counter, and began caramelizing.

In my first attempt, I ended up turning the crème brûlée a blackish color rather than the desired golden-brown. I quickly grabbed a spoon and scraped off the black. Problem was, since I was so focused on getting the burnt stuff off the crème brûlée before Jean-Pierre returned, I kind of forgot to turn off the blow torch. And I kind of held it against an apron. Which kind of caught on fire.

At the sight of the fire I gasped, and dropped the blow torch to the floor, which luckily turned the thing off. Telling myself to remain calm, I tried to think quickly. Like a flash, something I had learned in a fire safety class came to my mind. In the class, the teacher had said that baking soda was an excellent fire retardant. Frantically, I reached for some baking soda in a nearby glass container.

Unfortunately, however, it turned out that the white stuff wasn't baking soda; it was flour. And in that same fire safety class the teacher had mentioned that flour is actually quite flammable.

"Fire! Fire!" I heard myself screaming, as I backed away from the fire which had grown to the size of a frightening monster.

Two dressed-in-white sous chefs rushed into the room immediately. One of them grabbed onto me and moved me even further back away from the fire. The other grabbed a fire extinguisher from the wall and sprayed the white fire extinguisher foam on the flames. I closed my eyes to keep the foam from getting in them. When I opened my eyes, I saw that the fire was out. I also saw that my best suit was doused with white foam.

And then Jean-Pierre came back.

He stormed into the room, yelling at the sous chefs in French. The sous chefs pointed at me, and Jean-Pierre came over and got in my face. "Get out!" he hollered. "You are a disaster! Get out and do not come back!"

I backed away from Jean-Pierre and ran out of the restaurant much faster than I thought it was possible to run in heels.

The reception girls were giving me weird looks as I walked through the front doors of *Central Coast Living*, but I just didn't have the energy to care. I hadn't bothered to go home and change, because I had decided to do something—and somehow my doused suit seemed the perfect outfit to wear when I did it.

I had decided to tell George that I couldn't do it. I couldn't write the article. He was expecting a draft in a few hours, and I had nothing. I knew what that meant. It meant that I had failed.

So, I was going to tell him to give the assignment to Arvin and keep me as a recipe editor forevermore because I was obviously not cut out to write. I had wanted to do it so badly, and I had believed that I could, but apparently that just wasn't enough.

I walked straight to George's office, so I could get the whole thing over with.

"George is not in today," Gidget informed me when I told her I needed to see him. Her eyes settled on my suit, and she looked almost pained at the sight of the blotchy silk.

"Where is he?" I asked.

"He has pneumonia. I tried to call you earlier. His doctor wants him home at least until Friday, so he won't be able to look over your article today. He said to leave him a voicemail if you need anything, and he'll get back to you."

"But I really need to talk to him about something. Can I call him at home?"

"He's not taking calls at home. But he is calling in to check his messages. I can leave a message for him to call you."

"Thanks," I said. "I, um, I'm not feeling too well myself. I think I'm going to go home."

"All right," Gidget said. "And here," she jotted something down on a piece of paper, "this is the number for the dry cleaner I've been using for years. If anyone can save that suit, they can."

I was at home, dressed in a pair of wide-leg sweats and a baggy tee, shoving large spoonfuls of Cold Stone ice cream into my mouth when the phone rang.

"Hello?" I answered wearily.

"Annabelle Pleasanton?"

"Yes."

"This is Joseph Noir, the maître d' at La Bonne Violette. I have your purse here."

"What? Oh, yeah, I must have left it when I ran out," I

muttered softly. I was too disheartened by the occurrences of the day to really care that I had left my bag somewhere.

"I'm sorry?"

"Oh, nothing. I'll be there in fifteen minutes to pick it up."

I stored the ice cream in my freezer, changed into a pair of wool pants and a button down shirt, and went back to the place I had been banished from just hours earlier.

"Thank you," I said to Joseph as I grabbed my handbag and turned to rush out of the restaurant.

"Wait!" Joseph called out to me. "Jean-Pierre wants to see you."

I froze in place. "Um . . . what?"

"Jean-Pierre would like to see you in the kitchen. Go on back."

I swallowed hard. He probably wanted to hand me a big fat bill for the fire damage. "Okay," I relented as I began walking back to the kitchen, my shoulders drooping.

I saw Jean-Pierre standing in front of the large range in the kitchen, and I almost fled, but he spotted me before I could.

"Perfect. Mademoiselle Pleasanton, I am so glad you returned," Jean-Pierre said in a jovial tone.

What? He was glad I returned?

"Hi, Jean-Pierre. Joseph told me you wanted to see me." My voice was slow, hesitant.

"Yes, yes. I wanted to apologize for shouting at you earlier today. As a chef I know that accidents happen."

"You . . . you do?"

"Yes, I do. And I want you to know, I still would like to do the interview."

"You would?" I sounded like a girl who just got asked to the big dance by the coolest boy in school.

"Yes. But you must do something for me first."

"Of course, of course, anything," I promised without thinking. And, let me tell you, if I had been thinking, I probably would have kept my little mouth shut.

"My nephew Patrique has just moved here from Santa Cruz. He does not know the area yet. He is showing his art at two different venues, one tonight and one tomorrow afternoon, and I am going out of town and will not return until Sunday evening, so I cannot accompany him. Go with him."

"I . . . well . . . I don't," I stuttered.

"I'll go fetch my nephew," Jean-Pierre said briskly.

Jean-Pierre returned with a younger man, I guessed late twenties. The guy had dark curly hair, a goatee, and dark eyes. The look in his eyes seemed to scream, "I know you think I'm handsome." This immediately made me think just the opposite.

"Chérie," Jean-Pierre said to me, "this is my nephew, Patrique."

I gave Patrique a stiff smile. "Hi, Patrique, I'm Annabelle."

"Enchanté," Patrique said, kissing me on my hand. It kind of shocked me, and when he removed his lips from the top of my hand, there was a blob of saliva just sitting there. He looked at me as if he had left it there as some sort of treat for me.

I tried to hide my disgust as I wiped my hand on my pants. I almost felt sorry for them. I mean, they were nice pants. But it was either them or me.

"I . . . I just remembered . . . I'm going to be really busy over the next couple of days," I announced, suddenly determined to find some plans. Anything would do.

"That is a shame," Jean-Pierre said, giving me a look I couldn't quite decode.

"Please," Patrique said in accent-free English. "I would love to be accompanied by such a luscious creature."

"Excuse me?"

"I think you are loveliness in the flesh," Patrique said.

Uh, you better keep your eyes off my flesh, mister, I thought, disgusted.

Patrique continued. "I saw you this morning, and thought

there could be no one better to accompany me to my first Monterey Bay art shows. When my uncle sent you away, I begged him to give you another chance." Patrique moved close to me until he was practically touching my face with his. I backed away slowly.

"Oh, thanks," I said without emotion.

"Will you please come, chérie?" Patrique asked. He again moved incredibly close to me.

I looked at Jean-Pierre. He was giving me a look that said, "If she cares about her article, she'll go."

I was silently fuming. How rotten of Jean-Pierre to use my need for an interview to get me to entertain his slime ball nephew. But, of course, I knew that in the magazine business it was customary to schmooze.

I thought for a moment. If I did this, my dream would be alive again. George would never know how close I was to giving up, and I would write the best article that had ever appeared in *Central Coast Living*.

"All right," I said finally.

Patrique moved away from me, a satisfied look on his face.

"And when you get back into town we can finally do the interview, right?" I asked Jean-Pierre.

"Monday morning at nine o'clock," Jean-Pierre said, shaking my hand as if to seal the deal. Then he quickly disappeared from sight.

"I guess I should go home and get ready then," I said to Patrique.

"No. We must leave now."

I looked at Patrique and, like Dad had taught me to, I listened for any feelings inside of me that were warning me that he was dangerous. I didn't get the sense that he was. Slimy, but not dangerous.

"All right then," I said reluctantly. "Where is your car?"

Patrique made a face. "I don't want to take my car. Gas is so expensive. And my car is a real guzzler. Do you have a car?"

Patrique asked as he shoved some packages of expensive soup crackers into his pockets.

I just stood there, watching him in disbelief.

"Well, chérie, do you have a car?" Patrique repeated.

"Yes, I have a car, but—"

Before I could finish my argument, a woman came up beside me. I recognized her as the kind lady who had given me directions to the restroom following the, uh, Refrigerator Locker Incident. "Do not make this poor girl drive you around town," she said to Patrique. "You can take a catering van."

"Fine, Jacqueline," Patrique whined.

"Thank you," I told the woman I now knew as Jacqueline, grateful for her kindness.

"I'll need it back by nine," Jacqueline said. "I have to take down a party."

I looked at my watch. It was three o'clock. Of course we'd be back by nine. This thing couldn't take more than a couple of hours. I looked over at Patrique, waiting for him to say something.

"All right," Patrique groaned.

Jacqueline looked at me with sympathy as she wordlessly handed Patrique the keys to the catering van. Patrique then looked at me and said, "I'll be right back," before disappearing from sight.

"I really appreciate you helping me out," I said to Jacqueline. "I've been . . . I've been having a bit of a hard time working on this article, and it's nice to have a friendly face around."

"It is my pleasure," Jacqueline said. "I probably would not want Patrique in my car either." She smiled at me knowingly.

Just then a pretty girl who looked about fourteen and who wore her dark curly hair in a pony tail at the back of her head appeared at Jacqueline's side. "Where do I need to put the silverware?" the girl asked, and as she spoke I noticed a thick layer of shiny gloss on her lips.

I smiled at the teen and she smiled back.

Jacqueline answered the girl's question and then introduced

me. "This is my daughter, Amber. Amber, this is Miss Pleasanton. She's writing an article about the restaurant."

"Call me Annabelle," I said. "What kind of lip gloss is that?"

"Foxy Glossy," Amber answered.

"I've gotta get myself some of that," I said.

"It's my favorite kind."

"It looks really pretty on you."

Amber looked at the ground and touched her lips gently. "Thanks," she whispered.

Jacqueline put her arm around Amber. "Amber helps me do catering so she can buy all of the cosmetics and shoes she insists she needs."

"I know exactly how that is," I said with a grin.

"So, do you work for the newspaper?" Amber asked.

"No. I work for a magazine called *Central Coast Living*."

"My dad reads that," Amber said.

"Hopefully he doesn't stop reading it after he sees my article."

"I'm sure you'll write a really good article," the girl said as if she were talking to a friend.

"Thanks," I responded, looking at Jacqueline and Amber. At least two people at La Bonne Violette didn't think I was a total loser.

Patrique returned and told me to follow him. I said good-bye to my new friends and followed Patrique into the dining area where he grabbed onto my hand. I quickly moved my hand away.

Sluggishly, I followed Patrique as he walked to a table and in one swift motion grabbed some violets out of a vase and handed them to me.

"Thanks," I said lifelessly as I took the flowers. I mean, were violets stolen from a restaurant table supposed to impress me? Give me a hand-picked box of Milk Duds any day.

Patrique led the way to the back parking lot of the restaurant where we found two catering vans with the words

"La Bonne Violette" painted on them in purple letters outlined in gold. Patrique looked at a number stamped onto the key chain he was holding and matched it to the number on the van parked closest to us.

"Why don't you drive," Patrique said. "I need to meditate."

"Fine," I grumbled, grabbing the keys from his hand. But then I realized that being nice to the slime ball was probably important for the sake of my article, and I changed my tone. "I mean, of course."

I buckled myself into the driver's seat and Patrique lounged in the passenger's seat. "I'll wait until we're in traffic to meditate," he said, giving me a creepy look. "That way I can sit next to you for a while."

I completely ignored the comment. "So where are we going?" I asked flatly. I couldn't believe I didn't already know the answer to that question.

"Monterey. Del Monte Avenue. I'm showing some of my paintings at an art gallery there. It's a one-day show." Patrique looked at me like this was supposed to impress me to no end.

"Cool," I said breezily, trying not to encourage him.

We drove to Monterey in silence. About halfway there, Patrique moved to the back of the catering van and sat in a meditation pose. Once, I took a quick glance in the rear view mirror to see what he was doing back there. He appeared to be in a trance.

As I pulled onto Del Monte Avenue, I brought Patrique out of his trance by swerving wildly when a motorcyclist came out of nowhere and pulled out in front of me. Patrique went flying, and hit the side of the van with his shoulder.

I apologized like crazy, afraid that if his temper was anything like his uncle's, I could be in for some fierce words.

But Patrique surprised me by his reaction. Rubbing his shoulder, he moved to the front of the van. "That was the universe's way of giving me pain, so I can feel my art."

"Oh," I said, nodding my head. I had thought it was my bad

driving, but, hey, whatever.

"Turn left at the next light, and park on the street," Patrique instructed. "The gallery is right up there." He pointed to a building with peeling tan paint.

I parked the van on the steep hill, pushed the emergency brake all the way to the floor, hopped out of the van, and joined Patrique on the sidewalk. We both gazed down the hill at the bay. As I glanced at the gorgeous waters, I thought of Isaac. I would have loved to be seeing the view with him.

Patrique interrupted my thoughts by gesturing toward the gallery. "Let's go inside."

I took a deep breath and followed Patrique into the building.

The gallery was small with a beat-up wooden floor and art displayed on drab gray walls. As we stepped inside, an attractive woman with dark, wild hair shot me a hateful look.

"Do you know that girl over there in the tight black dress?" I asked Patrique quietly.

"Yes, that's Tempest," Patrique answered. "My ex."

"Tempest, huh? The name suits her."

"It should. She came up with it. Her real name is Bertha. Come with me." Patrique held out his hand, and I pretended I didn't see it. He walked toward a large painting against a back wall in the gallery.

I stared at the painting. It was a mass of black and deep blue with neon green body parts—arms, legs, and I think maybe a liver—floating around in the mass. Faces that appeared to be cackling were painted in white in the corners, blood dripping from their open mouths. I looked at the title of the piece: *Le Cauchemar.*

I turned my eyes from the painting. I have been moved by art before. But this was the first time I was moved to nausea.

"What do you think?" Patrique asked, as if I were standing in front of a national treasure.

"I think . . . I think I'm going to be sick." I teetered over to a nearby metal chair.

Patrique smiled wildly. "Yes!" he exclaimed. "It got to you!"

"What does *Le Cauchemar* mean?" I asked weakly, covering my mouth with my hand.

"The nightmare," Patrique answered, putting tremendous emphasis on each syllable.

It was pretty much the perfect name for the painting, I decided. "Could you please get me something to drink, Patrique?" I asked, thinking maybe some liquid would help.

"Of course, chérie," Patrique said, his voice enthused. "It really got to you!" he cried as he walked away.

Patrique returned with a glass of wine.

"Oh, Patrique, I should have been more specific," I said. "I actually wanted water."

"No wine?" Patrique asked, furrowing his brow.

"No wine."

"Okay, I'll get you water then."

Patrique brought me a bottle of water and sat down next to me on the metal chair that really only had room for one. I opened the bottle and sipped.

"Do you want to see my other paintings?" Patrique asked.

"Maybe later," I answered quickly.

I took a sip of the water and noticed the woman named Tempest walking toward us. Patrique immediately put a scowl on his face. "Hi, Tempest," he growled.

"Who is this?" Tempest asked, pointing to me.

Patrique put his arm around me. "This is Annabelle," he said.

I smiled at Tempest as I removed Patrique's arm.

Tempest looked at me with disdain. "Obviously, she's not an artist," she said to Patrique.

"Actually, I'm a—" I began to explain that I was a writer.

But Tempest cut me off. "It's a good thing. That way you can't steal her ideas."

This statement piqued my interest. What did she mean by that?

Patrique let out a huff as he stood up. "Come on, darling," he said to me, the "darling" obviously for Tempest's benefit.

Tempest spun around and walked to the other side of the gallery, her heels clicking on the floor as she walked.

"You still have a thing for her," I said to Patrique once Tempest was gone. It was so obvious.

Patrique was silent. The silence said yes.

"But if you have a thing for her, why all the mushy talk and touchy-feely stuff with me?" I asked.

"My soul may belong to Tempest, but I am still a man," Patrique replied.

I rolled my eyes.

After a few moments of uncomfortable silence, Patrique led me to the other side of the gallery, where I stood in the shadows as the business of selling and buying art unfolded before me.

For two and a half hours.

I made up a song in my head. I came up with tons of ideas for Carrie's bridal shower menu. I played a few games of Skydiver on my cell.

I was trying to top my high score when the phone rang. I checked the caller ID: unknown number. I ducked my head and answered the call anyway.

"Hello?" I whispered, wanting to kiss the person on the other end of the line for giving me something to fill the time.

"Annabelle, it's Isaac."

Yep, I definitely wanted to kiss the person on the other end of the line.

"Isaac, I'm so glad you called."

"Are you busy right now? I was thinking we could have dinner." Isaac's voice was so gorgeous, I could barely contain myself.

My eyes scanned the gallery. I didn't see Patrique anywhere. I could disappear for an hour and he probably wouldn't even notice. But then again, what if he sold all of his paintings and came looking for me? A story from Patrique to Jean-Pierre about how I just up and left would probably not help my working relationship with Jean-Pierre very much.

"You have no idea how much I would love dinner," I said.

"It sounds like you're about to say 'But . . .'" Isaac predicted.

"No, I was about to say 'However . . .'" I said with a laugh. "However . . . I'm a little tied up with work right now."

"You can't get un-tied-up?" Isaac asked, sounding cu-ute.

Then I heard a female voice in the background on Isaac's end of the line. "Mwa she mwa go mwa you mwa me mwa mwa mwa mwite mwagether."

Since I am pretty fluent in girl-in-the-background-ese, I could make out that the female voice was saying something along the lines of, "If she can't go then you and me can get a bite together."

"Who's that?" I asked Isaac.

Please say your Mom. Or a gray-haired woman you're helping across the street. Or a gray-haired anyone.

"That's Rona. We're just finishing up getting some shots of a huge house on 17 Mile Drive."

A vision came to my mind. In the vision Rona and Isaac were driving along 17 Mile Drive—which for those of you non-Monterey-residents is this gorgeous, long coastal drive that's so incredible you have to pay to drive on it, unless, of course, you live in one of the mansions it leads to.

Okay, so back to the vision. Rona's perfect hair was blowing in the wind as she drove her snazzy little convertible. She was smiling over at Isaac, and Isaac was smiling back. Then the two of them drove to a quaint little café in Carmel, and there wasn't a fluorescent light in sight, so Rona looked flawless. Then Isaac looked at Rona and said, "I'm so glad you aren't engaged anymore because . . ."

No, no, I can't let this happen!

"What do you know, Isaac, I just got un-tied-up," I said quickly, hoping he wouldn't catch on to the fact that Rona was the main factor in my quick change of heart.

But if you remember from before, Isaac doesn't really pick

up on these things too well. And this time was no exception.

"Great," he said, completely believing that somehow, although I hadn't spoken to anyone, made any type of phone call, or yelled out some version of "I'm outta here," I had gone from busy to un-busy in three point five seconds.

"I'm down by Cannery Row. Do you think we could meet there?" I asked hopefully, not sure what I would do if he said no.

"Sure, I'll meet you at the little amphitheater thing where all the musicians perform. Say in about half an hour. Then we can pick a place to go. Sound good?"

"Yes," I answered. "That sounds so good."

"All right, I'll see you in half an hour."

"I'll be looking forward to it," I said.

Smiling, I flipped my phone closed. Now I just had to sneak out of the gallery and hope that no one bought Patrique's paintings over the next hour and a half or so—and it seemed pretty unlikely to me that anyone would.

I was making a plan of escape when I saw Patrique looking around. I silently begged him not to be searching for me. But no such luck. He caught sight of me and called me over to where he stood. I made my way toward him slowly.

"Annabelle, I really need a Rolaid," Patrique said, rubbing his chest.

"Oh, sorry," I said, not quite sure why he was telling me this.

"Can you go buy me one?"

"You want me to buy you one Rolaid?" I asked slowly.

"No," Patrique said, his voice agitated. "You'll probably have to buy a pack."

"But are you sure it's a good idea for me to . . ." *Wait a minute. Why am I arguing? This is perfect. The perfect opportunity to get out of here.* "Yes," I said. "I will go buy you a Rolaid."

"Great," Patrique said.

I stood next to Patrique for a second, waiting for him to hand me some cash.

"What are you waiting for?" he asked, sounding annoyed.

"For you to give me some money," I answered.

"Oh, I don't really have any cash on me. Can you spot me?"

I groaned to myself. "Sure."

After all, buying Patrique his chalky round antacids was my ticket out of that gallery. My ticket to see Isaac.

Chapter 11

"Hello there," I greeted Isaac.

He was sitting on one of the benches in the amphitheater, watching a long-haired musician play a wind instrument. The mellow music was accompanied perfectly by the sound of the ocean waves in the distance.

"Hello," Isaac said as he stood up from the bench. He put his arms around me for a hug and my heart started pounding like crazy. "Do you want to eat now, or do you want to stay and listen to the music?" he asked as he pulled away from me.

"Could we eat now? I'm starving." A girl can only live on bottled water for so long.

"Sure. I have an idea."

"Oh yeah, what is your idea?" I asked, sounding quite flirty.

"Why don't we have a transient dinner?"

"A what?"

"Why don't we walk Cannery Row and get food along the way. We'll be sure to get the basics from the food pyramid. Of course, the food won't be the most nutritious . . ." Isaac sounded like he was losing confidence in his idea.

"I love it!" I exclaimed. "Can we start with a jumbo pretzel? I smelled them on the way over and ooh they smelled so good."

Isaac smiled at me, and I noticed that the sea breeze was making the hair on the right side of his head stand straight up. It was quite possibly the cutest thing I have ever seen. "All right," he said, "let's go get some pretzels."

Isaac took hold of my hand, lacing his fingers through mine. It felt so natural, yet as incredible as I remembered. We chatted as we walked to the nearby pretzel vendor.

Then, with our huge, warm pretzels in hand—well, a large portion of mine was already in my mouth—we walked down Cannery Row in the direction of the Monterey Bay Aquarium.

"So what were you up to when I called?" Isaac asked as we strolled.

I pointed to my mouth to indicate to Isaac that it was full.

He smiled. "You are so cute," he said, and the words made my insides flutter.

I chewed the pretzel in my mouth and swallowed as quickly as I could. "You don't want to know what I was doing," I replied before taking another bite of my pretzel.

"Sure I do."

"Okay. I was trying to get on Jean-Pierre's good side by going to an art show with his nephew."

"His nephew? You know, come to think of it, I heard Ethan saying something about Jean-Pierre's nephew moving here and working in the restaurant."

"Apparently his other job is painting. And if you ask me, he should probably stick with working in the restaurant."

"So how was the art show?" Isaac asked.

"Actually it's still going on." I bit my lip, feeling a sense of anxiety come over me. How long would I be able to be gone without Patrique suspecting that I had done more than just search for his Rolaid?

"Do you need to go back?" Isaac asked.

"No, not yet," I answered. I moved closer to Isaac to let an older couple pass us on the sidewalk. "I really want to be with you. I'll take my chances."

Isaac let go of my hand and pulled me close to him. "Good," he whispered in my ear.

A shiver went through my entire body. "Thank you," I said breathlessly. "For saving me, I mean. I don't know how much longer I could have stayed at that art show."

"Don't thank me. I was hungry," Isaac answered. He was still holding onto me.

"You could have gotten food without seeing me," I said. *In fact, I remember Rona Bircheck inviting you to get some with her.*

"Yes, but I wasn't just hungry for food," Isaac explained, his voice low.

I turned my head down nervously, pulled away from Isaac, and began walking again, watching my feet as they moved on the sidewalk.

After strolling in silence for a while, Isaac and I stepped into this large mall-type building that is full of shops and is home to John Steinbeck's Spirit of Monterey Wax Museum. We found a bench on the main floor of the building and sat down to finish the last bites of our pretzels. When my pretzel was gone, I wadded up the wax paper it had been wrapped in and tossed it into a trash can about five feet away. The paper went into the can like a basketball going through the hoop.

"Nice shot," Isaac praised.

I stood up and gave Isaac a little curtsy. "So, do you want to look at the shops?" I asked.

Isaac shook his head. "I actually like what I'm looking at right now."

I smiled shyly and took the wax paper from his pretzel out of his hand. I crumpled the paper up. "Let's make a friendly wager," I suggested.

"Sorry, betting is against my religion," Isaac teased.

"All right," I said, shrugging my shoulders. I got ready to shoot the paper into the trash can.

"No, wait," Isaac called out. "A *friendly* wager is probably okay."

I smiled. "What should we wager?"

Isaac looked up at the ceiling like he was deep in thought. "If you don't make it, you have to show me that pink notebook you wouldn't let me see the other day."

My body tensed at the suggestion. I couldn't show him my Pink Notes. I just couldn't. He'd think I was a lunatic and run away for sure. But, of course I wasn't going to lose. I mean, it hadn't been hard at all the first time. Plus, I already knew exactly what I wanted to collect when I won.

"Okay," I agreed. "And if, I mean *when*, I do make it, you have to give me a photograph that you've taken of the ocean."

"Deal," Isaac agreed.

With exaggerated movements, I got into a wax-paper-shooting stance. I smiled at Isaac. "Prepare to lose," I said.

Then I shot.

And I missed.

"Yeah!" Isaac hollered.

I gave him a dirty look. "That wasn't fair," I argued. "You probably did something to your paper when I wasn't looking. Weighted it with salt or something."

"A bet's a bet," Isaac said. "Looks like I get to see that book." Isaac rubbed his hands together quickly and grinned a satisfied grin. "Is it in there?" he asked, looking at my handbag.

"Actually it's not," I said. I was suddenly grateful that I had picked that day to use my tiny fancy bag and not my everyday bag, and thus had left my Pink Notes at home.

"That's cool. You can show me later," Isaac said. Then he leaned close to me and added, "And don't plan on me forgetting."

I nodded slowly. "Let's walk around," I suggested. *And while we walk I'll think of ways to make you forget about our bet.*

We walked side by side for a while, perusing the shops inside the building. But I have no recollection whatsoever of what I saw in those shops.

Why? Because all I could think about was the fact that Isaac wasn't holding my hand like he had before. Had he thought I was lying about not having the notebook, and thus decided that he wanted nothing to do with me? Had my hand sweat too much the last time and totally grossed him out?

Finally, I couldn't take it anymore. We were inside a photo gallery, and Isaac was commenting on some photos of cypress trees when I blurted out, "Will you hold my hand again, please?"

Isaac grinned at me. "I would love to." He took my hand, and I savored the sensation.

We continued looking in the shops, and when we stepped into a candy store, my eyes widened with glee. In the corner of the shop, a teenage girl stood behind the counter, dipping shiny red apples into a creamy caramel sauce. I watched the process, mesmerized, my mouth salivating as if I were one of Pavlov's dogs.

"Would you like one of those?" Isaac asked, noticing my wide-eyed look.

"Well, we should get something from the fruit and vegetable group for our dinner," I answered with a grin.

"You're right. It would be un-nutritious of us not to."

Isaac politely asked the girl behind the counter for two caramel apples. When the girl handed the apples to us, I offered to pay for them, but Isaac insisted on paying.

We were walking out the candy shop door when I spotted a barrel of chocolate covered gummy bears. "Ooh, milk chocolate covered gummies. I love those." I moved my feet toward the exit of the shop, but my head was turned toward the barrel of gummies.

"Come on." Isaac chuckled as he led me back into the shop. He grabbed a cellophane bag and began scooping generous scoops of the gummy bears into the bag. With each scoop my smile grew wider.

"That's enough," I said finally. "But I'm getting these." I practically raced Isaac to the counter, frantically unzipping my handbag to retrieve my wallet.

"Nope," Isaac protested, smacking a twenty dollar bill that

seemed to appear out of nowhere onto the counter. "Dinner is on me. The milk chocolate on these should cover the protein group." Isaac pointed toward the chocolate on the gummy bears.

What a horrible dinner we were eating. A delicious, wonderful, horrible dinner.

With my gargantuan bag of gummy bears in hand, I alternated between taking bites of the gooey caramel apple and the chewy bears as Isaac and I walked out of the building and onto the sidewalk.

"Thank you so much for everything," I said after swallowing the first delicious bite of my apple.

"You're welcome," Isaac replied.

I popped a gummy bear into my mouth. "Do you want one?"

"No, thanks. Those are for you."

"Wanna walk up the hill?" I asked. "It's a great view from up there. And I should probably be heading back up to the gallery anyway."

"Sure," Isaac replied. "But I have to tell you, I really don't want to say good-bye." We crossed the street and began heading up the hill away from Cannery Row. "When can I see you again?" Isaac asked me.

"Anytime," I replied.

Isaac stopped abruptly on the sidewalk. "Do you really mean 'anytime'? Because I'll take you up on that. I can't seem to get enough of you, Annabelle."

Thank goodness we weren't walking anymore because that comment made me momentarily unable to move. "Yes, I mean anytime," I assured Isaac in a soft voice.

"Then I'll call you tomorrow."

Isaac and I resumed walking, and Isaac took the last bite out of his caramel apple. He then tossed the core and stick into a nearby trash receptacle. Trying to finish my apple as well, I took a very large bite out of it. An unladylike amount of juice from the apple dribbled onto my chin. I wiped at it with a napkin I had grabbed on the way out of the candy shop.

"These aren't exactly the most glamorous things in the world to eat," I said, feeling myself get flushed with embarrassment.

Isaac looked at me tenderly. "Glamorous or not, you're adorable."

In a nervous reaction to Isaac's comment, I raised the apple to my mouth to take another bite. But Isaac's hand covered mine and stopped me in mid motion. He looked intently into my eyes. "I really want to kiss you," he said.

"I would like that," I said breathlessly.

Isaac tucked a strand of hair behind my ear. Then he gently took my face in his hands. His hands smelled sweet, like candy apples. Slowly, he moved his face in toward mine. I closed my eyes, eagerly awaiting his kiss.

"Annabelle?"

"Yes, Isaac," I whispered.

Wait a minute? That voice was coming from too far away to be Isaac. And it sounded an awful lot like . . .

"Patrique!" I exclaimed, my eyes shooting open. I spun around and saw Patrique standing behind me. "Why . . . um . . . why aren't you at the gallery?"

Patrique held up a pack of antacids to let them answer the question for him.

"Oh," I said flatly.

Patrique folded his arms across his chest. "So I guess you must have gotten lost while looking for my Rolaids." He waved the antacids in the air.

I don't know why, but I almost started laughing. I mean, read Patrique's sentence again and tell me it isn't hilarious.

"I was so hungry, Patrique," I explained, holding back my laughter. "I was ready to start eating the fermented fruit off one of the sculptures at the gallery."

"Yes, well, it looks like you have your food." Patrique's eyes surveyed my nearly finished caramel apple. "Who is this?" Patrique asked, looking at Isaac. "Besides someone who can't buy a lovely lady decent food."

I glared at Patrique. If it hadn't been so important for me

to be nice to him, I just might have smacked him.

"Isaac Matthews." Isaac introduced himself, a slightly pinched look coming onto his face. Then he turned to me. "I should probably get going, Annabelle."

No, please don't leave. You were about to kiss me, remember?

"Okay," I said softly. "Call me?"

"I will," Isaac said. Then he gave a halfhearted wave to Patrique. "Good to meet you."

"Yeah," Patrique grunted.

I watched Isaac walk into the distance. He was so incredibly handsome. Then I turned to Patrique. I studied his sliminess and the package of Rolaids in his hand.

Just one more day, I told myself. *Just one more day and then this whole nightmare will be over, and on Monday I will get my interview.*

"So what is Isaac?" Patrique asked. We were back inside the gallery and I noticed that Tempest was watching us from across the room.

"He's a photographer," I said.

"No, I didn't ask what he does. I asked what he is."

"I don't know, English, maybe part Irish."

"No," Patrique said, sounding impatient. "I mean what is he to you?"

"Oh." I pondered the question for a moment. "I guess we're dating," I replied. The words made me feel quite giddy.

"How nice for you," Patrique said with a false smile.

Not wanting to talk to Patrique anymore, I took out my cell phone to play a little Skydiver. It was then that I noticed that the time was 9:05. "It's after nine!" I exclaimed. "We were supposed to get the catering van back by nine. We're late!"

"I can't leave now," Patrique said.

"But—"

"You can take the van," Patrique said with an edge in his voice. "I'll find a way home." Then suddenly he softened.

"I'll see you tomorrow. I'm showing my art at the Festival of Local Art at the fairgrounds. Meet me at the main fairgrounds entrance at one thirty."

One more day, I repeated in my mind, *just one more day.*

"Fine," I agreed stiffly. "See ya."

I quickly made my way to the door. But before I could make a clean break, I was stopped by Tempest.

"Annalynn is it?" she asked.

"Annabelle," I said. I hated correcting people. I would much rather let it slide. I didn't much care what people called me. Unless it was a food name, like Apple or something; that's just too far for me.

"Annabelle," Tempest began, sounding serious. "I need to warn you about Patrique."

"Warn me?" I asked, without emotion. I knew better than to put much stock into anything an ex-girlfriend has to say about a guy.

"Yes. Patrique gets what he wants from his women."

I stifled a laugh. "Oh, I am not one of Patrique's—"

"If he doesn't get what he wants he will try to sabotage you," Tempest interrupted in a sinister voice.

"But you don't understand, our relationship is simply work—"

"He does it subtly," Tempest said. "I had just begun a new painting when we broke up. After things were over between us, I moved out here to Monterey and starting dating someone else. When Patrique found out, he stole the subject of my painting for a painting of his own. And now he's moved here, I think to steal my clientele."

I looked toward the exit. "Okay, thanks for the tip," I said quickly.

"Fine," Tempest huffed. "If you don't want to listen to me, you'll just have to learn the hard way."

"Okay, bye," I said, dashing to the door.

But honestly, looking back, I really should have paid a little more attention to what Tempest was telling me.

Chapter 12

Thursday morning, I walked into the cardio room at the gym and decided to do a little stair stepping. I had no idea why I wasn't conserving all of my energy for my trip to the Festival of Local Art; I knew I was going to need it.

I wrapped my cell phone in a towel and set it on the floor next to the machine. Isaac had said he would call, so I was not letting my phone out of sight.

As I worked out on the machine, my mind went back to the scene on the sidewalk near Cannery Row. The one where Isaac had almost kissed me. The very thought made me feel like I was going to explode with eagerness. Why didn't anything ever come easily to me? I couldn't even seem to manage a first kiss.

I was in the middle of mentally imagining what it would feel like to kiss Isaac when I noticed a woman looking at me. I don't think I even have to tell you. It was Rona Bircheck. Rona Bircheck in all of her non-engaged glory.

Does she live at the gym or something? I wondered. And from the looks of her toned physique, I guessed I wasn't too far off.

Rona came to my side and stood there, staring at me.

"Uh, hi, Rona," I said. I ceased stepping but remained high on the machine, and thus, a good two feet above Rona. "I meant to call you," I said. I had received a voicemail from Rona the night before, in which she asked me about the catering for Carrie's shower, but I hadn't exactly returned her call.

Rona remained motionless and wordless.

"About the caterer . . . um . . ." I paused. I should just come clean. I should just tell her that I was living and breathing my impossible article and that I just hadn't been able to get too far in my search for a caterer. I should just tell her that at this point I was leaning toward going with my original idea of fruit and veggie trays and Costco rolls. But instead I continued to stammer. "I've been . . . thinking . . ."

Rona cut me off. "Look, Annabelle, I thought I could count on you. But the party is in two weeks, and I'm beginning to think I should just relieve you of the responsibility."

Oh, no you don't. You already stole the party from me. You will not take the caterer. "I have it under control," I said.

Just then I heard the beautiful sound of my cell phone. "Excuse me," I said to Rona. I stepped down to retrieve the phone from its towel wrap. I was kind of hoping she would leave.

"Hello," I said into the phone.

"Hi, cute girl," I heard Isaac say.

Cute girl, I repeated in my mind. The words made me feel wonderfully dizzy. I immediately wondered if Rona had heard them. I glanced at her, but it didn't look like she had. Too bad.

"Hi," I said into the phone, my voice sweet.

"What are you up to?" Isaac asked.

"I'm at the gym." I noticed that Rona had hopped onto the stair-stepper that was next to me and was stepping vigorously. "How about you?"

I glared at Rona out of the corner of my eye. If she hadn't been there, I just might have used my most flirtatious voice and asked, "When will I see you again, so we can finish what we started last night?" But since she was there, I was stuck with, "How about you?"

"I'm helping Ethan put together the programs for the recital tomorrow. Are you going to come?"

"I wouldn't miss it," I answered, wondering how inappropriate it would be if our first kiss was in front of a room of recital-goers.

"Could you hang on for just a second, Annabelle?" Isaac asked. "I think Ethan is one key stroke away from Adobe Photoshop implosion." I could hear Ethan yelling in the background on Isaac's end of the line.

I laughed. "Sure."

"Is that Isaac?" I heard Rona ask.

I nodded, a stony look on my face.

"I need to talk to him," Rona said as she stopped stepping on her machine.

Was she serious? She wanted me to hand over the phone so she could place it against her not-one-hair-out-of-place head and talk to Isaac, the guy who—I think—likes me?

"Annabelle, can I talk to him?" Rona repeated, reaching for the phone.

I held up a finger. "Just a sec." I waited for Isaac to get back on the line.

Finally Isaac's deliciously deep voice returned. "Sorry about that, Annabelle."

"No problem." I turned my eyes toward Rona who was still waiting for me to hand over my cell. "Um, Isaac, Rona wants to talk to you," I said, gritting my teeth.

Rona smiled widely as I handed her the phone.

"Hey, Isaac," Rona cooed. "We're still meeting at two o'clock, right?"

Meeting?

I strained to hear Isaac's response to the question. But I heard nothing. I kicked myself for not turning up the volume on the phone before handing it over to Rona.

I tried to make sense of the conversation from what I was hearing from Rona. "Okay, I'll show you." Pause. Giggling. "Oh, that would be so great." More giggling. "I can't wait." Pause. "Okay, I'll see you then. Just inside the entrance of the grounds." Giggles. Pause.

It's for work, I tried to convince myself. *They're meeting for work.*

"Okay, bye. I'm handing you back to Annabelle." Rona handed the phone back to me. "Thanks," she said, her smile sickeningly bright. "I tried to get a hold of him last night, but I couldn't reach him."

Yeah, because he was with me.

"No problem," I replied, forcing a smile.

"I'm gonna go do weights now," Rona said. "Call me no later than tonight about the caterer."

"All right," I agreed weakly.

A trail of turning heads followed Rona into the weight room.

I put my ear back to the phone. I wanted to ask Isaac what in the Sam Hill was going on. That's a real saying, right? I think I heard Mom say it once. Anyway, I wanted to ask Isaac that. But with our relationship nearing the kiss stage, I didn't want to mess with a good thing. Of course, my intentions not to mess were one thing. My mouth was an entirely different thing. "What are you and Rona doing today?" I blurted into the phone.

"I'm not quite sure," Isaac said slowly.

Thanks, Isaac, very reassuring.

"How can you not know?" I said, trying very, very hard to keep my tone light.

"Because Rona never really said."

"Oh," I said stiffly.

"Is something wrong, Annabelle?" Isaac asked.

Uh, yeah! Don't you see what Rona is trying to do? She's free as a bird now, and she wants you! Open up your eyes, Isaac!

"Nothing you did," I muttered. I find that if you say this, most guys drop the subject.

Of course, Isaac isn't like most guys. "Then what is it?" he asked.

"There's this girl," I admitted. "For some reason, she's always had something against me. And she's giving me grief."

I waited for Isaac to put the pieces together. I figured his train of thought should go something like this: I was talking to Annabelle. Then I talked to Rona. Rona giggled uncontrollably and irritatingly the whole time. Then I got back on the phone with Annabelle and explained to her that I was doing something with Rona and had no idea what it was. Then Annabelle seemed upset and started talking about some girl who was giving her grief. So that must mean Rona is the one giving Annabelle grief. And that I shouldn't do anything with her or any other girl ever again but should marry Annabelle and . . .

But Isaac didn't quite put the pieces together. "I'm sorry," he said. For a second, I admired that Isaac seemed to be completely guileless. But after that second, I couldn't help thinking, *Oh come on!*

"It'll work out," I said, giving up on the whole thing. "Let's talk about something else."

"All right. Let's talk about what you're doing tonight. I really want to see you."

"I have plans with Carrie," I told Isaac. Miles had to work late, so Carrie and I were actually going to be able to have Paint and Popcorn night. "But maybe we could have an early dinner?"

"Uh, I don't know. I have no idea how long this thing with Rona is going to take."

I forced myself to breathe deeply. I needed to believe that what was meant to be would be. I needed to believe that Isaac really did care about me, like he was acting like he did, and he wouldn't just drop me for Rona Bircheck. "Okay," I said weakly. "I guess I'll see you at the piano recital tomorrow then."

"Yeah. But hey, come to think of it, maybe you could help us set up for the recital. We'll probably start at about four o'clock. If you come early, that means I'll get to spend three extra hours with you."

I smiled into the phone even though Isaac couldn't see me. "That sounds nice. I get off work at five, so I can help after that."

"Great. And after the recital we can do something," Isaac

said. I was almost sure that I could hear some "such as finally manage our first kiss" undertones in his voice.

"That sounds wonderful," I breathed, feeling an ache at the thought of not seeing Isaac until the next day.

"All right, then, I'll see you tomorrow," Isaac said.

"See you tomorrow," I echoed.

Of course, little did I know, I wasn't going to have to wait that long to see Isaac.

Patrique led me into the cement-floored fairgrounds building, which smelled like animal feed. Just inside the doors, I noticed a sign that said Fine Visual Art in block letters.

"Wow," I said, surveying the place as we stepped inside.

Large eggshell-colored partitions were placed strategically on the open floor, displaying oil paintings, watercolors, and photographs. Also dotting the floor were wooden pedestals on which were displayed sculptures of everything from seagulls to bicycles. Obviously a lot of preparation had gone into the festival, and a lot of talented artists had come to exhibit their work.

"I see Tempest over there." Patrique unbuttoned the two top buttons of his silk shirt. "She's showing some of her things here today. I'll be right back."

I gave Patrique a weak wave and began slowly walking the perimeter of the building. I had just finished admiring a group of gorgeous oil paintings of various seascapes and was looking at a sculpture of a sea lion when the sound of something behind me caught my attention. It was a giggle. A giggle that sounded oddly familiar. I turned around, looking in the direction of the sound.

And then I saw them.

Rona and Isaac. Standing next to some photos that looked like the ones I had seen in Ethan's piano studio. I gasped and quickly ducked behind the sea lion sculpture. The solid wood stand was just tall and wide enough to conceal my crouched body as the sea lion perched atop it hid my face.

So this is where you two were going today, I thought.

I watched. My eyes narrowed. "Now I can see just what you're up to, Rona," I whispered, almost scaring myself with how much I sounded like a witch from a Disney movie. "And I can see how Isaac reacts to it."

Soon, a woman, probably in her fifties, with long, graying hair and a multi-colored crepe dress appeared at my side. "Trying to get a better look?" she asked in a kind, soft voice.

"Uh, yeah" I said, my voice strained due to the unnatural position of my body.

"This one took me a year to finish," the woman said, her voice filled with nostalgia. "I found a group of naturalists who were studying a sea lion they called Arnie. I studied alongside the group. When I finished the sculpture I just knew I had to name the sculpture after Arnie." The woman pointed to a plaque attached to the front of the pedestal which read *Arnie of the Sea.*

"Oh, so you made this?" I asked, still crouching.

"Yes," the woman answered. "Viola Waters," she added, introducing herself.

"Good to meet you. It's lovely." When I didn't stand up to talk to the woman like any normal person would have, she looked at me curiously.

Just then I saw Rona put her hand on Isaac's arm. I immediately clenched my fists.

"You're looking at the whiskers, aren't you?" Viola asked. I had forgotten she was standing there.

"Um . . ." I muttered as I counted the seconds that Rona's hand was on Isaac's arm. Three. Four. Five. Six. Could she be any more of a floozy?

"They were by far the hardest part of the sculpture," Viola said.

"Finally," I mumbled when Rona removed her rotten little hand from Isaac's arm.

"I'm sorry?" Viola asked.

"Oh, nothing."

"Are you interested in buying the sculpture?" Viola asked, a wrinkle of confusion in her brow.

"I don't think so," I answered, watching as Rona began giggling.

Viola turned to walk away. "Okay. Enjoy looking."

Moments after Viola had left my side, I noticed that my back was aching. I kept a close eye on Isaac and Rona as I stepped about three feet to the left where I concealed myself behind a tall partition and tried to un-kink my back. I was about to return to my hiding spot so I didn't miss a second of spying, when Patrique approached me with a pale-looking, dressed-in-black Tempest by his side.

"Hi, my dear," Patrique said to me.

Ignoring the "my dear," I replied with a flat "Hi."

"Hi, Anna Lou," Tempest addressed me.

"Hello," I said, not bothering to correct her.

"Patrique tells me you work for *Central Coast Living*," Tempest said.

"Yeah," I replied quickly. I needed to get the conversation over so I could get back to watching Isaac and Rona. Anything could be happening between them while I was stuck behind that partition.

"I've been thinking about running an ad in there for my online business," Tempest said.

"Oh, okay, I can give you the marketing director's number, if you'd like," I responded, my words brisk.

"Do you have it now?" Tempest asked.

"I need to move," I said senselessly as I moved back over to the sea lion sculpture and ducked behind it again. Tempest and Patrique watched me, bemused looks on their faces.

Back in my spot, I noticed Rona gesturing what looked like a good-bye to Isaac. Then it looked almost like she was going to hug him, but he quickly offered her his hand to shake. I sighed heavily in relief. Rona began walking away from Isaac, and I felt hope rising inside of me. But a few feet away from the exit, she stopped short and turned back around.

"What are you doing? I was asking you a question," Tempest said as she moved closer to me, looking at me as if I were vermin.

"I . . . I really like this sculpture," I replied as I watched Rona talk to Isaac, keeping a close eye on the position of her hands the whole time.

"Well, that's great. But I was talking to you. Can I get that number from you?"

"What? What number?" I looked up at Tempest confusedly for a second.

"The marketing director's number," Tempest said slowly, as if talking to a child.

"Oh, I don't have it right now. I'll have to get it to you later." I turned my eyes back to Isaac and Rona.

Tempest looked at me like I was the most useless creature on the planet.

Patrique moved to my side. "Annabelle, why don't you give me the number and I could get it to Tempest," he suggested.

"All right," I replied. I was so distracted with spying that I probably would have agreed to just about anything.

"I'll call you," Patrique said to Tempest.

Tempest said a few things back to Patrique, but I wasn't listening because Rona finally made her way to the exit and left the building.

After Rona had gone, a man in an olive-colored suit approached Isaac. The man and Isaac began talking, and as I watched Isaac my mind conjured up a daydream.

In the dream, I was the one talking to Isaac. He was explaining to me that he couldn't wait one more second to kiss me. So he took me in his arms and kissed me deliciously.

Then Rona came back because she had forgotten her handbag, and she saw the whole thing. Her entire face turned red, and she walked off in a huff that Isaac of course didn't notice because he was too busy confessing his undying love for me.

Then Isaac asked me to marry him and put a huge ring on

my finger. Everyone in the fairgrounds building clapped, and some women cried at how moving the proposal was.

We got married and bought a house in Carmel and had two girls, three boys, and a beautiful thoroughbred horse named Snickers—after my second favorite candy bar, since I don't think Milk Dud would be a very good name for a horse.

"You know, you two really are perfect for each other," Tempest's edgy voice came into my ears.

"I know," I said dreamily.

Tempest shook her head at me and walked away dramatically.

It only took me a second to snap back to reality and realize that Tempest was referring to me and Patrique. "Wait!" I cried out in utter disgust at the thought. "What I meant was—"

Patrique shushed me. "Don't ruin it! She really thinks we're a couple. And it's getting to her, I can tell." He gave me the weirdest, creepiest look and added, "I can't believe you did that for me." Then before I knew what was going on, he had pulled me up from my crouched position and was hugging me in a not-quite-platonic way.

The shock of it all made me momentarily frozen. But when sensation returned to my limbs, I pushed Patrique away forcefully, looking in Isaac's direction, making sure he hadn't seen. I didn't want him jumping to any conclusions.

Little did I know, the forceful push I gave Patrique was about to cost me a pretty penny.

It all seemed to happen in slow motion. Patrique's body slamming into the pedestal. The pedestal wobbling from side to side and then toppling over. *Arnie of the Sea* falling, heading straight for the ground.

Suddenly Viola came out of nowhere, she too appearing to be in slow motion. She threw her body under the sculpture and cried out, "Arnie!" And all of a sudden, as if some sort of crazy adrenaline had taken over, she extended her arms above her head bench-press style and caught Arnie in the air—and let me tell you, that sea lion looked pretty heavy. The pedestal made a loud bang on the cement floor just beside Viola. Heads turned, and the whole building seemed to become silent.

My mouth dropped open, and I blinked slowly.

Patrique and a female bystander in a very tight dress reached down to help Viola off the ground. The bystander and Patrique then picked the wooden stand up from the floor and set it upright. Viola placed the sculpture atop the slightly cracked wood, her hands shaking.

"I'm, so, so sorry," I cried. "I'm so sorry."

"It's, all right," Viola said quietly, her voice shaky.

"No, really, I, I . . ."

"Annabelle?"

I looked up and saw Isaac standing in front of me.

"What happened? Are you all right?"

"Um, I, I nearly killed Arnie," I said, leaving out the part about Patrique hugging me and me pushing him away.

"Ah," Isaac said as if he had knocked over a sea lion sculpture just yesterday and completely understood my predicament. "But you're all right?"

Before answering, I quickly glanced over at Patrique. He was chatting with the tight-dressed bystander, acting as if he had nothing to do with Arnie's near-death experience. I was angry, but at the same time glad that Isaac and I could talk without Patrique's interruptions. "Yeah, I'm fine," I answered. Then I turned to Viola. "Are you okay?"

"I'm all right," Viola answered. "I do Pilates. It gives me good core strength." Viola forced a smile.

"Is the sculpture okay? I mean, is there any damage?"

Viola began inspecting the sculpture. "I don't think so." Then suddenly she fell to her knees. I had no idea what she was doing until she whispered, "A few of his whiskers fell off."

Viola looked up at me from her kneeling position. She held up her hands, and in them were four whiskers that had fallen to the ground. As she inspected the whiskers in her hands, her shoulders hunched forward, and she looked smaller somehow.

"I'm so sorry, Viola," I said. "I'll pay for the sculpture."

"It's all right. Maybe I can solder them back on or something," she muttered.

"No, I'm buying *Arnie of the Sea*," I insisted. I had just deposited a bit of money into my account, so it wouldn't be a problem. "How much do I owe you?"

"He was priced at seven hundred seventy five," Viola explained.

Oh. Well. I hadn't quite deposited that much. I bit my lip.

"Will you take a post-dated check?" I asked Viola hesitantly.

"I usually don't but . . ."

I glared at Patrique. I considered this to be just as much his fault as mine, maybe even more his fault. He should cough up some of the money.

"Patrique," I called out, trying to snap his attention away from Miss Tiny Dress.

Patrique looked at me. Then it seemed like he noticed Isaac for the first time and a strange look crossed his face. "Yes," he answered, raising his eyebrows.

"Do you have any money I can use to pay for Arnie?"

"All I've got are two twenty spots," Patrique said, pulling two dirty, wadded twenties from his pocket.

I rolled my eyes.

"I can loan you some money," Isaac offered.

"No, Isaac, I could never ask you to. It's way too much."

Isaac touched my cheek gently. "I want to help," he said.

"Are you sure? I asked, Isaac's touch making me feel suddenly lightheaded.

"I'm sure."

"I'm so sorry. I'll pay you back when I get my check next Friday." I sighed heavily and looked into Isaac's eyes. "Thank you. You're always saving me." I threw my arms around him gratefully.

At that moment, Patrique's attention left the woman in the tight dress, and he focused wholly on me and Isaac. He watched us with an odd, glaring look on his face. But Patrique was always making weird looks, so I just ignored it.

Chapter 13

I was driving to Carrie's house for Paint and Popcorn night when my cell rang. Keeping my eyes on the road, I answered the phone quickly without checking the Caller ID. I hoped it would be Isaac. He had left the art festival early so he could go check out a photo gallery that was interested in his work, and so we hadn't really gotten much of a chance to talk.

But it was Mom's voice I heard on the line. "Annabelle, do you know who—"

"Oh, Mom," I interrupted in my best voice of lamentation. "Why do these things always happen to me? How am I going to come up with eight hundred dollars?"

"We can talk about that in a minute but first—"

"It wasn't even my fault that I almost killed Arnie," I said, cutting poor Mom off again. "It was Patrique's fault. All I was doing was hiding behind Arnie so I could see Rona and Isaac through his whiskers."

"Who's Arnie?" Mom asked.

"He's a sea lion."

"You were looking at Rona and Isaac through a sea lion's whiskers?" Mom said, sounding confused. "And you almost . . . killed the sea lion?"

"Yes. But like I said, it was Patrique's fault. That's why I had to buy Arnie. But it's okay. I'll find a place for him."

"You bought a sea lion?" Mom said the words slowly, as if she were waiting for me to correct her.

"Yeah. Hey Mom, listen, I just got to Carrie's house, so I've gotta go. Carrie was expecting me about an hour ago, but I had some trouble getting Arnie to the car, and he was pretty difficult to transport, so I'm pretty late and . . ."

"The sea lion is in the car with you?" Again Mom's words were slow, bewildered-sounding.

"Yes. But don't worry. He's small; I can handle him. I've really gotta go, Mom."

"But wait—"

"Oh, sorry. What did you call me for?" I asked.

"I was calling to see if you knew the final Jeopardy question," Mom said in a hurried voice. "But that doesn't matter. What matters is—"

"Oh, sorry about the Jeopardy thing Mom," I said. "I'll call you later. I have so much more to tell you."

With no further comment, I flipped the phone closed with my chin, put the car in park, and headed toward Carrie's front door.

"Tell me how the wedding plans are going," I instructed Carrie as I painted my toes carefully.

Carrie was doing Yoga on the living room floor and was practically folded in half in Head to Knee Pose, which I think should be called Hamstring Torture Pose. I'm pretty sure that Carrie must have been the inspiration for both Gumby and Pokey.

Carrie sat up from her position, and I looked at her white cotton yoga pants and matching white tee. Although a white on white outfit would make me appear to be that huge marshmallow man in Ghostbusters, Carrie looked like the angel of yoga. I instantly hated her. Until I remembered how much I loved her.

"Let's see . . ." Carrie began. "I've chosen the colors for the reception: yellow and white. And I think I've chosen the kind of cake I want. It's made with a blend of whole grain flours and sweetened with vegetable glycerin rather than sugar."

"So in other words, I should definitely bring a pack of Twinkies to your reception," I joked.

"I bet if I hadn't told you, you wouldn't have even noticed," Carrie said.

Carrie's always telling me stuff like that. Like she's always saying that soy ice cream tastes just like real ice cream and tofu tastes just like meat. Yeah right, and yellow paper tastes just like banana cream pie.

As Carrie leaned further and further forward into her pose, she told me between yoga breaths that she was researching caterers in the Oakland area. This instantly reminded me of the fact that I had told Rona Bircheck that I would call her about the caterer for the shower. I really, really didn't want to call. But what I wanted less was for her to "relieve me of the responsibility," as she had suggested she would. So I decided to go for it.

"I have to go make a call real fast. Be right back," I informed Carrie. "Then you have to tell me all the rest of the details."

"Okay," Carrie said as she moved into Staff Pose.

Walking on my heels so I didn't get any polish on the bamboo-fibers area rug, I made my way to my bag, which I had left by the front door. I bent down and located my phone. I moved into the bathroom down the hall so Carrie wouldn't hear me talking and stood there for a second, thinking.

In my thinking session, I decided that I was going to tell Rona the truth. I was going to tell her that the caterers I had checked out were entirely too expensive, and that I was still searching, but I would think of something. I would tell her she could trust me, I would come through for Carrie.

I flipped open the phone and dialed Rona's number. On the second ring, she picked up. Now, if you promise you won't judge me, I'll tell you the rest.

Do you promise?

All right.

I hung up. I heard Rona's voice and hung up.

I just couldn't do it. I could imagine her condescending tone as she told me how she had depended on me, and I had failed. She would remind me that the party was in little more than two weeks and it would be nearly impossible to secure a caterer now. Then she would tell me she would just take care of it herself. Then she would wish that she could un-invite me, and would be mad that since I was Carrie's best friend she couldn't.

No. I was going to find a caterer before the night was over. And it was going to be the best caterer in the whole Monterey Bay area.

I tapped the side of my mouth with my phone as I thought of who I could call at eight o'clock PM about a caterer. Then I had an idea: Jacqueline from La Bonne Violette. She had to know tons about the catering business. Plus, she was really nice.

I dialed the number I had for La Bonne Violette. No answer. I disconnected the line with a frown on my face. I wondered who else I could call. Immediately, Patrique's name came to mind. He would probably know Jacqueline's number.

You probably shouldn't call him, my brain immediately said to me. *He's bad news. Think of something else.*

But it's just a phone call, I argued with my brain. *What can happen over the phone?*

I dialed Patrique's number—which he had given me just in case I couldn't find him at the fairgrounds—and reached his voice mail. "Bonjour, you've reached Patrique Poitier. If you are calling for business please leave your name and number, and I'll return your call as soon as possible. If you are calling for pleasure please leave your name and number, and I'll return your call as soon as possible. And if you're a beautiful woman calling for business or pleasure, please leave your name and number, and I'll return your call immediately."

Now I bet you're expecting me to say that I'm just pulling your leg about that being Patrique's outgoing message. But that really and truly is his message. In fact, if you want to, you can call him and see for yourself. His number is 555-0987.

The tone sounded, and I left a brief message. "Patrique, it's Annabelle Pleasanton. Please call me back as soon as you get this message."

Willing Patrique to call me back before the night was over, I went back into the living room.

"Ready for a movie?" Carrie asked as I sat down on the couch and stretched my arms over my head.

"Definitely," I answered.

Carrie put *Father of the Bride* into the DVD player, and I popped a bag of all natural popcorn. It wasn't exactly the most balanced dinner, but hey, corn's a vegetable, right? Or maybe it's a grain. I don't know.

As Carrie and I sat on the couch watching the movie, I felt my eyes beginning to grow heavy. I leaned back into the cushions and gave into the heavy feeling. I was half-asleep when I heard a faint electronic ringing sound coming from Carrie's front door.

That's funny, I thought in my cloudy state, *Carrie's doorbell has the same ring as my cell phone.*

"Annabelle, it's that Patrique guy," I heard Carrie say. Her voice sounded far away. And like she was in a tunnel.

"Is corn a vegetable, Mom?" I mumbled in a weird, half-conscious voice.

Carrie instantly began giggling. The giggling brought me to full awareness, and I sat up, rubbing my eyes.

I looked over at Carrie. "Was I talking about corn?" I asked groggily.

"Mm hmm," Carrie replied, still giggling.

This happens to me a lot. In fact, back when I was in Young Women and went to girls' camp, the favorite nighttime activity of the girls in my cabin was to get up in the night and listen to the crazy things I said. I heard that by my fourth year at camp, girls were requesting to be in my cabin for this reason alone.

Carrie handed me my cell. "It's Patrique," she said, stifling a laugh.

"Hey, Patrique," I said into the phone. "Did you get my voice mail?"

"Yes," Patrique replied. "And I saved it so I can listen to that succulent voice anytime I want to."

"Whatever. Listen, I was wondering if you could give me Jacqueline's phone number. You know, the woman who does catering at your uncle's restaurant?"

"I know who she is," Patrique said. "What do you need to call her for?"

"Well . . ." I stood up from the couch and went back into the bathroom down the hall so Carrie wouldn't hear the conversation. "I need to ask her something," I said as I sat down on the bathroom counter.

"You need to ask her what?" Patrique prodded.

"I have a question about catering."

"Why?"

"Because I'm looking for a caterer for my friend's bridal shower," I said, sounding a bit irritated.

"Why bother calling Jacqueline? I can arrange it for you. I work in catering at my uncle's restaurant too."

"Oh, no, I'm not talking about having La Bonne Violette cater. I could never afford that. I only have a couple hundred dollars to work with."

"That's no problem," Patrique said. "I can get you a really great deal."

"Are you messing with me?" I wondered aloud. "Because that's just mean."

"No, I'm serious."

"What's the catch?" I asked warily.

"No catch. You've done so much for me. More than you know. It's the least I can do for you. When's the party?"

"Two weeks from Saturday," I said hesitantly. "At noon."

"How many people?"

"About twenty."

"No problem," Patrique said. It sounded like he was smiling. "After your meeting with my uncle on Monday, you and I can meet and set it all up."

I sat in silence. Two emotions were building inside of me. First, I felt extreme relief. And second, I felt a strange worry that I couldn't seem to ignore.

"Annabelle," Patrique began, obviously sensing my hesitance, "I want to do this for you."

"And there's no catch? I don't understand . . ."

"Tempest called me," Patrique explained. "She told me that seeing you and me together made her realize that she misses me. She wants to get back together."

"Oh," I replied slowly.

"And when Tempest told me that, I felt something, something . . . unexpected. And it's all because of you. So please let me do this for you."

"Okay," I said, wondering why I felt so reluctant. "I accept your offer."

After saying good-bye to Patrique, I sat on the bathroom counter, envisioning Carrie's shower.

In my little vision, smiling women walked into the shower and were instantly drawn to the food table. They piled their plates high with the delicious fare and then turned to me and said, "Oh, Annabelle, this food is delish. How did you *ever* manage to get La Bonne Violette to do the catering?"

I told the women that I personally knew Chef Jean-Pierre and that he had given me a marvelous deal on the food. The women were highly impressed and told Carrie that I was a jewel of a best friend. Carrie proceeded to tell the women that I truly was the greatest best friend ever, and everyone toasted their delicious nonalcoholic drinks "to friendship." Well, everyone toasted except Rona, who was in the background trying unsuccessfully to get some streamers to stick to the wall.

After the vision faded from my mind, I immediately dialed Rona's number. She must have been on the line because her voicemail picked up after one ring. I left a message telling her about the fabulous catering that I had secured and smiled to myself in satisfaction as I hung up. Things really couldn't be working out any better.

So why did I feel so worried?

Chapter 14

"Hi there," Isaac said in his ever-gorgeous voice when I answered my cell phone on Friday afternoon.

I was sitting at my desk and was supposed to be editing a page of recipes for the Anniversary Issue, since in all the craziness of writing—or at least trying to write—I had gotten a little behind on my regular work. But although I was supposed to be editing, what I was actually doing was typing Annabelle Matthews on my computer in different fonts.

When I heard Isaac's voice, I quickly closed the document as if I were afraid he could see it through the phone.

"Hi," I said in a sweet voice. "What are you up to?"

"We just started setting up for the recital."

I leaned back in my office chair. "You still want me to come help, right?" I asked.

"I sure do," Isaac replied, his voice all low and insinuating.

"I can probably leave work a little early and come over," I said, feeling excitement bubble up inside of me. "You're at Ethan's studio, right?"

"No," Isaac replied. "We're at La Bonne Violette. In the Rouge Room."

"The recital is at La Bonne Violette? That must cost Ethan a fortune."

"Actually, Jean-Pierre lets him use the room for free. And he gives him a really great deal on catering."

"That's cool. Pat—" I stopped myself. I had been about to say that Patrique was getting me a similarly great deal on catering for Carrie's shower, but I decided against it. No sense bringing creepy Patrique into our pleasant conversation. So instead I finished my sentence with, "Pat . . . Pat him on the back, that's great." It made no sense, but Isaac didn't seem to notice.

"Yeah it is," Isaac said. Then he lowered his voice and asked, "Do you like surprises?"

"Of course. I love surprises."

"I was hoping I could surprise you with something after the recital. It should be over at about eight."

"Hmm . . . I don't know," I said in a playful, flirty voice. "Should I agree to this?"

"Yes, you should," Isaac said, flirting right back.

"Well . . . I suppose that would be all right."

"Good. So when can I expect you over here?"

"Let's see," I said, playing with the mini stapler on my desk. "I'll probably leave here in about twenty minutes or so. Then I'll run home really fast to change, and then I'll head over. So about an hour."

You might be wondering why I wanted to take the time to go home and change instead of just rushing over to see Isaac. Well, it was possible-kiss day. And being such, I needed to wear something that said, "Don't you want to kiss me? Well, go ahead and do it baby." And not my work clothes which said, "Do you want to run down to Kinko's with me and make some copies?" So you see, I definitely needed to change.

"Okay, then I'll see you in about an hour," Isaac said.

"See you in an hour," I echoed.

I was about to add something extremely cute and enticing that would leave him barely able to wait until he saw me, when my office phone rang. "Isaac, can you hang on for a sec?" I asked.

"Sure."

"Hello," I said into my office phone.

"Pleasanton, George Kent here. I need to see you in my office."

"Of course, I'll be right there."

Without another word, George hung up.

I put my cell phone up to my ear. "Isaac, I have to go. I'll see you soon."

"Okay. Remember, come prepared for a surprise."

"Oh, I will."

I took a deep breath as I opened George's office door. He was on the phone, so he motioned for me to come in and sit down. I lowered myself into the chair across from George and looked at a picture of him and his wife and son, which was sitting at an angle on the desk. I also noticed two walls had been painted a nice calming shade of blue since the last time I had been in the office—Arvin's handiwork, I guessed.

George ended his phone call and spoke to me. "Pleasanton," he began. "How are you?"

"I'm good, thanks. How are you doing? Are you feeling better?"

"Much better, thank goodness. Now, I called you in here to talk about your article," George explained. "When I came back, I had an email from Jean-Pierre waiting for me. He sent the email last Friday, after you first met with him. In the message he complains about your professionalism."

"What?" I asked, dumfounded.

"Let me read it to you." George opened a file on his computer and began reading.

George,

I have some concerns about the young woman you have sent to interview me. From what you and Ingrid told me, I was expecting someone with more experience. But this girl, she is not what I expected. I let her into my kitchen and she made a very big mess and ruined some very expensive Roquefort cheese. Please see that nothing of this nature happens again.

Jean-Pierre

"Annabelle," George began, using my first name. "Am I going to regret putting my faith in you?"

"No, no, of course not," I responded, feeling the sting of the words. It wasn't my fault Jean-Pierre's refrigerator was a trap of death.

"Never mind about the email," George said. "Have there been any other problems?"

"Um . . ." I stammered, remembering the fire. "There was one little thing. But everything is fine now. I'm still going to get the interview."

"What do you mean you're *going* to get the interview?" George asked, leaning forward in his chair.

Oops. I didn't mean to let that slip.

"I mean . . . I . . ."

"Are you telling me you haven't gotten the interview yet?" George looked at me with an appalled look on his face. "What have you been doing this whole time?!"

"I've been . . . it's been really hard and . . .I do have some of it and . . ."

"I can't believe this," George said, rubbing his temples with his fingers.

"It's not as bad as it sounds. I have everything under control."

"Everything under control? You have had an entire week to work on this and you have nothing. I should have known this was going to happen, especially after what happened last time."

Ouch. I knew I wasn't exactly the world's best writer, but I had worked hard. I had kept it together even after my first, and then second, meeting with Jean-Pierre had gone horribly. I had endured two excruciating trips to art functions with

Patrique. I mean, I deserved extra pay for having to subject my eyes to *Le Cauchemar.* And this point is the best of all, even after everything seemed to work against it happening: I was getting my interview. And then I was going to write a fabulous article.

"I can do this," I said, my voice confident.

"Well, there's nothing I can do about it now," George said in an aggravated tone. "I can't give someone else the assignment." He rubbed his temples again. "I'll just have to find a replacement article."

"No, you won't," I said. "I can do this."

George stared at me as if he were contemplating whether or not to tell me to pack up my cubicle and never come back, when the phone in the office rang.

"Hello?" George answered, still sounding perturbed. "Oh, hi, dear," he said, relaxing a bit. But the relaxation in his voice didn't last. "What do you mean they don't have any open rooms at Hotel Presidente for those days?!" he exclaimed angrily. "No, I don't want to stay anywhere else. What? Peter wants to go to Cancun? But we already decided on Cozumel. Hang on, will you?"

George covered up the receiver with his hand and spoke to me. "I'll leave you on this assignment," he said. "But only because I'm really not in the mood to fire you today. Remember, your deadline is a week from Tuesday, five o'clock. I want an absolutely pristine article. I mean perfect. And don't email it to me. Bring it to me on a USB drive. I'll look the article over Tuesday night and see if I need to run another one." George gave me an I-don't-want-to-look-at-you-a-second-longer wave and got back on the phone.

I slowly walked out of the office. I could hear George's words echoing in my mind: "Am I going to regret putting my faith in you?"

What had I been thinking all this time? That I could waste an entire week getting nowhere on my article and then put something wonderful together at the last minute? Of course that wasn't going to happen. How could I have been so stupid?

As I made my way back to my cubicle, I peered out the dirty windows in the office and saw a garbage man emptying the contents of a dumpster into his truck. *That's where I'm going to end up living*, I thought pitifully as I stared at the dumpster.

Back at my cubicle, I put my head down, trying to make myself invisible to my co-workers. Not like they would notice me. They were busy working. Probably doing a good job on their assignments. Probably being worthy of George's faith in them.

Fitfully, I grabbed my jacket from the back of my chair—a gorgeous little black one that I would probably have to sell for food money after next Tuesday—and headed to see someone who always had faith in me.

Someone who had faith in me even after I traded her antique garnet jewelry collection for Ice Skating Barbie. Someone who had faith in me even after I slept through the SAT. Someone who would have faith in me even if my article was the worst article in the history of articles, including the ones in the tabloids about alien babies.

I went home to Mom.

"What's wrong, honey?" Mom asked, taking one look at my face.

I plopped onto the couch rag-doll like, next to Mom who was reading a thick book. "I'm on my way to becoming . . . to becoming . . . a dumpster girl," I let out the last two words in a dramatic wail.

"Oh, honey, no you're not," Mom comforted, putting her arm around my shoulder.

"Oh yes I am," I said stubbornly. "I don't know what I was thinking. I'm going to get fired, and then I'll have to live in a dumpster. Just me and Arnie."

"Are you talking about the sea lion again?" Mom asked, her brow wrinkling.

I nodded.

"Annabelle," Mom began slowly. "Is everything all right?" She put a bookmark in her book and looked at me. "I could call Brother Kinsley." Brother Kinsley is a psychologist in my parents' ward.

"What? I don't need to talk to Brother Kinsley. Why would you say something like that?"

"First of all, there are the sea lion comments."

"What's wrong with talking about Arnie?" I asked, surprised by Mom's unwarranted concern for my lucidity.

Mom looked at me lovingly. "Remember in the movie *Harvey* when Jimmy Stewart kept seeing the life-size rabbit? I think it was because he needed a friend."

"What are you talking about? I'm not just seeing Arnie."

"It's okay, Annabelle," Mom assured me in a soft voice.

"What's okay? Arnie's real. I broke him, and the poor woman who sculpted him looked heartbroken, so I bought him. Actually, Isaac bought him, but I'm going to pay him—"

Mom cut me off. "Sculpted him?"

"Yeah. Arnie is a sculpture."

"A sculpture," Mom repeated, sounding relieved that she didn't have to call Brother Kinsley.

"I'm sure I told you that," I said.

Mom sighed. "You didn't."

"I'm sorry, Mom. I was just kind of going crazy last night. And now I'm going even crazier since I'm going to end up living in a dumpster in a matter of days."

"Why do you keep saying that?" Mom asked.

For the next twenty minutes I filled Mom in on what was going on. I told her that my article was doomed. Then I told her that even the things that were going well seemed like time bombs waiting to go off. Like my relationship with Isaac; Rona was an ever present threat to that. Then there was the catering for Carrie's shower; it was looking pretty good right now, but it was still in the hands of Patrique, and for some reason that left me feeling very uneasy.

"Honey," Mom said lovingly, "sometimes we think we have it all figured out. We know exactly how we want things to go. We make our lists, our plans. And that's good. But just remember that no matter what happens—even if it's completely different from what you planned—if you're living the way God wants you to, it will be for your good. Just remember that."

"I will," I whispered.

"How about some apple tarts?" Mom asked with a smile. "I made a batch yesterday."

I nodded. Twenty-four years old and Mom's treats can still do the trick.

I followed Mom into the kitchen where we sat at the breakfast bar and ate some tarts. "So where's Dad?" I asked as I sank my teeth into a scrumptious tart.

"He already left to go to the Giants game with Brian and Brett from work," Mom answered.

I nodded my head and reached for another one of the delicious pastries.

In the middle of my second, okay fourth, tart, I heard my phone ringing from the other room. I ran to answer it. The caller ID said Isaac. "Hello," I answered, my mouth still full of tart.

"Hi," Isaac said. "I was just calling to tell you not to eat anything. Part of my surprise is food."

Um, too late for that.

"I'll be sure to save room," I assured Isaac. "I'm heading over right now. So I'll see you in about twenty minutes."

"Okay. I'll be looking forward to it," Isaac said, a longing sound in his voice.

Isaac and I ended our conversation and I stood in place, smiling ridiculously.

"Mom," I called out toward the kitchen, "I've gotta go. See you Sunday."

Mom came out of the kitchen, wiping her hands on a

towel. "I'm making my chicken crescents and crème caramel for dessert," she said proudly.

"Mmm," I said, my salivary glands dancing. Seriously, Mom's crème caramel is pure deliciousness. "I can't wait."

I picked up my handbag and headed for the door.

"Where are you off to?" Mom asked, following me as I walked.

"I'm going to help Isaac set up for a piano recital at La Bonne Violette. Isaac's brother, Ethan, teaches piano to children with disabilities. One of his students invited me." I smiled as I remembered adorable little Angel.

"That's great," Mom said with a smile. "Have a good time. Tell Isaac I said hello."

"Okay, I will." I took Mom into a hug and added, "I love you, Mom."

"I love you too, sweetie."

I was walking to my car when I became painfully aware that I was still in my work clothes. But the twenty minutes I told Isaac it would take me to get to La Bonne Violette didn't give me enough time to run home and change into a suitable "kiss me" outfit.

Of course it didn't. From the second I met Isaac, I wanted to impress him, just like I desired to impress all of the other guys I dated, but it had never worked out that way.

Memories flashed through my mind like a movie. Me throwing a phone book at him. Me with a tomato-stained shirt and a stinky-cheese stench. Me shoving a huge bite of ham sandwich into my mouth. Me with a fat lip, wearing a pair of Isaac's drawstring pants. Me waddling out of the fairgrounds as I held one end of *Arnie of the Sea* and Isaac held the other.

I turned around and headed back inside.

"I'm gonna go change," I explained to Mom as I bounded back into the house.

I made my way to the closet of my old room, where I kept a stash of clothes I had been meaning to donate to Deseret Industries. I wouldn't find a "kiss-me" outfit in there, but I wouldn't look any worse than Isaac had seen me look before. And at least I would be more comfortable than I would be in my work clothes, which I had been spending entirely too much time in lately.

I flung open the closet and for some reason began singing the Mission Impossible song.

The mission: to find something to change into.

Task one: find a pair of pants.

I searched the closet, tossing pairs of pants behind me as I decided against them. A pair of Wrangler jeans I bought because Clint, a rodeo competitor I dated briefly a year earlier, said he liked them. No. Toss. The Karate pants I paid a fortune for when I was dating Bud the Martial Arts instructor. No. Toss. The vinyl jumpsuit I bought during the Hadwin days. No. Toss.

Finally, in the corner of the closet I found a pair of jeans I remembered leaving at my parents' house after I had helped Mom work in the garden. She must have washed them and put them in the closet. I kicked off the pants I was wearing and slipped the jeans on. Task one complete.

Task two: find a shirt.

I pulled shirts from their hangers and tossed the rejects behind me to join the pile of pants. A black tee with the words "Space Girl" written on it from when I was dating, who else, Hadwin. No. Toss. A shirt I wore the summer I worked at Happy Howie's hot dog stand so I could get enough money to get my nails done and hair highlighted like Rona's so Alex would regret not taking me to the prom. No. Toss.

Then I saw the shirt I got when I volunteered at the children's hospital. I grinned as I remembered that experience. I wrote a huge amount of Pink Notes in those three months. I removed my blouse and pulled the tee over my head. Task two complete.

Final task: locate a pair of shoes.

Since there weren't any shoes in my closet, I went and asked Mom if she had any I could wear. Mom said she did and sat on the king-size bed in her room as I searched her walk-in closet.

Mom's style is classic, with all the basics to mix and match: think JC Penney catalogue. I sat on the floor of the closet and looked through her shoes. Heeled leather boots in brown and black. No. Too hard to walk in. Leather slides in similar brown and black. No. Too easy to slide out of. Many a stumble has revolved around me and a pair of slides. Pumps with pointed and rounded toes. No. At least not for tonight. But I did want to borrow the pointed black sling-backs sometime.

Then, under a pair of brown boots, I saw some red flip-flops.

"These are cute," I said.

"You think so? They were on a 75% off sale at Penney's at the end of last summer," Mom said. Was I right about that JC Penney thing or what? "I haven't ever worn them though. They're a little too bright for me. You can have them if you want."

"Thanks," I said to Mom as I slipped the shoes on my feet. I glanced at my reflection in the mirror inside Mom's closet door and smiled. The outfit didn't exactly scream, "Kiss me, baby," but still I was pleased with what I saw: me.

I went into Mom's bathroom, smoothed some of her vanilla-flavored lip gloss on my lips, and put the tube in my pocket. Mom smiled at my klepto-like action. Half the stuff in my possession was snagged from my parents' house in a similar fashion.

"I'm really leaving now," I told Mom as I gave her a hug.

"Have a nice time," Mom said.

"I will."

I definitely will.

Isaac didn't see me come in.

So I crept up behind him, put one hand over his eyes and slipped my other arm around his shoulders affectionately.

"You better be who I think you are," Isaac said, feigning a tone of warning.

I uncovered his eyes and smiled sweetly at him. "Hi."

"Hi," Isaac echoed. "I like your shoes." He glanced down at the red flip-flops I was wearing. "You have cute feet."

"Thanks," I responded, wiggling my toes.

"You have cute everything," Isaac said. Then he pulled me into a hug and kissed me on the cheek softly. In front of everyone.

After the kiss, Isaac stared at me as if he were surprised at what he had just done, and I gazed up at him with a stunned, I'm-having-trouble-breathing expression on my face. I then looked around the room, expecting everyone's mouths to be dropped open at this momentous occasion.

But all the people in the elegant room had continued going about their duties—some draping red-silk cloth onto the tables, some setting out white rose floral arrangements, and others tying red bows onto the white chairs.

Didn't they realize what had just happened? Isaac had just kissed me—granted, not a mouth kiss, but I was sure he was just saving that for later—in public. And according to an article on relationships in a leading psychology research journal, that meant things were getting serious. Okay, so it was an article in *FAB* magazine, but still.

Isaac and I were exchanging shameless looks of flirtation when Ethan came up beside us. "Hey, guys," he said in a light tone that let me know that he, like everyone else, had missed the kiss. "Did you ever find the piano mike?" Ethan asked Isaac.

"I was just going to look for it," Isaac replied. Then he said to me, "I'll be right back," and turned to go.

"But what should I do in the meantime?" I asked.

Isaac looked at Ethan. "What still needs to be done?"

"You can help Jacqueline and Amber with the napkins," Ethan said. He pointed to a table where the two ladies were about to sit down, their arms loaded with white linen napkins.

"Okay."

"I'll be as fast as I can," Isaac said before he dashed away.

"So are you coming to the recital?" Ethan asked me.

"I sure am." I looked around the elegant room. "This is really gorgeous. All my piano recitals were in old VFW halls."

"You play?" Ethan asked me, sounding interested.

I shook my head regretfully. "I haven't played in years." I sighed and redirected the conversation. "You know, it's really great what you do for the kids, and for their families."

"They do more for me than I do for them," Ethan said poignantly.

I smiled a knowing smile. "Isn't it interesting the way that happens?"

"It is," Ethan agreed. "Well, I'd better get back to work. I'll see you."

"See ya."

The moment Ethan left I heard a small voice calling out, "Hey, Isaac's friend!"

I turned around and saw Angel zipping toward me in his motorized wheelchair. "Hey," I greeted the boy.

"Are you gonna watch me play tonight?" Angel asked, his eyes shining.

"You did invite me," I said.

Angel smiled shyly. "Um, I gotta go help my grandpa. I just wanted to say hi. Bye."

"Good-bye."

With a little wave in Angel's direction, I walked over to the table where Jacqueline and Amber were sitting. "Hi," I said with a bright smile as I took a seat across from the pair. "I've been sent to help with the napkins."

"Hi," the two said in unison.

"Have you folded napkins before?" Jacqueline asked me.

"Like in half?"

"No. Like this." Jacqueline placed a napkin that had been folded into a swan in front of me.

"Not quite," I said.

"That's all right. I'll show you how to do it," Jacqueline said.

"Don't worry, it's not that hard," Amber assured me with a sweet smile forming on her gloss-smothered lips.

"All right," I responded slowly.

I watched closely as Jacqueline demonstrated how to fold the napkin. It started out simple enough—a few triangles here, a basic fold there. Then suddenly it took a terrible turn. Octagons, hexagons, and other gons I don't know the names of took the place of the triangles. And flippy-inside-outy folds were being used instead of the basic ones.

"Are you getting all that?" Amber asked, probably sensing my distress.

"Not really. I don't get how . . ."

"I'm almost finished," Jacqueline said.

My mind became a muddle of geometrical complexities as I continued to watch Jacqueline's fingers move about capably. Then, when I was sure no earthy shape could be made out of all of the madness, Jacqueline set a perfect swan on the table.

What in this crazy world?

"Do you want to try one?" Jacqueline asked.

I bit my lip and willed my brain to give me a photographic memory. *Just this once, please brain. I've taken care of you over the years. I've never played any contact sports. I've eaten my leafy greens. I've read every book on my summer reading lists.*

But no such luck. I couldn't remember a thing. My brain completely let me down.

Just for that, no spinach for a month, I scolded my brain.

"Would you like to try?" Jacqueline repeated.

"Sure," I answered hesitantly. "I think maybe I can do it."

You big huge liar, my brain said.

But since my brain and I weren't on the best of terms at that moment, I ignored it. Plus, I figured I could do it. I could just follow Jacqueline's lead. I was sure I could get it by watching a couple more times.

Jacqueline, however, had other ideas in mind. "Good," she said, rising from her seat. "I have some flower arrangements to set out." She started to walk away.

"I lied," I blurted out. "I have no idea how to do it."

Jacqueline smiled. "It took me a while to learn how to do it too," she said. "You can watch Amber fold some more. If you can fold some, that is great. But if you cannot, that is fine too."

"Okay," I said, grateful for the kindness Jacqueline had shown me from the moment we met my first day at La Bonne Violette.

"I have something for you," Amber said after Jacqueline had gone.

"What? For me?"

Amber reached beneath the table and retrieved a small handbag. "I didn't know when I would see you here again, so I've just been carrying it around with me." Amber pulled a still-in-the-package tube of Foxy Glossy lip gloss from her bag and handed it to me. "This is for you," she said.

My mouth opened in surprise. "You are the sweetest thing!" I ripped into the package and swiped some of the gloss onto my lips. "Thank you so much!" I got up from my seat and went over to hug Amber. Her light-filled eyes sparkled.

"I bought it with the money I got from helping Mom on Wednesday."

"I can't believe you spent your hard earned money on me," I said.

"I like to be able to buy things for people. When I lived with my . . . with my birth mom I used to earn money babysitting. I hid the money in my room, but she always found it and took it to buy . . . not good stuff." Amber's bright eyes turned momentarily sad.

I sat silently, not sure how to reply.

"I guess we should start folding," Amber said, changing the subject quickly.

"Okay," I said.

I turned my attention to the napkins on the table and picked one up. I watched Amber's hands as I folded my first swan. When I was finished, I held up my swan and compared it to the one Jacqueline had folded, which was sitting on the table. Not even close. While the other napkin was undoubtedly in the shape of a swan, mine resembled an anteater that had grown a set of bat wings.

Amber looked at my creation and tried not to giggle.

"That was just a practice one," I said, quickly unfolding the anteater.

Moments later I looked at my second swan attempt. A little better. At least it looked like a bird. Kind of like a turkey. Why did it need to be a swan anyway? I mean, the turkey is a nice bird.

"How are you two getting along?" Jacqueline's accented voice came from behind me.

"Fine," I muttered, hiding my turkey among the collection of swans that Amber had successfully folded.

"Amber, Ethan was wondering if you want to go test out the piano," Jacqueline said.

"Of course!" Amber exclaimed.

"Amber plays the piano and sings in the school choir," Jacqueline said as she took a seat at the table.

"Really?" I asked, impressed. I pushed the unfolded napkins away from me. There really was no point in folding anymore. But if anyone needs some turkey napkins, call me, I'm your girl.

Amber blushed slightly at Jacqueline's comment.

"She has a solo in one of the songs for the end of the year concert," Jacqueline said.

"What song are you singing?" I asked.

"'This Little Light of Mine.'"

"No way! I love that song. It's one of my top-ten, make that top-five, favorites."

"Maybe you could come to the concert," Amber suggested.

"Maybe I'll just have to," I replied with a smile.

Amber stood up from the table. "See you later, Annabelle,"

she said. Then she hurried off to test the piano.

"She's such a sweet girl, Jacqueline," I said once Amber had gone.

"She really is. And she has had such a difficult life."

"So is she . . . is she your adopted daughter?" I asked carefully. I turned my head toward the piano when I heard Amber begin to play a Chopin piece. A piece I had tried to learn but hadn't been able to play.

"We haven't officially adopted her, but to us she is our daughter. Her mother, Holly, was my cousin. She left home at sixteen and became involved in some terrible things. She turned around for a while after Amber was born, but it did not last long. From the time Amber was six years old, Holly would drop her off at my house for long periods of time. Amber started calling me 'Mom' and my husband 'Dad' when she was seven."

Jacqueline paused for a moment, and I pondered how difficult that must have been for Amber.

Jacqueline continued. "Then Holly ended her own life two years ago, and my husband and I took Amber in permanently. She's been such a joy." A far-off look came over Jacqueline's face. "We never had children of our own."

"She's a very sweet girl," I said, rubbing my Foxy Glossy covered lips together.

"Yes," Jacqueline said softly. "She is very special. So, how did you fare with the napkins?"

"Not so great," I admitted. "I think I did more harm than good." I picked up my turkey and showed it to Jacqueline.

"It looks good to me," I heard Isaac's voice say behind me.

I turned around to face him. "Thanks," I said.

"Are you willing to spare her?" Isaac asked Jacqueline.

"She probably wants to get rid of me," I quipped. "I wasn't much help."

"Of course I don't want to get rid of you. But I see that this handsome young man wants some of your time, so I am willing to share."

I smiled at Jacqueline as I got up from my chair and stood next to Isaac. I noticed that he was holding a camera in his right hand.

"The recital is set to start in about fifteen minutes," he said. "I was wondering if you could come into the kitchen and help me bring out the food."

"Yes, I can. But just understand that Jean-Pierre's kitchen and I don't get along very well."

Isaac grinned. "I'll take my chances."

"Are you going to take photos of the recital?" I asked, glancing at the camera.

"I sure am," Isaac replied. He quickly snapped a picture of Jacqueline who was folding the last of the napkins. Jacqueline wagged a finger of reprimand at him.

"Okay. Do you mind if I meet you in the kitchen in a minute or two?" I asked. "I just have to do something really quick."

"That's fine," Isaac answered, looking at me like I was the most beautiful thing he had ever seen. The look made me feel terribly feverish. "See you."

"See you," I echoed.

I found a quiet, empty corner outside of the Rouge Room where I retrieved my Pink Notes from my bag and began writing.

Pink Note # 127
Name: Jacqueline
Why she's noteworthy: Jacqueline sees people who are in need and kindly goes about trying to help those people. She has done this for me as I've gone crazy trying to write an article on La Bonne Violette. But probably the best example is the fact that she took in her cousin's daughter and loves her as her own.

Pink Note # 128
Name: Amber
Why she's noteworthy: Amber has had a life that

> would leave many people lost and confused, or even hard and angry. But there is a light in her eyes, a brightness in her smile, which reminds me that there is something divine in each of us that allows us to rise above our circumstances and become the people God knows we can be. Plus, she gave me Foxy Glossy lip gloss!

Now if only I could get notes this good for my article, I thought as I left the banquet room and went to search for Isaac.

Chapter 15

"You're not peeking are you?" Isaac asked.

"How do you expect me to peek?" I fiddled with the blindfold that Isaac had secured over my eyes.

Of course, I didn't need to peek to know where we were. I could feel the sand between my toes. I could hear the sound of the waves and the seagulls in the distance. I could feel the wind, which was so cool that I pulled the sleeves of the sweatshirt Isaac had lent me over my hands.

Isaac held onto me, guiding my path until he declared, "Here we are," and removed the blindfold.

A huge smile formed on my lips as I took in the sight. Isaac had laid a large blanket on the shores of Marina State Beach. On top of the blanket sat a bouquet of tulips in a silver pail and a Coleman lantern, which supplemented the light of the fading sun. A large picnic basket was placed across from the tulips and lantern, helping to keep the blanket from blowing away in the wind.

"It's perfect," I said to Isaac as I hugged him. "But you've been with me at the recital, how did you . . . ?"

"Carrie helped me." Isaac held onto my hand as I sat down on the blanket and then took a seat across from me.

"Seriously?" I looked around, trying to spot Carrie ducking

behind a piece of driftwood, but she was nowhere to be seen. In fact, Isaac and I were the only ones on the beach except for a couple jogging along the water in the distance.

"She helped me with everything. Including traveling to Salinas to get our dinner." Isaac reached into the picnic basket and retrieved a white bag I immediately recognized. That bright yellow arrow. Those gorgeous red letters. An In-N-Out burger bag!

With a smile, Isaac opened the bag and placed a cheeseburger, an order of fries, and a strawberry shake in front of me. And even though I hadn't quite kept my word about saving room in my stomach and had sampled nearly every one of the delicious treats at the recital, everyone knows there's always room for In-N-Out. I took a bite of the burger, then a drink of the shake, then added a fry to my mouth. The tastes danced together on top of my tongue. It was pure heaven.

Isaac and I chatted as we enjoyed our food. Then, when the last bite was gone, Isaac looked at me. "I have something else for you," he said. He reached into the picnic basket and pulled out a package wrapped in silver paper. He placed the package in my hands gently. "This is for you."

Carefully, I peeled back the wrapping paper. Inside, I found a leather-bound album. I opened the cover of the album and nearly gasped at the beauty of what I saw: a breathtaking black and white photograph of the ocean.

"It was taken from nearly the exact same spot we're sitting in," Isaac told me.

I looked up from the photo and was carried away in the feeling of being in the very spot it was taken. "It's incredible. I can't believe you did this for me."

"Remember the bet we made on Cannery Row? You said this is what you wanted if you won, so I just had to give it to you."

"Even though I lost the bet?"

"Yeah, even though you lost," Isaac said, chuckling. Then he gestured toward the album. "There's more."

Slowly, carefully, I turned to the pages of the album, each featuring a beautiful black and white picture of the natural wonders of the Monterey Bay and Monterey Peninsula. Pictures of the rocky shores of Point Lobos. Photos of Pebble Beach. Shots of smiling children playing on the shores of Carmel Beach.

"Isaac, these are incredible," I whispered, deeply moved by the gift. It was at that moment that I knew what I had to do.

Gently I closed the album and placed it beside me on the blanket. Then I reached into my handbag and retrieved my Pink Notes. I held them tightly in my hand and spoke to Isaac. "I . . . I've never shown this book to anyone besides my family and Carrie, who is practically family. In fact, the thought of showing it to anyone completely scares me. But for the first time in my life, I want to show it to someone. I want to show it to you."

I began to hand Isaac the notebook, but immediately pulled it back again. "Please don't laugh. I know it may seem silly. But this book means a lot to me." With slightly shaking hands, I gave Isaac the notebook.

Isaac carefully opened the book and began reading. He flipped to my last entries and read what I had written about Ethan, Angel, Jacqueline, and Amber. I held my breath as I watched him, feeling like I had just handed him my beating heart.

Finally, Isaac spoke. "It's like a collection of word portraits," he said. "You write about the good in people so you can look back and remember."

I blinked a few times, staring at Isaac. "So you don't . . . you don't think it's dumb?"

"Dumb? It's amazing. Seeing the good in people and letting it inspire you is nothing close to dumb." Isaac paused for a moment. "This book is so . . . you. It captures the essence of who you are. A kind, caring, incredible woman. Annabelle, I . . ." Isaac began leaning close to me, and I felt my breath become shallow and my heart begin to beat faster.

This is it, I thought. *Our kiss is finally going to happen.*

"I have to ask you something," Isaac said. His tone made it sound almost as if he hadn't planned on saying the words. He slowly moved away from me.

Okay, so our kiss is going to happen after the question then.

"What's up with you and that Patrique guy?"

"What do you mean what's up with me and him?"

"Well, I know that he's Jean-Pierre's nephew and that Jean-Pierre wanted you to go to art shows with him. But is that all?"

"Of course that's all," I said, wondering how in the world Isaac could think otherwise. I mean, he'd met Patrique. How could there be any question?

"It's just that he seems so . . ."

"Creepy," I offered.

"Well, yeah. But the thing is . . . I saw him hug you at the art festival yesterday."

Oh. I was really hoping Isaac hadn't seen that.

"Isaac," I began, "I didn't know that was coming. I didn't invite it. Patrique is just a creep. He has no respect for anyone. And I pushed him away. That's how Arnie got knocked over. Did you see me push him away?"

"I saw it. But what I'm wondering is why he felt comfortable enough to hug you? And on Cannery Row he called you 'lovely' or something like that. If nothing's going on, why is he acting like that?"

"He's crazy!" I insisted.

"Did you know I was there?" Isaac asked.

"Did I know you were where?"

"At the art festival. Did you know I was there?"

I gulped. "Um, yeah, I had seen you a little while earlier. I was . . . I just . . . you were busy talking to Rona and then you were talking to that man in the olive-green suit, and so I just waited to come say hi."

"So it wasn't that you were avoiding me because you and

Patrique were on more than just a work-related outing?"

"Of course not! Isaac, I promise." I couldn't help laughing. "If you knew how much I detest Patrique we wouldn't even be having this conversation."

"I'm sorry," Isaac said. "I believe you. I just needed to make sure because I'm . . ."

"Because you're what?" I asked anxiously.

"Because I'm absolutely crazy about you," Isaac said in a deeper-than-usual voice.

"I'm a little crazy too," I confessed. "I mean about you," I clarified with a laugh.

An affectionate grin formed on Isaac's lips, and I knew it was going to happen. Our kiss.

My heart pounded as Isaac moved close to me and took my face gently into his hands. I couldn't breathe as he moved his lips close to mine, and closer still. Finally, our lips touched softly and I suddenly felt an incredible warm sensation pass over my entire body, like warm honey was being smoothed onto my limbs. The kiss was sweet and meaningful, like a promise, and lasted only a moment.

A perfect, beautiful moment.

That night, before I knelt at my bedside to pray, I did something I had never done before. I made a Pink Notes entry on a guy who I cared about in more than just a friendly way.

Pink Note #129
Name: Isaac Matthews
Why he's noteworthy: He is everything wonderful that a man can be. And interestingly, being around him makes me want to be everything wonderful that I can be. I think I'm falling in love with him.

As I wrote the last sentence, the craziest feeling took over my body. I traced the words with my finger, feeling the warmth of their meaning wash over me. It was true. I was falling in love with Isaac.

Okay, one more time, just so I can hear myself say it: I was falling in love with Isaac.

Chapter 16

"Just a minute," I called out toward the front door of my condo. I quickly headed to the gas grill I had set up on the balcony and flipped the barbecue ribs over one last time.

It was six o'clock Saturday evening, and I was making Isaac a special dinner. I had asked him what his favorite food was and without hesitation he had replied "barbecued ribs." So I had called Dad, who is a barbecuing genius, and asked him for step-by-step instructions for ribs. He not only gave me his rib secrets, but also let me use his homemade barbecue sauce and prized grill.

With the ribs flipped, I made my way to the front door.

"You're early," I said with a smile as I swung the door open, not bothering to check the peephole.

"I am?" the person at the door said. The person who was Patrique.

"What in the world are you doing here?" I glared at Patrique and saw that he was holding a bouquet of violets—probably stolen from La Bonne Violette—and a slightly large painting that looked like it was still wet.

"Aren't you going to invite me in?" Patrique asked, stepping inside my apartment without being invited. He kicked the door closed behind him.

"You have to go," I said briskly. "I'm expecting company." *And disaster could strike if Isaac finds you here.*

"I can see that," Patrique said as he looked at the long candles burning on the dining room table.

"What do you want?" I asked Patrique, my words rushed.

"I wanted to give these to you." Patrique handed the flowers to me.

I didn't move my hands forward to accept the flowers. Instead I said, "You really should be giving those to Tempest, not me."

"Actually, that's why I'm here." Patrique took off his jacket and draped it on the back of my couch. He set the violets on the coffee table, carefully propped the painting against the table, and sat down on the couch.

"Listen, Patrique," I said, "whatever you want to talk about, it's going to have to wait until Monday."

"It can't wait until Monday," Patrique said. "Please sit down. I have something to show you."

"I'm not sitting down. And you are not staying." I looked at the front door and then at the clock. Isaac would be arriving any minute.

Patrique stood up from the couch and I relaxed a bit, thinking that perhaps he was going to leave. But he had other plans. He picked up his painting and walked toward the wall where I had hung three of Isaac's photos the night before.

After our wonderful night at the beach, at my insistence, Isaac had driven me to MainFrame where I had bought some gorgeous frames. Isaac had then helped me nail the photos to the wall in my condo, kissing me softly on the cheek after each one had been hung.

Patrique took down the photo of the children playing on Carmel Beach and hung up the painting in its place.

"What are you doing?!" I shouted. I took the painting down, shoved it into Patrique's hands, and put my beautiful photograph back on the wall.

"I'm hanging up your painting. And be careful, it's still a

little wet." Patrique looked at the painting admiringly, almost adoringly.

I glanced at the painting, finding it hard to decipher what it was. I had just decided it looked an awful lot like a horse head when Patrique said, "It's you."

"What?" I asked, staring at the portrait. I didn't look like that. Did I? I suddenly had a very strong urge to find a mirror just to make sure I hadn't taken on the look of horse without knowing it. "It's great and all Patrique, but I liked what I had on the wall."

"Those are poor excuses for photos. This is real art!" Patrique removed the photo once again and hung the painting on the wall.

"Take that down, and leave!" I ordered.

Just then a knock sounded at the door. I froze in place, moving my eyes from Patrique to the door and back to Patrique, trying to figure out what to do.

Just open the door and let Isaac inside. You aren't doing anything wrong, my brain instructed.

But obviously Patrique is a sore spot with Isaac—what if he thinks something? I argued with my brain.

The knocks repeated.

"Aren't you going to answer that?" Patrique asked in a horrifically loud voice. I threw my finger to my lips in a "shush" gesture. Why was he screaming all of a sudden?

"Do you know anything about ribs?" I asked Patrique quietly, desperately.

"What?"

"Ribs," I repeated as I pushed Patrique toward the balcony. "I was hoping you could tell if they were done. You know, since you know so much about food and all."

"Well, I do know a few things . . ." Patrique began.

But before he could finish I quickly led—well, more like shoved—him onto the balcony and said, "Could you turn off the grill too?" Then I quietly yet swiftly pushed the sliding glass door shut.

I had about thirty seconds to find a way to make sure Isaac didn't find out that Patrique had been in my apartment giving me flowers and a painting in which I looked like a horse. It just wasn't worth the risk. It was better that he didn't know.

I exhaled quickly and scurried to the front door. "Hi," I said, stepping onto the concrete steps outside my condo and closing the door behind me.

"I know I'm early, but I couldn't wait." Isaac handed me a cellophane bag full of chocolate-covered gummy bears and gave me a kiss on the cheek.

"Thank you," I said with a smile as I took the bag. Then, without missing a beat, I added, "So, I was thinking we could go out to dinner."

Isaac smiled. "Dinner didn't quite work out the way you hoped?"

"Yeah," I replied, justifying the statement by telling myself that it was technically true.

"So, I was thinking Italian," I said. I grabbed onto Isaac's arm and lead him down the five concrete steps and onto the sidewalk, hoping he wouldn't notice I was wearing a pair of green frog slippers and not proper shoes.

But he did notice. He stopped walking and looked down at my feet. "You know that I think you're adorable no matter what, but are you really going to wear your slippers to a restaurant?"

"Sure. Why not?" I resumed walking, leading Isaac a few feet down the sidewalk.

"What's going on?" Isaac asked, stopping yet again.

"N-nothing," I stammered. "I just really want to get Italian food." As soon as the words escaped my lips, I felt horrible about not being completely honest with Isaac. So horrible that I almost considered telling him everything. But then I remembered the look on Isaac's face, the sound in his voice when he had been asking me about Patrique the night before, and I lost my nerve.

"I don't even think you locked the door," Isaac said. Then,

before I could stop him, he began moving quickly back toward my condo.

I tried to follow after him, but my frog slipper jumped off my right foot, and nearly killed me. Finally, I got the thing back on and ran like a crazy person up to Isaac.

I reached the front door just as Isaac opened it. "See, you didn't lock it, sweetie," he said.

"Oh, yeah, I guess I didn't," I responded, reaching for the door. Quickly, I tried to close it.

But it was too late.

Inside the condo, Patrique was emerging from the balcony, casually saying, "They look good Annabelle."

"What's he doing here?" Isaac demanded, glaring at Patrique.

Patrique halted just inside the sliding glass doorway and returned Isaac's glare. "What are you doing here?" he asked Isaac with a territorial sound in his voice that infuriated me.

I pulled Isaac outside, slamming the door shut behind me. "Isaac . . . I didn't . . . he just . . ."

"Is this why you wanted to leave? Did I come too early and interrupt something?" Isaac gazed at me, the look in his eyes a mixture of confusion and anger.

"No, you didn't interrupt anything. Patrique came over unannounced and . . ."

"He came over for what?"

"To bring me something," I answered vaguely.

"To bring her the painting," Patrique declared, swinging the door open. He made it sound like I had requested the thing.

"Patrique, please!" I snapped. I grabbed the door and attempted to close him inside again.

"What painting?" Isaac asked, his voice strained.

"It doesn't matter," I said.

"Doesn't matter!" Patrique shouted, flinging the door open widely. "That's not how you were acting on Thursday!"

Patrique's statement caught me by total surprise, and I

was too shocked to come up with a rebuttal.

"Thursday," Isaac repeated. Then the look in his eyes seemed to change from confusion to understanding, as if he had just figured out the last word in a crossword puzzle. With an injured expression on his face, he shook his head gently.

"Patrique, get out of my house and leave!" I hollered when I found my voice.

Patrique opened his mouth to reply, but it was Isaac's voice that I heard. "No, I'll leave."

Isaac stepped down one step and I grabbed onto his arm. "Please don't go," I pleaded, a suffocating panic filling my chest.

"Let go, Annabelle," he said icily, pulling his arm out of my grip.

"Isaac, don't go," I repeated.

"I have to," Isaac said. There was a finality in his voice that terrified me.

Isaac quickly descended the stairs and began jogging toward his Firebird, which I could see parked in the guest parking lot. I hurried down the sidewalk behind him, the pounding of my feet on the cement in sync with the pounding of my heart.

I caught up to him just as he was putting the keys in the car door. "Isaac, please just let me explain," I pleaded.

Isaac continued to unlock the car door, and it looked like he was going to get into the car and drive away. But all of a sudden he turned and faced me. "Explain what? Explain why he was there? Explain why he gave you a painting? Explain why he seems to think you reciprocate his obvious feelings? Explain why you lied about him and about what is going on between the two of you?"

"No, Isaac," I cried in a strangled voice. "I didn't lie."

Isaac looked at me and I saw a pain in his eyes that ripped my heart apart. "I believed in you. I trusted you. But you just stood outside your house and lied to me about why I couldn't go inside. I can't do this, Annabelle. Not again."

I suddenly found it hard to breathe. Like someone was holding me under water with great force. "What are you saying?" I asked, my voice nearly inaudible.

"I'm saying I can't do this. It's over."

"No," I whispered, feeling like I was going to be sick. "But I can explain. It's not what you think," my voice was rushed, panicked.

Without another word, Isaac got into the car and slammed the door shut. He then looked at me through the window, and for a minute I thought he might open the door. But he didn't. He started the ignition, gave me a move-out-of-the-way look, and sped away, squealing his tires as he pulled out of the parking lot.

An overwhelming wave of nausea overtook me, as if I had just been beaten up. I crouched down in the spot where Isaac's car had been, and hugged my knees tightly. Tears began to fall to the ground, leaving tiny dots on the pavement.

I'm not quite sure how long I stayed in that position, but after a while the sound of a car horn made me look up. An elderly couple driving a Crown Victoria wanted the parking spot I was blocking. I stood up slowly, feeling numb and dazed, and walked out of the parking space.

For the first few steps, I continued to feel numb, shell-shocked. But as I drew nearer to my condo, I felt fury welling up inside of me. My footsteps grew quicker and harder and my blood grew hot in my veins.

"You have three seconds to get out of my apartment," I said furiously when I found Patrique still in my condo, sitting on the couch eating a huge barbecued rib.

"I'm not leaving until I tell you what I came here to tell you," Patrique said.

"No, you're leaving now." I tore the rib from his hand.

"But I came here to tell you how I feel about you. It started on Thursday, when you made it look like we were a couple in front of Tempest. That made me realize how magnificent you are."

"That whole thing with Tempest was an accident!" I nearly screamed.

"It doesn't change anything. I still adore you."

"Adore me!" I shouted. "So you come here and ruin the one thing that matters the most to me in the world!"

"You'll get over that wimp. I'll help you." Patrique moved close to me, a slimy look on his barbecue-sauce smudged face.

"Get out!" I yelled. "And take your painting with you." I ripped the painting from the wall and threw it out the still-open door. I was frenzied. I was seriously a Judge Judy case waiting to happen.

"My painting!" Patrique cried as he rushed outside. Seizing the opportunity, I ran to close and lock the door. But I was not fast enough, and Patrique speedily stuck his foot inside, preventing me from closing it.

He pushed his way into my home, holding the painting and studying it thoroughly. With the painting still in his hands he got into my face, a fiery look in his eye. "You fool," he spewed. "You are so lucky the painting is not damaged."

Patrique set the painting down on the coffee table and began pacing around me in circles, like a lion circling its prey. Finally he stopped pacing and got back in my face. "Dear Annabelle," he said sardonically. "It looks like I need to remind you of something: you need me. For your article. For your friend's little party." Patrique was spitting the words at me. He smiled at me sinisterly.

Suddenly, Tempest's words came to my mind, the ones about how if Patrique didn't get what he wanted, he would try to ruin me. I hadn't put much stock into the words at the time, but now it appeared that they were right on. And I was afraid. Afraid of how much Patrique could ruin.

But just then, someone else's words came to my mind—Mom's words. Mom had told me that as long as I lived the way God wanted me to live, everything would work out for my good. And with Mom's words echoing through my mind, I knew what I had to do.

It was time for me to start acting out of integrity rather than fear when it came to my article. It was time for me to think about Carrie instead of my feelings toward Rona as I searched for a caterer. And it was time for me to be honest with Isaac, time to stop trying to show him only the things that I wanted him to see.

And if I did that, if I did what I knew was right, my article, Carrie's shower, maybe even this big misunderstanding with Isaac would work out. I didn't know how, but I knew that they would.

"No, I don't need you," I said firmly.

"Fine," Patrique spat. "Don't even bother coming to La Bonne Violette on Monday. I'll make sure my uncle doesn't even speak to you. And even if Jacqueline is your friend, she can't authorize a catering order for someone on the Do Not Serve list." Patrique then added in an evil voice, "Poor Annabelle, you lost everything that meant something to you in one day."

Finally, Patrique lifted the painting from the coffee table and walked out of the condo casually, arrogantly.

I slammed the door closed behind Patrique and locked it quickly. Then I blew out the candles on the dining room table, fell onto couch, and sobbed.

Chapter 17

I probably looked like a crazy person standing on Isaac's doorstep at eight thirty at night, frog slippers on my feet and mascara stains on my cheeks. But I didn't care. Isaac had to know what had really happened. And once he did he would take back the awful words he had said. He would tell me that it wasn't really over. Because it couldn't be over. It just couldn't.

I knocked on the door and Ethan answered. "I'm sorry, Annabelle," he said the second he saw me. "Isaac doesn't want to talk to you." It was obvious he had been instructed to send me away if I came to the house.

"Isaac!" I yelled through the cracked door. "Please, just listen to me!"

Ethan put his hand up to silence my yells. "I don't think he can hear you. Wait here just a minute."

Ethan turned around to go into the house. He left the door cracked open a bit, and I was tempted to enter without permission, but I didn't want to make things any worse than I had already managed to make them. I strained to hear any sounds from inside the house. I couldn't hear a thing.

Ethan returned to the door with a regretful look on his face. "He said he wants you to go away."

"Please Ethan, just let me inside. If he'll just listen to me then—"

"I don't think that's going to happen," Ethan explained.

"Isaac!" I yelled into the house again. "I'm not leaving until you talk to me!"

"I'm sorry. He's not going to come. I'm sorry." Ethan looked pained as he slowly closed the door on me.

I stood on the doorstep feeling stunned for I don't know how long. Then I slowly began to walk back to my car.

I stopped short when I heard something. It sounded like a bouncing ball, and it was coming from Isaac's backyard. Quietly, I crept along the side of the house, hiding myself behind some bushes as I moved in the direction of the sound.

And then I saw Isaac.

He was on the basketball court in the backyard, still dressed in the nice slacks and button-down shirt he had been wearing when he had come to my condo. My heart ached as I watched him furiously dribble the basketball and then make equally furious shots. With each shot, the ball swished cleanly through the net.

I came out from the side of the house, revealing myself to Isaac as I walked closer to him. "I heard you back here," I said, attempting a neutral greeting.

Isaac continued dribbling and shooting without saying a word to me. He shot a basket that bounced off the backboard and flew behind him. He tried to jump and catch it, but it was too high. It bounced a few feet in front of me and finally rolled toward my feet.

I stepped on the ball with the toe of my slipper. "Please talk to me."

Isaac wordlessly walked over to me. He bent down to retrieve the ball, but I pushed my foot downward, making the retrieval difficult.

"Can I have my basketball, please?" he asked harshly.

"Yes, if you'll talk to me."

"Okay, I'll talk to you. Please get off my property. There, I talked."

Isaac grabbed the ball from beneath my foot, sending me teetering. He then dribbled the ball toward the hoop, shot, and missed. The ball bounced off the rim, and Isaac caught it. He moved to the free-throw line and got ready to make his next shot.

"I can't leave, Isaac," I said. "This can't be it. I can explain everything if you'll just listen to me."

Isaac turned his head slightly, and looked at me. "Listen to more lies?" His voice was like ice—the kind that's so cold it stings.

He looked away from me and shot the basketball angrily. He missed. We both watched as the ball bounced off the court and onto the backyard grass.

I walked onto the court and stood in front of Isaac. I looked into his eyes pleadingly. "Isaac, this is all just a big misunderstanding," I said.

"So I misunderstood that you lied to me so I wouldn't go into your condo and find Patrique there?"

"No, but—"

"I don't want to hear it," Isaac cut me off.

"So you're just going to leave things like this because you're too stubborn to listen to me?"

"Stubborn?" Isaac said incredulously. "You think I'm being stubborn because I expect you to be honest with me? You have problems, Annabelle."

Isaac's words were like darts. He had once been so tender and kind, but now he was cold and callous. I had thought that maybe he loved me like I loved him, but the anger in his voice and his demeanor let me know he never had.

I stood silently for a moment and watched as Isaac moved away from me and continued to shoot baskets as if I weren't even there.

The sound of Ethan's voice broke the silence. "Isaac, Rona's here," he said cautiously.

Isaac told his brother that he would be inside in a minute and Ethan nodded and went back into the house.

"I see you didn't waste any time," I said bitterly.

Isaac didn't say anything.

"All right, I'll go," I said. "You know, Isaac, all this time I've been thinking that you're pretty much perfect. I've been wondering when I would find a flaw. Well I guess I've found one. . . . You don't care about me enough to believe in me. You say that I lied to you, but you know what, Isaac? You're the one that lied to me, when you said you cared."

Isaac looked at me and with everything in me I yearned for him to say something, to do something that would tell me that I was wrong, that he did care.

But all he did was say, "Good-bye, Annabelle," and turn around and walk away.

I was sitting on my couch at home, pretending to watch television, but really staring off into space, when my home phone rang.

"Hello," I said into the receiver. "Isaac?"

"No, it's Mom."

"Hi, Mom," I said, forcing myself to sit up, and trying to sound upbeat. I noticed that it had grown dark outside, but I didn't bother to flick on a light. I sat in the darkness.

"Annabelle, are you okay?" Mom asked slowly, knowingly.

"He doesn't love me back," I said.

"Oh, honey," Mom said, sounding as if her heart were breaking right along with mine. "What happened?"

"I made ribs for Isaac with Dad's stuff. Gorgeous ribs that smelled so good . . ."

Tearfully, I told Mom the rest of the story, trying to deal with the pain by purging myself of the words that Isaac had spoken and the images that were in my mind.

When I was finished recounting the horrid details, I wiped my face on the sleeve of my powder blue shirt, leaving traces of makeup and tear-juices on the fabric. Then, sounding like a small child I whimpered, "Mommy, will you take care of me?"

"I'll be there in fifteen minutes," Mom said, and the line went dead.

I spent Saturday night sitting on the couch, dressed in an old New Kids on the Block t-shirt and a pair of grungy sweats, watching a box set of *I Love Lucy* episodes that Mom had brought over. Mom sat next to me on the couch, laughing at the funny parts. But I couldn't laugh. Not even during the episode where Lucy tries to speak Spanish to Ricky's mom.

I finally moved from my spot on the couch, which by then had a permanent indentation in the shape of me on it, to ride with my parents to their church meetings on Sunday at two o'clock. I went with them because I knew I couldn't handle singles ward. I could only imagine that Rona would be all over Isaac, fighting off all the other girls who surely knew that our brief courtship had not lasted.

After church, I felt slightly better, as if the Spirit had begun to wash away the darkness. But still, I was not quite up to Sunday dinner and asked Mom to drop me off at my condo.

Silently, Mom drove me back home. Then, after she had made me enough of her famous chicken soup—using ingredients I didn't know I had in my kitchen—to last me a week, she moved toward the front door to leave. I walked with her.

With her hand on the doorknob, Mom asked, "You're sure you'll be all right?"

"I'll be fine. I have to be. And even if I can't be fine on my own, the Lord will help me." I felt a warming feeling inside as I said the words.

Mom squeezed me tightly before leaving. "Call if you need anything," she said about fifteen times.

I thanked her for everything and said good-bye.

Seconds after Mom left, my home phone rang. It was the first call since Mom had called the night before, and I dared to dream that it was Isaac. I rushed to the phone and with a pounding heart I pushed Talk.

"Hello?" I answered hopefully.

"Why weren't you at church today?" It was Carrie.

I released a breath and moved into my bedroom, where I plopped on my bed, which Mom had slept in the night before since I had refused to leave the couch. The bed linens smelled like Mom's fragrance, and I breathed in the comforting smell. "Isaac and I . . . we . . . I think it's over," I said weakly. "So I went to my parents' ward."

Carrie was silent for a moment. "Do you want to talk about it?" she asked, her voice filled with love and consideration.

I gave Carrie the short version of what had happened.

"Maybe he just needs some time," Carrie said.

"Thanks," I said. "Anyway, how was church?"

"Good. Arvin, that guy from your work, he gave a talk. He compared life to surfing."

"Oh, that sounds interesting," I said hollowly. I then found myself desperately fighting the urge to ask about Isaac. Was he at church? Where did he sit? Who did he sit with? How did he look? Did it seem like he had been crying?

"How about I come over and we play a game and eat ice cream," Carrie suggested. "I'll even try that Cold Stone stuff you've got in your freezer that you keep telling me is so good."

"I think I'm just going to go to bed," I said.

"It's not even six o'clock."

"I know, but I'm just so tired." I yawned a wide, loud yawn.

"Call me if you need anything," Carrie instructed. "Anything at all."

"I will. But I'm going to be fine. I'm going to get through this, with the Lord's help."

Carrie sighed. "Well, get a good night's sleep. And call me."

"Okay. Love ya."

Carrie and I ended our conversation, and I sat on my bed with the phone in my hand. My thoughts turned to what I had told Mom before she left. And what I had said to Carrie. I had said that the Lord would help me. But had I asked Him to?

Instantly, I slid off the bed and fell to my knees, resting my hands on top of my bed. I prayed aloud, pouring my heart out, tears falling down my cheeks as the words fell from my lips. I asked for forgiveness for my shortcomings. I asked for help with everything that was going on in my life. And I thanked my Heavenly Father for blessing me with Isaac, even if only for a short time, because I knew I was better for having known him.

Then I told God my desire for Isaac to find out the truth about what had happened and for us to work things out, but assured Him that I would accept His will.

I ended the prayer and waited. I don't really know what I waited for. Well, in all honesty I think I was waiting for Isaac to call. But no call came. Something else did.

I was suddenly overcome by the feeling that someone had wiped the clouds out of my mind and replaced them with warm sunlight. And I knew that things were going to be okay.

Overcome with the wonderful feeling, I took a long, hot shower and dressed in a clean, pretty pair of silky pajamas, snuggled into my bed, and slept peacefully.

Chapter 18

"Listen, Jean-Pierre, I don't care what Patrique told you. You assured me that if I attended two art functions with Patrique you would grant me this interview. It was a contract. I kept my end, and now you have to keep yours. In fact, a friend of mine, who is an attorney in New York City, has informed me that a verbal agreement between a journalist and an interviewee is a legal one. So with that said, shall we begin the interview?"

Pretty good speech, huh? I thought so. I particularly like the part about my lawyer friend, who, just between you and me, is a character in a mystery novel I read about a month ago. I mean, hey, a character in a book can definitely be considered a friend.

I was practicing this speech in my head as I weaved through La Bonne Violette's kitchen at nine o'clock on Monday morning. The plan was to find Jean-Pierre, deliver my speech, and then leave the restaurant with the best interview ever.

The only problem was, after searching through the entire restaurant, I couldn't find Jean-Pierre anywhere. Maybe he hadn't arrived yet. Or maybe he was in some super-secret chef's room. I decided to ask someone.

I spotted a teenager mopping the floor in front of the

walk-in refrigerator. He was listening to a tiny MP3 player and had earphones stuck in his ears. I could hear the music he was listening to—a very bass-heavy song saying something about "bling."

"Excuse me," I hollered so I could be heard over the music.

The teen looked up from his mopping, his eyes almost completely covered by the beanie he was wearing on his head. He removed one of his earphones and looked at me. "Yeah," he grunted.

"I'm looking for Jean Pierre," I explained. "Have you seen him?"

"Who are you?" the teen asked.

"I'm Annabelle Pleasanton. I work for *Central Coast Living* magazine."

"*Central Coast Living*. I think I saw Missy Phat in there once. She looked hot. She came in here once, but I was on my lunch break. I was so mad, man. It would have been so tight to clean her table. She's hot."

"Yeah, yeah, Missy Phat's hot. But listen, I really need to talk to Jean-Pierre."

"I thought I told you not to come here," I heard a voice behind me say.

I spun around and my eyes met with Patrique's. I glared at him, trying to make myself appear fearless. "Yes, but I know Jean-Pierre is not going to refuse to do this interview simply because of the dispute between you and I." *Wow, I sounded pretty official just now.* "Jean-Pierre and I had a verbal agreement, and I'm sure he intends to keep it. Plus, it is in Jean-Pierre's best business interest to do this interview."

Patrique wasn't impressed. "Ha!" he roared. "You think my uncle cares about an insignificant local magazine. He only agreed to do the interview because he was dating Ingrid, your editor-in-chief. But he's getting tired of her."

I opened my mouth in shock. George had not told me anything about that. "I think I'd like to hear this from Jean-

Pierre," I said. Then, without another word, I began to walk away.

Patrique caught hold of my elbow and held me in place forcefully. "He's not here," he informed me in a nasty voice. "He's in Reno. And don't bother trying to get his number or anything because I called and told him that you've been replaced by another writer since yesterday you checked yourself into a drug rehab center." Patrique smiled ominously to himself. "I liked that one. My uncle said that the drugs must have been why you were so clumsy and stupid. I told him that the writer who replaced you is going a different route on the article and doesn't need an interview."

"You, you made that all up," I muttered in disbelief.

"Pretty inventive, don't you think?"

"But I'm sure if I call back and explain and . . ." I mumbled, talking mostly to myself.

"There's no point. He'll just think it's the drugs talking." Patrique laughed.

I glanced at Patrique who was looking all smug, and expected myself to be upset, sad—something. But strangely, I didn't. Instead, the peaceful feeling I had felt the night before began to swell inside of me. And I knew that somehow everything was going to be just fine.

"Well, thanks for your assistance," I said to Patrique as if I were talking to a bank teller. "Have a nice day."

Patrique stared at me, obviously angry that he hadn't affected me the way he had planned. I spun on my heels and walked toward the exit of the kitchen.

"You'll never be able to write anything decent!" Patrique called out after me. "You can't do anything right!"

I refused to react to Patrique's words and just continued to walk.

I had nearly reached the exit when someone holding a large stack of tablecloths ran into me. "Oh, I'm sorry," the tablecloth-carrier said from behind the pile of linen.

"Jacqueline?" I said, fairly certain I had recognized the voice.

"Yes, it's me."

"Here, let me help you with those," I offered.

I took a few of the tablecloths from the stack and helped Jacqueline carry them outside to one of the catering vans. As I placed my portion of the cloths into the vehicle, I saw that Amber was standing inside the van, arranging some carts.

"Are you playing hooky?" I asked, raising my eyebrows.

"It's a teacher inservice day," Amber replied. Then she looked at my pinstripe pants—a great designer pair that my older sister Cammie bought for way too much and then gave me after she had her first baby—and added, "I like your pants."

"Thank you," I said. Amber's kindness was like a warm light in the dreary awfulness of my experiences at La Bonne Violette. "You know," I added with a sigh, "you and your Mom are so sweet. If only I could write about you . . . Oh my goodness!" I exclaimed, my eyes wide. "That's it!"

Jacqueline and Amber looked at me like I was nuts, and I continued to speak what definitely appeared to be nonsense to them. "Obviously Jean-Pierre is okay with someone doing an article that doesn't revolve around an interview with him. Someone taking 'a different route' like Patrique said. So why can't I? I mean, I can still put in stuff about him and some quotes and . . . Oh man, this will be perfect. And I even have . . . oh my goodness, I even have notes, my Pink Notes! And I'm sure all those people will answer a few questions. And it's what I've always wanted to write. It will be so perfect!" I was speaking very quickly, and I didn't take a single breath until after the very last thought was out of my mouth.

"Is everything all right?" Jacqueline asked me. She sounded concerned, as if she had heard the rumor about me being on drugs and was beginning to wonder if it were true.

"Yes, everything is perfect!" I replied ecstatically, trying to catch my breath. "Listen, I have to go but, um, do you mind if I call you later? Will you be at the restaurant in say, two hours?"

"Yes," Jacqueline said, giving me a sideways glance.

"I'll talk to you later then," I said, already turning to go. I needed to get to work quickly, while I had all the ideas swimming in my mind.

"Bye, Annabelle," the two said in unison.

Then, before leaving, I hopped into the van to hug Amber, and then hopped out of the van to hug Jacqueline. "Thank you so much for being who you are," I said to them. "And if I have anything to say about it, a lot more people are going to be blessed by knowing you."

Without another word, I waved and dashed away.

I spent the rest of the day frenziedly making calls, getting interviews, and writing an article that came together like nothing I had ever written before.

You see, I had realized something while talking to Jacqueline and Amber. I had realized that during all my trips to La Bonne Violette, I thought I was getting nowhere on my article, but actually I had been discovering an incredible article-worthy story: the story of the people who were part of the restaurant.

So I took a risk. Using my Pink Notes as a jumping off point, I switched the angle of my article from the glitz and glamour of La Bonne Violette to the beauty behind all of that. The beauty in the people who worked there: Ethan and his story of perseverance, Jacqueline and Amber and their examples of family and love, even Jean-Pierre, who opened the doors of his restaurant for a piano recital where students like Angel uplifted others with their music and bright spirits.

Sure, I still included all of the important bits about the restaurant and Jean-Pierre, but to those bits I added something I felt was truly meaningful, something I thought could inspire the reader.

Before I knew it, I was sitting on my couch at home, smiling as I clicked Save on my laptop and watched as the little green light on the USB drive indicated that my article was being stored safely. Everything was finally going just right.

Well, except for one little thing.

Since I had decided to change the angle of the article, and the new angle was going to be a lot different than what I had previously discussed with the photographer, I needed to call the photographer and let him know. And, as I'm sure you remember, the photographer assigned to my article was none other than Isaac Matthews. Isaac Matthews who I hadn't seen or spoken to since the day he told me it was over.

As I thought about the prospect of calling Isaac, a whole mess of emotions swirled around inside of me. I had successfully—well, almost successfully—buried the feelings inside of me as I immersed myself in my writing. But now they were all back: hurt, longing, anger, and yes, love.

Still, although I was feeling all of those things, I had to put them aside and do my job. I had to call Isaac and let him know I had changed the article. So, I would just act as if he were any other photographer. Yes, that's what I would do.

With shaking hands, I picked up my cell phone before I could talk myself out of calling. I pushed the number three button, which was still programmed to speed dial Isaac's number.

Isaac picked up on the first ring. "Hello?"

"Uh, hi," I said in a weird voice.

"Annabelle?" Isaac said, and I thought I sensed something in his voice. It sounded almost like gentleness.

"Yes. It's Annabelle. I'm calling about the article. I just want to let you know that I have changed the angle of focus a bit. I'll email you a copy of the article so you can see the changes. Well, see ya." I moved to hang up the phone.

"My email has been down all day," Isaac said quickly.

"Okay. Do you have a fax machine?"

"No."

"All right then, I guess I'll drop it off at your house." I tried to sound professional, but inside I ached as I thought about the last time I had been at Isaac's house.

"How about I come to you?" Isaac suggested. I wondered why he didn't want me at his house. He probably took a whole bunch of photos of Rona Bircheck and had them all over the walls or something. Big, glossy photos in heart-shaped frames.

"That will be fine," I replied, still trying desperately to sound professional.

"I'll be there in about half an hour."

We hung up and I started to feel anxious at the prospect of Isaac coming over. How was it going to be to have him at my home again after what had happened? Would we talk about it? Or would we just continue to act as if nothing had ever happened between us, good or bad?

I didn't have much time to dwell on the thoughts though, since my apartment was in shambles. I hadn't had time to clean it up all week, and it showed. My New Kids on the Block t-shirt and sweats were in a not-too-pleasant-smelling heap on the couch. Half-eaten bowls of chicken soup sat unwashed in my sink and in various places around the living room.

Then there was a box I had marked "Burn" when at one point my sadness had turned to fury and I had filled the box with everything that reminded me of Isaac. Not like I would ever burn it. But making the box had been, I don't know, cathartic or something.

I wasn't sure if Isaac would even come inside, but if he did, I needed to make the place presentable. So I began printing a copy of the article and quickly started tidying up.

I had just finished stashing the Burn box into the hall closet when my cell rang. I checked the caller ID, and it was Mom.

"Hi, Mom."

"Hi, hon, how are you doing?"

"Actually I'm feeling pretty good today," I replied. "Thanks for all you've done for me lately."

"That's what I'm here for," Mom said caringly. "Do you need more chicken soup?"

I smiled. "No, I still have a little left."

"Dad and I were wondering if you were up to coming over and playing a few games for family home evening. Unless you're going to the singles ward FHE."

Yeah right, like I was going to set foot at a singles ward activity.

"That sounds nice," I replied. "But I'll be about an hour. Isaac's coming over."

"For what?" Mom asked tentatively.

"Work stuff."

"Oh," Mom said. It was obvious she wanted to ask more, but she didn't. It was like somehow she knew that I didn't want to talk about it.

"Yeah, and this place is a mess, so I better go, Mom."

We said our good-byes and I set the phone on the coffee table. I quickly went to wash the dishes in the sink and heard the phone ring again.

With wet hands I picked up the phone, after checking the caller ID. "Carrie, can I call you back?" I asked without a greeting. "Isaac's coming over, and I need to straighten up."

"Did you two—" Carrie began to ask hopefully.

"No," I cut her off quickly. "But he's still the photographer for my article. So I'm giving him a copy of my article because it changed a lot since the last time we talked about it."

"Well, call me later," Carrie instructed.

"Okay. You know, we should go to Shrimpy's on Saturday." Shrimpy's is this great seafood restaurant that Carrie and I go to sometimes. They have quite a few dishes that Carrie likes and the best lobster I've ever tasted.

"That would be great," Carrie said.

Carrie and I quickly made tentative plans to go to Shrimpy's, and the second I hung up with her, there was a knock at the door. I ran and looked through the peep hole. It was Isaac. I grabbed the printed article and went to open the door.

"Hi," Isaac said. He looked uncomfortable, and I wondered

if he too was thinking about the last time we had been on the steps outside the door.

He didn't look too eager to come into my condo, and the place was still a disaster anyway, so I didn't invite him inside. Instead, I stepped my bare feet outside and let the door close behind me.

"Hi," I said. "Here's the article."

Isaac reached out for the paper. "Thanks."

But just as Isaac's hand clutched the document, a strong gust of Monterey Bay wind tore it away from him, sending it flying to the ground. We both dove for the paper, and in the struggle to capture the flying article, we brushed shoulders. I felt a shiver at the physical contact. A slight flicker in Isaac's eye made me wonder if he had felt something too.

Isaac finally got hold of the paper and gripped it tightly. He looked at me like he was about to say something, but he remained silent.

"Well, I'll see ya," I said briskly, afraid that if he stayed a minute longer I would not be able to stop myself from crying out, "I love you Isaac, please let's work this out," which would be pointless, because it was over. Isaac had told me so, and he had meant it.

Isaac waved weakly and started to walk away.

I turned to walk into my condo, and discovered something not too great: the door was locked. I jiggled the knob, sure that I hadn't locked the door.

Just then, a vague, fuzzy recollection of Mom saying something about how she had adjusted the lock on the door so it would lock whenever the door closed, as a matter of safety, came to my mind. I hadn't been listening to her when she'd said it since I was sitting on the couch, dazedly staring down at Donnie's head on my New Kids on the Block shirt.

So now I was locked outside with no shoes on my feet and no spare key hidden in a clever little spot. I mean, I've always been afraid to hide a spare key outside. With my luck I would hide my key in the exact spot that a serial killer hides his.

I glanced to the left and saw Isaac walking down the walk. I began wiggling the knob and banging on the door as if someone were inside and would come and open it for me. Then, desperate, I threw my body against the door. Hey, I'd seen it work in cop movies. Unfortunately, though, it didn't quite work out for me.

Isaac halted on the walkway. "Having problems?" he asked.

"Nope, everything's fine here," I replied with a too-bright smile. I rubbed my shoulder.

Isaac resumed walking. "All right."

"Wait!" I hollered. "Do you maybe have a credit card or something I can use to try and open it?" Again, this idea was inspired by cop movies.

Isaac approached me, reached into his wallet, and handed me a gym membership card. I took the card and began trying to jimmy the door open. Isaac stood at the bottom of the steps, watching me try to break into my own home.

Amazingly, I got the door open in just a few minutes. "I got it!" I exclaimed when the door came open. And then I made a mental note to tell my landlord that I deserved a discount in rent since my condo was obviously terribly insecure.

"Thanks for letting me use this," I said. I went down the steps to return his gym card. I felt a pang inside as I took a quick glance at him, all gorgeous-looking and no longer mine.

I moved to hand the card to Isaac and realized that I had pretty much destroyed the thing. "Uh, sorry," I said. "I'll pay for a replacement card."

"Don't worry about it," Isaac replied.

"Oh, okay, bye." I turned to head back up the steps into my condo.

"Why did you do it?" Isaac asked seriously.

I turned to face Isaac. "It's not like I did it on purpose. It's just kind of hard to get the card in the right spot, and . . ."

"No, I'm not talking about the card," Isaac said, looking

into my eyes. "You could have told me you're seeing Patrique. You should have told me."

"I'm not seeing Patrique!" I practically yelled. "Nothing is, was, or ever could be, going on with me and that slime!"

"Then why didn't you want me to know he was here?"

I let out a long breath. "I was afraid. Afraid of what you would read into him being here. I didn't want to ruin our evening."

Isaac laughed humorlessly. "You didn't want to ruin our evening, so you lied to me?"

"Stop saying that! I didn't lie. I just knew this was going to happen. I knew you would think something was going on, and I wanted to avoid all of this craziness. So I panicked. People panic. But they should be forgiven for doing it and shouldn't be called liars."

"I really want to believe you," Isaac said, his voice suddenly soft.

"You can, Isaac," I said just as softly. "You know me."

"But it's all just kind of hard to believe," Isaac said. "It really looked like something was going on."

"Well, if we're going on appearances, then something was going on between you and Rona Bircheck," I said under my breath. I was sure there was no way Isaac heard it.

Wrong.

"Rona Bircheck?" Isaac snorted.

"Yes, Isaac," I said loudly. "Rona Bircheck. I mean, let's see, where do I begin? 'Come to dinner with me, Isaac,' 'Come to a surprise place with me, Isaac,'" I imitated Rona unflatteringly. Then, to put in one last punch, I added, "'Let me touch your arm, Isaac.'" I put my hand on Isaac's arm and felt a shiver at the touch. I moved my hand away quickly. Then I imitated Isaac, "'Okay, Rona, whatever you say.'"

"This is ridiculous," Isaac said.

But I was on a roll. "And then, the day you end things with me, 'poof' Rona appears at your house. What an interesting coincidence."

"She was returning something I left in her car," Isaac said.

"Oh, something you left in her car, huh? That doesn't sound good, Isaac. How do I know what was going on in her car? How can I believe you when you say it was all innocent? How do I know you're not ly-ing?" I sounded like I was about five years old.

"Because it's true—whether you believe it or not."

"Hmm, sounds familiar," I said snottily.

Isaac frowned. "It's different."

"Sounds the same to me."

"It's not the same, because Rona knew about our relationship, and more importantly, she respected it."

Rona Bircheck? Respected our relationship? That's a good one. Right up there with the one about the chicken crossing the road.

"There's a lot about Rona that you obviously don't know," I blurted, and soon as the words escaped my lips, I regretted them.

"So now you're talking bad about your friend?" Isaac asked, surprised.

"Forget it," I snapped.

"Fine by me," Isaac snapped back. "I don't even know why I bothered trying to talk to you. I'll see you around."

"Fine, see you around."

Isaac walked away angrily and I stood in place just as angrily, but deep down inside of me there was a tiny bit of relief. After all, "I'll see you around" was much better than "Good-bye."

Chapter 19

I nervously played with the cherry red USB drive in my hand as I waited for George to return to his office. Gidget had let me inside after informing me that George had stepped out for a moment and would be back shortly.

I was early. George had said he wanted the article at five o'clock, but the clock on the wall, which I noticed was a fancy new chrome one, said one-thirty.

Writing had helped me get my mind off Isaac, so I had spent most of the night putting the finishing touches on my article. And I really thought it had turned out well.

"Well, Pleasanton, it looks like you've beat your deadline," George's booming voice came into my ears. I heard the door close loudly behind my back.

"Yes, I've finished early." I fumbled with the plastic cap on the USB drive in my hand as I watched George take his seat and set a Coke down on the desk in front of him.

"Good. Now I don't have to spend my whole morning tomorrow making sure it's suitable to run," George said.

"It's suitable," I promised.

"Great. You know, just yesterday I was reading an article about La Bonne Violette. It was a feature piece in the newspaper."

"That's cool," I said, not sure how else to react to the information.

"Actually, it wasn't cool. It was awful. The writer did a terrible job. I thought I was reading about Peggy's Pancake House, not a world-class restaurant!" George's tone was the same one that men in black and white movies use when they say "Preposterous!"

I bit my lip. My article didn't exactly focus on the "world-class" aspect of La Bonne Violette either. Was that what George had wanted, the glitz and glamour article I had decided not to write? I began to feel like I had made a terrible mistake.

"I'm so glad you have more sense than the dimwit who wrote that article," George said. He reached forward over the desk, waiting for me to hand over the USB drive.

But I didn't move. I sat there staring at my hands, my mouth suddenly dry. "I . . . I just realized I have to . . . I have to do something with the article really fast," I stammered, sounding like I had a wad of cotton in my mouth. I stood up quickly, and headed for the door.

"Is there a problem?" George asked.

"No, no problem. I'll . . . I'll be back." I dashed out of the office and toward my cubicle, ignoring George who was calling out after me.

Inside my cubicle, I paced back and forth, covering the eight by eight space many times over.

What was I thinking, I wondered ruefully. Of course George didn't want my touchy-feely article. I was writing for *Central Coast Living*, not *Chicken Soup for the Restaurateur's Soul*. How could I have ever believed that the silly little notes from the silly pink notebook that I carried around would be of any worth in writing an article for a reputable magazine?

My mind ran away from me, conjuring up a horrible vision. In the vision, I was sitting in a conference room at *Central Coast Living* and all of my colleagues were sitting around me reading my article, laughing. George was laughing the hardest.

Wiping the vision from my mind, I plopped into my office

chair. I searched my top desk drawer until I located the black USB drive where I had stored notes and outlines for the article that I had tried to write at first. The kind of article that George was clearly expecting.

I inserted the drive into the port on the computer and got to work.

At 4:50, I knew I was in trouble.

I had managed to write something much more in line with what George wanted, but although the research and writing were decent overall, some parts of the piece consisted of ramblings mixed with lines like, "Many celebrities dine at La Bonne Violette, such as hip hop artist Missy Phat, who, according to a member of the La Bonne Violette staff, is hot."

I watched the clock change to 4:51 and realized that I had a decision to make. Did I go back to George's office and give him the touchy-feely, heart-strings-tuggy, chicken-soupy article? Or did I go in there, hand him the Missy-Phat-Is-Hot article, tell him about my struggles in writing the piece, and hope for a miracle?

I saved the Missy Phat article to the black USB drive. I then slowly set the drive down on my desk next to the red one. I looked down at the two drives, thinking of the consequences of handing George either one.

If I gave George the heart-strings-tuggy article on the red drive, he would think that again I had gotten my assignment all wrong, and it would be the French Toast Fiasco all over again. He would look at me the same way he had back then, and would tell me that I obviously wasn't made for writing.

On the other hand, if I handed in the Missy Phat article on the black drive, at least he would know that I had tried very hard to write the kind of article he expected. I would just have to admit that it had been difficult because of circumstances I couldn't control. And maybe, just maybe, he would give me an extension and I could polish the article to perfection.

I drew in a breath and made my decision. I was going to hand in the black drive. I was going to hand in Missy Phat. I clicked the cap onto the black USB drive, made a note in my planner to tell Isaac that I was going back to my original idea, and geared up to go see George.

I was reaching for the black drive when I heard someone say, "Hey," from the doorway of my cubicle. It was Patty, dressed in a revealing black outfit. There was something different about her, but I couldn't quite put my finger on it.

"Hi!" I exclaimed, motioning for Patty to come inside.

Patty perched herself atop my desk. "You will not believe the call I got from my mother this morning." Patty opened a jumbo box of Junior Mints and popped a few into her mouth. She handed me the box and I gladly poured a few of the creamy mints into my hand.

"What did she say?"

"Well, she just entered retirement so she's been a bit bored lately. So she's taken up a new hobby: signing me up for online dating services. She called to tell me that she signed me up for MatureMatch.com and that she described me as a petite blonde with a love for literature. I said to her, 'Mother, I'm not petite, I'm short, and the only literature I read is the TV Guide.'

"Just for kicks, I checked the computer this morning and I had gotten a hit from a guy named Bernie who said that since he recently got laid off from his job as a computer programmer, he now spends his time inventing. He said he just invented a contraption you put around your neck so you don't have to hold your electric toothbrush with your hand. But he can't put it on the market since it was found to pose a strangulation hazard. He asked me if I wanted to buy one anyway."

I couldn't help giggling. "Are you going to email him?"

"Maybe if his next invention can shave my legs for me," Patty said.

"I might have to start inventing stuff after George reads my article and fires me," I said pitifully.

"That's right, I heard George had you write for the

Anniversary Issue." Patty popped a Junior Mint into her mouth. "It can't be that bad."

"It is," I replied in a miserable voice. Then I brightened a bit and added, "Hey, now that you're back, maybe you could take my notes and write something."

"Don't think so. I'm still technically on sick leave."

Out of the corner of my eye I noticed the clock change to 4:59. "Well then, Patty, it's been nice working with you." I got up from my chair and slowly walked out of the cubicle. I was a few steps away when I realized I didn't have the USB drive.

I spun back around, and when I reached the doorway of the cubicle I asked Patty, who was still sitting on the desk eating Junior Mints, to hand me the USB drive on my desk.

Patty picked up the red USB drive and handed it to me.

"Thanks," I said, distracted by my pounding heart as I accepted the drive. "I'll be back in a minute."

Gidget wasn't at her desk so I knocked softly, timidly, on George's office door.

"Come on in," George bellowed.

"Hi, George, I . . . I have the article."

"You all right Pleasanton?" George asked, looking up from the mess of papers on his desk. "You practically ran out of here earlier."

"Actually, no, I'm not all right," I confessed.

George gestured toward the chair opposite his desk, and I sat down. I cleared my throat nervously about three times. "I drove all the way to the San Joaquin Valley for that Portuguese cake," I said.

"What?"

"The Portuguese cake you asked me to bring to the Anniversary Issue meeting. I drove for hours in the heat to get that cake."

"I'm not quite sure why you're telling me this," George said, sounding perplexed and slightly impatient.

"Because I want you to know that I tried. I drove in the stifling heat for that cake so I could show you that I was a serious, dedicated employee. I was hoping that you would give me another opportunity to write. And then you did." I paused before repeating, "I just want you to know that I tried."

George leaned back in his chair and laced his fingers together behind his head. "What are you getting at here, Pleasanton?"

I gently set the USB drive on the desk. "Here's my article. But I don't know what you're going to think of it. I tried, George, I really did, but in the end a whole bunch of stuff happened that made the article extremely difficult to write. I even tried to write a whole different article, but the focus was all wrong." I looked down at my hands. "I guess now you regret putting your faith in me."

George let out a long breath, obviously to calm himself. "Is there anything usable on there?" he asked, pointing to the drive.

I nodded. "A lot of it is good. It just needs some polishing. Maybe if I had a little more time—"

George cut me off. "No. Looks like I'd better do it." He picked up his Coke, took a sip, and slammed the can onto the desk in front of him. I jumped slightly. "Guess I'm getting up early tomorrow after all!" he shouted. "Why didn't you tell me you were having trouble?! I thought maybe you were when I got that email from Jean-Pierre, but you assured me you could do the assignment!" George ran his fingers through his hair, and I almost thought he was going to start pulling hair out. "I can't believe this."

"I'm so sorry," I said, feeling like I could cry.

"Why don't you just go home," George said.

"Are you . . . I mean . . . am I f-fired?" I stuttered, my voice shaky.

"I don't know yet. Take the rest of the week off." George spoke in an I-just-don't-want-to-deal-with-you-anymore tone. "I'll figure out what to do with you after I see how bad the damage is."

"I'll never try to write again, George. I'll stick to editing. Please just let me keep my j—"

George cut me off. "I'll be in touch."

I hung my head. Tears began building up in my eyes. "Thanks," I said without looking up. Quickly, I got up from my seat and exited George's office. I rushed to my cubicle, trying desperately to fight the tears.

When I reached my cubicle, I saw that Patty was gone. She had left a brand new box of Junior Mints on my desk, on which she had drawn a big heart in her bright lipstick. Then she had signed her name in the lipstick. I knew it said Patty, but it kind of looked like Putty.

I smiled slightly at the gift, but for some reason the smile made the tears in my eyes increase. The stinging tears blurred my vision as I swept a few items off my desk into my handbag, slung the bag over my shoulder, and rushed out of the office.

No one answered the phone at my parents' house. Carrie didn't answer her phone either. So not only was I practically jobless, but I was also parentless and friendless.

Not wanting to go home to my empty condo, I went to the gym to clear my head of the mess I had managed to make out of my life—and to use my free gym membership for maybe the last time.

I was changing into my sweats when my cell began ringing loudly, causing a girl who was changing next to me to jump about a mile.

"Hello?" I answered hesitantly, not recognizing the number on the caller ID.

"Annabelle, it's Rona. I'm sorry I didn't return your call sooner, but I got your message about La Bonne Violette doing the catering, and that's great."

Oh man. I had left that message over a week ago, before the whole thing had fallen through. And in all the craziness of everything else in my life falling completely apart, I had forgotten to call Rona and tell her that it wasn't going to happen.

"Um, Rona, listen," I began, "I'm at the gym right now so can I call you back later?"

"No need. I'm on my way to the gym right now. I'll see you there. Bye."

Rona hung up before I could protest.

I sighed as I flipped the phone closed, and decided that I needed more than ever to run on the treadmill. I approached the treadmills in the cardio room and noticed that all but one of them were in use. I sauntered up to the unused treadmill and saw a small sign posted on it: "Danger: This machine has been having electrical problems. Run at your own risk."

What's the worst that could happen, I thought as I hopped onto the treadmill, not wanting to wait for the other machines. I set the machine and began running vigorously, hoping to release all of the distress from my mind.

"That looks like an angry run," I heard a voice say after I had been running for about fifteen minutes.

"Oh, shut up," I said, thinking the voice was my brain.

"Excuse me?" I heard the voice ask.

I turned my head and saw Rona Bircheck standing beside the treadmill. "Oh, sorry, I was talking to myself," I said as I pushed Stop on the machine.

Problem was, the thing didn't stop. It automatically started increasing in speed and kept increasing no matter how many times I pounded on Stop. Finally, with a scream, I lunged off the thing and landed on the ground beside Rona.

"Ow," I said as I picked myself up off the ground.

Rona started laughing.

"It wasn't that funny," I said coolly.

"Sorry," Rona said. She moved her lips around all weirdly, trying to wipe the smile off her face.

I rolled my eyes, thinking that Rona wouldn't see it.

But she did.

"Annabelle, did I do something to offend you?" Rona asked,

the laughter gone and a serious, almost hurt tone taking over her voice.

"Well, it's not nice to laugh at someone when they fall," I said, rubbing my now rug-burned elbow.

"I think it's more than that," Rona said.

"What makes you say that?"

"For quite a while, I've sensed some . . . I don't know . . . tension between us, I guess."

I gulped.

It's time to get things out into the open, my brain told me.

No way, I argued with my brain. *Nothing good will come out of that.*

It's the right thing to do, my brain pressed.

Whatever, I decided finally. *I guess it's not like my life can get any worse.*

"Well," I began, speaking to Rona without looking at her. How was I supposed to start the conversation I had successfully avoided for six years? "If you sense tension it's probably . . ." I paused when I noticed a blonde girl who was jogging on one of the treadmills turn her head slightly, obviously listening to our conversation, hoping to hear something juicy. "Do you wanna get a smoothie?" I asked Rona, eager to relocate.

"Okay," Rona replied slowly.

Silently, Rona and I made our way to the juice bar where Rona ordered a Fat Buster and I ordered a Weight Lifter's Choice since it has the most protein. Okay, mostly because it has the most frozen yogurt. I charged both smoothies to my account, and Rona and I chose a secluded booth to sit in.

We sat sipping our smoothies in silence until Rona spoke. "Did something happen between you and Isaac?" she asked.

I didn't reply. Like I was going to tell her so she could make a play for him. Yeah, right.

"I was just wondering because he seemed really upset on Saturday night after you left," Rona said.

Again, I didn't reply. I was too busy trying to prevent myself from blurting the sarcastic, "Yeah, and I'm sure you comforted him real nice," comments that were on the tip of my tongue.

"I have a confession to make," Rona said.

I think my heart stopped beating. As soon as the words came out of her mouth, I knew what she was going to say. She was going to tell me that she and Isaac were in love. That they were the ones who were going to buy the house in Carmel and get the horse named Snickers.

But that's not what she said.

"I've noticed this . . . weirdness between us for a long time," Rona began. "And that's one of the reasons I decided to plan a shower for Carrie. I was actually going to ask you to plan it with me. But I chickened out, and just asked you to take care of the catering."

So she hadn't been trying to edge me out as Carrie's best friend? No. That couldn't be right. I looked up at Rona. "I would have loved to plan the party," I said. "In fact, I felt a little sad that I wasn't in charge of the shower. It made me feel like a crummy friend." I looked at my smoothie, wondering if there was some sort of truth serum in it or something.

"But," Rona said, "when I was about to ask you to help me plan the shower, I felt that familiar tension, and I didn't think it would be a good idea for us to work together."

"What do you mean? It would have been fine." I paused. "Okay, it would have been a little . . . weird maybe." At this point I took the lid off my smoothie and looked inside. Seriously, what was in there?

"Do you remember the senior trip?" Rona asked out of nowhere.

"The senior trip? Yeah, sure, I remember that. Why?"

"You and I shared a seat on the bus down to Disneyland. Remember? We talked the whole time and read magazines, taking all the little quizzes. We even shared an In-N-Out shake."

The memory came to my mind. Carrie was sitting with her latest admirer—Carrie has always had tons of guys after her—and so Rona and I sat together. We really did have a lot of fun on that trip. But that was a long time ago. And more importantly, it was pre-prom. Things change. "That was pretty fun," I said finally.

"So what happened?" Rona asked.

"What do you mean?" I said, although I was pretty sure I knew what she meant.

Rona sighed. "Forget it," she relented, taking another sip of her Fat Buster.

I looked across the booth at Rona, and all of a sudden I could see the girl I sat with on the bus. And I saw her sipping not a Fat Buster smoothie but an In-N-Out shake. I pushed my smoothie away, deciding there was not only a truth serum in there but also a hallucinogen.

Then I took a deep breath and told the truth. "You want to know what happened? I thought you were my friend, Rona. But then Alex Michaels happened. The senior prom happened. After getting my heart broken, I decided you weren't much of a friend." For some reason, when the words came out of my mouth, they sounded strangely petty. They had seemed a much better reason to dislike Rona in my mind.

Rona's eyes started filling with tears. "I'm sorry I did that to you," she said softly.

What in this insane world? I looked at Rona's smoothie. Did someone put something into hers too? I peered over at the juice bar. There *was* something iffy about the teenagers working behind the counter.

"W-what?" I stuttered, staring at Rona.

"I'm really sorry, Annabelle," Rona said meekly. Since when was Rona meek?

"You are?"

"Do you know why my Mom and I moved to the Monterey Bay?" Rona asked quietly, dabbing at the tears in her eyes with a napkin.

My mind was blank. I really didn't know why. "I don't think so," I said.

"My dad died from cancer that year. We moved here to live with my grandma. It was the worst year of my life."

Before I knew it, I was reaching for Rona's hand. And at that moment something happened. I can't really explain what it was, but I knew that things were going to be different between us from then on.

"I'm so sorry," I said. "I had no idea. I should have known."

"How could you have known? I didn't tell anyone. Anyway, without my dad, I went maybe a little crazy. I looked for a guy to take his place or something." Rona looked at me, unsure, as if she regretted this admission.

"Oh," I said softly. "So you didn't, you know, purposely take my date or anything; you just wanted a guy."

"Well . . ." Rona said slowly. She took a tiny sip of her smoothie.

"So you did do it on purpose? Why did you hate me so much? I don't understand."

"Hate you? Are you kidding? I wanted to be you. I was totally jealous of you."

"What?" My mouth was slightly open as I said the word.

"Come on, like you didn't know that."

"How can that be?" I asked. "You were the one with everything. The looks, the guys. In fact . . . I may have had an envious thought about you every now and then." I shook my head slightly. "I can't believe how dumb this all sounds."

"Well, we were kids."

"Yeah, but I've let it go on. I'm really sorry, Rona. I haven't been very nice to you the past few years."

"I don't think it's that we haven't been very nice," Rona said. "I think it's that we haven't been very honest."

Rona was right. Now, how many of you over the course of this story thought that you would ever hear me say something like that?

"Yeah," I said, responding to Rona. Then I continued, "So maybe it's time to, I mean, maybe we could . . ."

"Start over." Rona and I said the words simultaneously.

"Okay," I committed.

"Okay," Rona echoed.

We both took sips of our smoothies, and smiled at each other. There was no hug. No plans to go shopping together were made. But the tension was gone. And I realized at that moment how much it had eaten at me all those years.

After a few quiet moments of smoothie-sipping, Rona got a very serious look on her face. "I just realized how things may look to you, but I want you to know that I don't have any interest in Isaac. That's the honest truth."

Could I really believe that? I mean, maybe my bad feelings toward Rona had tainted my ability to see things clearly, but some things were just not mistakable. "Oh, I never thought you'd go for Isaac," I said.

Liar, my brain scolded.

"You didn't?" Rona asked.

"No," I replied.

Liar, liar, liar, my brain chastised.

"Okay, maybe for a second," I admitted. "You do always . . . well, Rona . . . you're always flirting with him," I blurted.

Rona turned her head downward and played with the straw in her smoothie. "There's something you should know," she said seriously.

"Okay," I replied, not sure I wanted to hear what she was going to tell me.

"I wanted Isaac to like me."

All right, not exactly what I wanted to hear.

"But not for the reason you think. I did it because I . . . well . . . I like Ethan."

"Who's Ethan?" I asked stupidly.

"Isaac's brother."

"What? You like Ethan?" I stared at Rona, completely flabbergasted—I don't usually use that word because I think it sounds ridiculous, but it's honestly the only way to describe how I felt at that moment.

Rona nodded and grinned.

"Since when?" I asked, completely shocked, and, I have to admit, relieved. It was nice to know that I wouldn't have to see Rona and Isaac sitting together holding hands in the singles ward any time soon.

"Since a while," Rona replied. "It's a pretty crazy story."

"I'm all for a crazy story," I said. *Especially since it's about you liking someone other than Isaac.*

"Well, my friend Lupe is in the Spanish ward, and sometimes I go to church with her. I minored in Spanish in college, so I really enjoy attending Spanish services. I got to know Ethan in that ward, and I really liked him, but we were just friends since I was engaged.

"Then Tristan broke off our engagement. After I cried for way too long, Lupe intervened and told me she was taking me to her favorite Portuguese restaurant. She forced me to shower and put on makeup and took me to the place, which was called Vaz Plaza.

"After we ate, we were about to leave the restaurant when Lupe told me she saw Ethan's brother, Isaac, who she said was a photographer. So I started scheming. I wanted to get to know Ethan better, since I was free of that idiot Tristan. And seeing as I really needed a new property photographer, I thought it was the perfect opportunity to get to know Ethan through his brother.

"So I came over to the table where Isaac was sitting with you and gave him my card. The next day, I invited Isaac and Ethan to my house for lunch, and things just happened from there."

I remembered that day. I had assumed Rona was inviting Isaac to lunch and that it would be just the two of them all comfy and cozy. Could it really be that there was a different explanation for that lunch and maybe even for everything else that had happened?

"So it wasn't Isaac—it was Ethan," I muttered to myself.

"Yeah, it was Ethan," Rona said, responding to the words

I hadn't quite meant to say out loud. "But it's not like you had anything to worry about anyway. Isaac's obviously crazy about you."

I closed my eyes and sighed. "Maybe he was, but he definitely isn't anymore."

"How can that be possible? All I've heard since the day Isaac and I started working together is Annabelle this, Annabelle that, Annabelle is perfect in every way."

"Well, he doesn't think that anymore, that's for sure. It's over between us." My voice was sad. I sounded an awful lot like Eeyore from *Winnie the Pooh.*

"I guess it's none of my business anyway," Rona said quickly. She picked up her smoothie and scooted to the edge of her seat. "Thanks for the smoothie. So, I guess I'll see you next Saturday."

"Oh yeah, about that. I've been meaning to tell you, the catering kind of fell through. But don't worry, I'll come up with something." I grimaced, awaiting Rona's reaction.

Rona released a breath. "That's okay. I know Carrie will love whatever you come up with."

That was not the reaction I expected. "So you don't want to take care of it yourself?" I asked, referring back to when Rona had suggested just that.

Rona smiled slightly. "I know I was a little uptight about it before, and I apologize. I don't think anyone will do a better job than you," she said.

"I hope you're right."

Rona picked a napkin up off the table and put it into her empty smoothie cup. "I'm really glad that we talked," she told me. "Not just about the shower, but about everything."

"I am too," I said.

Rona stood up from the booth. Then she looked me in the eye. "I may be overstepping my bounds here, but I just have to say that you shouldn't give up so easily. You should fight for Isaac. Fight for your man." It took only a second for Rona to realize what she had said, and the connotation it held for the two of us, and her face flushed with embarrassment.

I gave her a don't-worry-I-didn't-take-it-badly wave and stared at a painting of a seagull on the wall. "I don't see any point fighting for this," I said in my Eeyore voice.

But the thing was, deep down, I really did want to fight.

Chapter 20

I didn't know what to do with myself.

It was like I had gotten used to hanging out with Isaac and had completely forgotten how to be by myself in the evening. So I opted to put on my pajamas, eat ice cream right out of the carton, and watch *The Price is Right.*

I was shouting at the woman on the television, telling her that she bid way too much on her showcase, when my phone rang.

"Hello?" I answered, shaking my head at the television when the woman stuck to her astronomical bid.

"I'm calling to see how you're holding up," Mom's voice came on the line.

I opened my mouth to tell Mom the latest when I heard a loud crash on her end of the line followed by, "Stupid thing!"

I muted the television. "Mom, are you all right?" I asked with concern.

"I just dropped the mixer. I'm sorry you had to hear me talk like that," Mom said, apologizing for her use of the word "stupid."

I chuckled to myself. "What are you doing?"

"I'm making some hors d'oeuvres and desserts for Elise Stapleton's pre-rehearsal-dinner party."

My goodness, how many parties does one girl need? I wondered. I was a bit surprised that the Stapletons had asked Mom to make any more food after, well, you know, the almost-fight. But then, of course they called Mom; she was the best.

"Of course!" I exclaimed into the phone.

"Well, yes, the party is tomorrow," Mom responded slowly, obviously confused by my outburst.

"I can't believe I never thought of this before!"

"I'm not sure what you're—" Mom began.

"And all that wasted time. All that worrying over nothing. When the answer was right in front of my face."

"What are you talking about, hon?" Mom asked.

"Mom, will you cater Carrie's shower for me?" I asked, my mind already swirling with menu possibilities.

"Well, I've never really done all the food for a party. Usually I just do a few things. Unless you include your sisters' weddings. Or Aunt Margaret's retirement party. Or your graduation party. Or . . ."

I smiled. "Like I said, will you cater the shower?"

"When is it?"

"Saturday," I answered hesitantly. It really was short notice. But she was Mom. If anyone could do it, she could.

"I'll need your help," Mom said.

"Of course, anything you need. So does that mean you'll do it?"

"Sure," Mom agreed. "But you'll have to help me come up with the menu, and help me find recipes. I know Carrie has very particular taste."

"Okay," I promised. "Thank you so much, Mom. This is so perfect!"

"You're welcome. Annabelle, I'm really proud of you. You're finding your own way. Not everyone else's way, but your own way."

"Yeah, well, I don't really have a choice," I muttered.

"I better get back to the desserts," Mom said. I heard her

turn on the electric mixer. "I'm making my special white fudge squares."

"Will you save me a few?" I asked, speaking loudly so I could be heard over the sound of the mixer.

"Sure," Mom replied in an equally loud voice. And I could tell she was smiling.

Glad to have something to do other than sit around and watch people try and win new cars and RVs, I threw myself into the project of brainstorming for Carrie's shower menu.

I pulled out my planner and started jotting some thoughts down. I began a Carrie likes/Carrie dislikes list, which I thought would be a good jumping off point.

Carrie Likes:
Tofu
Frozen desserts made with rice milk
Anything with organic vegetables
Seafood

Carrie Dislikes:
Anything with refined sugar (which is basically my staple food)
Chocolate
Anything with refined flour
Most red meat

I smiled as I realized that Mom was right—I was finding my own way. Not Anna Medici and Company's way. Not La Bonne Violette's way. But my own way.

I saved the list to my computer's hard drive and then decided to back it up on a USB drive. Not that it was a difficult list to remember, but just between you and me, I kind of get a thrill out of using those cute little drives.

I reached into my handbag and fished out my black USB drive. I inserted the drive into the computer, and a screen naming the files that were on the drive popped up. I was about to close the screen when I saw something funny. I saw a file with the name Très Bonne: An Inside Look at Carmel's Premier French Restaurant.

Horrified, I quickly opened the file and sure enough, there was my Missy Phat article. The one I was sure I had given to George. And if I had the Missy Phat article, that meant George had the . . .

Oh. No.

I jumped up from the couch and started pacing back and forth, my heart pounding and my stomach suddenly feeling sick. As I paced, my mind flashed back to me asking Patty to hand me a USB drive, and me not even bothering to check the color. Why hadn't I bothered to check the color?! By the way, bonus points for those of you who picked up on this back when it happened. But seriously, why didn't you tell me I was making the hugest mistake ever?!

I peered at the clock on my living room wall and saw that it was eight-fifteen. George was probably at home. I could just call him, tell him I gave him the wrong drive, and arrange to give him the correct drive. Everything would be just fine.

With unsteady hands, I found George's home number in my cell phone's directory and dialed the number. The answering machine picked up. "Hello, you've reached the Kent residence. We can't come to the phone right now, so please leave your name and number and we'll get back to you." Beep.

Panic grew in my chest as I left a slightly frantic message. "George, this is Annabelle Pleasanton. Please call my cell phone number immediately when you get this message."

Next, I tried George's cell. He didn't answer, and I hung up midway into the voicemail's outgoing message.

Then, formulating a plan in my mind, I grabbed my jacket, slipped it on over my pajamas, and headed for the office.

My heart was pounding like crazy as I walked through the large glass doors of *Central Coast Living*, which thankfully were still unlocked.

Just inside the doors, I paused and reached into my bag to make sure—for about the fiftieth time since I left my condo—that the black USB drive was in there. When my fingers clutched the device, I released a long breath.

Suddenly my mind was filled with a whole mess of what-if-I-can't-fix-this scenarios: me coming back to work after my "days off" to find that my cubicle had been cleared of my stuff and transformed into a game den complete with a foosball table. Me trying to walk into my cubicle and seeing a girl that looked just like me, but wasn't me.

Stop it, I told myself. *Everything is going to be fine.*

My pace quickened as I got closer to George's office. As I hurried along, I saw a few late workers sitting at their desks, hunched over their computers, munching on candy and granola bars. Some of them glanced up at me as I zipped past, and it didn't even seem to faze them that I was running around the office in my pajamas.

When I reached George's office, I pressed my face up against the glass window in the door. A small security light illuminated the room just enough for me to see everything inside. I thought that was a little bit ironic.

After a moment of visual scanning, I spotted a pile of papers. A single, red USB drive sat on top of the pile. It had to be mine. I put my hand on the doorknob, looked to my left and then to my right to make sure no one was coming, and turned the knob. I did this because I once saw a news report that said many robbers gain access to homes and offices through unlocked doors. Not that I'm a robber or anything. But even if I had been a robber, it wouldn't have mattered because the door was locked.

Just then, I heard the sound of keys jingling in the distance. I moved my ear in the direction of the sound. It sounded like it was coming from the janitorial closet. I immediately had an idea.

Quickly, I approached the janitorial closet. A sinewy, older man with thinning grey hair was moving a supply cart into the closet.

"Hi, um, Bill," I said, looking at the name patch on the man's shirt.

"I'm Gilbert. Bill's shirt fits me better than mine, so I wear it." Gilbert's voice was gruff. It didn't really sound like a Gilbert voice to me for some reason.

"Oh, of course," I said.

"Do you need something, missy?" Gilbert asked. "Is the ladies' room out of paper?"

"Oh, no. Actually I need you to unlock a door for me." I made sure to speak extra sweetly.

"Do you work here?"

"Yes."

"I've never seen you before," Gilbert said, eyeing my pajamas suspiciously.

"Well, I do work here. In fact, my cubicle is right over there." I pointed toward my cubicle.

"Show me your Employee Identification card." Gilbert spoke as if he were a secret service agent guarding the Oval Office.

"I don't exactly have it," I said, biting my lip. That card was in my satchel, which I hadn't thought to grab on my way out of my house.

"If you don't have your card, I don't think I can help you." Gilbert grabbed a bottle of sanitizer and a rag off of a shelf in the closet and turned to leave.

"Wait. If you just come over to my cubicle for a second, I can prove that I work here."

"I really don't have time for this," Gilbert said.

"Please. I really need your help." I played the damsel in distress card.

To my surprise, it worked like a charm. "All right," Gilbert agreed. He placed the rag and sanitizer on a small table that was covered in various knobs and gizmos, and he followed me to my cubicle.

"See there's my name plaque." I pointed to the fake-wood, fake-gold plaque with my name on it. I plucked my driver's license from my bag and showed it to Gilbert. "And here's my license. Annabelle Pleasanton. See, I do work here."

"Okay," Gilbert said. "I need to get my keys."

Gilbert led the way back to the custodial closet. He reached for a ring of keys that were hanging on a peg on the supply cart. "So what door do you need me to unlock? The copy room? The kitchen?"

"Actually, I need you to open George Kent's office."

Gilbert frowned. "Sorry. No can do."

"What do you mean?" I asked.

"I mean I can't open that office for you."

"I just need to put something in there," I explained. "It will only take a second. You can keep an eye on me and make sure I don't mess with anything."

Gilbert made a face that said he was considering my words. But in the end he turned me down. "I'm sorry," he said. "I could lose my job."

Gilbert placed the key ring on the cart and picked up the rag and sanitizer. He left the closet and whistled what sounded an awful lot like a Madonna song as he walked away.

Away from the key ring.

I looked over at the shiny keys. Why had Gilbert left them there? Didn't he realize how much of a temptation it would be for me to take them? But then, maybe he wanted me to take them. Maybe he was trying to tell me that he couldn't "give" them to me, but if I just happened to take them, well that was that. I decided that had to be it, and grabbed the keys.

I was tiptoeing out of the custodial closet when I saw a pair of beady little eyes staring at me from a nearby shelf. It only took a moment for me to realize that the beady eyes belonged to a small, grey mouse. I tried to be calm, tried not to be one of those crazy females who screams and jumps on a chair or table at the sight of a mouse. I mean, come on, a mouse versus a human, who's going to win?

The mouse, that's who!

My scream was accompanied by the sound of the keys crashing on the concrete floor. And with a swiftness I didn't know I had in me, I somehow hopped on top of the table with the knobs and gizmos on it, keeping a keen eye on the mouse's every move. I clutched my bag close to me as if I thought that maybe the mouse would climb in it. Or maybe steal it.

My teeth began chattering as I watched the mouse slink around. He was just so creepy, all small and rodenty. Sure, all those Disney movies make mice seem cute and friendly, with their little outfits and their cute little songs, but I'm telling you, this guy was not in a little outfit, nor was he singing. I had to get out of that closet.

So, with my eyes tightly closed and a scream coming from my lungs, I hopped off the table and dashed out the door. I slammed the door closed and let out another squeal. Quickly, I ran away from the closet.

That's what you get for trying to steal that old man's keys, my brain scolded.

Oh be quiet, I said to my brain.

Far, far away from the janitorial closet, I tried to come up with another solution to my predicament. I decided to try to call George again. I dialed his home number, and on the second ring a woman answered. "Hello?"

"Hi, is George there?"

"No, sorry, he's not here right now. Can I take a message?"

"Is this his wife?" I asked.

"Yes," the woman replied slowly. "Who is this?"

"My name is Annabelle Pleasanton. I work with George at the magazine."

"Ah yes, I believe we met at the Christmas party. Aren't you the one who showed up with that lovely Portuguese cake?"

"Yes, that's me," I said with a sigh. "So, um, would you happen to know how I could get a hold of George? It's important."

"He's at his weekly poker game. Even *I* can't get a hold of him." Mrs. Kent laughed a strained laugh.

"Oh, okay. Thank you very much." I hung up the phone and suddenly a thought came to my mind: I knew someone who had a key to George's office.

I found Arvin's number in my cell phone directory and dialed it, my heart pounding.

"Hello?" It was Arvin's roommate Clay, who is also in the singles ward.

"Hey, is Arvin there?"

"Nope. Who is this?"

"Annabelle. I really need to reach him. Does he have a cell number?" The last I heard, Arvin thought a cell phone cramped his surfer lifestyle.

"No," Clay answered. "But he's at the Pine Hills golf club for the singles activity. He left with six girls and a dude about twenty minutes ago. Didn't you plan the activity with him?"

"No, I didn't." I had been so busy with everything else in my life that I had been slacking on my activities committee duties. "How long do you think they'll be there?" I asked.

"A couple of hours," Clay answered.

"Great. Thanks."

"No problem."

I hung up the phone and tapped my toe on the floor. The Pine Hills golf club was only about a mile away. I could just drive over there, find Arvin, get the key, and switch the drives without George knowing a thing. It was the perfect plan.

Or so I thought.

I was about two feet away from an exit door when I felt something brush against my shoulder. I was absolutely positive it was the mouse, come to get me back for locking him in the closet.

"Eee!" I screamed, brushing my shoulder and jumping around like a madwoman.

"Annabelle?"

I screamed even louder. Now the mouse was talking to me.

"Annabelle, it's me," the mouse said.

Okay, okay. At this point it began to register that it wasn't the mouse talking to me, but a human. And guess which human. I'll give you a hint: it rhymes with Misaac.

"Don't ever do that again," I panted, my teeth chattering wildly.

"I'm sorry," Isaac said. The green light of the nearby exit sign illuminated him. And of course, even in green exit light he was gorgeous.

"What are you doing here?" I asked, trying to catch my breath.

Isaac held up a black portfolio. "Working. I'm basically living here for the next week. What about you?"

"I left something here by mistake," I answered. "But speaking of work, I've decided to go with my original article. That is . . . I think I am."

Isaac furrowed his brow. "So the focus changed back?"

"Well . . . I'm not sure yet," I said, sounding like a complete ditz. "I'll email you. Is your email working?"

Isaac nodded.

"Then I'll email you if I go with the original article."

"But as of now you're gong with the article you gave me? Because that's the article I submitted photos for today." Isaac scratched his head, which made his hair get all messy and adorable. I quickly turned my attention to a weird yellow spot on the wall behind him.

"Yeah, I guess I'm going with the one I gave you for now," I said, still staring at the yellow spot. I tightened my jacket around me and turned to walk away. "Well, I've really gotta go."

"Wait, Annabelle," Isaac called out, reaching for me.

"Why should I wait?" My voice was much more biting than I had intended.

"Because I don't want it to be like this between us," Isaac said.

I cocked my head to one side. "And how do you want it to

be between us?" I asked, my voice still full of bite.

"I . . . I don't know," Isaac replied.

"Well, I don't have time for *I don't know* right now," I said. I put my hand on the exit door.

"What if I told you I think I made a mistake?" Isaac said.

I turned and looked at him. "Do you think that?"

"Well, I think that maybe I was wrong to refuse to forgive you."

"Excuse me? Forgive me? Aside from trying to keep you out of my condo so you wouldn't get angry, I didn't do anything wrong. How many times do I have to tell you that? Because frankly, it's getting exhausting!" I pushed the exit door open furiously, and stepped out into the cool evening.

Isaac followed me out the door. "Come on, Annabelle. I saw how that creep acted around you, and you never said a thing. Then the guy is in your house, and I'm supposed to believe that nothing is going on?"

I got in Isaac's face. "Do you want to know what was going on?" I shouted. "Okay, I'll tell you what was going on. Yes, I never said anything to Patrique about the way he acted around me, but only because Jean-Pierre made it very clear that the future of my article depended on me being nice to him. And yes, he was at my condo, but only because, like I told you before, he's crazy. And yes, I didn't want you to know he was there, but only because I was terrified of losing you. Because for the first time in my life I felt like someone really saw me. I've spent so many years of my life trying to show people the parts of me I thought would please them. But not with you. I couldn't do that with you for some reason. You saw me, all of me, and still you stuck around. And when that happened, I wasn't so afraid to be me anymore. I was stronger.

"And that night, after you left, and I wasn't even sure I would ever see you again, I put everything on the line and stood up to Patrique. Because of you. Not only because of how I feel about you. But because of how you made me feel about myself."

A gentle look came into Isaac's eyes, and he moved very

close to me. Time seemed suspended, as if it were waiting for us to make something of the moment.

But just then, a man in a heavily wrinkled suit bounded out of the office building, talking loudly on a cell phone, and the moment was gone.

"Well, I better go," I said in a voice that sounded nothing like me.

"Yeah, uh, me too," Isaac said.

We exchanged quick good-byes, and headed in opposite directions.

As I walked to my car, I saw the man in the wrinkled suit getting into a car in the distance. And I couldn't stop myself from wondering what might have happened if he had come out of that exit door just a few moments later.

Chapter 21

"I am very sorry, but we have a dress code. Slacks and a collared shirt are required." This blond-haired kid, who looked about fifteen, was refusing to let me onto the golf course because I wasn't dressed properly. I looked down at my pink Barbie pajamas: I didn't see the problem.

"Listen, I'm not going to golf," I said. "I'm just looking for someone."

"I cannot let you onto the course unless you are dressed properly."

"Okay then, do you rent clothes here?" I asked.

The teen looked at me like I had just asked if he would share a piece of chewing gum with me. "No, we do not rent clothes. However, you are welcome to purchase clothing in our Pro Shop."

"Okay, thanks."

I made my way to the clubhouse and stepped into the Pro Shop in search of something "proper" to wear. But as is usually the case with shops like this—ones that exist for the ridiculously inflated purchases of items that people should have gotten at a normal store—everything was in two styles: 1) Who in their right mind would wear this? 2) Who in *any* state of mind would wear this?

I was thumbing through a rack of ladies' plaid pants when I saw a woman walk by wearing an outfit that was dress-code appropriate, yet was actually something I might wear again.

"Excuse me," I said to the woman.

"Yes," she replied with a stiff smile that revealed the straightest, whitest teeth imaginable.

"Where did you get your outfit?" I asked. Maybe it was within driving distance.

The woman made this little pouting face like she was trying hard to remember where she got her outfit. "In London. At the most darling little boutique not too far from Cambridge."

"Oh," I responded, nodding my head. For a split second, I tried to calculate how long it would take me to get to England. "Thanks."

"Of course." The woman walked away with the poise of a runway model.

I moved from the plaid-pants rack to a rack of shirts. I was seriously considering a bright purple polo shirt with a sick-looking seagull embroidered on it when I decided to forget the clothing search. Like the place had golf cops that would come and cuff me for not observing the dress code.

I walked down onto the golf course, which was illuminated by tall, wooden-posted lights. I looked out at the course and was overwhelmed. All I saw was a sea of green grass for what seemed like miles. I had no idea how I would ever find Arvin in the green sea.

Luckily, I spotted a map nearby. After consulting the map, I decided to start searching for Arvin at the first hole and make my way to the eighteenth. Personally, I think golf is a little silly that way. Why waste time and energy walking all over a course? Why not just use the same hole eighteen times?

I was walking toward the third hole, when I was approached by another blond teenager, this one with a set of eyebrows that were sculpted into a perfect arch that I could only dream of.

"Excuse me, Miss. Can I help you find something?" the teenager asked.

Good, I thought, *someone who is helpful rather than obsessed with the dress code.*

"Yes, I'm actually looking for someone."

"Did you miss your tee time?"

"I'm sorry?" I asked, not quite sure what tea had to do with golf.

The teen rephrased his question. "Is your group already on the course?"

"Um, yeah, I think so," I answered.

"Well, I have been instructed to inform you that in order to be on the course, you must be in accordance with the dress code."

Man, what was with these kids speaking better English than me? *I have been instructed to inform you? In accordance with?*

I was coming up with a proper Englishy response, using what I thought Miles would say as a reference, when, over the top of the kid's head, I saw Arvin. He was pretty far in the distance, surrounded by a group of six girls who I didn't know very well and one guy named Peter who was nineteen and had just received his mission call to Argentina.

"Arvin!" I yelled.

He didn't hear me. So, without a second thought, I took off running. I had only run a few yards when a golf cart pulled up and formed a sort of blockade in front of me. A big, burly man in a security uniform got out of the cart and approached me.

Behind me, I could see the blond teenager with the nice eyebrows yelling, "Code Green! Code Green!" into an expensive-looking walkie-talkie.

"Miss, I'm going to have to ask you to leave the course," the burly security man said, approaching me. The teen peered over at me, obviously content with letting the burly man handle the situation.

"But I really have to talk to that guy over there." I pointed to the green where Arvin was watching while a tall, dark-haired girl practiced her swing.

"Is it an emergency?" the burly man asked.

"Um, well . . ."

"If it's not an emergency you're going to have to leave."

Now, you're going to be proud of me for this one. I did not lie. I wanted to make up some great emergency, to tell the man that I needed to inform Arvin that his prized surfboard had been stolen by a serial surfboard-stealer, but I didn't.

You're not going to be quite as proud for this one, though. While I didn't make up an emergency, I did take off running full speed away from the golf course worker, toward Arvin and the singles group.

After running a few yards, I cut to the left to get around the golf cart, and as I did I lost my footing. I went flying face down onto the grass and landed with a big thud.

"Are you okay?" the burly man asked heartlessly. Underneath the question I could sense a whole lot of that's-what-you-get.

"I'm fine," I replied, standing up. I soon noticed that grass stains covered my Barbie pajama pants. I frowned. It had taken me forever to find a pair in my size. "Look," I said to the man. "Can't you see that I'm willing to go through quite a lot to talk to this person? I just ruined a really good pair of pajama pants. Could you please just bend the rules this once?"

"There's no such thing as bending the rules once." The man sounded suddenly philosophical.

"There is if no one knows about it."

"But I'll know," the man said, keeping up the philosophical bit.

"What's your name again?" I asked.

"Chuck."

"Please, Chuck," I pleaded, using his name for effect. I then attempted to bat my eyelashes. But for some reason, I found it incredibly hard to bat. It was as if my eyelids were suddenly made of lead.

"What's wrong with your face?" Chuck asked.

"Excuse me?"

"Your face is . . . weird."

Look, buddy, I know I'm not perfectly groomed like most of the golf club crowd, and I know you might be a little mad at me for trying to run away just now, but there is such a thing as verbal decency. I pouted and looked away.

"I mean it. Look." Chuck plucked a shiny golf club from the back of the golf cart/blockade and handed it to me putter—or wood, or chipper, or whatever it was—side up. "Look," he repeated.

He wanted me to use the club as a mirror so I could look at my weird face? That was just cruel. I pretended to look into the club. I could go home and look at my weird face in the mirror, thank you very much.

"Your arms are weird too," Chuck said.

My arms? What's wrong with my arms? The man was brutal.

"Fine, I'll leave!" I hollered.

I did an about-face on my heels and took a quick glance at my arms. "My arms are weird!" I gasped, turning back around.

"I told you," Chuck said.

I inspected my arms. They were covered in this puffy red rash that seemed to be growing right before my eyes. "What's wrong with my arms?!"

"Maybe we should go to the first aid office," Chuck suggested. "Dr. Schneider is still there since we have a night tournament going on."

"Okay," I whimpered, not taking my eyes off my arms.

Chuck helped me into the golf cart and whisked me to the clubhouse. Once inside, he left me sitting on a plush couch outside a door that was labeled *First Aid* in fancy scrolling lettering.

I was pretending to read *Golf for Women* magazine, but mostly staring at my arms, when an attractive, blond-haired man sat down next to me to the couch.

"I'm Dr. Schneider," he introduced himself. "So what do we have here?" He didn't ask me to go into the room, and I was glad since I'm not too big on exam rooms.

I held out my arms.

Dr. Schneider looked my arms over. "How long ago did this rash appear?

"Just a few minutes ago."

"And what about your face?" Dr. Schneider asked.

Look, people, maybe I don't have the money to go to the spa for a facial every week like the other ladies around these parts, but that doesn't mean there's anything wrong with my face. "I think my face is just fine, thank you," I said defiantly.

"I'm not so sure about that," Dr. Schneider said. He disappeared into the first aid room and for a second I thought he was going to come out with a coupon for the on-site aesthetician. Instead, he appeared with a mirror. Likely to show me how in need I was of the aesthetician.

I tried to fake a glance into the mirror, just as I had faked a glance into the golf club, but It caught my eye: this horrible, red, puffy rash that looked like poison oak on steroids. I think I may have screamed, but my memory of the moment is blocked due to the sheer trauma.

"Do you have any allergies?" Dr. Schneider asked.

"Not that I know of," I choked out.

"Did you touch or eat anything unusual today?"

"No, I don't think so."

"Does the rash itch or burn?"

"No."

Dr. Schneider brought his hand to his chin in a thoughtful gesture. "My guess is that you're having some sort of allergic reaction. Unfortunately, I don't have any prescription strength antihistamines. I ran out last week."

"So what should I do?" I asked, distraught.

"I think you should go to the nearest urgent care center or emergency room. But you had better hurry because I think your eyes are swelling shut."

I looked in the mirror again. The sight was even more mortifying than the one I had seen just moments earlier. Sure enough, the puffiness around my eyes was increasing. I was beginning to look like something that would scare young children.

Quickly, I stood up from the chair. Time was of the essence. In the back of my mind, I thought of my purpose for being at the golf course in the first place. I needed to get that key from Arvin.

But one more glance in the mirror made me forget about that.

I knew I couldn't drive when I tried for five minutes to get into the wrong car. I flipped open my phone and pushed the number one to speed-dial my parents' home number.

"Hello?" Dad's voice answered.

"Hi, Dad."

"Hi, Bellie."

"Are you busy?" I asked hesitantly.

"No. Your mom and I were just eating some peach cobbler."

"Tell her I made it with my own canned peaches," Mom called out in the background.

"Did you hear that?" Dad asked.

"Yep," I replied, smiling. Well, as much as my face would allow me to smile. "Listen, I need help," I said, my tone suddenly serious.

"Is everything okay?" Dad asked worriedly.

"I'm fine. I just have a bit of a rash. I need to go see a doctor, but my eyes are swelling shut and I can't really see, so I can't drive. Some people from singles ward are here, but I don't know how I'd find them, and plus I look pretty scary so . . ."

"So you need a ride?"

"Yeah, if you could."

"Where are you?"

"I'm at the Pine Hills golf club, in the front parking lot." I tried to look around through the blurry slits that were my eyes. *At least I think I'm in the front parking lot.*

"See you in fifteen minutes." Dad hung up the phone.

Less than fifteen minutes later both Dad and Mom showed up in the parking lot. Mom jumped out of the car before Dad had even fully parked.

"Oh, honey!" she exclaimed, rushing to me.

"That looks pretty bad," Dad said, following behind Mom.

Mom gave him a little don't-say-that hit with her hand. "Why don't you get in the car," Mom instructed. She held onto my arm, guiding me into the backseat of the tan station wagon.

After a little bit of debating, we decided that since the hospital was close by, we should go to the emergency room rather than to an urgent care center. With ambulance-like determination, Dad drove to the ER.

"Okay, thanks for the ride," I muttered once Dad had pulled up to the curb. "I'll just call when I'm done, I guess." My words said I'm-an-independent-woman, but my tone was pure I-need-my-mommy-or-daddy-to-stay-with-me.

"Don't be silly," Mom pronounced. "I'm staying with you." She jumped out of the car, opened my door for me, and offered me her arm.

"Do you want me to stay too?" Dad asked.

"We'll be fine," Mom told Dad, her words rushed. "Besides, I think I might have left the oven on."

"Then I'll pick you ladies up later. I'm sure everything is going to be fine."

"Thanks, Dad," I said.

Mom said a quick good-bye to Dad and then hurriedly guided me through the ER's automatic doors.

Once inside the waiting room, Mom filled out the registration forms for me, and we found a pair of unoccupied seats in a corner. Through my blurred vision, I could see that there were about ten other people in the waiting room besides Mom and me.

I reached for a magazine on a nearby table and held the magazine close to my face so I could read the cover. It was a three-month-old issue of *Central Coast Living*. Like a flash, my switched-article predicament returned to my mind. I slapped the magazine back onto the table, flipped open my phone, and dialed George's cell phone number. Voicemail. I didn't leave a message. Reluctantly, I dialed his home number. Answering machine. I hung up before the beep.

This horrible anxious feeling took over my chest. It was the feeling I woke up with the morning I slept through the SAT. I tried to breathe and told myself that George had to get home sometime, and that when he did I would get a hold of him and this whole thing would be on its way to being over.

Then, to get my mind off of things, I busied myself by attempting to read a pamphlet on preventing athlete's foot, and prepared for the long wait.

The very long wait.

The ridiculously long wait.

Finally, Mom—who I think had read four entire issues of *Good Housekeeping* from cover to cover, including the ads in the back for things like tanning beds and padded underpants—approached the curly-haired receptionist at the front desk. "Do you have an idea how much longer it will be?"

"What's the name?" the receptionist said in a tired voice.

"Annabelle Pleasanton."

"It looks like there are a few people still ahead of you. We only have one doctor on staff right now, so it might be a while."

"Thanks," Mom said. She walked back to my side, looking tired. "There are still a few people—"

"I heard," I said. "I'm sorry I'm ruining your night." I looked at the cracked clock on the wall. I moved my head into various positions, trying to read the clock with my blurry sight. "Does that really say it's after midnight?" I asked.

"Yes," Mom replied wearily. "I need to move around. I think I'll go to the vending area. Do you want anything?"

"Chocolate," I answered quickly.

Mom smiled, and headed to the vending area a few yards away, rolling her shoulders slightly as she walked. She returned with a package of Reese's Peanut Butter Cups and a bag of pretzels. I ripped into the candy while Mom daintily ate a few pretzels.

"What were you doing at the golf course anyway?" Mom asked.

I shifted uncomfortably in my chair. "Can we talk about that later?"

"Annabelle Pleasanton?" The deep voice of a male nurse seemed to boom through the waiting room.

I stood up, and Mom took my arm, leading me down a hall and into a room where she helped me step onto a scale. She stood behind me as the male nurse proceeded to call my weight out loud enough for the entire hospital to hear.

Once my blood pressure, pulse, and temperature were taken, the nurse directed Mom and me down the hall to another room. I tried to make out what was inside the room. I saw several blurry hospital beds separated by equally blurry curtains that hung from the ceiling. Mom helped me sit down on one of the beds and then she sat down on a chair beside the bed. The nurse stood at the foot of the bed.

"So what are you seeing the doctor for today?" the nurse asked.

Um, can't you see me? Isn't it obvious? "I have this terrible rash." I held up my arms and pointed to my face.

The nurse took down some notes and said, "The doctor will be with you shortly." He pulled a curtain closed around my bed and disappeared.

I leaned back into the inclined bed. "Mom, you can go if you want." I released a heavy sigh.

"I'm not leaving you here," she stated simply.

"I was trying to track down a key to my boss's office," I said.

"What?"

"That's why I was at the golf course. I really messed up this time."

"I thought you didn't want to talk about that right now," Mom said, fluffing the lumpy pillow that was behind my head.

"I gave him the wrong article. And if I don't somehow get him the right one soon, I think I might lose my job."

"What do you mean you gave him the wrong—" Mom began.

I cut her off. "But do you want to know a secret? Deep down, I'm almost glad it happened this way. Because the article I wrote, the heart-strings-tuggy one, it was good. It really was. Not because of anything I wrote, but because of what I was writing about. My whole life I've wanted to write something like that."

Mom opened her mouth to speak, but before she could say anything, the doctor, a woman whose face I could barely make out, pulled back the curtain. She took one look at me and began asking me a whole lot of questions.

After some discussion, it was concluded that I had probably suffered from an allergic reaction to the fertilizer used on the grass at the golf course. Apparently it was this new high-tech stuff that a lot of environmental groups were trying to get banned. And a whole bunch of people were having reactions to it, though none as severe as mine. The doctor knew all of this because she was a regular at Pine Hills.

I was then given a powerful antihistamine. And the last thing I remember was mumbling something to Mom about how when we left the hospital I would need her to take me to *Central Coast Living* and could she pick up some camouflage for me to wear so the mouse wouldn't see me when I tried to steal Gilbert's keys again.

Chapter 22

I woke up in my own bed.

I sat up groggily, rubbed my eyes, and realized with glee that I could see again. I looked down at my arms. The rash had cleared up a bit, but some not-too-lovely traces of it still remained.

Mom was sitting at the foot of the bed, reading the bridal magazine I had bought to do research for Carrie's shower. I silently hoped she hadn't found the ad where I had written "Me" under the picture of the bride and "Isaac" under the picture of the groom.

"Good morning, honey," Mom said, looking up from the magazine.

"Good—" *Wait a minute, did she just say . . .* "Morning? Oh. No." I threw the blankets off of me and sat up straight. "What time is it?" I asked frantically.

"Oh, about eleven," Mom replied.

Eleven. Too late. By now George had read my article and had discovered that it was completely off the mark, that none of it was usable, and that he would have to run something in its place. My cubicle was probably being cleared out and turned into a game den as we spoke. I leaned against my bed's padded headboard and put my head in my hands.

Mom set the bridal magazine down and came to my side. "Oh, honey, what is it?"

"I tried," I said pitifully. "I worked so hard. I put up with Jean-Pierre and then Patrique, and I even lost Isaac, and it was all for nothing. Nothing. By now George has read my stupid mushy article, wadded it up, and thrown it in the trash. I completely failed."

Mom put a loving arm around me. "I'm not so sure about that," she said. "You told me that you were happy with what you wrote. In my book that is the definition of success. Now how about I make you some breakfast?" The nurturing tone in Mom's voice was soothing.

"Well, it has been a long time since I had your waffles," I whimpered.

Mom smiled and left for the kitchen. I sank into the pillows on the bed.

"Oh, before I forget," Mom called out. "Your boss called this morning."

I jumped out of the bed and hurried to the kitchen. "What! What did he say?"

"I let the machine get it," Mom answered.

I hustled to the answering machine and pushed Play. "George Kent here. I tried your cell phone first but got no answer. I was hoping to get in touch with you. I'll try back later."

I cringed. It was so obvious in his voice. He was going to fire me. He was going to fire me, and I would end up going door to door selling those electronic-toothbrush-holding contraptions that Bernie, Patty's MatureMatch.com admirer, invented. And I would be a horrible saleswoman because I would always end up telling the people that the things weren't safe. And then Bernie would fire me and I would be known as the girl who gets fired from everything and . . .

"After I finish breakfast," Mom's voice broke into my thoughts, "I'm going to get your prescription filled."

"My what?" I plopped onto a chair in the dining room.

"Your prescription. The doctor said you should take some antihistamines for the next couple days."

"Oh," I sighed. "I can pick up the medicine, Mom." Might as well do something to keep my mind off of my crumbling life. "Plus, I'm sure you want to get home to Dad."

"Okay. But first let's eat."

Ah. My life may have been falling apart, but those words definitely helped cushion the fall.

A bell dinged as I walked into the pharmacy located in the Green Meadows shopping center near my condo. I walked to the back of the store and handed my prescription to the pretty, young pharmacy worker. She took one look at the traces of red rash on my arms and face and shot me a sympathetic glance.

The young woman informed me that it would take a few minutes to fill the prescription, and so to pass the time I made my way to the magazines in aisle eight and began flipping through an issue of *Cutting-Edge Coifs*. I was looking in awe at a picture of a woman whose hair had been styled into a peacock, complete with feathers and everything, when I heard someone calling my name.

"Annabelle?"

I turned around and saw Rona, looking like she had just come from a photo shoot for one of the magazines on the rack.

"Rona," I said, snapping the magazine shut. "Hi."

"What happened to you?" Rona asked.

A few days earlier I would have begrudged the question and known for sure that Rona was glad that I looked so terrible because it would mean that I was less competition for her if she changed her mind about Ethan and decided to go for the other Matthews brother. But I didn't think that at all. Okay, almost not at all. Hey, change doesn't happen overnight.

"I had an allergic reaction to a chemical the Pine Hills golf club uses on their grass."

"Does it hurt?" Rona asked. "It looks like it does."

I shook my head. "It doesn't."

"Well, I'm glad I ran into you," Rona said. "I was just next door at Anne's Partie and Paperie looking for decorations for Carrie's shower, and I have no idea what I'm doing. I came here for a pick-me-up." Rona held up a bag of peanut M&Ms.

"Well," I said. "My prescription is going to take a few minutes. I could go next door with you if you want." I was a bit shocked that those words came out of my mouth. Yes, we had shared smoothies together and decided to start over and all. But I wasn't exactly planning on becoming buddy-buddy with Rona. Was I?

"That would be great," Rona said with a relieved sigh.

Rona and I went next door to Anne's Partie and Paperie, which is this gorgeous store with classy event decorations and paper products—the kind of stuff that you would find in the entertaining section of a glossy, chic magazine.

Once we were inside, I turned to Rona. "So what exactly are we going to be decorating?" I asked. "A living room? A banquet room?"

Rona looked at the ground. "Well, there's been a little problem with that. The owner of a summer home I sold about a month ago had agreed to let me use his beachfront property for the shower, but his daughter just finished her first year at Berkley and decided she wanted to have a vacation there with her friends. And I can't have it at my house because I'm getting the carpets replaced the day of the shower. So I put TBA on the invitations, and I've been searching for a place but . . ."

"We can have it at my condo," I offered easily.

Rona's face registered surprise and relief. "Really?"

"Of course. I would love to have it at my place."

"Perfect," Rona said. "I'll call all of the invitees tonight."

"I can help you call if you want," I offered, surprising myself.

Rona sighed gratefully. "Thanks."

"All right. So now that we know what space we're working

with, let's check out the decorations."

"Yes, let's," Rona echoed.

For the next thirty minutes Rona and I walked through the aisles of the store. Rona pulled decorations down from the shelves and held them up for me to see, and I shook my head at nearly everything she held up. Nothing was quite right.

Then we found an entire aisle that seemed to scream Carrie. It was filled with earthy decorations, many with Asian influences. As Rona and I walked into the aisle, I raised my eyebrows and looked over at her. She was nodding her head as if she too thought the decorations were perfect.

With huge smiles on our faces, we began scooping up paper lamps, floating candles, and bamboo wall hangings with Chinese characters painted on them. I even found a mini bonsai tree that I just couldn't resist. We topped things off with thick, recycled napkins in an earthy green, and bamboo plates.

"Oh, this is going to be so perfect," I cooed.

"And I just remembered I have some pillows in a similar style," Rona said. "I could bring them and everyone could sit on them."

I smiled giddily at Rona. This party was going to be incredible! We giggled as we approached the check-out counter.

"I'll get these," I offered as we set our items on the counter. I might as well spend my last hard earned dollars from *Central Coast Living* on my best friend.

"It's on Miles," Rona said. She retrieved a wad of cash from her wallet. "He said he has to make things up to Carrie. Something about almost ruining her wedding dress."

I grinned to myself as the checkout girl smacked her gum loudly while scanning each of the items.

Bags in hand, Rona and I left the store. I was looking into one of the bags I was holding, engrossed in the goodies inside, when I ran smack into a man who crossed our path on the sidewalk.

"I'm sorry," I said, looking up at the man I had just run

into, a man I immediately recognized. "Isaac," I whispered.

Now, dear reader, I have been in your spot before. The spot where you think, "Yeah right, like she'd run into all these people she knows at some little shopping center in an area as big as the Monterey Bay." But I'm telling you, the world is small. And apparently even smaller when one is covered in a red, splotchy rash.

"I, uh, I'll see you later, Annabelle," Rona said. She handed the bags she had been carrying over to me. "Why don't you take these to your place, and I'll call you later." It was painfully obvious that she wanted to leave me and Isaac alone.

"Um, okay," I said.

"Good to see you, Isaac," Rona added casually. She stepped behind Isaac and made motions like she was boxing—apparently referring back to when she told me to "fight for my man." I shot her a cut-it-out-he-might-see-you look. She grinned and strutted away. I stood frozen, not knowing what to say or do.

Isaac looked at the rash that covered arms and face. "What happened? I mean . . . are you okay?"

"A broken heart affects me badly, apparently." *What in the world? Did I really just say that?*

Isaac looked down at the ground. "Annabelle, we need to talk," he said.

"We do?"

"Yeah, I—"

"Ready to go, Isaac?" An attractive blonde came and hooked her arm through Isaac's. She was carrying a take-out box from the cute little Italian restaurant at the south end of the shopping center. She regarded me and shot me a look that said, "Oh you poor blotchy thing; it's too bad you aren't as pretty as me."

"So are you ready?" the woman repeated. She looked at Isaac, awaiting his reply.

For a moment, Isaac looked at me like he was torn, like he didn't know what to do. But the look soon disappeared. He cleared his throat and glanced at the woman. "Sure," he said. "I'll talk to you later, Annabelle."

Isaac began to walk away, and my mind filled with things I wanted to call out to him. *Wait! When will we talk? What do we need to talk about? Who's the blonde?* But the only words that came out of my mouth were tiny whispers even I could barely hear. *I love you, Isaac. I still love you.*

Chapter 23

Beep, beep.

I was sitting at my parents' dining room table, planning the menu for Carrie's shower with Mom, when I heard the sound of my cell phone indicating that I had a voicemail message.

"That's weird," I said. "I didn't even hear the phone ring."

Mom shrugged her shoulders, and I casually got up from my seat and dug through my bag, which was sitting on the opposite end of the table. I located my cell and looked at the number on the Calls Missed screen. Isaac had called.

"No!" I hollered at my phone.

Mom raised an eyebrow at me, but didn't say anything. She continued flipping through her Asian cookbook.

I checked the message. "Hi, it's Isaac. I . . . I guess I'll try back later."

"No!" I hollered again.

My heart racing, I quickly moved into my old room, plopped onto the bed, and dialed Isaac's number. As I listened to each ring, I began to imagine how our conversation might go.

Me: Isaac, I got your message.

Isaac: Oh, Annabelle. I'm so glad you called back. I don't know how much longer I could have waited to talk to you.

Me: Really?

Isaac: Yes. I need to tell you that I'm so sorry that I didn't believe you about what happened. I know you would never lie to me. You are the most wonderful woman I have ever known. And I can't live without you.

Me (indignantly): Then why were you out with someone else today?

Isaac: I wasn't out with her. She's a crazy stalker who saw my photos in a gallery and became obsessed with me. You're the only one for me. And just so you know, I think you look really beautiful with a rash.

Me: Oh, Isaac.

Isaac: I am crazy for you, my little spring blossom.

I was so into my imagined conversation that I was startled when I heard the phone go to Isaac's voicemail. "Hi, this is Isaac. Sorry I can't take your call right now . . ."

As I listened to the outgoing message, I quickly started debating about whether or not I wanted to leave a voicemail. I had pretty much decided on not leaving one, when the tone sounded, leaving me no choice.

After a second of silence, I began to leave my message. "Hi, this is Isaac. I mean, uh, um, hi, Isaac. I'm just returning your call. So, call me." Then, almost as an afterthought, I added, "Oh, this is Annabelle."

I hung up the phone and buried my face in a pillow on the bed, wondering why I could never seem to leave a normal, regular, "Hey this is Annabelle, call me back," message on Isaac's phone.

"Annabelle?" Mom's voice came from the doorway of the room.

I jumped a bit at the sound and sat up. "Yeah."

"I have to go in for my volunteer shift at the library in about an hour. I was wondering if you could call Carrie and somehow find out what she thinks about the menu we've chosen for the shower. Without letting her know that's what you're doing, of course."

Mom handed me the menu we had put together, and I looked it over.

1) Grilled shrimp with Asian flavors
2) Asian hot and sour noodle soup
3) Baby greens with orange-sesame vinaigrette
4) Asian stir-fried asparagus

"Sure," I said with a grin. "I think I can figure out what she thinks of this."

I punched the number for Carrie's health food store into my cell. Mom leaned against the door frame and waited as I called.

"Fresh Food Fanatics, this is Moonbeam," a perky voice answered.

"May I please speak to Carrie Fields?" I asked

"Oh, hi, Annabelle," Moonbeam said. "Sure. I'll get her for you." If you haven't guessed by now, I call Carrie at the store a lot. Probably more than I should.

Carrie's voice came on the phone after a few moments. "Hello?"

"Carrie, is that you?" I joked. "I forgot what your voice sounded like."

"I'm sorry," she said, and I could hear her smiling. "Planning a wedding is hard work. I've never been busier in my life. Not even when I was opening the store."

"Are we going to get together tomorrow for Paint and Popcorn night?" I asked.

"I don't think so," Carrie answered apologetically. "Miles and I just signed up for a couples' yoga class that is only offered on Thursdays. It's supposed to help relieve the stress of planning the wedding."

"Okay," I said, trying to hide the disappointment in my voice. "But we're still going to Shrimpy's on Saturday, right?"

"Yes, of course."

"Good. How about I come and pick you up at your house and I'll drive us over."

I hoped Carrie would agree. Usually, Carrie and I would just meet at the restaurant, but that wouldn't work this time, because we weren't actually going to the restaurant.

You see, while we were shopping for decorations, Rona and I decided on a plan. According to the plan, I would say I was driving Carrie to Shrimpy's for our already-planned Saturday outing. But I would actually drive her to my condo where—surprise!—her party would be waiting.

"Okay," Carrie agreed. "If you want to drive, that's fine by me."

"Great," I said. "So . . . speaking of Shrimpy's . . . don't you wish they had Asian shrimp? You know, grilled shrimp with Asian flavors." I read the name of the dish straight from the paper in my hand.

"I don't think they serve Asian food at Shrimpy's," Carrie said.

"Yes, but if they did, wouldn't that be great?"

"Uh, sure. I love Asian shrimp."

I flashed Mom a thumbs up sign, grabbed a fuzzy pink pen off the nightstand, and put a big circle around grilled shrimp with Asian flavors.

Onto the next menu item. "You know, I was thinking. When we go to Shrimpy's, I think I'm going to get one of those yummy nonalcoholic specialty drinks."

"Those things are like 90 percent sugar," Carrie cautioned.

"Yeah, I guess that's true. But you know what's not 90 percent sugar . . . Asian hot and sour noodle soup." I sounded like a very bad actor trying to read lines.

"I've never had that before," Carrie said.

"Yes but do you think you'd like it?"

"Probably," Carrie said slowly. "I love hot and sour food."

"Cool."

I circled Asian hot and sour noodle soup.

"I ordered my dress yesterday," Carrie said. I think she wanted to stop my babble.

"Oh, Carrie, I'm so excited for you! I got the pictures you emailed me. It's gorgeous. Call me the second it comes in."

"I will," Carrie promised, sounding like one very excited bride.

Silently, I tried to think of how to get the topic back to food. After all, I only had two items left to investigate. "You know how your dress has little flowers embroidered on the bodice?" I began. "Well, I think lettuce looks like flowers. Especially when it's in a salad. Maybe a salad with, I don't know, say, orange-sesame vinaigrette."

"What are you talking about?" Carrie sounded seriously perplexed.

"I'm saying that I like salad with orange-sesame vinaigrette."

"Sesame oil is really hard for me to digest," Carrie said.

"Oh."

"And it's pretty gross."

"Oh," I repeated, this time making it a two syllable word.

I crossed off the salad.

"You know what's not gross, though," I said. Just one more menu item to go. "Asian stir-fried asparagus."

"What's with you and Asian food?"

"Well, it's just that talking about Shrimpy's made me get food on the brain. And I just realized that it's been a while since I had some good Asian food. Like stir-fried asparagus."

"I'll make some for you sometime. That's one of my favorite dishes."

"Oh it is, huh," I said in a weird voice as I circled asparagus on the list.

"Annabelle is something—" Carrie started to ask.

"Well, I better let you get back to work," I said quickly. "Bye."

I hung up before Carrie could say anything and let out a long breath. "Well, I think I pulled that off," I said to Mom. "Now let's get to work."

"Oh, no. I just remembered I left something at my condo," I said when Carrie and I were pulling into the parking lot at Shrimpy's.

The plan had been for me to pick Carrie up and take her directly to my condo, but Rona had called and told me she needed more time to set up, so I had to keep up the pretense that we were going to Shrimpy's.

"What did you forget?" Carrie asked.

"My, um, my . . ." I looked out my window and saw a middle-aged woman, obviously a tourist, wearing a tennis visor. "My visor," I said.

"Your visor?" Carrie asked. "I've never seen you wear a visor."

"That's because it's new," I replied quickly. "I just got it to . . . protect my eyes from the sun's harmful rays."

"But we're going to be eating inside," Carrie said.

"Yes, well . . . fluorescent lights are just as harmful, you know."

"Really?" Carrie asked with interest. "I've never heard that before."

"It's true," I said with feigned expertise.

"Can't you just get a visor somewhere around here? I'm sure they sell them."

"I know," I began. "But it's not just any visor. It's a special visor. I got it from, uh, my eye doctor. They won't sell them around here. It's called a . . . Rayofilter visor," I said, kind of proud of the little name I came up with.

"Okay, well if you really need it," Carrie said. "I know how important it is to protect ourselves from the harsh environment."

Carrie was so sweet and gracious, I felt terrible lying to her.

As Carrie and I drove back to my condo, I explained, at Carrie's request, how the Rayofilter visor worked. As I made stuff up, Carrie frowned at me a couple of times, as if to say that what I was saying made no sense, but she didn't say anything.

When I was within five minutes driving distance from home, I made a call to Rona's cell. "Yes, hello, Blockbuster, I'm calling to see if you have any copies of *The Karate Kid Part II,*" I said into the phone.

That was the code Rona and I had set up beforehand. Because, you know, the movie is set in Japan and the shower had an Asian theme and . . . Anyway, we thought we were pretty clever, so just go with me on this one.

"Yes, we do," Rona replied with a laugh.

"Great," I said and flipped the phone closed.

"The Karate Kid? You hate *The Karate Kid."* Carrie looked at me. "Annabelle, what's going on?"

"I just have a hankering to see it," I fibbed.

After a few more minutes of Carrie questioning why I wanted to see *The Karate Kid Part II* and if I was going to make her watch it, we reached my condo, and I parked in the parking lot. When I started getting out of the car and Carrie didn't follow, I asked, "Aren't you going to come in with me?"

"Why do I need to come in?" Carrie asked.

It was a good question. It didn't exactly take two people to fetch my fictional Rayofilter visor. "Well," I stammered, trying to come up with something, "I need you to carry the . . . the battery pack. Yeah, the visor requires a battery pack, and I need you to carry it. It's pretty heavy."

"It's so heavy that you can't carry the visor and the battery pack at the same time?" Carrie narrowed her eyes. "I'm serious, Annabelle, what's going on?"

"Nothing," I said, trying my best to conceal my mischievous grin as I got out of the car.

I led a very reluctant Carrie to my condo and was practically bursting with excitement as I put my hand on the knob of the front door. I started talking really loud to let everyone inside know that we were there. "So, I'll grab the visor and you grab the battery pack!" I hollered.

"Okay," Carrie said slowly. She was definitely catching onto something.

My hand itching with anticipation, I flung the front door open. "Surprise!" eighteen women screamed the second the door was ajar.

Carrie stepped inside slowly, a dumbstruck look on her face. "You guys," she said as her eyes settled on the huge "Congratulations Carrie and Miles" banner on the wall. Her voice was choked with emotion. "I can't believe you did this."

Carrie looked into the smiling faces of her closest friends and family: her mom, Miles's sister Clarissa, my mom, Rona, Carrie's friends from Fresh Food Fanatics, and other women of all ages who had come to know and love Carrie.

We all watched as Carrie moved around my living room enjoying all of the party elements. The décor. The scrapbook table where Rona had placed pictures of Carrie and Miles so all of the party-attendees could make scrapbook pages for Carrie. And of course, the food, which included everything I had asked Carrie about plus some extras, like the homemade fortune cookies Mom had made from organic ingredients.

"It's amazing," Carrie said, looking at everything in awe. She then made her way around the room, hugging every one of the women there.

After the hugs, Carrie inspected the food table. She read the label in front of the plate of fortune cookies and held one up. "These are organic?" she asked Mom.

"One hundred percent," Mom replied with a smile.

Carrie grabbed a bamboo plate on which she set two of the fortune cookies. Then she said, "I don't know about all of you, but I'm going to eat."

And with that, the party began in full swing. Everyone talked and laughed as we ate the delicious food, oohed and aahed as Carrie opened her gifts, and then played Miles and Carrie trivia.

I was in the kitchen putting ice into a pitcher of water when Carrie came up beside me and slipped something into my hand. She hugged me tightly and said, "This is for you." I noticed there were tears in her eyes. Then as quickly as she had appeared, she disappeared.

I opened my hand and found a small fortune. The fortune said, "You are a true, cherished friend."

Soon, there were tears in my eyes too.

Chapter 24

Mom and I were plopped on the couch in my living room, exhausted from after-party cleanup, when my cell rang. Quickly, I hopped up to answer it. I immediately recognized the number on the caller ID. And while I'd love to say that it was Isaac's, it wasn't. It was George's.

Filled with at least the confidence that I would still have people who loved me after I lost my job, I answered the call. "Hello," I said weakly.

"Pleasanton," George's powerful voice greeted me. "I have been trying to get a hold of you since Wednesday. I need you to come down to the office as soon as possible."

"But it's Saturday," I said.

George laughed humorlessly. "The Anniversary Issue is out in less than a week. I'm in the office twenty-four seven until then."

"Well, okay, I'll be down in a few minutes."

"Great," George said, and he disconnected the line.

I guess he wants to fire me in person, I thought miserably.

I told Mom I had to go to the office, and she hugged me good-bye and left for home, leaving me with a refrigerator full of leftover party food. I was suddenly grateful that the shower venue had changed to my condo.

After saying good-bye to Mom, I dressed in my best please-let-me-keep-my-job outfit, a pair of sleek black pants and a cream-colored designer top, which I got for less than twenty bucks at a charity sale in Carmel. Then I headed out the door, munching on my second, all right sixth, homemade fortune cookie.

On the way to the office, I turned on the radio in an attempt to distract myself. I pushed Preset 1, which was set to my favorite station.

"Out of work?" a commercial blared. "Call our experts at Temployment, and they'll find you work to help you make ends meet."

I groaned and punched Preset 2.

"Can't get that dream job because you're not qualified? At Westside Technical Institute we provide you with the training you need to get the job you've always dreamed of. Call or visit us online at . . ."

I hit the radio off and drove the rest of the way in silence.

I pulled into the parking lot at *Central Coast Living* and felt strangely like a high school senior on the last day of school. Was this the last day I would be here?

I made my way to George's office. The door was wide open, and I could see George motioning for me to come inside. Reluctantly, I stepped into the office.

"Please sit down," George instructed.

"I'd rather stand," I replied. After all, it would only be moments before I was sent on my cubicle-clearing way.

"Okay," George said. "I called you down here to tell you—"

"Wait," I cut George off. "I know that you're disappointed in my article. Maybe even angry. But I want you to know, I accept that I'm not cut out for writing. I accept it, and I'll never ask to write again. Nor will I run around the sweaty heat of the San Joaquin Valley looking for a cake to impress you so I can trick you into letting me write. But if you'll let me keep my job editing, I'll be the best editor imaginable. I will."

A smile formed on George's lips. I found it kind of offensive that he was getting so much joy out of firing me.

"Can I speak now?" he asked, the smile growing.

I nodded, readying myself for the blow.

"I called you down here to tell you that I thought your work was great."

"And another thing—" I began. I had more things to explain. More begging for my job to do. More . . . "Wait, what did you just say?"

"I enjoyed your article. We're going to run it."

I sat down. "What?"

"When you came in here on Tuesday and told me how much trouble you'd had writing and that you needed more time, I was expecting something awful. But when I read the piece, I was nicely surprised. You really came through for me, Pleasanton."

I stared at George. "I . . . I did?"

George nodded.

"But that article . . . it wasn't what you wanted."

"You're right, it wasn't," George replied, raising his eyebrows. "But the thing about your story is that it puts the human element into an article about food. We've been trying to come up with a way to do that for years. Ever since those *Chicken Soup for the Soul* books came out and sold like hotcakes."

I couldn't help laughing. "Really?" I asked in disbelief.

Okay. So let's just recap here. I had a horrible, awful time trying to write about the glitz and glamour of Le Bonne Violette and ended up not being able to get an interview with Chef Jean-Pierre. So I wrote another story about the restaurant, the story that deep down I really wanted to tell.

But then I lost my nerve and didn't want to give that story to George. However, somehow, in a strange twist of events, George ended up with it anyway. And he thought it was good. And it was going to be in the magazine. My story was going to be in *Central Coast Living*! Not the story I thought everyone else expected me to write, but the story I truly believed in.

"And to think I tried to give you Missy Phat," I muttered under my breath.

"Excuse me?" George asked.

"Nothing. Let's just say, this is, well, this is craziness."

"Craziness?" George repeated, and it was obvious he didn't often use the word.

I gave George a never-mind wave. "It's a long and boring story, and I don't want to waste your time."

"All right then," George said. "The next item of business is the Anniversary gala. It's this coming Friday evening. Invitations have been sent to you, your family, and the individuals featured in your article."

"I'll be there," I said.

George nodded. "Good."

I smiled at George, not quite sure whether I was excused or not.

I was about to say good-bye when George spoke. "You know, Pleasanton, the best thing about your article is that it hits home. Folks want to know people like the ones in your story. That part about that woman Jacqueline who took in her cousin's kid, well, that part was good. My son is adopted, you know." George paused for a moment and picked up the picture of him and his wife and son.

"I was working for a national magazine, doing a piece on orphanages in Romania. It was . . . heartbreaking. I wanted to bring them all home with me." George's voice was filled with emotion. It was the first time I had ever heard him speak like that. "Later I went back with my wife, and we brought home our son. He turned eight yesterday."

"I had no idea," I said reverently.

"Not many people do," George replied as he set down the photo. "So," he said, his voice returning to normal, "like I told you, our readers are going to love your story. They'll eat it up like cake. And I have a feeling they're going to want seconds."

"What are you saying?" I asked, my eyes wide.

"I'm saying you should plan on writing a lot more in the future."

I smiled to myself, already beginning to plan which Marjorie Pleasanton recipe I would include in my next article.

After leaving George's office, I was halfway down a deserted hallway when I was suddenly overcome by a deep, warm sense of gratitude.

I was grateful that once I had asked God to help me in my endeavors, He had done just that. He had helped me write something meaningful, something inspired by the goodness in some really incredible people. Silently, I thanked Him for the opportunity, for helping a fallible girl like me use her talents for good.

The sense of gratitude was soon accompanied by giddiness. A giddiness that for some reason made me want to sing. So, I did—I started singing. I mean, there was no one around, so it was fine.

Before I knew it, I was singing to the tune of "Popcorn Popping." But that's not all, my friends. I wasn't just singing the cute little song. No. I was making up words of my own, singing in a hard rock voice, my hands playing, well, they were playing the air guitar.

"I came to the office and what did I see," I belted as I strummed the air guitar, my eyes tightly closed.

"George is publishing an article by me.

"Is it really so?

"Yes it seems to me.

"George is publishing an article by me!"

At this point, I played a solo on the air guitar, my head bobbing in an oh-yeah kind of way.

"I don't think that's how the song goes," a voice came into my ears.

My eyes shot open, and I stopped strumming my invisible guitar. Isaac was standing in front of me, smiling. No, it was more like chuckling.

I turned my head down toward the floor, thinking, *Okay floor, this is where you swallow me up*. But the floor just stared back up at me.

"Isaac," I choked out in humiliation, "I, um, didn't know you were there."

"Well I'm glad you didn't because you looked so . . ." Isaac made a weird face and cleared his throat. "So . . . is George in his office?"

"Yeah, I just talked to him." I wanted to tell Isaac everything. To tell him about my conversation with George. To tell him about how everything had somehow worked out. But I didn't. I couldn't.

"Good. I have to ask him something before I leave."

"Leave?" I asked.

"Yeah, I'm going out of town for the week. I have some projects to finish up in Los Banos."

"Oh," I said simply.

Right here there was a very long pause.

"So . . ." I mumbled uncomfortably.

"So . . ."

"Are you going to the gala?" We both asked the question in unison.

"Yeah, I'm gonna go," I answered first.

"Me too," Isaac said. "Maybe we could go together."

My eyes suddenly got all wide and doe-like. "Really?"

"Yeah. We did work on the article together. So it might be good to go together. You know, as friends."

"Yes, of course, as friends," I said, nodding my head a little too emphatically.

Isaac played with a button on his shirt. "So, I'll pick you up a little before seven on Friday?"

"Okay," I agreed.

"Great," Isaac said, beginning to walk away.

"Yeah, great," I echoed. *Just great.*

Chapter 25

I hate friends.

Okay, I don't exactly hate friends. I just really hated that I was being forced to be friends with Isaac. It was too hard. I didn't know how to act. I didn't know what to say. And I certainly didn't know how I was supposed to go to the Anniversary gala with him and not think about how handsome he was, how much I wanted to hold his hand, how much I wanted to kiss him, how much . . .

I put an abrupt end to the thoughts and focused on my reflection in the full length mirror in my room as I smoothed some Foxy Glossy onto my lips. He was just Isaac. Isaac my friend. My friend Isaac. My buddy. My pal. My chummy chum.

I smacked my lips together and did one last mirror check of my red party dress, the fabulous strappy shoes I found on clearance at Macy's, and my hair and makeup, which I had gotten done by Kiki, the stylist I go to for special occasions.

Satisfied by my reflection—after all, it's always nice to look good for one's friends—I went into the living room to distract myself from my thoughts on Isaac by doing my new favorite activity: looking at my article in the Anniversary

Issue of *Central Coast Living*. It had provided me with many moments of joy, so I thought it would be a good diversion.

I flipped to the article—which by then the magazine pretty much fell right open to—and reminisced about the moment George had called me into his office and handed it to me. I had taken it into my hands carefully, almost ceremoniously. Then I had walked to the privacy of my cubicle and done four things.

1) I sniffed it. Though I'm not quite sure why.
2) I looked at the gorgeous, glossy cover and just soaked in the fact that my article was inside.
3) I quickly turned to my story, and stared at the words printed near the top: Written by Annabelle Pleasanton. It was such an exhilarating feeling.
4) I made up this little game where I closed the magazine and then timed how long it took me to turn to my article. I did this repeatedly, until I had the time down to just a little over a second.

All right. Since we're friends and all, I'll tell you one more thing that I did.

5) I looked adoringly at the photos Isaac had taken. They were absolutely incredible. Somehow Isaac had captured every one of the people in my article perfectly, shooting images that seemed to give all of my words more clarity, more poignancy. It was amazing.

Yes, amazing, I thought as I ran my fingers across Isaac's name underneath the photo on page 63. So much for using the magazine as a diversion. I flipped the magazine shut and was about to turn on the television when I heard a knock at the front door. I got up from the couch and looked through the peephole. Isaac was standing on the doorstep, looking delicious in a black suit. And I mean delicious in a purely friendly sense, of course.

I exhaled deeply and swung the door open. "Hi," I said, my

voice sounding very weird.

"Man, you look gorgeous." Isaac fixed his eyes on me for a wonderful moment, but then quickly looked away. "So, uh, are you ready to go?"

"Yes, I'm ready."

I grabbed my wrap and my dressy handbag and locked the door from the inside. Delicately, I stepped outside, and Isaac offered me his arm. I rested my hand on his muscular forearm, and was instantly overcome by the electric sensation that filled my body. And for the first time, I was afraid.

Afraid that I wouldn't be able to stop myself from telling him how handsome he was, how much I wanted to hold his hand, how much I wanted to kiss him, how much I . . . loved him.

Say something friendish, I instructed myself.

Isaac and I were sitting at a lovely blue-silk-covered table in a lavishly decorated banquet room at the Carmel Heights Hotel. I was watching the people on the dance floor in the middle of the room as they danced beneath the twinkle lights that hung from the ceiling, and Isaac was looking out the large bay window, gazing at the ocean as it sparkled in the moonlight. And I couldn't think of a thing to say.

Well, that's not entirely true. I could think of plenty of things to say. But they weren't the sort of things a friend says to a friend. They were all *Isaac will you hold me close as we glide across the dance floor* and *Isaac let's go walk hand in hand along the beach.* Definitely not friend-like.

"So this is, um, a really great party," I said finally.

"Yeah, it is," Isaac agreed, turning to look at me.

"Is your family coming?" I asked.

"They couldn't make it. But Ethan should be here a little later. He's bringing Rona. But who knows, he took her out to dinner first, and the way they've been lately, they'll lose track of time and won't end up coming."

"So they're getting pretty serious then, huh?"

"Practically inseparable."

"Good for them," I said, suddenly feeling ridiculous about how far off I had been about Rona's love interest, and wondering if Isaac remembered the things I had insinuated about the matter.

"Is your family coming?" Isaac asked.

"Yeah," I replied.

As if on cue, at that moment, I saw Mom and Dad enter the room. Mom was dressed in a black dress with a sprinkling of sequins that shimmered like diamonds under the lights in the room. Dad was in his church suit and a silver tie. I've never in my life seen my dad in a silver tie. It was kind of weird.

I excused myself—not like it mattered since Isaac and I weren't really talking anyway—and quickly went to say hello to my parents. When I reached them, they told me yet again how proud they were of me. Then, in a hushed tone, Mom asked me where Isaac was. I pointed to the table where Isaac now sat alone. Mom asked how things were going, and with a shrug I said they were just fine. She looked at me like she didn't believe me.

So I was about to tell Mom that things weren't fine, and I was going to ask her how I could make Isaac love me, when the band started playing some song that had significance to Mom and Dad. They started talking about listening to the song on some road trip they took in the sixties or something, and Dad asked Mom if she wanted to dance. With a shy smile Mom accepted, and they went to the dance floor.

I watched them go and then stood in place pathetically.

"Come dance with us," I heard someone say. It was Patty, and she and Arvin were dancing around the floor together. It was a crazy sight if I ever saw one.

"Oh no, I don't think so," I protested.

But before I could object any further, Patty dragged me into the mass of dancing people. Soon I was moving my body around freely, trying to get Isaac out of my system. When the band began to play an even faster song, I invented this great move where I kind of punched the air from different angles. I was really into the move, punching and punching, when I smacked some girl in the back of the head with my flying fists.

"I'm so sorry," I apologized immediately.

The girl, who I think I recognized from marketing, rubbed her head and looked at me with contempt. Then she relocated on the dance floor.

The band began playing a nice slow song, and I started to walk back to the table where Isaac was sitting. Maybe by some miracle he would ask me to dance.

"I saw that," I heard a giggling voice say behind me as I walked. I spun around and saw Amber, all dolled up in a black knee-length dress.

"Saw what?" I said innocently.

"You know what," Amber said. "Come sit with us." She motioned toward a nearby table where Jacqueline, dressed in a blue dress, was sitting alone.

"Okay," I said, quickly glancing over at Isaac who was still sitting at our table, playing with a napkin.

"We enjoyed your article very much," Jacqueline said with a smile after I had taken a seat. "Though I am not sure I deserved all of the things you said about me."

"Yes you did," I insisted. "You both did."

"Are you wearing your Foxy Glossy?" Amber asked me.

I rubbed my lips together. "Of course."

"Amber!" I heard a young boy's voice calling out.

I turned and saw Angel waving his hand at Amber. Julio was standing behind Angel's wheelchair, holding a glass of water with a lemon in it.

"I'm coming!" Amber called out to the boy. Then she turned to her mother. "I think it's time to go get ready to . . ." She looked at me and paused. "You know, do the thing."

Jacqueline nodded, and I wondered how in the world she knew what her daughter was talking about.

"I'll come with you," I said.

"No!" Amber said a little too loudly. "I mean, we have to do it alone."

"Okay. I just wanted to say hello to Angel." My voice was slow, confused.

"Oh, okay," Amber said.

I followed Amber and Jacqueline as they walked over to where Angel and Julio were waiting.

I smiled widely at the pair. "Hi."

"Hi," Angel echoed.

Julio nodded his head politely. "Hello, Miss Pleasanton."

"Don't you look sharp," I said, looking Angel over. He was dressed in a little black suit complete with a tie, and his dark hair was neatly combed.

Angel beamed. "Grandpa bought me a tie. I never wore a tie before."

"Angel was honored to be in your article," Julio said to me.

Angel smiled and started talking quickly. "Yeah. Before I got sick, I played t-ball and I got a trophy and Grandpa made me a shelf to put it on. My friend Peter has a shelf in his room too, and he has a whole bunch of trophies on it and he told me it's dumb that I have a big shelf with just one trophy on it. But Grandpa took the story you and Isaac made, and he put it in a frame and put it on the shelf for me. He said that being in the story is just like getting a trophy."

"Your grandpa's right," I said meaningfully.

Amber put a hand on Angel's shoulder. "Angel, we should probably go now," she said.

Angel nodded his head, and the foursome said their good-byes to me before disappearing from view.

Finding myself alone, I seized the opportunity to visit the buffet tables in the back of the room. I loaded one plate with mini shrimp skewers, bruscetta, and stuffed mushrooms. And then I filled another plate with chocolate-covered strawberries. Yum.

I returned to the seat next to Isaac. "Don't these strawberries look great?" I asked.

Isaac looked up from the napkin he was still messing with and glanced at the strawberries. "Sure."

And at that moment, something inside of me snapped. I just couldn't take the one syllable responses and "friendly" conversation anymore.

"Isaac," I blurted, not giving myself time to think. "I hate this. Friends stinks." *Friends stinks? That doesn't even make sense.* Quickly, I tried to come up with my next words, seriously hoping that they were better than the last ones I uttered, but Isaac spoke before I could.

"Annabelle, I—" he began. Then he stopped. Some muffled sound was coming from the front of the room, and it distracted him. He became suddenly quiet.

"What, Isaac?" I asked snippily. "You know what? I don't care what you have to say. It's very obvious that you don't really want to be here with me. What happened, Isaac? That blonde couldn't come with you?" I knew I sounded ridiculous, but for some reason I just couldn't stop myself.

"Candy?" Isaac asked. His voice was no more than a whisper.

"What? Why would I want candy? I'm trying to talk to you!"

"No, I mean her name is Candy." Isaac's voice was still whispery soft.

"Who? What are you talking about?"

"Annabelle," Isaac whispered. "Maybe you should lower your voice."

"No, I will not lower my voice!" I hollered.

Isaac leaned back in his chair and pointed straight ahead. With a scowl on my face, I turned my head to see where he was pointing. And that's when I saw Ingrid Chandler, editor-in-chief of *Central Coast Living*, standing at a podium in the front of the room.

When did that podium get there? I wondered. *And when did the band stop playing?*

Just about everyone in the room had stopped what they were doing and they were all looking at me, looks of disgust on their faces. And I think I saw Mom mouthing, "Where are your manners?" at me.

I bit my lip and could feel my face turning scarlet red.

"All right, now that I have everyone's attention," Ingrid said. She was staring right at me. "Thank you all for coming tonight to celebrate the Anniversary Issue with us. Many individuals dedicated much time and effort to make the issue a success, and I believe it is one of our best ever. We will now take a few minutes to hear from our deputy editors."

By the time George got up to speak, I have to admit, I had zoned out a bit. I was staring at one of the strawberries on my plate, letting my vision get all blurry until the strawberry looked like a chocolate blob with a green thing on top, when I felt Isaac gently touch my shoulder.

"Your boss is talking about you," he said.

I looked toward the front of the room and tuned in to what George was saying. "One of the best works produced in our department was an article by Annabelle Pleasanton. It has been just three days since the issue hit newsstands, and the public response to Miss Pleasanton's fresh and heartfelt article on La Bonne Violette has been unprecedented. I already have a stack of emails in praise of Miss Pleasanton's work."

What? Emails? People had written in about my article?

George continued. "We received one rather unusual request from some fans of Miss Pleasanton's work, and we couldn't help but comply. So without further adieu, allow me to introduce two of our guests who would like to present Miss Pleasanton with a special gift: Amber Metz and Angel Sanchez."

Completely surprised, I watched as Amber and Angel emerged from a door along the wall behind the podium. Then, as if out of nowhere, a woman appeared with a microphone, and two men appeared pushing an upright piano. Angel zoomed over to the piano, and the woman holding the microphone handed it to Amber and disappeared from view.

With a slightly shaky voice, Amber spoke. "Annabelle gave us something very special when she wrote about us, so we wanted to do something special for her. She wrote about the people she met through La Bonne Violette because she saw something good in us. Well, we saw something good in her too. And that's what this song is about—sharing what we have inside with the people around us and trying to make the world a brighter place." Amber's words were flawless and obviously carefully memorized. I felt the beginning of tears in my eyes.

I watched as Angel moved his tiny fingers to play the opening line of "This Little Light of Mine." The melody was simple, and Angel missed a note or two, but in my mind, no music had ever been so perfect.

The room grew impossibly hushed as Amber joined in with a voice so pure and beautiful it seemed to pierce me.

This little light of mine
I'm gonna let it shine . . .
Let it shine, Let it shine, Let it shine

Hide it under a bushel? No!
I'm gonna let it shine . . .
Let it shine, Let it shine, Let it shine

I couldn't stop the tears that filled my eyes as I listened to the music. Amber had remembered that this was one of my favorite songs. And she and Angel had obviously spent a whole lot of time practicing their presentation. I have seen masterful performances by trained musicians, but nothing was ever more beautiful than the song performed by my two young friends that evening.

After the last note of the song sounded, a soft, reverent applause filled the room. I looked at the audience and noticed that I was not the only one with tears in my eyes. After a moment of soft applause, the clapping grew louder until all had stood up from their seats and were uproariously cheering.

Angel made his way to Amber's side, and the two of them

smiled at the audience, and then looked directly at me. My mouth turned up in a smile that couldn't possibly reflect what I was feeling.

The applause continued for a long time, and as it did I glanced around the room, looking at the cheering crowd. It was then that my eyes settled on someone across the room: Jean-Pierre. My first reaction was to turn away quickly, but I noticed something strange: Jean-Pierre was smiling at me as he clapped. A smile that seemed to say he was proud to be a part of all of this. I couldn't help smiling back.

The clapping went on until George approached the podium and said, his voice cracking, "Thank you. That was quite a treat." Then he cleared his throat and looked toward the band. "Well, that's a tough act to follow, but I guess you'll just have to try."

Laughs filled the room, and the band proceeded to play a slow Louis Armstrong number.

I watched Amber and Angel make their way to a table where their loved ones greeted them with smiles and hugs. "I'll be right back," I said to Isaac before dashing off to add my own smiles and hugs.

"You guys were amazing," I said, hugging them one after the other. "I can't believe you did that. It was so wonderful."

After a moment, Isaac was at the table as well. "You have a beautiful voice," he said to Amber. "And Angel, buddy, you were like a pro up there."

"I messed up at the beginning," Angel admitted bashfully.

"You were perfect," I said. "Just perfect."

Suddenly I felt Isaac come up beside me. He placed his hand on the small of my back and moved his face so close to mine I could feel his breath on my cheek. "Will you dance with me?" he asked.

I felt as if my legs might give out under me, and every inch of my skin felt hot and prickly. "Yes," I whispered.

Isaac and I said our good-byes to the group, and he led me

out to the dance floor. The band was still playing the Louis Armstrong song as Isaac placed one hand on my waist and held up his other hand for me to take. I shakily clasped his hand, and we began swaying to the music.

"I think you did it," Isaac said.

I furrowed my brow. "What?"

"I think you did what you wanted to do with your writing. I remember you telling me that you wanted to write something with meaning, something to counteract the junk that's in the media. Well, from what I've seen tonight, I'd say you did it."

"I can't believe you remember me telling you that," I said softly.

"Of course I remember."

I wanted to reply to Isaac's words. To tell him what that meant to me. To ask him what that meant for us. But the song ended, and the people on the dance floor began clapping for the band. I turned toward Isaac. "Thanks for the dance," I said briskly. I began moving off the dance floor.

"Come outside with me," Isaac said suddenly.

I looked into his hazel eyes and said nothing.

"Please, Annabelle."

After a pause, I found myself nodding slowly, hesitantly.

Isaac offered me his hand, and we walked outside and made our way to a cobblestone walkway that led to the beach. As we drew closer to the shore, the sound of the music from the hotel grew softer, and the gentle roll of the waves took its place. When we stepped onto the sand, I took off my shoes and held them in my hand. Isaac did the same.

Almost immediately I began to shiver in the cold wind. My thin cashmere wrap, which I had picked up from the coat check on the way out of the hotel, wasn't doing anything to shield me from the cold.

Isaac removed his jacket and placed it around me.

"Thanks," I said, pulling the jacket around me tightly.

For a moment, we walked silently along the shore, the moist sand beneath our toes. I listened to the soothing sound of the sea and looked up at the moon in the sky.

"Annabelle, there's something I need to tell you," Isaac said, breaking the silence.

His voice was so deep and serious I knew just what he was going to say: He was in love with the blonde. He had realized it as they ate at the little Italian restaurant in the Green Meadows shopping center. And they were going to get married. And he was wondering if I would ghostwrite a poem to her from him, now that I was an established writer and all.

"I want you to know that I'm sorry," he said.

"It's okay," I sighed. "You have to move on."

"Move on?"

I traced tiny circles in the sand with my toes. "Yeah. I know what you're going to tell me. You're going to tell me that you've found the girl for you. And I'm happy for you, I really am."

Isaac watched my feet. "I guess that's part of what I was going to tell you."

"Well, good," I said. "I hope that you and Caramello are very happy together."

"I'm not talking about Candy," Isaac said. "My overly concerned mother set me up with her because she thought I was sulking around too much. I'm talking about you, Annabelle." Isaac paused for a moment and looked into my eyes. "You, the girl who would drive hundreds of miles for a cake. You, the girl who applauded Angel's 'La Cucaracha.' You, the girl who went to The Artichoke House to comfort your best friend. You, the author of the most incredible article I have ever read."

"You mean me, the liar," I said.

Isaac shook his head intently. "No, I don't."

The sea breeze picked up and whipped through my hair. I brushed the brown strands out of my face. "Wait? Are you saying you don't still think I lied to you about Pat—" I stopped myself from saying the name. "About pat . . . the pat . . . the patchwork of stuff that you thought I lied about." I'm not quite sure there is such a thing as a patchwork of stuff, but it was better than saying the name of slime.

A serious expression came onto Isaac's face. "I know you didn't."

"You really know that?" I asked, almost afraid to believe him.

"It's because I know *you*," Isaac said. "Remember that night when I ran into you at *Central Coast Living*?"

"Yes, I remember." I had thought he was a mouse.

"Remember how you told me that for some reason you could never hide from me?"

"Yes."

"The thing is, I loved everything that I saw. I loved . . ." Isaac let his voice trail off. "Anyway, I think I used the whole Patrique thing as a reason to run away from something I was afraid of. I blamed you when I was the one to blame. You were nothing but wonderful and beautiful to me, and all you wanted was not to upset me, and I was a total jerk to you. I am so sorry." Isaac tentatively touched the apple of my cheek.

I pushed his hand away. "You really hurt me, Isaac," I said rigidly. "Do you expect me just to forget all about that and go on like nothing happened?"

"No, I don't," Isaac replied. "There's no excuse for the way I treated you. I let my insecurities cloud the truth, and I will do everything in my power not to let that happen again. And if you can't forgive me now, then I'll wait. I'll wait until you can."

"What if it takes me a week?" I asked, folding my arms across my chest.

"I'll wait."

"What if it takes me a month?"

"I'll wait."

"What if it takes me a year?"

"A year," Isaac said slowly.

"Okay," I said, a sudden softening taking place inside of me, "maybe it won't take that long."

Isaac touched my arm gently. "I'm so sorry, Annabelle."

"I know."

And the thing was, I really did know.

Wordlessly, Isaac and I both turned to gaze at the sea, and Isaac gently touched my fingertips with his, as if he were asking permission to hold my hand. Slowly I laced my fingers through his, and it felt even better than I remembered.

"Annabelle?" Isaac asked.

"Yes?"

"I really want to kiss you."

Isaac turned to face me, gently put his arms around me, and leaned toward me slowly, purposefully. When he was inches away, I closed my eyes and let myself be carried away in the moment. His lips were so close I could almost taste them.

But before our lips met, I found myself blurting, "So do you believe everything I told you then?"

Isaac pulled away and looked at me, obviously surprised by my untimely outburst.

What are you doing, making me ask questions at a time like this? I asked my kiss-ruining brain. *Don't you know he was about to kiss me?*

"Yes, I do," Isaac assured me.

"Why?" my brain made me ask.

No more questions, I begged my brain. *Kiss. Focus on the kiss.*

"Because I'm in love with you, Annabelle."

The words were so beautiful they made me gasp.

Okay, brain, given the circumstances, I'll forgive you this once.

"You love me?" I asked. "Cheese-smelling, can't-play-tennis, made-you-pay-for-a-sea-lion me?"

Isaac tightened his arms around me. "Yes, you."

The most incredible warm sensation filled my entire being. "Oh, Isaac, I love you too. So much. You are the kindest, best man I have ever known. And the first man who has ever truly known me."

Isaac looked at me the way I have always dreamed a man would look at me and softly traced my lips with his finger. Then he took my face into his hands and kissed me. The kiss I had been longing to feel on my lips for much too long. The sweetest kiss imaginable. And when it was through, I was smiling and crying at the same time.

"Do you want to know a secret?" I asked Isaac.

Isaac kissed me softly on the forehead. "Yes."

"I put you in my Pink Notes." Of course, I had, in a moment of anger, crossed off Isaac Matthews in the entry and replaced it with Jerky Jerkins, but that could easily be fixed.

"I have a secret too," Isaac said.

"What?"

"I took a photo of you talking to Angel when we were setting up for the recital. And I put it in my wallet."

"No, you didn't."

"Yes, I did." Isaac reached into the back pocket of his suit pants, and showed me the picture in his wallet. "I wanted to capture the look you get in your eyes when you're talking to him. You get the same look when you talk to any of the people you write about in your notes."

I turned my head down, embarrassed.

"It's beautiful," Isaac said. "One of the things I love most about you."

Isaac put an arm around me, and I gently rested my head on his shoulder. I listened to his breath as we silently stared out at the moonlit sea.

"You know," I said pensively as I looked out at the water, "it's crazy, really. Everything that's happened. That day when I went out to the San Joaquin Valley looking for that cake, I had no idea what was in store for me. I was looking for a cake, but in the end I found so much more. I found so many wonderful people, and their incredible stories. I found you. I found parts of myself that I think I might have lost for a while. And all of that was . . . the icing on the cake."

Isaac kissed the top of my head. "Well, according to this really amazing girl that I know, the icing is the best part," he said.

I lifted my head slightly and smiled up at Isaac. "Yes," I said. "It sure is."

The End

Elodia Strain

Elodia was born in Alaska, and grew up in California. She graduated cum laude from Brigham Young University, where she majored in advertising and minored in English.

She currently resides in Spokane, Washington, with her husband, Jacob. When she's not writing, she enjoys reading, doing yoga, playing the piano, and listening to her husband play guitar.

She firmly believes that laughter is the best medicine, and in this world of troubles and trials, she hopes to bring laughter to readers through her writing.

Say hello at www.elodiastrain.com.

0 26575 70114 2